The
Foster Child

Lawrence Peter

This is a work of fiction. Names, characters, places, and incidents are either products of the author's imagination or are used fictitiously. Any resemblance to actual events or locales or persons, living or dead, is entirely coincidental.

ISBN: 0615573568
ISBN-13: 978-0615573564

DEDICATION

To Karen, Zack and Aaron – my fuel.

ACKNOWLEDGMENTS

Thanks to my family for infinite understanding and constant support. Special thanks to my wife Karen for serving as my editor, proofreader, friend, confidante and lover during this long process. She is responsible for my maintaining the integrity of the characters — especially in giving voice to Marian.

Thanks to my Aunt Barbara Paulin, who first inspired me to write and got me started on the path to spiritual enlightenment. And thanks to Enid Vien and her philosophy of Dynamism for showing me how to complete the journey. Thanks also to two wonderful friends, Jim Land, Sr. and Angela Payne for their encouragement to publish this story.

parthenogenesis (pär-thə-nō-jĕn-ə-səs)

noun: A form of reproduction in which an unfertilized egg develops into a new individual, occurring commonly among insects and certain other arthropods.

From the Greek *parthenos*, meaning *virgin*.

PROLOGUE

Have I ever lied to you?

A reasonable question, even though you don't know me from Adam. You've been lied to all your life – by those you trusted to tell you the truth – and beginning a new relationship with a clean slate is quite important. At least it is to me.

You wonder how we got to this point – how this brave new world came into being? Well, I'm the only one who can tell this story in the way it needs to be told.

I was there when the deal went down. I saw the struggles of all involved, and will tell you details you never heard on the news, or will read in the history books. It's a more amazing story than you imagine.

We have to begin the journey several years in the past. As in much of history, the good that has finally emerged had its origins in the lowest aspects of the human condition.

So before we continue, let me ask again: Have I ever lied to you?

Maybe, just a bit. But at least I can be honest in my deception.

After all, this is a game…

CHAPTER 1

"Dr. Foster, another rhesus monkey . . . um . . . exploded. Group 12 again. Something's really wrong with this bunch. I'm trying to get the mess cleaned up before Prevost shows, but it was bad this time. I really need you here now. Shit. Please get in here as soon as you can."

Marian Foster lifted her head from the toilet as the answering machine clicked off. It was her assistant, Carl. His pleading carried little weight with Marian this morning. After spending two hours weighing the benefits of death against the agony of her uncontrollable retching, trading places with an exploding monkey was an attractive proposition.

She yanked a foot of toilet tissue from the roll and raked it across her mouth. Tossing the tissue into the commode, Marian leaned back against the wall and stretched her legs. The cool tile brought a brief respite from the incessant waves of nausea.

Marian felt another spasm rippling through her abdomen, a mild aftershock she prayed would bring an end to the tsunami of bile and acid. She watched the rhythmic rise and fall of her midsection, trying desperately to block the dark visions of the monkey experiments.

Several had produced viable embryos, but Group 12 was problematic. The rhesus monkeys in this group developed tumors with such a high metabolic rate they grew in a matter of hours to a size the body couldn't contain. The image of the first monkey's death was still burned into her mind - the pitiful look of surprise on the creature's face as its abdomen stretched, then burst, unable to contain the cancerous mass.

She shook the image from her mind. *That's not me. Too many days have passed.*

Marian gingerly lifted herself from the floor and stood staring at the stranger in the mirror. Dabbing at her puffy eyes, she began a third attempt to put on makeup. She drew close to the mirror but her trembling hands made it impossible to apply the mascara.

The fear was growing again. Her life and her career were both in jeopardy. She had crossed the line into the realm of B-movie mad scientists. She had experimented on herself.

Marian slammed her fists on the porcelain sink. *I am in control! I KNOW what I'm doing!*

The pain flaring through her hands restored her usual state of swaggering confidence. *Just put on the gloves and get in the ring,* she thought. *This meeting won't be any different from the rest, and that means you've got a fight on your hands.*

A woman in a brawl with a room full of men needs every weapon at her disposal. Marian knew her two most powerful weapons were her intellect and her looks. A second glance in the mirror reminded her she might be fighting short-handed today.

Marian ran her fingers across cracked lips and swollen jowls. *Shake it off, Foster. It's from the hormones. It'll pass.*

She let her robe drop to the floor and ran a hand across her smooth stomach. *You're twenty-nine and you still look damn good.* That thought was quickly erased by a more pressing concern. *If it worked ... how long before I begin to show?*

No time for worrying now. In ninety-three minutes Marian was due to address the Board of Directors of BiEnCo Pharmaceuticals. She would be lobbying for continued funding of her current research project – a very controversial human fertilization procedure.

The results of the latest animal experiments had been promising. With Dr. Prevost's continuing support, she had been confident of approval – at least until the recent outbreak of detonating monkeys. This had to be kept quiet. Group 12 was the only group showing adverse effects, and the refined procedure used on more recent subjects was producing normal embryos. So far.

The question that haunted Marian was: Why had she risked career suicide and attempted the procedure on herself?

So I can take those fat-fingered bean counters and shove their faces into the shit they've been giving me for the past eighteen months, that's why.

Their arguments against funding her research had become an endless loop of motivation that bordered on obsession. The taunts of her colleagues rang in her ears day and night.

You must be kidding! Human parthenogenesis? You can't create a human embryo without an egg <u>*and*</u> *a sperm. Did you sleep through Biology 101?*

Marian had believed since medical school that human parthenogenesis *was* a possibility. It takes twenty-three pairs of chromosomes to make a human, and every egg and sperm contains exactly half of what is needed. Sex is determined by only one chromosome pair. Two X chromosomes make a female, an XY combination makes a male. Female egg cells contain only X chromosomes; sperm cells contain a fifty-fifty mix of both X and Y. If you could entice two egg cells to combine, you'd have twenty-three perfectly good pairs of chromosomes. And the pairing of two X chromosomes would guarantee that the result would always be female.

French scientists had proven several years ago that by tweaking a single gene, spontaneous egg cell division could be triggered in mice. Their efforts produced only two embryos out of a thousand attempts, neither of which could be brought to term. Marian knew their failure was a result of doubling the genetic material inside a single egg. Natural human conception requires genes from two separate donor cells, and she had engineered an enzyme that would allow genetic material from a pair of egg cells to fuse together in the same way an egg and sperm combined.

She often questioned why we need sperm. Some biologists theorized that the Y chromosome that causes the condition known as "male" was originally a flawed mutation of an X chromosome. She kept that tidbit in her arsenal of arguments for female superiority. Men were simply women with a debilitating genetic condition. A disease of sorts.

Marian's obsession with proving her theory was now overwhelmed by a need to keep that proof secret – if, indeed, she was carrying a viable embryo. And there was only one way to tell: Extract it and examine it.

Plans for an illicit abortion could wait for another day. First on the agenda was this morning's meeting with the board. It was time to get the game face on.

Marian went to her closet to select the uniform of the day. White button-up blouse. Good. Conservative, but just a bit snug in the chest for that "straining to get out" look. The gray skirt that hung just short of the knee, showing just enough leg to keep the more ignorant ones' attention. Flats or heels? Did these bastards deserve her fuck-me shoes? Marian decided the continued funding of her project warranted so.

Dressing hurriedly, Marian glanced at the clock. She still had plenty of time to make the meeting, but was anxious to get outside into the fresh air. The smell of sickness that hung in the bathroom was starting to make her queasy again. She rushed toward the door, stopping in front of her bedroom dresser for a last look at herself. *Damn smell's all through the house.*

A second glance at the mirror revealed the true source of the odor. Marian saw a sizeable chunk of yellow vomit clinging to her hair just above the left shoulder. That's when the tears came.

*   *   *

"Fuck! Asshole!"

Just getting warmed up. Marian slammed her fist firmly down on the horn as she let loose a stream of free-form cursing. Marian cursed like John Coltrane played the sax. Rapid bursts of improvisation in contexts never before considered. Fiery and emotional passages in disparate rhythms that cut across the grain of a monotonous sonic background. Atlanta traffic on this morning was inspiring new riffs on well-known themes. A light-blue Corolla swerved into Marian's lane, causing her to brake suddenly.

She spat through clenched teeth, "Son of a cock-biting ass-whore!"

Marian and the errant driver exchanged a one-finger salute, and she returned to her mental rehearsal of the upcoming presentation. As she took the turn off I-85 into North Druid Hills, Marian's attention was captured by a rotating billboard. The side facing her was a bright blue sky overlaid with a golden text reading, "God Loves You, Atlanta!" Before she could conjure up a cynical thought, it had rotated to its reverse side, which displayed an empty photo album beneath the headline, "An Aborted Baby's Scrapbook."

Marian snorted in disgust. "Brought to you by the Church of the Latter-Day Morons." Then, patting her stomach added, "Hey kid. That's you."

Marian's mood sobered as the severity of her situation settled in once again. Her logical mind had always been able to find an escape route from dangerous situations, but in this case logic was drawing a blank. Following the trail of cause and effect is the basis of logical problem solving. And the cause of this situation was the stumbling block. Marian had absolutely no idea why she'd done it.

What could have possibly driven her to bypass stages of animal testing and perform a dangerous experiment on herself? She knew she was lying with each adamant declaration of the necessity to *prove she was right*. The animal tests would have proven it in two months. So why?

Marian exited Piedmont Road and accelerated her Lexus through the parking lot, then skidded to a halt, maneuvering her car diagonally across three parking spaces. Snatching her briefcase, she made a dash toward the entrance to the building. The blinding sun glinting off the chrome and glass of BiEnCo's office tower almost caused Marian to trip as she jumped the curb. By her watch, the meeting had started three minutes ago. Marian barreled through the front door, shoving her security pass into the face of a startled guard.

"I'm late!" she shouted as she passed the guard. Marian took the left turn down the hallway at a full run. She lost her balance for a moment, barely catching herself against the wall. *Why did I choose the heels?* Approaching the conference room, Marian paused outside the door to quickly adjust her blouse and straighten her hair. Satisfied, she entered, determined to look as dignified as possible.

Dr. Gordon Prevost was addressing the group seated around an large oval conference table. He mustered a very unconvincing smile upon Marian's entrance. "Glad you could join us, Dr. Foster."

All eyes in the room turned to Marian. Prevost was obviously covering for her, as he had done so often in the past. He was a surrogate father to Marian. A mentor, protector and confidante, as well as the man who signed her paychecks. He also had the fatherly talent to totally disarm Marian with the raise of an eyebrow that signaled disappointment.

"I've just been briefing these gentlemen on the status of your project," Dr. Prevost continued. "Perhaps you could take over now and fill them in on the details."

"I'd be happy to," Marian responded, striding confidently to the front of the group. She briskly typed a command on the keyboard stationed at the podium and her PowerPoint charts came to life on the projector screen. She opened her mouth to begin her presentation but was immediately interrupted by a thin, balding man with thick glasses. It was Alvin Hedstrom, BiEnCo's Chief Financial Officer.

"Dr. Foster, a moment please. Now, I try to be sympathetic when one of our personnel has such passion for a research project, but I'd like to remind the board this is a pharmaceutical business. Key words being *pharmaceutical* and *business*."

Hedstrom paused dramatically and removed his glasses.

"This is not a chemical compound that can be put into easily swallowed pills, it's a complex medical procedure. Our company does not sell medical procedures. And even if we did, how many times is an individual going to use this product? Give me another Valium. A new antidepressant. Something that's taken three times a day and refilled ad infinitum. That's where profits come from."

Marian's face flushed with anger. The anger grew stronger as she saw the nodding men around the table being drawn into Hedstrom's spell. Prevost stared into space, nervously fingering his beard.

Hedstrom continued, "I have a hard time seeing a return on investment from research that makes it easier for single women to bear welfare children. Anyone here want to try selling this product on the Lifetime Channel?"

He looked around the room defiantly. "Our research capital should be spent on new medicines we can sell, not on left-wing social experiments. Gentlemen, let's stop wasting our time and money. I move that funding for this project be discontinued immediately."

Marian steadied herself against the podium. The bastard was trying an end-run before she even began her presentation.

Hedstrom was one of the few original investors who actually held a position within the company. He had lobbied hard for CEO only to have the board decide that a doctorate in medicine was more appropriate for that position. Butting heads with Dr. Prevost at every turn was his way of coping with the defeat.

Marian took a deep breath and began, "Mr. Hedstrom, this project is research in the purest form, not product development. We all were aware of that when the project was initially approved. As we discover more about the mechanics of conception and cell division and find ways that process can be chemically manipulated, we come closer to understanding and treating inherited birth defects, cancer, schizophrenia, epilepsy. . ."

Hedstrom broke in, "Can you deny that one of the goals of this research, if you are indeed successful, is that single women - even teenagers - can have babies without the knowledge, consent or input of any other person?"

Marian's eyes narrowed as her gun sights lowered on Hedstrom. *You stupid little fuck. You dare to use morals as an argument against my work?* Her brain filter flipped to the "off" position and she began her assault.

"Did you actually just say 'input', Mr. Hedstrom?" she heard herself saying, a bit too loudly. "Interesting euphemism for the act of sex."

Hedstrom blushed, "That's not -"

Marian continued, pacing behind Hedstrom's chair, "No more good, old-fashioned *fucking*. Is that what you're worried about?"

Marian feigned an expression of awe and continued sarcastically, "Or perhaps you're afraid the world will eventually be overtaken by women, because the procedure only creates female embryos. That," she said, leaning over the back of his seat, "is what I'm *really* after - world domination by women, of course."

Marian chuckled as she turned her back to Hedstrom and began a slow walk to the podium.

"No worries, Mr. Hedstrom. The act of copulation is safe. Even if there are other ways of becoming pregnant, it's still quite a bit of fun for most of us."

Following a lengthy moment of silent stares, there was a contagious outbreak of nervous paper shuffling and tie adjustments around the table.

Marian continued, "Now, if we could please get serious again. I'll direct the rest of my presentation to the men of science in the room, rather than the bean-counters."

Hedstrom, red-faced, glared at Marian. She returned the glare with a small smile. Marian knew the psychology of human groups was no different that that of any animal pack. She had asserted her superiority over the small man through sheer intimidation and knew the adrenaline was surging through the group as they awaited the kill. She was in control of the room. Now was the time to bring the rest to her side, to appeal to their need to be on the Alpha dog's team.

"I know *most* of you understand the importance of this project. Not only for medical and pharmaceutical reasons, but for the importance to a free society as well. Freedom is not a left-wing issue. And freedom is what this is about. Our company, BiEnCo, can offer women the freedom to be personally responsible for satisfying their desire to bear children.

"Consider a successful businesswoman who bypassed marriage to focus on her career and now wants to have a child. Of course, adoption is a possibility, as is a sperm bank. But each of those leave in doubt the genetic makeup of the child. In the case of adoption, she knows nothing about either parent. With a sperm bank, she knows nothing about the father's ancestry. If she conceives through egg-cell fusion, she knows all the child's genes come from her family tree. And there are those women who simply don't want or need the burden of a relationship with a man."

Hedstrom chimed, "I think they're called lesbians." Soft chuckling around the room was quickly covered with throat clearing and coughs as Marian's face flushed with rage.

An angular young man in a less powerful seat spoke up, "I've just recently come on the board, and I'm not a scientist. But I just don't see how this is different from human cloning, which has already been banned."

"The difference is", Marian replied through clenched teeth, "that cloning would involve taking a mature cell from a woman and creating a genetic duplicate of her. What I'm attempting is to cause a combination of genetic material from two of her egg cells to combine and begin mitosis, which is the cell division that causes embryos to grow."

Marian's anger subsided as she continued her explanation, "All the egg cells in a woman's ovaries are genetically different from one another. They all contain some of her genes, but also genes from her father, mother, grandfather, and so on. The combination of genes from two eggs would create a totally unique human. Also, all embryos conceived in this manner would be female, since it takes a Y chromosome to make a male, and that only comes from a male's sperm."

The young suit seemed satisfied with her explanation and nodded as Dr. Prevost cleared his throat to speak.

"Well, this discussion certainly got my blood pumping. Perhaps a bit too much for a man my age. Given that funding has already been approved through the end of this quarter, I'm going to close further discussion of egg-cell fusion until next month and move on to a subject that should be of interest to all present, since it has to do with both pharmaceuticals *and* profits.

"Dr. Foster is heading up this project as well, so please keep the floor, Marian. Let's hear an update on the progress of the new monoclonal antibody tests."

"Certainly." Marian nervously advanced her PowerPoint presentation to the appropriate charts.

"Oncostatin is showing great potential both in animal testing and early clinical trials as a primary therapy against Non-Hodgkin's lymphoma. In initial studies we're seeing average tumor size reduction of up to 65% after seven weeks. We also appear to have induced a total remission in one case. Detailed reports on the study are in these folders."

Excited murmuring spread through the group as Marian passed the documents around.

"These were limited trials, but very promising. Next week we begin a six month double-blind study at Bardstown University Hospital. We have 120 patients involved, which should give us a much clearer picture of the potential."

Prevost's prediction was spot-on. The room was electrified by the prospect of Oncostatin's future profits. Concerns about bizarre fertilization procedures were buried beneath fantasies of stock portfolios growing and expanding like malignant tumors.

As Marian exited the conference room she spied Dr. Prevost waving her closer. Marian bit her lip and prepared for a painful dressing-down. Gordon Prevost could bring a man to tears without lifting his voice above a whisper or relinquishing his smile. Stubby fingers combed through his graying beard as he watched Marian approach.

"Marian, I probably have enough clout to ensure the continued funding of your pet project for another three months."

Marian replied contritely, "Thank you, but -"

"But I don't have enough clout to save your career if you continue to perform like that. I'll admit you're damned good at molecular biology. You've got a talent for coaxing DNA to bend to your will. Your work could earn this company a lot of money, but don't forget that what you've already done is owned by the company. The 'bean counters' never forget that."

Prevost leaned close to Marian's ear and continued in a stern whisper, "Oncostatin might be big enough for them to let you become someone else's problem child. Your future potential means nothing to them, since you might have already made them all billionaires."

Prevost softened his tone slightly. "Luckily, Marian, not only do I respect your work - I actually like you, although I truly don't know why sometimes You just need to learn to keep your filthy little mouth shut until your brain comes on-line."

"I'm sorry, Dr. Prevost," Marian said softly. "I don't know what came over –"

"And another thing," Prevost interrupted, "I know you're close to human trials on your egg-cell fusion project. I expect you to maintain complete secrecy. Not a word of this leaks out until we've got real pharmaceutical benefits to show. The media already portrays us as the evil drug company that robs elderly widows of their pensions and deprives impoverished children of their medicine. I don't want us to be known as the ushers of the New World Order as well."

He gazed sternly at Marian, as if considering how to continue, then sighed and turned to enter his office.

"And Marian, it seems that the Group 12 rhesus monkeys have an accounting problem. Your records show a population of eight in that group and there are only three monkeys in the kennel tagged as Group 12. Obviously an error in your records, yes?"

As he closed the door he added, "I would take care of that quickly if I were you. And bleach the floors. Your lab is disgusting."

A handsome young man in a lab coat rushed up to Marian as she walked sullenly down the hallway. Carl Fontenot was hired as her assistant shortly after she began at BiEnCo. His boyish look, charming demeanor and eagerness to please made him an irresistible target whenever Marian felt a need to vent.

"Well, boss, how did it go?"

"Just fucking peachy. I might as well be teaching quantum physics to cavemen. Is the lab clean this time?"

"Lemony fresh. You'd never know that two hours ago all the equipment was covered in monkey –"

"Carl, I've seen it. I know what happens," Marian snapped. "Is there something else you need?"

"Uh, yes – do you have a projected timetable for human testing? Eight of the Group 14 fetuses appear viable this time. I'm assuming when we bring them to term, we'll be ready to start screening candidates."

"Human testing is already in progress," Marian said softly.

Carl grinned, but saw that his boss appeared to be serious. "No, come on…"

"I've decided that I should be the first human subject."

Carl's grin melted into an open-mouthed stare. He was waiting for the punch line to a bad joke, but Marian's expression was unchanging.

"You've got to be kidding!" Carl exclaimed. "You don't have Prevost's blessings on this. You're putting yourself and the company in danger. We're not even sure this is legal! There's a lot to consider here!"

Marian turned down the hall. "Then you should start considering," she called over her shoulder, "because I'm three weeks late."

*　　　*　　　*

Gordon Prevost slowly closed the door to his office and sprawled out on the black leather couch, wondering if he had bet the farm on the wrong horse.

God, I'm getting too old for this. He was battered and worn from his incessant defense of an abrasive employee he had guaranteed would bring untold success to BiEnCo. He glanced at the wall clock, wondering if it was too early for a drink.

Prevost had placed great hopes in Dr. Marian Foster. She was one of those rarities who, after completing a doctorate in medicine - top of class no less, chose research over a lucrative career in Oncology.

From the beginning, though, he'd had concerns. Marian seemed to enjoy a bit too much the persona she'd created – the attractive female genius whose purpose was to show men their true position in the hierarchy of life: A position somewhere between bacteria and crawling mollusks. Even before she began blowing up monkeys it was hard to find a team willing to work with her.

Marian had also come to BiEnCo with strings attached – her demands for an independent research grant for a highly controversial fertility procedure. Fortunately, along with the animosity she provoked, she was also responsible for developing a drug that had the potential to put BiEnCo on par with Pfizer in the world of pharmaceuticals.

Yes, Marian Foster still held some promise for the company. And Prevost knew that his career depended on her delivering on that promise. With another glance at the clock he deduced that it was 5:00 PM in Norway right now. Holding that thought, he went to his desk and pulled the bottle of Glenfiddich from the bottom drawer.

CHAPTER 2

Cancer wards smell like shit. And death.

Each new trial of a cancer drug reinforced Marian's choice of research over medicine. With every hospital visit she remembered the real reason for her decision: The smell. So much human waste and decay that it couldn't be overpowered by disinfectants. It just made it worse.

Marian's mood was foul on the day she began screening candidates for the Oncostatin study. Although her disposition rarely approached anything that could be called cheery, she was suffering heavily from the effects of the fertilization procedure she had performed on herself. Months of hormonal manipulation to stimulate her ovaries to release egg cells in pairs had created a personality that gave new meaning to the term "bipolar." Add to that the pain and irritation from weeks of inserting protein cultures from sperm cell coatings into her uterus and you had one turbocharged bitch.

Marian's role today was not so much that of a scientist, but of a football coach making roster cuts in an attempt to ensure a winning season. The first order of business is to try to eliminate those patients who stand the poorest chance of responding to the drug. Once the testing starts, you have to play the hand you're dealt. Always better to stack the deck if the opportunity presents itself. And the old woman in bed 34 definitely was not a top draft pick.

"Why is this woman a candidate?" Marian asked indignantly. "Her prognosis is three month survival!"

The nurse gave a thin smile and shrugged as Marian flipped through the patient's charts.

"My God, you're about to stop radiation *and* chemo on her and she's supposed to respond to my drug?"

The nurse's smile grew wider as she nodded toward the patient. Marian looked down at a skeletal old woman, wide awake and listening intently to their conversation. Angry at herself for the breach of decorum, Marian made a perfunctory attempt at proper bedside manner.

"Ma'am, have you noticed any additional nausea or dizziness today?"

The woman replied weakly with a smile, "Honey, I puke almost as often as I breathe. And when I *stop* being dizzy, I just hit the morphine pump again."

Marian impatiently reached to check the woman's pulse. As she touched the patient's hand, the woman's eyes rolled back in her head. Her hand clamped down on Marian's like a vise.

"Nurse! I need some help in here!"

As Marian called for the nurse, the old woman's body stiffened and she quickly progressed to grand mal seizure. Marian frantically searched for something to put in the woman's mouth to prevent her from swallowing her tongue. Nothing was within reach and she was unable to escape the woman's grip. The old woman convulsed violently, but amidst the panting and heaving, a faint chuckling sound grew louder. The seizure soon began to weaken and it became clear that the old woman was laughing.

As the spasms finally released their hold, a tear rolled down her right cheek as she softly whispered, "It's gone." Her raucous laughter then resumed in full force, only to be briefly interrupted by exclamations of "Sweet Jesus" and "Thank you, Lord."

Marian shook herself free of the woman's grip and angrily stormed from the bedside.

"Just great," she snarled to herself. "First notes: 'Patient shows possible side effects of FUCKING PSYCHOSIS!'"

The woman's laughter haunted Marian throughout the remainder of her examinations. *It couldn't have been my drug. No psychological side effects have ever been reported. Maybe the morphine or. . .*

As the day wore on, a new sound replaced the laughter that echoed through Marian's head. A soft whisper. *It's gone.*

*   *   *

After a night of troubled sleep, Marian arrived at the hospital to continue her rounds when a young radiologist waved her down.

"Dr. Foster, you need to see this."

Marian followed him into the lab as he continued, "One of our test patients was scheduled for a follow up MRI this morning."

He spread the MRI images across his desk. "These are from four weeks ago. And these are from this morning."

As Marian examined them closely, she felt her temper rising.

"This is absurd." She flipped rapidly through the images, then glared suspiciously at the radiologist.

"The tumor on this patient's pancreas must have weighed four pounds and you're trying to tell me that today it's gone?"

"Guess which patient," the radiologist asked, smiling. "The old woman who went crazy on you yesterday."

Marian narrowed her eyes, "If this is a joke, I swear you'll be looking for a job before lunchtime. You expect me to believe that a terminal patient went into remission after one treatment?"

The radiologist was laughing now, "No, it's better than that! She didn't get the treatment. She's in the group that got the placebo. She says that... that you cured her."

The young man dramatically laid his hand on Marian's arm. "With a touch!"

His laughter echoed through the ward as Marian stormed angrily down the hallway. The radiologist shouted after her, "Feel free to touch a few more patients on your way out!"

*   *   *

Marian's mood soured as she completed her rounds. Upon returning to BiEnCo, she stalked the halls, desperately in need of a victim to vent her rage. Finding the hallways empty, her sights, as usual, were leveled at Carl.

Marian entered her office and found her assistant hunched over his laptop surrounded by stacks of documents, one of which had infiltrated the corner of her desk. With a stroke of her arm she swept the stack onto the floor, scattering the papers.

"Your desk!" Marian declared, pointing at Carl's desk. "My desk!" she continued, gesturing at hers. "Do you think it's possible to make that distinction?"

"Sorry. Jeez," Carl muttered as he attempted to reassemble the stack. "This is the data from the rhesus monkey embryos. There's a lot to go through."

"Your job is to keep the data in order. I suggest you do it."

The sight of a handsome young man on his knees was already bringing Marian a bit of relief.

"How's it going with the Oncostatin trial?" Carl asked, placing the stack of research on his chair.

"Thank God I was smart enough to choose research over practice," she spat, throwing her files onto the floor.

"Listening to patients whining all day, searching for uncollapsed veins to pump useless pain-killers into soon-to-be corpses. . ."

"Must have gone really well," deadpanned Carl.

"Let's just focus on the fusion project, shall we?" she said, glaring at him.

"Got it. I suppose it's time to begin documentation on human trials, given your. . . status. Who's going to be your attending physician during pregnancy?"

"Dr. Waters."

Carl shuffled through an employee roster, looking puzzled, "We don't have a Waters on staff."

"God, those deductive neurons are just firing away aren't they, Carl? You make me so proud," she said condescendingly.

"Jennifer Waters. She's been my gynecologist since. . . for a long time."

Carl couldn't believe what he was hearing. "You can't go outside the company for this! You know we can't afford any leaks."

"I don't see any women certified as OB/GYN's on staff do you? The day I let a man —" Marian took a deep breath and regained her composure. "Final word: I don't want any further discussion and I don't want her name in your notes. The subject won't even be brought up until the experiments are complete."

"Whatever you say."

Carl removed a stack of forms from the printer and placed them inside a new file folder. "If you don't mind me asking, how does it feel to become a mother under these circumstances?"

"What the *hell* are you talking about?"

"Well, I mean, as experiments go, this is a pretty long one. Nine months, plus eighteen years – if they move out on schedule." Carl smiled.

"It sounds like you expect me to give birth."

Carl was perplexed. "Isn't that the desired result of this experiment?"

"*This* experiment," Marian asserted, "is to determine whether the procedure can cause spontaneous mitosis and form a healthy human embryo. Carrying to term will be phase two of testing."

"So you're planning to abort?"

Marian's eyes narrowed, "You have a problem with that?"

"Well . . . yes, I do. We're not talking about a used hypodermic needle. Human beings aren't exactly disposable."

Marian felt her blood pressure rising. "This 'human being' as you call it, is no more than a clump of cells the size of a tadpole, not even distinctly – "

She broke off and a smile crept across her face. "I can't believe it. Right under my own nose and I missed it. You're a goddamn Right-to-Lifer!" she laughed.

"And I thought I chose an assistant who might be slightly more evolved than the other Neanderthals."

Marian glared at Carl in disgust. "How could I have been so stupid? Handsome young Carl, the player!" she sneered sarcastically.

"I've seen those sperm banks you call women picking you up after work. A different one each week. Being God's gift to the female sex, of course you think you should have control over our sexual decisions."

Carl flushed, "You're out of line, Doctor. You don't know anything about me. I'm the one who uses contraception. I believe in safe sex."

Marian rose from her chair, overcome with blind rage, "Safe sex? If you're serious about safe sex, then I'd suggest castration. That would make us all feel a bit safer!"

She slammed the door on her way out.

*   *   *

"I don't know whether to feel flattered or insulted. A renowned scientist comes to me asking for a free pregnancy test." Dr. Jennifer Waters closed the examination room door behind her.

"I know this is no surprise to you," she smiled, "but I'm at least going to go through the motions of doing my job. Congratulations, Dr. Foster. You're seven weeks along."

"And this is where it ends," Marian replied sharply. "I'm going to need an extraction of the complete embryo. Whole and undamaged. Any suggestions on someone who can be discreet about this? And quick as well."

Jenny Waters had known Marian since grade school. Marian considered Jenny to be her closest friend. Jenny considered Marian to be – well, someone she had known since grade school. At one time she would have said they were best friends, but something had changed in Marian as they grew. By the time they graduated med school, Marian had become like a machine. An automaton driven by an endless loop of programming: Push harder. Harder. . .

Aborting a fetus for medical experimentation would land both of them behind bars. With the documentation required for a research project of this magnitude, it would be virtually impossible to cover their tracks. Unfortunately, Jenny knew from past experience that changing Marian's mind was usually a waste of energy.

"Marian, I know what you're trying to accomplish. This work is very important," she empathized. "But you really need to find someone inside the company. I can't be a part of this and I don't know of any reputable doctor who would –"

Marian interrupted, "I can't go to the company. I haven't told anyone that I've even begun human experimentation, let alone that I'm pregnant. There's already a lot of opposition to my work. They'd pull my funding instantly."

Jenny rose from her seat, "Do you know what you're asking? Forget about lost funding – you'd go to jail *and* be unemployable when you got out. And the same would happen to me if I help you."

Marian looked at Jenny desperately, "I've got money set aside. I could pay a surgeon more than he'd get for a organ transplant."

She decided it was time to play an ace. "I went out on a limb for you!"

The bitch had to bring that up again. Every time Marian needed a favor, especially something unethical, she used it. Jenny had struggled with her board exam while trying to become certified as an OB/GYN. But she never asked Marian to produce a stolen copy of the test for her. She did that on her own. *Damn this bitch.*

"Okay. There might be someone... " Jenny bit her lip nervously. "But I'll only ask him to call you. Nothing more. I refuse to get involved in this."

"Jenny, please. I need to have an intact embryo."

Pressing both thumbs into her temples to stave off the migraine that was taking root, Jenny reluctantly surrendered.

"I'll see what I can do."

*   *   *

In a dim corridor of the surgery wing at Sisters of Mercy Hospital, Dr. James Markham reviewed the night's schedule with the supervising nurse.

"So you're sure that there are three surgical suites available tonight in case of emergency patients?"

"I'm sure," the nurse replied. "But I don't understand why you're requesting an O.R. at 2:30 in the morning. With your reputation, I think you could get a kidney transplant rescheduled if you needed to remove a splinter."

Markham laughed, "That's kind. But the truth is that this is a favor of sorts – a charity case for a rather proud woman. This will allow her to remain anonymous and also make sure that O.R.'s are available for our paying clients. And you wouldn't want your patients seeing a retired old coot like me roaming the halls. Might scare them off if they think I'll be carving on them."

The nurse laughed with him.

"So who's going to assist?" The nurse asked.

"I'll be bringing in my own team."

"For a charity case? This must be important to you."

"Well, it'll be a reunion of sorts. The team I formed when I was chief of OB/GYN."

"Doc, you can't call it a reunion if there's no potato salad and Budweiser," the nurse laughed, "but this room is yours at 2:30. Good luck." She waved as she walked away.

"Yes. Luck," Markham whispered to himself.

*   *   *

At 2:30AM, Markham and three other men in surgical scrubs joined a sedated Marian Foster in the operating room.

Markham questioned the group, "No one was seen on the way in?"

The men shook their heads.

"Well, then, you know what we're here for. Let's get started. Vitals?"

An elderly assistant squinted through coke-bottle glasses, "Everything good. B.P. 108 over 74, pulse 53, O_2 is 3.7."

"Alright, speculum." Markham ordered. He took the chrome instrument in his hands and bent forward. Blinking several times in confusion, he shuffled sideways in a feeble attempt to stand upright.

His eyes shot open wide. A gray pallor spread across his face and a trickle of blood ran from his left nostril. Markham's knees slowly buckled as he fell forward. The blood formed a pool beneath his cheek as he lay on the tiled floor.

The other men in the room ran to where he lay. One quickly placed two fingers on Markham's neck.

"Jesus. There's no pulse!"

"Flip him! Start chest compressions!"

The doctor's body was rolled over and a second man began pumping his chest with both hands. "Can we get a crash cart in here?"

With each chest compression, thick streams of blood pulsed from the doctor's nostrils.

"It has to be an aneurism that ruptured. That's a hell of a lot of blood."

The men silently stared at one another as the gravity of the situation suddenly sank in.

"Fuck!" the anesthesiologist shouted.

"Shut her down, quick," he pointed toward Marian. "And somebody get the lights   Start cleaning up!"

*   *   *

Marian awoke shivering from the cold steel of the operating table. The room was dim and silent. She was alone. That probably wasn't a good sign. Still groggy, she stepped down from the table and felt a stickiness beneath her bare feet. She tripped over something large and fought to regain her balance. Her eyes were adjusting to the darkness and she was able to see that it was the body of an elderly man, lying in his own blood. A scream was about to escape her lips, but was stifled by a hand that quickly covered her mouth.

Jennifer Waters' voice spoke, "We've got to get you out of here!"

Jenny struggled to get Marian into her car, then swiftly drove off muttering, "Why do I even have to know you? God, the shit never ends! Why did I let myself - "

Marian began to emerge from the anesthetic, "What's going on? Where's the embryo?"

Jenny shouted, "Embryo? Worry about the goddamn embryo from your jail cell! That's where we'll both be soon!"

Marian replied angrily, "You said Markham could get this done! You said he had enough pull at the hospital to do this without being questioned."

Jenny shot back, "Markham has no more pull! Or didn't you notice that when you stepped on him?"

Marian's mind started to clear and she now remembered the body on the floor. "What the hell happened?"

"I got a call from one of his team telling me I needed to rush over and get you out. The guy wasn't too chatty, as you can imagine, but he thinks Markham had an aneurism that burst and bled out."

"He'd scheduled the room for a 'charity case.' So, if everything had gone well, there would've been no questions asked. His team brought in all their own instruments, right down to the anesthetics, so there wouldn't be a record of any equipment or supplies that could have been used for an illegal abortion."

Marian began to assess the gravity of the situation. "What about the doctors who assisted? Won't the hospital conduct an investigation?"

"Most of the 'doctors' who assisted don't even have licenses. They were old acquaintances of his. Abortionists from the days before Roe v. Wade. They were experts with techniques that today's surgeons never even learned."

Marian slumped against the door, her mind was spinning wildly.

"Yeah, you didn't know prestigious Dr. Markham had such a colorful past, did you. Before he was head of OB/GYN at University, he made his first million saving rich debutantes from embarrassment at their Sweet Sixteens."

Jenny sped toward I-85, anxious to leave the vicinity of the hospital. She drove on silently, her mind churning through the details of the evening.

She finally broke the silence. "Maybe there's a chance we can get away with this. The O.R. was clean. Nothing out of place. Somebody was smart enough to get Markham out of his scrubs. From all appearances, he arrives early to check the room, keels over, bleeds out. Nobody knows who the patient is or why they never show up."

"I never dreamt anything like this could happen," Marian said shamefully.

"Oh, of course not! What could possibly go wrong? Setting up an illegal abortion at the largest hospital in the state. Four men who could be jailed for practicing medicine without a license. Now we have a DEAD BODY! Fuck!"

Jenny pounded the steering wheel with her fist. "Fuck. Fuck!"

"You've been nothing but trouble since we were kids. I can't believe I ever listened to you! Here's your apartment. Don't call me. Don't text me. I don't want anything to do with you."

"But. . ." Marian stopped herself. She knew better than to bring up the embryo. Instead, she finished, "I'm sorry."

"Just get the hell out of my car."

*   *   *

In a small row house at the edge of Washington, D.C.'s Shaw district, a bearded man peers through the tarnished aluminum slats of the blinds covering his front window. The shining dome of the distant Capitol building towers above the sea of tenements that make up his neighborhood. Typical of the United States to parade the affluence of the powerful before the masses of the poor.

The man had lived alone for three years in this rat-infested house. Three years of watching, learning about America's capital city. What he saw sickened him. But his time of solitude was coming to an end; he soon would be entertaining guests. Guests bearing gifts.

Tiny leaden boxes containing bits of plutonium would start arriving soon. Quantities as small as 10 grams at a time. Amounts small enough to go unnoticed when pilfered from research facilities, university labs, and legitimate weapons manufacturers. But they would be coming. Combined, the amount of plutonium would total almost exactly sixteen pounds. Enough so that if compacted by a precise configuration of C-4 explosive, the resulting chain reaction would vaporize fifteen square blocks.

The Capitol was farther away than that, but the heat, radiation and firestorm of debris would instantly kill everyone inside, even if some small shell of the building remained. In seconds, the government of the United States would vanish. Everyone in the chain of succession to the presidency would be inside.

The man walked down the narrow steps to his basement and flicked on the light. Gleaming in the corner was a shining steel cylinder the size of a water heater. The man ran his hand across its polished surface and thought how beautiful it was. He turned eastward, sank to his knees, and gave thanks to Allah for being alive.

CHAPTER 3

Two weeks away from her office was becoming an eternity. Marian hadn't taken a vacation or sick leave in over three years and for a brief few days, the break felt good. Soon, though, the hours alone in her apartment were unbearable. Too much time to think Too much time to reflect. Marian hated reflecting.

The same old questions kept buzzing around her head like a swarm of hornets. *Why are you still alone? Why no relationships? Why is it that the only people who associate with you are the ones who are paid to?*

Marian wanted to scream, *Alright! I know, damn it. It's all because of me!*

She'd always used her childhood to justify her destructive behavior. Her father's abuse and eventual desertion. Her mom's death. Friendless except for Jenny. Marian knew these were hollow excuses. She'd made far too many decisions on her own that helped bring her to this point. How to change the situation remained a mystery, but she knew she had to get out of this damn apartment.

Returning to BiEnCo, Marian entered her lab and found Carl at the computer.

Without taking his eyes off the monitor, he asked, "So I assume your leave of absence resulted in something I need to begin processing right away?"

"Carl, I'm sorry."

"No need. It's just part of the job."

"I mean for the way I treated you. That was wrong."

Carl, stunned at the apparent apology, turned to her. "I'm listening."

"There is no embryo to examine. It's still in me."

Marian sat on the leather sofa and continued in a soft voice, "A man died trying to remove it."

Carl cautiously sat beside her. "What happened?"

"The doctor who was trying to extract the embryo died from an aneurism before he could perform the procedure."

"Everything about this project is going sour," she added quietly. "I was willing to risk everything – my career, other people's careers. I'm hiding in shadows like a criminal. Hell, I guess I am a criminal!"

Carl saw the tears glistening in Marian's light blue eyes.

She went on, "You know, it's not just the man who died. Turns out he was a bastard, anyway. But, I think I've lost the one thing that really meant something to me. I did actually have a friend."

The tears were now streaming down her cheeks. "Can you believe it, Carl? I had one friend. One. I'm twenty-nine years old and there was one person in the whole goddamn world that cared about me. And I used her again, like I've been using her since we were kids."

Marian was now sobbing heavily, "I can't stand being like this! I don't have anything in my life except this damn job."

Carl edged closer to Marian but resisted the urge to place his hand on her shoulder.

Marian stared at the floor and continued, "When we first started working together, you tried to be a friend to me. I forget now how I pushed you away. Did I insult your masculinity, or was it your intelligence? It's all become so automatic."

The silence grew so heavy Carl finally felt compelled to speak.

"I don't know all the details about your past. But the legend around here is that you had a pretty rocky start. You've accomplished everything on your own. I had help and support from a wealthy family and I'm lucky to have a job as a research assistant."

Carl fidgeted with the papers in his hand. "I guess what I'm getting at is, any time you'd like to talk . . ."

Marian wiped her eyes and chuckled, "Open up to another person? Seriously?"

She stood and tried to compose herself. "Let's take this one step at a time. Oh, and not a word about my crying. I can still fire your ass."

Marian flashed a hint of a smile as she walked away. Carl thought the smile might have been real.

*   *   *

Over the next weeks Marian's enthusiasm for work returned. The Oncostatin trials were exceeding expectations and the accolades of co-workers were starting to feel genuine. Her focus on the cancer drug also served to push thoughts of her egg-cell fusion project into the background.

Marian didn't want to be reminded she still had no embryo to examine and no clue what to do if her pregnancy was discovered. On the day that Jenny Waters called, Marian was hesitant to speak with her.

"I didn't think you'd ever speak to me again," Marian began nervously.

"Neither did I. But I guess friendships are hard for me to let go of. Even destructive friendships."

"I'm glad you called."

"I hope I don't regret it. I've been trying to decide if I really care for you or if I just pity you. You're a pathetic human being."

"Yeah," Marian sighed, "I had a similar discussion with my assistant."

"I know your childhood sucked, but you have to let go of it. You have to stop making the rest of us pay for it. We didn't do anything to you!"

The familiar justifications began to surface in Marian's mind.

"I've been staring at a mountain of obstacles all my life," Marian said. "The only way through them was to be a bulldozer."

"Everyone's tired of being run over," Jenny offered. "I'm the only one you have left. Thank God I have a few memories of you when you still had some redeeming qualities."

"Jenny, the years I lived with your family were the best years of my life."

"Yeah. Mine too. Oh, God! Remember junior prom?"

"Not the prom!" Marian laughed.

"I can't believe that I let you take me to the prom," Jenny chuckled. "I had real dates waiting in line!"

"Wasn't it worth it, just to see everyone's faces? I thought I made a handsome man."

"Oh yeah, my dream guy has shoe polish sideburns and mustache. I know it didn't bother you, but I resented being labeled a lesbian my entire senior year."

They both laughed.

Marian grew serious. "Jenny, I'm so sorry for dragging you into this. I know you've heard too many apologies from me, but . . . I can't afford to lose you as a friend."

"I could have said no. I'll take my share of responsibility. But we didn't get caught. History repeats itself."

Jenny decided it was safe to move into dangerous territory. "So how are you? How is the pregnancy going?"

"As far as I can tell from blood work and our piece-of-crap ultrasound imager, fine. But as soon as I start to show, I'm sunk. If I was sure that internal organ development is going OK, I'd just go ahead and ask for approval for human testing."

Jenny asked, "I don't understand why you won't follow standard procedure. The human testing phase is where you find those kinds of things out."

"Because I have one shot, Jenny. If one problem shows up, my funding's gone. BiEnCo won't give me a second chance."

"Marian, when has a procedure this complex ever gone off without a hitch?"

She replied adamantly, "Why do you think I've taken this so slowly? I was working the biochem part out while I was still in med school. I've had three straight successes with the rhesus monkeys. But you know the political climate. I'm screwing with Mother Nature and the will of God and at least a dozen other sacred cows. No, there can be no hitches."

There was a long pause before Jenny drew a deep breath and spoke. "Okay. The other reason I called is because I *might* have an idea. One that's legal. Almost. In several other countries where there are looser constraints on abortion, they've been experimenting with drug combinations to reduce recovery time as well as the risk of infections. There's one - a combination of RU486, ptocin and a cocktail of hormones, that can cause the detachment of the placenta and a complete expulsion without the need for a D & C."

Marian's excitement grew. "And this is legal?"

"The drugs are legal. The combination and intent to use them for abortion is not. But if you'll mix the drugs, I'll set up an IV you can administer yourself, Kevorkian style. If you're caught, you could still go to jail, but it would be your ass, not mine."

"How soon?" Marian's heart was pounding.

"I can probably get everything together by Monday. It'll have to be at your apartment. If I need to intervene, the story is: You did this all on your own, then panicked and called me. Deal?"

"Deal."

*   *   *

By early afternoon Jenny and Marian had set up the network of IV tubes and attached the appropriate mixtures of chemicals. A petcock valve on the IV tubing hung next to the bed so that Marian could begin the flow of the drugs herself. When everything was prepared, Marian got in bed and threaded the IV needle into a vein on her left forearm.

Jenny took a seat in a chair across the bedroom and signaled thumbs-up. Marian returned the sign and turned the valve on. They both watched as the clear liquid crept through the tube, growing closer to her arm. Marian lay back on the bed, and as the first drops of liquid reached her arm she felt an intense burning. Her chest was instantly numb and she gasped for breath. The growing red stain that clouded her vision meant she was bleeding inside her eyes.

As her body stiffened she could barely make out Jenny's silhouette calling frantically, "Marian! Oh God ..."

Then everything went black.

The darkness became an infinite field of dazzling white which dissolved like lifting fog to reveal a young boy around three years old. He ran down a polished hardwood hallway, giggling as his socked feet pounded the floor. The boy turned a corner and entered a beautiful study with a large picture window looking out onto a lake surrounded by maple trees in golden autumn glory. In front of the window was a woman typing at a computer, her back to the boy. The child ran toward the woman shouting, "Mommy, Mommy!"

The woman turned and scooped up the laughing boy, burying him in a bear hug. The woman was Marian. The white fog engulfed the scene again and dissipated, this time to reveal a busy metropolitan street.

It might have been New York City, except for the lack of filth. The streets were spotless, storefronts bright and clean. The throngs of people seemed to be engaged in animated conversation as they walked, rather than shuffling along with eyes down. An elderly Italian man was lifting an African-American baby out of a carriage as the mother looked on, smiling. A teen boy with spiked hair held a boom box as a Japanese girl and a Jamaican girl rhymed in unison. Scenes of fellowship and laughter unfolded in Marian's dream. Missing were the poor, the homeless, the hopeless. The white fog rolled in again, this time dissolving to darkness as Marian entered a deep sleep.

*　　　*　　　*

The darkness finally lifted, this time revealing Jenny's face.

"Finally waking up?" she asked as she lifted Marian's eyelid.

Marian squinted at the beam from the penlight in her eyes. "Follow my finger," Jenny said coldly.

"Where are we?" Marian asked dreamily as she watched Jenny's finger move from left to right.

"Hospital. You've been here two days. Looks like you're going to make it."

It was clear that Jenny was angry.

"Obviously I screwed up again. Can you tell me what happened?"

"Anaphylactic shock. I thought you were dead. You had a reaction to that cocktail the instant it entered your vein. Luckily, you didn't get enough for it to be detectable in the blood work. I was able to tell them it was a reaction to penicillin."

"Thank you," Marian replied weakly. "Again."

Jenny folded her arms and stared intently at Marian. "Unless you tell me the truth about everything, and I mean *everything* right now, I'm walking out for good. Find a new sucker."

"I . . . don't understand," said Marian.

"Don't even start with the lies. I took the liberty of doing an amnio."

"Damn it, Jenny, amnio could damage the fetus and I need – "

"You needed me to be sure you didn't have a dead baby in you," Jenny sharply replied, "But you were afraid of what I would find, weren't you?"

Marian began to respond, then stopped, a look of confusion on her face.

"I just don't get it," Jenny continued. "It's hard to believe that you'd go to such extremes just to cover up an unwanted pregnancy. Or that you're demented enough to want an undamaged fetus as some kind of souvenir. But on the other hand, I think you're smart enough to stop having sex if you're going to be using yourself as a guinea pig in a reproductive experiment."

Marian's mouth moved, but no sound emerged.

"OK, I'll play along. You wanted confirmation that your procedure worked? Well, it didn't work," Jenny snapped.

"I don't – "

"Your embryo is male. Your procedure can only produce females and *you* are pregnant with a boy."

Marian's brain rejected the word. *Boy. She didn't say that.*

Jenny went on, "You'd think my feelings for you would be gone by now, but what hurts the most is that you never told me. After all this time, you finally had a relationship and you never told me."

Marian was frozen in a blank stare. "This isn't possible."

"The sample never left my hand from here to the lab. I did all the tests myself. These are the facts: You are pregnant and your embryo is male. Now, give me answers or I'm out of here."

Marian began to cry now, "I'm still a virgin, Jenny. You've got to believe me. I've never had sex with anyone. None of this is possible."

Jenny's face softened a bit but not her voice, "Look. I've been your gynecologist since we both got out of med school. As far as the dictionary definition of 'virgin', you haven't been one since the first time I examined you. You'll have to do better than that."

Marian said softly, "As close as we were growing up, don't you think I would have told you about my first time?"

Jenny pondered, then replied coldly, "Yeah, I thought about that. But you always had a line that couldn't be crossed, no matter how close we were. There was a lot about you I never knew."

Marian's tears flowed down her cheeks as she continued, "I don't know exactly when it first happened. Either I've blocked it out or . . . it was when I was too young to remember. You knew things were bad at my house."

Jenny's hand flew to her mouth, "My God, Marian, you told me your Dad hit you, but – oh, Jesus – didn't you tell me he left when you were *nine?*"

"It had been going on a long time. How long, I have no idea. He would come to my room after I had gone to bed. He would be drunk. And… and…he'd tell me to close my eyes -" Marian choked as she fought the urge to vomit. "And it would hurt. My God, it hurt, Jenny."

Jenny embraced her friend as Marian collapsed onto her shoulder, sobbing loudly.

"I am so sorry."

Marian struggled to speak through her tears.

"Why do you think I'm like this? Why I've never had a relationship? Why I'm scared to have a man look at me, let alone touch me?"

Jenny held Marian as she wept. There was a whole new set of questions to be answered, but those could wait. Right now, nothing was more important than holding her friend.

CHAPTER 4

Marian spent the morning poring through old research files. She must have missed something. Some amphibians could spontaneously change sex during their youth, but was there a mechanism that would allow for this in higher animals? A male fetus wasn't possible with her procedure. DNA remnants in the sperm coating proteins? No. Every sample had been irradiated and double-checked. Nothing but amino acid-based proteins.

She slammed the last file shut. There was nothing here. Perhaps it was *her*. Marian made a note to schedule a ovarian biopsy to double-check the genetics of her own eggs. Nothing left to do except satisfy her caffeine jones. Coffee break.

As she walked through the lobby, she was met by Carl, waving a stack of papers excitedly.

"Have you seen this? Of course not – I just got them. You gotta see this!"

"If you stop waving them around, maybe I *can* see them." Marian took the papers and quickly began shuffling through, her eyes widening.

"Five weeks! Only five weeks in!" Carl grabbed the papers back and flipped frantically.

"Look - look at this - 2 complete remissions! Over here – average decrease in size of tumor 23%. Less than 5% not responding to treatment. Worst side effects - nausea and increase in frequency of urination! You did it!"

"*We* did it, Carl. We're a team. But remember, this study still has months to go. Sometimes side effects don't crop up for years. Never forget Thalidomide."

She studied the results a moment more, then turned to Carl with a huge grin, "*We did it!*"

Little work was done that day as BiEnCo took an unofficial holiday in celebration. A conga line of employees filed by Marian at lunch offering reserved congratulations.

She knew they despised her. They were all praying for side effects. As the line thinned, Dr. Prevost joined Marian at her table.

"I'm not even going to bother congratulating you. Your back's probably bruised from all the patting."

Marian smirked and rolled her eyes.

Ignoring her reaction, Prevost continued, "Instead, I'm going to ask that you lend some of this positive energy to another project. Ruben's team is coming up dry with the research on T-cell inhibitors. I think they may be in over their heads."

He smiled broadly, "I want to insert you and Carl in their team. I can't bust Ruben's balls by officially putting you in charge, but unofficially, you will be. I'll need you to report directly to me, and I'll make clear to them that your instincts are to be acted upon."

"Well, thank you," Marian replied, "but we've still got five months to go on Oncostatin, and my fertility project - "

"You can supervise the rest of Oncostatin with your eyes closed. I'm not concerned about that. And your fertility project has just completed animal testing, so this would be an ideal time to get away from it for a bit. If your input on Ruben's team is as valuable as I think it will be, I can assure you an increase in staff *and* funding on the remainder of the egg-cell fusion research."

Marian hesitated, "I'm just not sure - "

Prevost offered an unnerving smile, "I've never seen you show a lack of confidence before. It's somewhat endearing, but unnecessary with me. Your ego's as big as any doctor I've ever seen. So put your chip back on your shoulder and go get Ruben's team moving."

Prevost patted her arm and was gone.

* * *

"Thanks for seeing me. I'm about to drive myself crazy."

"And you needed me to join you in your journey to insanity?" Jenny sighed.

"This is impossible," said Marian, "unless we're totally wrong and it's more than just a Y chromosome that makes a male. But if we're wrong on that, then we might as well close BiEnCo. We're operating under the assumption that we actually understand genetics."

Jenny was glad to see that Marian was finally accepting her situation, even though no logical answers were apparent. She was also relieved that Marian's focus was no longer on harvesting the fetus.

"You're sure nothing in the animal testing pointed to this as a possibility?"

"Nothing," Marian replied. "Over forty successful fusions producing viable embryos – all XX female. Now I have three healthy female rhesus adolescents that appear to be perfectly capable of reproduction after they mature. I've been constantly monitoring blood cell formation as well as their immature egg cells and there is absolutely no evidence of abnormal mutations.

"I don't know what to do," she continued, biting her lip. "I don't think I can abort this. . . baby. Something's happening to me and I'm a little scared. I rely on logic, and logically, I should get this - the baby - out and see what's happening.

"I just can't stop thinking about the dream I had in the hospital. I saw that this baby was a boy, I saw myself as its mother, and it felt good. For once, everything felt right." Marian eyes began to glisten.

"I keep telling myself to forget about it," she said sternly, wiping her eyes, "but I can't. Every time I think about the damn dream, I can remember what it feels like to really care about something."

She looked up at Jenny. "And the whole world in my dream seemed...different. As if my having this baby had changed everything. The people were different. The feelings were different."

"What do you mean, the 'feelings' were different?"

"I could sense what the people were feeling. There was no more fear."

"Fear? Of what?" Jenny asked.

"Of anything. No fear at all."

Jenny began chuckling to herself.

"What?" Marian asked.

"I'm sorry." Jenny said, regaining her composure. "But when I add your dream into this equation, the story starts sounding familiar."

Marian looked at her, puzzled.

"A virgin becomes pregnant with a 'miracle child' and sees in a dream that her son will change the world? Please don't decide to give birth in a barn."

"Damn it, don't talk like that!"

Jenny exclaimed, "It's a joke, Marian! I just thought the parallels – "

"You've got me worried now." Marian pulled anxiously at a stray lock of hair. "I've risked my whole career on this project. Years of my life. And you're right, it sounds like an Internet fable from the Jesus nuts."

Marian ran a hand lightly over her stomach. Four months of incredible luck had passed, but she was finally beginning to show.

"How could I do this? When word of my pregnancy leaks out, I am so screwed. I've got to get that stupid dream out of my mind. I wish I had never told you about it. Please don't say a word to anyone. Promise!"

"Don't worry, " Jenny replied, "I promise."

A smile crept back to her face. "The rosary just wouldn't be the same: 'Hail, Marian, full of grace, the Lord is with thee...' "

"Just shut the fuck up."

Outside the examination room, a nurse was scribbling furiously on a notepad. Placing her ear to the door and hearing laughter still ringing in the office, she quickly went to Jenny's desk, grabbed the top page from Marian Foster's file and stuffed it into the copy machine. Retrieving the copy, she replaced the page into the file folder and ran from the office.

*   *   *

In a remote valley in Eastern Iran, the serenity of a majestic sunrise is broken by a sonic boom. A single missile rises over the Western mountains and descends toward a rock-walled compound in the center of the valley. Farmers and shepherds in the nearby foothills look upward to see the vapor trail spiraling downward, ending in a fiery explosion that collapses 200 feet of the stone wall and damages several buildings in the interior of the compound. The shepherd nearest to the compound is able to see a flurry of activity around the detonation as armed men emerge from the remaining buildings in the compound.

The shepherd watches as the men rush toward the impact site and, one by one, collapse to the ground in mid-stride. In his peripheral vision he also notices something spreading up the hillside toward him like a wave. His sheep are toppling over where they stand, as though blown over by a wind that could neither be felt nor heard. He stares in wonder as the sheep nearer and nearer to him topple to the ground like rows of dominoes. Before he has time to ponder the cause of this strangeness, he becomes aware that he cannot breathe, followed immediately with the realization that he can no longer move. His mind empties of thought and as his face strikes the ground he feels no pain, for he was dead before he had even begun to fall.

*   *   *

Marian and Carl joined a growing crowd in the BiEnCo cafeteria to watch a breaking newscast. A missile carrying nerve gas had struck a suspected terrorist training camp in Iran. Satellite and radar stations in the Eastern hemisphere had triangulated its origin as Israel.

The Israeli defense minister would not comment on the attack, but instead launched into a diatribe on Israel's right to defend itself. He focused on the previous week's assassination attempt of their Prime Minister by a terrorist group believed to be headquartered in Iran.

The newscaster reported that an emergency meeting of the U.N. Security Council had been called and several members were already demanding Israel's expulsion from the U.N.

The BiEnCo employees fell into a heated discussion preventing any of them from hearing the final news tidbit of the broadcast: Scientists had discovered a new comet that would pass within 2 million miles of Earth in five months, at which time it would become the brightest object in the sky.

CHAPTER 5

The morning sun glinted off the minarets of the Motahri Mosque in downtown Tehran as thousands of people poured into the streets. Some were lost in devout prayer, most were lost in anger. The news of the Israeli attack had quickly spread. A mob of protesters soon dwarfed the already immense crowd gathered in prayer outside a nearby hospital where their beloved Imam, Muhimir al-Akmed lay dying. For seven days he had lain in a coma and the throng of citizens anxiously awaited any final words from their spiritual leader.

In a small hospital room, his inner circle of Mullahs held a death vigil while debating the future of the ongoing Jihad. Ayatollah Al-Akmed had given his blessings to their holy war and his second-in-command, Kalil el-Hamir, was eager to accelerate the timetable for a massive attack.

An orderly rushed into the room. "Come quickly! He awakens."

The men crowded around their dying leader, who spoke to them in a strained voice with tears streaming down his cheeks.

"We have taken the wrong path. The violence must end. Immediately!"

The group glanced nervously at one another as the Ayatollah continued in a stronger voice.

"I was shown a vision by the Prophet himself. I have walked in His footsteps. Led to the feet of Moses, where a message was given to me: Allah sends the final teacher to walk among us. In his honor, the world must be cleansed of hatred."

The Mullahs looked at one another in disbelief. The leader-to-be, el-Hamir, spoke with a weak smile.

"You're feverish, Holy One. Muhammed was the Seal of the Prophets. This was Allah's decree. No more prophets will come. Do not speak blasphemy on your deathbed."

"This one is not a prophet," the old holy man whispered. "He is the great teacher who prepares us for the day of judgment. As was the prophet from Judea, he shall be born of a virgin. Signs in the sky and on the Earth will signal his coming. Governments will crumble. The religions of the world shall unite in His Name. He will lead the world into order. His coming brings the end of the Holy wars. The end of *all* wars. Peace will rule the land and he will guide us and all people into the final days. 1000 years of peace."

El-Hamir spoke angrily, "Holy one, this very morning, Israel has launched a chemical attack on our homeland. The infidels have no love for God or for our people. You have led our fight honorably for many years. I will carry on for you and destroy the devils that dare to stand against God's people. Their day of reckoning is fast approaching."

The Imam's voice softened. "These are my words to you and to our people: Make peace with our foes. Open your hearts and open your doors to those who were our enemies. Cleanse the land of hatred in honor of He who shall come."

Fire flashed in el-Hamir's eyes.

"We are close to destroying our oppressors! I will not lead our people into shame. Cursed are those who preach abandoning the Holy path!"

The Imam grasped the arm of el-Hamir.

"I have led us in Jihad for twenty-three years. Do not speak to me of the Holy path! Above all else, I am Allah's servant, and this is His will."

The Imam drew el-Hamir even closer and whispered, "I was shown what the world will be. It. . . is. . . beautiful."

The Imam fell back on his bed and with eyes open wide, breathed his last. All heads turned from the dead man to el-Hamir.

"This is my first message to our people: The Imam, Muhimir al-Akmed, died at ten forty-five this morning. With his last breath he promised to avenge the slaughter of our fellow Muslims. In Allah's name he swore that the infidels will meet with a fiery death. Go and tell the people."

The men hesitated, glancing uncertainly at one another.

"Go!" he shouted.

One man, Bashir Pezek, loitered behind the others. Bashir was not a Mullah, but a member of the Imam's elite personal guard. In all his years of service to the Imam, he had never seen such a look in the holy man's eyes. Gone was the fire that had burned as he had given his rousing speeches of Jihad and domination of the infidels. Gone was the passion for blood that had spurred Bashir into battle against the devils from the West.

As the Imam spoke his last words, his eyes shone only with the light of peace, of someone who had truly seen. Bashir had loved the old man and had pledged his life to him. He looked at the frail body in the hospital bed. Bashir was certain the man had seen something. What could it have been?

CHAPTER 6

Marian was dreading her first day with Dr. Ruben's research team. She knew too well the resentment that came when management inserted a new face into an existing team - especially when the face was that of an ambitious woman.

Marian strode confidently into the lab, "Good morning, everyone. We can skip the formalities for now. I'm sure everyone's aware of our new configuration. Can I get an update of our timeline?"

No one turned from their workstations to acknowledge her request, but a lab tech briskly passed her and slapped a newspaper into her hand.

She unfolded the paper to see the front page of a tabloid, The Global Enquirer, with the headline: "The New Madonna? Bioengineering technology leads to Second Coming of Christ. The Virgin Mother's dream of a New World Order."

With mounting fear, Marian frantically turned the pages.

The workers in the lab began to snicker.

Dr. Ruben approached Marian, "Normally we leak information to a publication such as *The Journal of the American Medical Association* or *Science*, but, I guess when you're desperate for funding any press is better than no press."

Marian's eyes tore through the two page article. *"Inside source reveals. . . gynecologist affirms her claims of virginity. . . the mother's prophetic dream of a new world."*

Surely not. Jenny couldn't have. . .

"Bold move for a researcher who hasn't begun human testing yet," Ruben continued, casting a glance at Marian's abdomen, "or is there something we don't know?"

Marian ran from the lab, not slowing as she exited the BiEnCo complex. She hurried across the parking lot, wiping away tears as she slid into her car. She had to get away from everyone, to have time to think. Marian couldn't bear to answer any questions from Prevost. She needed time to read the whole article. And to call Jenny.

*   *   *

"I've seen it," Jenny said sullenly. "My nurse was the 'unnamed source'."

"Fuck! Are you sure?"

"I found a copy of your medical records in her desk, and when I confronted her, she confessed. She didn't give them any hard evidence; she told them everything she overheard in our conversation on Monday, but was holding out for money before giving them documents."

"She gave them enough," shouted Marian, "They had your name!"

"They star-sixtynined her call and when the receptionist answered they got my name. But they don't have yours. She was holding that until she got cash."

"This is just fucking great! Along with all the quotes from Revelations about the final days, there were enough facts in the article to let everyone at BiEnCo know exactly who they were talking about. Jenny, that whole stupid dream was in there! I'm ruined. And God help me if BiEnCo's name turns up anywhere."

*   *   *

In the darkened offices of The Global Enquirer, a single flickering desk lamp cast a greenish aura on the photos of human freaks and gargantuan garden vegetables that were tacked haphazardly across the walls. The machine-gun cadence of fingers on a computer keyboard was occasionally interrupted by muted cursing and frantic adjustments to the lamp switch in an attempt to coax a few more moments of illumination from the dying appliance. Stan Wallace was on a roll.

The odor of blood was in his nostrils. This story could destroy careers. And the plot was of a genre that his readers loved. Profiteering pharmaceutical companies, self-deified scientists, corporate cover-ups. No god-forsaken, tarnished-brass, Goodwill-reject of a lamp was going to keep him from his literary character assassination. A hearty twist of the power cord brought a rejuvenated glow from the bulb.

A few phone calls and promises of Braves tickets on the first base line was all it had taken to get the passwords into local hospitals' admissions records. Stan chuckled to himself as he typed "anal_fissure" and was rewarded with a scrolling screen of personal privacy invasion.

Browsing through the records, he made a note of every name that had "J. Waters, M.D." in the column labeled "attending physician." The lamp flickered again as Stan made an illogical sexual reference to its mother.

*   *   *

Upon arriving at BiEnCo, Marian was greeted with the receptionist's curt message that her presence was required immediately in Dr. Prevost's office. She expected this. Hopefully she hadn't lost all her powers of reasoning. Last night was spent concocting a series of well-woven lies she hoped would buy her enough time to decide what to do next.

She entered Dr. Prevost's office. "Good morning, Marian," Dr. Prevost said cheerily, gently placing yesterday's copy of the Enquirer on his desk.

He smiled broadly. "What the hell is going on?"

Marian began, "I … made a huge error in judgment."

Dr. Prevost's smile was quickly fading, "Tell me about this. . . error."

"I needed an outside opinion on problems that might come up when we begin the human testing phase. I went to my personal OB/GYN because our staff physicians haven't seen the range of pregnancies she has. We've known each other since childhood and I knew I could trust her. Unfortunately, her nurse overheard us and thought she could make a quick buck by selling the story of the research to the Enquirer."

"Damn it, Marian, I told you to keep this inside the company!" Prevost bellowed. "What the hell possessed you to go to your personal physician?"

"None of our staff have ever attended an entire pregnancy. They've only worked under lab conditions. I needed to talk to someone who dealt with unexpected complications as a matter of course."

Prevost calmed slightly, "There was little detail about the research in that article. Mostly religious ravings about the next messiah."

Marian continued, "The Enquirer wasn't interested in paying her for a story about fertility research. Obviously, the writer she spoke to used the little information he had and built a story around it that was more... suited to their readership."

"Is there a remote possibility the nurse overheard the name of the company you work for?"

"I've relived the whole conversation several times, and I can definitely promise you that BiEnCo was never mentioned," Marian said, looking straight into his eyes.

"Now I'm going to ask straight up – are you pregnant?"

"Are you serious? You actually think I would experiment on myself?" Marian feigned indignancy.

"There have been several comments about recent changes in your wardrobe," Prevost replied, fingering his beard.

"So this is what a woman has to tolerate in this company if she gains a few pounds?" Marian's voice grew louder. "I don't suppose anyone has asked if you're carrying twins?"

Prevost sheepishly straightened his posture and attempted to suck in his gut a bit.

"Am I going to see any more stories about this?"

Marian closed her eyes and exhaled. "Unfortunately. . . probably so. Tabloid stories seem to have a lifespan proportional to their level of absurdity. How often have you seen Bat Boy on the cover?"

Prevost winced at the mention.

Marian continued, "But, I can promise the nurse won't give out any more information. Dr. Waters fired her and she's been threatened with arrest."

Prevost paused and rubbed his face with both hands.

"You're a laughing stock around here right now. Whatever grief the staff gives you, you deserve triple. God only knows what I'll hear from the investors."

He turned away from Marian and began shuffling through research reports.

"I haven't decided yet how to deal with you about this. Get back to work. You'll hear from me soon."

Marian hastily exited his office, wondering how much time she had just bought.

*   *   *

Stan Wallace was examining his list of patients admitted to area hospitals in the last two months by "J. Waters, MD". Most were easily dismissed. Deliveries of full term babies obviously had no bearing on the story   Ultrasounds for married women were also crossed off. Only one patient didn't fit the normal pattern. Marian Foster.

Length of stay was two days. Treatment for anaphylaxis due to penicillin allergy. Why would a gynecologist be the attending physician on a patient with a penicillin allergy?

Stan opened a browser window on his computer and searched "Marian Foster, Atlanta." His eyes widened as the pages of results quickly topped twenty.

He scanned the first few hits. Articles published in the Journal of the American Medical Association. Magna cum laude, NYU 2003. M.D. from Harvard Medical School. A press release on her hiring at BiEnCo Research, a pharmaceutical and bioengineering firm in 2006. *Bioengineering!*

Stan smiled. "Gotcha," he muttered, "Tampering with forces beyond man's understanding. Meddling in God's affairs."

Stan was a pro at working these kinds of stories. Leave it to the rest of the hacks to create the tales of aliens controlling the pope's brain. He could weave in enough truth that his stories had legs. Stan Wallace stories lived on and became urban legends, tales told around campfires and spread on the Internet.

He felt he had at least enough to go on to make a credible case for devilish experimentation on human embryos. But something told him to push further. Something bigger was hiding here.

On page two of the search results, he found a press release that he read in its entirety. A double-blind study was currently being conducted on a new cancer drug at University Hospital, headed up by

Dr. Marian Foster of BiEnCo Pharmaceuticals. Early results seemed to be very impressive. Name of the drug: Oncostatin.

On a whim, Stan typed in "oncostatin" in the search bar. Perhaps he would luck out and discover some bizarre side effects that would be helpful in building a case against a satanic drug manufacturer.

The results page showed only two hits. The first was the same press release on the study he'd just read. The second was a link to the on-line bulletin for the Mt. Vernon, Arkansas Evangelical Church of Christ. Only one choice here, Stan thought as he clicked on the link.

He scanned down the page and shouted, "Yes!" and pumped his fist. "He shoots! He scores!"

". . . the congregation erupted in shouts of praise as Mrs. Wilma Barnhardt, 78, testified to her miraculous healing from terminal cancer. Mrs. Barnhardt had been participating in a study on a new drug called Oncostatin at Bardstown University hospital and had been pronounced completely cured.

"Wilma testified, 'I was touched by God's grace. I knew I was cured even before the doctors told me. They were shocked because I was one of the patients who didn't really get the drug. They gave me a fake, but I knew exactly what had happened. There was a young woman doctor named Foster who touched my hand and filled me with God's healing power. She has the gift. I knew right then that I was cured. That doctor is one of God's miracles.' "

Stan was ecstatic, "This calls for an interview! We need to hear this straight from the horse's mouth."

He flexed his fingers and placed them on the keyboard. Pausing in thought for a moment, Stan abruptly stood and grabbed a windbreaker from the chair.

"Hell, I'm so happy I'll even go talk to her before I write it." He left his apartment whistling merrily.

* * *

In a hastily-called meeting of the United Nations Security Council the Iranian ambassador was demanding Israel's expulsion from the Council and the General Assembly. The ambassador claimed no responsibility for the Scud missile launched into downtown Tel Aviv yesterday morning.

"The Israelis should be expelled immediately! They are criminals! This is the first use of chemical weapons since the Second World War. The missiles that were fired upon our country were launched from Palestinian territory that has been illegally occupied by Israel since 1967. We have no such weapons to defend our country. The West has seen to it that we remain defenseless."

The American ambassador asked, "When you refer to the first use of chemical weapons since World War Two, do you mean *other* than their use by Islamic countries against their own citizens?"

"Lies! More insane rumors of 'weapons of mass destruction.' Another excuse to invade our lands and find nothing!"

The Chinese ambassador rose to speak.

"The Israelis have initiated an unprovoked attack on a nation very close to our own borders. We support their expulsion and Beijing is adamant that such weapons will not be tolerated in our part of the world. I can promise you, another attack on Iran will be viewed as a threat to China's security. And we *will* take action."

The Iranian spoke again, "At Friday's General Assembly, Iran and 32 other nations will walk out in protest. Some of the nations who are joining us will surprise you. The United Nations does nothing to protect the interests of small countries against aggression from the rich and powerful. We will take matters into our own hands now. And you shall see what small nations do when they're tired of being stepped on."

The ambassador gathered his notes and stormed out.

The Israeli ambassador stood and addressed the remaining members, "My colleague spoke one bit of truth. The United Nations truly does little for the smaller nations. It's nothing but a façade – a game we've played because we've been afraid not to.

"Since the creation of the State of Israel, our borders have been under constant attack. We've been cajoled into compromising away our settlements and have fought constantly for our very existence. My government has informed me that we are withdrawing from the Security Council and the General Assembly."

The American ambassador looked shocked, "If you withdraw from the U.N., I can't promise continued American support!"

The Israeli ambassador stood and closed his attaché.

"Our people have survived 3000 years without American support. We can certainly do without it now."

*   *   *

The phone rang at Marian's desk.

"Marian Foster."

"Dr. Foster," the voice on the phone responded, "you need to speak with me right away."

Annoyed, she replied, "I'm not interested in anything you're selling. So, if you'll excuse me – "

"I need to talk to you about your baby."

"What?"

"Quite a miracle, isn't he. And quite a big secret, too."

"Who is this?" Marian snarled into the phone.

"Come meet with me and find out. You'll be interested in how much I already know about your little baby bump."

Marian felt her insides turn to ice. She inhaled deeply, struggling to keep her composure.

"Where?"

"Varsity Grill. 8:30. Table in the back corner by the bathrooms. And don't be afraid, Marian. I just want to be your friend."

Stan hung up the phone, stretched and leaned back in his chair.

"Some days my job is just too easy."

CHAPTER 7

After the six hour drive to Atlanta, Stan's back was killing him. Even after several stops to relieve the numbness in his legs, the agony was peaking. He had blown a disc out in his back almost seven years ago. After hearing what would be involved in surgery and recovery, he opted to just deal with the pain.

Most days it was bearable. He had accepted the reality that getting into a car sometimes took five minutes. He had become used to relying on the handrails to get himself up and down stairs. He had even decided his slight limp added a bit of mystique to his personality.

But today there were no such happy rationalizations. The sporadic jolts of pain caused him to curse out loud. He desperately wanted to kick someone's ass. The thought of Marian Foster seated by a reeking bathroom in a hot dog joint, waiting nervously for him to arrive and ruin what was left of her life brought Stan a brief smile.

He never knew how these interviews would go. Tears. Shouting. A broken nose, perhaps. At least he had already filed a follow up story that would be in tomorrow's edition. Anything he gained tonight would be gravy. And he had a feeling this story had a future. A big one.

As he pulled into the parking lot of the Varsity, Stan dug in his glove compartment for his fake press credentials from the Atlanta Constitution. He had phonies from every major newspaper in the country. They seemed to help people open up to him.

Stan entered the Varsity and headed toward the rear. He immediately noticed a young, slender blonde sitting at the corner table glancing around nervously. Not too hard on the eyes at all. He walked to the table.

"Are you Marian Foster?" Stan asked.

"*Doctor* Foster. You're late and I'm giving you five minutes, so get to the point."

"I apologize for my tardiness. Name's Stan Wallace."

He extended his hand but Marian didn't return the gesture. Stan offered a patronizing smile and seated himself across from Marian.

"You've received some disturbing press in the tabloids about your pregnancy and I thought you might be anxious for someone to tell the truth about it. To tell your side. You know, the real story."

Marian was wary, "I really don't know what you're talking about, and I don't read tabloids."

"You're pregnant," Stan began as he opened a pocket-sized notebook, "you're 29. Dr. Jennifer Waters is your gynecologist. You were treated at University Hospital by her on March 12th and 13th for a severe reaction to a penicillin allergy. Yeah, right."

Stan glanced up at Marian, smiling, and continued, "You were in Dr. Waters' office for an appointment on March 15th where you were overheard by a nurse named Ruth Batson. You work at BiEnCo Research where you developed a drug called Oncostatin and while overseeing tests at University Hospital, touched and healed a dying woman of cancer."

Marian glared at him through narrowing eyes.

"I found all that out in 10 minutes on the Internet. You can be sure the Enquirer has this information too. You need to tell your story before you become a national laughing stock."

Marian thoughtfully considered all she had just heard, then spoke, "Who do you work for?"

Stan reached into his breast pocket for the press credentials and offered them to Marian.

"Atlanta Constitution."

Marian reached to take the I.D. and as her fingers brushed Stan's, an electric jolt shot through his body. A memory from long ago flashed briefly in his mind, then evaporated.

Marian examined the I.D. and handed it back to Stan, who was studying his hand closely. He slowly turned and looked cautiously at Marian. He reached forward, and instead of taking the I.D. back, grabbed Marian's hand forcefully. The electricity shot to the top of his head and he began breathing heavily, a look of terror on his face.

Marian shouted, "What are you – LET GO! Let go of me!"

But Stan was gone. He was sitting in the office of the Dean of the School of Journalism at Ole Miss. The year was 1982.

"You could have a future in journalism, Stan, but you need to change your style. The student body enjoys your flamboyant hyperbole, but this is no substitute for actual reporting. Appealing to the lowest common denominator won't earn you any respect in journalism."

The Dean's office dissolved and in an instant, Stan found himself reliving his interview for a position with U.S. News and World Report.

The editor was saying, ". . . good background at the dailies you've written for, but your style really isn't appropriate for us. Our philosophy is: the story exists. You don't need to create it. Just report it."

Stan found himself instantly back in the noisy restaurant as Marian jerked her hand free.

"What the hell is the matter with you!" she shouted.

"I lied to you," Stan said, trying desperately to catch his breath. "I work for the Enquirer. I'm the one who wrote that story."

Marian slapped him hard across the face, stood and shouted, "If you ever come near me or call me again, I'll have you arrested! I swear to God!"

She hastily turned and left.

Stan barely felt the pain from the slap, which left a distinct handprint across his left cheek. His heart was still pounding, his vision blurred. He slowly stood and walked to the parking lot, his mind a blank, unable to conjure up one thought to fill his empty head.

Stan lumbered to his car like a zombie. He turned the keys in the door lock, opened the door and instinctively braced himself for the pain that always accompanied entering the front seat of a car. But it never came.

The missing pain shocked Stan back into reality and his mind instantly flooded with thoughts. He stood back up and sat again. Still nothing. A third time. He jumped out of the car and stood in the parking lot. Stan braced himself for agony and began leaning forward, bending at the waist. He continued downward until his fingers touched his toes for the first time in seven years.

"Jesus Christ!"

Stan broke into a cold sweat as he jumped in and started his car. "Jesus freakin' Christ," he said as he sped off.

*   *   *

The next morning, Marian was once again greeted at the door of BiEnCo with a request to go immediately to the CEO's office. This time when she entered the office, Prevost was not there. Instead, at his desk sat Alvin Hedstrom.

"Where's Dr. Prevost," Marian began, "I have a meeting with him."

"No, your meeting is with me," said Hedstrom, "and it will be brief."

He offered a piece of paper to Marian.

"I'm pleased to inform you that you are no longer an employee of BiEnCo."

Marian was stunned. "What? I want to speak with Dr. Prevost!"

"He is no longer a member of our little family either. He resigned yesterday. Saw the writing on the wall, I guess. The board of directors felt that he was leading this company down an unsavory path. Our stock took a big hit with the publishing of the latest article in the Enquirer this morning."

"*This* morning?"

Marian was momentarily confused, but quickly regained composure.

"You have no grounds to fire me. It takes more than a rumor in a tabloid to dismiss an employee with tenure."

"Oh, definitely. You're absolutely right. It takes things like $80,000 in funds missing from your research account."

It was the money paid to Markham for the unsuccessful abortion. Marian's heart sank.

Hedstrom went on, "And I've audited your inventory and found the drugs and equipment that you took home for your little experiment. Leaving a signed receipt for several liters of human semen in your desk drawer was really stupid for a woman of your education. So we have: theft, fraud, unauthorized human testing, and divulging confidential company information. You're through here. Just one other little matter before we part ways."

He reached into a desk drawer and pulled out an inch-thick document.

Marian looked at the top page titled, "Petition for Ownership of Intellectual and Physical Property."

"What's this?"

Hedstrom smiled, "Just some light bedtime reading. A little reminder that in your employee contract you signed an agreement that, should you ever leave the company, all knowledge and materials developed in the course of company funded and sanctioned research immediately becomes, now and forever, company property."

"No problem," Marian shot back, "Take Oncostatin. Take it all! I won't even clean out my desk."

Marian rose to leave.

"What you have of ours isn't in your desk," Hedstrom said gravely, gazing into her eyes.

Terror struck as Hedstrom's demand clarified in her mind.

"You're insane! This is a baby. This is a human being!"

"That's not a certainty at all. Until genetic tests are done, we don't know what it is. And it doesn't meet the legal definition that affords protection to human embryos. It was not conceived by 'natural or medically proven means.' It doesn't even contain any genetic material from a male. This is totally the result of BiEnCo funded research and it is now our property."

"No court will ever allow you to take a baby as property. You're off your fucking rocker!"

Hedstrom smiled, "We look forward to presenting our case in court. If you left here with a computer chip implanted under your skin, or an experimental pacemaker, or a cloned kidney, we would have the legal right to demand it back. It's our position that this is no different. And we're putting this on a fast track, Marian. We have friends in District Court that assure us we'll have a decision very soon."

"Talk to my lawyer if you have anything further to say!" Marian shot back as she rose and headed for the door.

"Oh, we will. You have something of ours, Marian, and we're going to take it back."

*   *   *

As Marian drove from the parking lot, she called from her cell phone to an inside line.

A voice answered the phone. "Hello, this is –"

"Carl," she interrupted, "it's me."

"Dr. Foster! I just heard what happened."

He continued in a whisper, "Goons from the management office are tearing this lab apart. They're taking everything concerning the fertility project."

"Shit. Is there anything left in my desk? The file you and I started two weeks ago?"

"Your desk is empty. I have everything that was in it. I got it as soon as I heard you'd been sacked."

"Thank you," Marian said gratefully.

"Can you get it out of there? I'll call you later and arrange to meet up, O.K.?"

"I think I can get it out. They haven't put snipers at the door yet, but with Hedstrom in charge, it's only a matter of time."

Marian sped through traffic to the office of Waldham and Barnes law firm. Meeting with Susan Barnes, she quickly explained the background of her pregnancy as Susan looked over the legal document Hedstrom had given Marian.

"I'm four months pregnant, Susan. There's no way they can get this through the court system before the due date."

Susan continued to read the document quietly.

"Is there?" Marian pleaded.

"I'm not going to make odds on this one, Marian. We're in new territory here. There's no precedent for a case like this. If they believe they can convince a judge you're carrying a future freak show attraction, then your due date will become the timeline for this case. If you give birth to a healthy baby, no court will take it away and BiEnCo knows that."

Susan took a deep breath. "You have to realize that there are a lot of judges who are dying to have a high profile case like this. District and Circuit Court seats are just political stepping stones, not careers for most. These guys have political ambitions and they want their names in the paper. This case will get into court quickly, no doubt."

Marian felt the world closing in on her.

Susan continued, "What happens after that, well, that's the mystery - and the troubling part. My best guess is, this case will be appealed all the way to the Supreme Court. With the fast track this case demands, it conceivably could be in their hands within five months. Given the current makeup of the court, I think they'll shy away from making such a controversial decision. they'll probably refuse the case. Which means the decision of the last Federal judge to hear the case will probably stand."

"So what will you do?" asked Marian.

"Just try to finesse the game. We have to make sure we can get the case heard by the right judge when it reaches the end of appeals. If we have to lose a decision, we want it to be early on."

Tears began to form in Marian's eyes. "How can this be happening?"

Susan tried to comfort her, "Just get away for a few days. Try to relax. It's my job to do the worrying now. Let me spend some time on research, find out where they're going to try to have the case heard, and when I need you again, I'll call you."

"I won't let them take my baby," Marian said softly.

Susan tried to hide her doubts. "We won't let them," she said.

*   *   *

As Marian entered her apartment, her phone was ringing. She walked across her living room and answered.

"Hello."

"This is Stan Wallace. Please don't hang up —" Marian slammed the phone down.

It immediately began ringing again. Marian walked into her kitchen and began looking in the fridge for dinner. She heard the answering machine pick up.

"Marian. You don't have to talk to me, but, please just listen to this message. I don't want to write any more about your story. I just need to find out what you did to me.

"I've had a ruptured disc in my back for seven years. I could barely walk. When I grabbed your hand last night, all my pain went away. I just got back from my orthopedist and he told me my disc has been repaired. I've got the MRIs right here in front of me.

"I talked to Wilma Barnhardt too — the lady that says you cured her of cancer. According to her, when you touched her she flashed

59

back to a period in her life a long time ago, like she was reliving it. When you touched me, the same thing happened. I'm really confused and – "

His voice was straining at the edge of desperation.

"I just have to know what you did to me! That dream you were telling your doctor – "

Marian grabbed the phone. "Let me begin by telling you, I don't believe a word you say. Secondly, I don't give a damn what you do or what you write. I have nothing more to lose! You've already cost me everything, including my baby!"

"NO!" Stan interrupted, "You have to have this child!"

"Well, thanks for the support, but it's not in my hands anymore because of you. This is now a court case. My company is claiming the baby as their property!"

"They can't do that! No court will stand for it!"

"Well, my lawyer's not so sure. . . What am I even talking to you for? Good bye!"

"No, please! Wait! Do you believe in God?"

"What? I don't know. What does this have to do – "

"Just meet with me. Please. I'll do anything. Sign anything. I'll meet with you and your attorney, or. . . anything! I know you think I'm scum, and you're right. But I wasn't always like this. I remember now."

I wasn't always like this. Marian struggled with the feelings resurrected by that sentence. They were quickly swept away by a new thought that rose like a bubble to the top of her consciousness.

A voice in her head was whispering, "Do it."

"All right. I'll meet with you. If you're lying to me, I swear I'll castrate you."

"Thank you, Dr. Foster. I'll even bring the knife."

*   *   *

The following evening, Marian met with Stan Wallace in her apartment, his MRI pictures and research covering her desk. Stan spoke passionately about his experience when he touched Marian. Slowly, reluctantly, she found her cynicism dissolving away.

"Either you're a great actor, or you're not as much of a slimeball as I thought you were," Marian said critically.

"You're not far off," Stan offered, "I am a slimeball, and I've been a good enough actor to cover it up when it suited me."

"So, I'm supposed to believe that with the touch of my hand, you've become a changed man. What's next? Do you plan on joining a monastery?"

Stan stared at Marian as he considered his next question.

"Do you remember the moment when you first decided you wanted to be a doctor?"

Marian eyes met Stan's and she quickly looked away

Stan asked again, "Do you remember the feelings that made you want to be a doctor?

Marian carelessly thumbed through the papers strewn across the desk.

"I was just a kid then. I didn't have any idea what being a doctor was all about."

Stan continued, "I bet you did it for a good reason. Kids make decisions like that for a good reason."

He leaned forward so their eyes could meet again.

"I remember. I had my reasons for why I began writing. But I can't come up with a single good reason why I've ended up the way I have. I have to make that up to myself."

"So you had good reasons once? What were they?"

Stan sat down, rubbed his eyes and smiled.

"My dad never would listen to my stories."

Marian shifted uncomfortably in her seat as he continued.

"My dad was Mr. Blue Collar. Not a bad father, I guess, but typical for the time. Ten hour days, worked most weekends. In his world, home was *his* time, no one else's. He put in his time for family at the factory. Food on the table was his contribution. After supper was TV, beer and bed. One night a week out with the guys.

"I would write stories for him when I was little. Hide 'em in his lunchbox. He never said anything about them. When I finally asked him if he liked my stories, he just said, 'Never been much into fiction, kid'."

Stan went on, "The only thing I ever saw him read was the U.S. News and World Report. That was the only magazine we got at our house. I finally figured out that if he was ever going to read one of my stories, it would have to be in that magazine.

"So I decided to go into journalism, but could never get the storyteller in me to shut up. So I wound up in the only branch of journalism that loves fiction."

"The Enquirer," Marian smiled weakly.

"Yeah, the Enquirer. I just wanted my dad to finally read one of my stories."

Marian stared vacantly into the distance.

"I remember."

The words began to fall under their own weight. She tried, but couldn't stop their momentum.

"My mom was a heroin addict. When I was thirteen, she tried to kick. I stayed with her, locked in the house for six days. In between the screaming and puking and trying to keep her out of the knife drawer, that's when I decided I wanted to be a doctor."

A tear ran down Marian's cheek. "I wanted to be able to make people stop hurting."

Stan nodded, "Maybe you finally got your wish."

*   *   *

In a hastily called emergency session, 46 countries including China, France, Saudi Arabia and Pakistan joined Iran in leaving the General Assembly of the United Nations. What remained were mostly Western bloc nations. The world watched fearfully as the organization which had prevented World War Three for over half a century slowly crumbled.

In the White House, President Mitchell Stanton was meeting with Secretary of State Hugh Turner and foreign affairs advisor Judith Cromwell. Turner had the floor.

"It looks like the rest of the African nations and Middle East are going to pull their ambassadors on Monday. Russia's economic arrangements with several of these countries make it quite embarrassing for them to remain."

"I guess this is it, then," the President began. "It lasted over a half-century longer than anyone originally expected. What can we do in the short term? We need, at the very least, an informal way to keep the communications flowing."

A uniformed man briskly entered the conference chamber and handed a paper to the Secretary of State before saluting, turning on his heels and exiting.

"Damn. It's starting. OPEC has called for an immediate embargo on oil shipments to the western countries."

"Surely Kuwait didn't join?" Cromwell inquired.

"They're probably the only ones from that region we can count on for now. Even with what we can squeeze from the Saudis, things are going to get tight."

The uniformed man made another appearance to deliver a brief to Cromwell.

"More good news?" asked the President.

Cromwell scanned the document.

"Military action on the India - Pakistan border. No certainty yet, but it appears India is the aggressor. Also, satellites show troop movements reinforcing the borders of all the countries that have withdrawn from the U.N."

"Everyone's scared. It's to be expected," offered Turner.

"Not from China. Their borders have always been secured at wartime levels. The number of troops they're moving right now point to a pending offensive strike."

Silence fell upon the room, but was sharply broken by President Stanton's order:

"I want you to set up a meeting for me with Tom Hunt."

"Mr. President, I have to advise against that," Turner said forcefully. "He's still convinced you stole the election from him and he's building an ideological war chest for next time. This will do nothing more than give him fuel."

"And confidence," Cromwell added.

"You can both stand down," said the President.

"Your loyalty is duly noted. Both of you know we've got a lot worse to worry about than an election that's two years away. Do you think it's easy for me to admit that arrogant son of a bitch can deal with China when I can't? He's responsible for almost every trade agreement we have with Beijing and I need him now."

"Do you really think China will talk, even to him?" asked Cromwell.

"Officially, no," said the President. "But unofficially, he can get people on the phone who won't speak to me."

"I'll go make the call," said Turner.

"There's something else I want to talk to him about," added Stanton. "Thirty years ago, when he was a freshman Senator, he floated around this idea for a global economic union. His position was that the U.N. would soon be obsolete, that monetary crises would quickly become more dangerous than political ones. Of course, he wasn't taken seriously. In those idealistic days, no one wanted to consider that money might be the solution to all evils. It was the *cause*. I think the time has come to take another look at his ideas."

"Yes, sir." Cromwell and Turner replied in unison, and sharing an uncertain glance, left the room.

CHAPTER 8

Marian was quite surprised at herself. Her yielding to Stan Wallace's request for another meeting defied all logic. She had been abused by a man once again, her privacy invaded and her career in shambles, yet she was agreeing to help him make sense of a troubling personal situation.

Don't I have enough problems without playing Good Samaritan to a slimeball journalist?

One part of her mind was telling her to watch her back, keep her guard up. Another unfamiliar part kept pushing her forward. For the first time in her life, Marian's logical side was losing an internal battle. The sound of her doorbell raised the hairs on the back of her neck. *En garde!*

"Come in," she said, her tone as cold as she could muster.

"Thanks for seeing me again," Stan said as he entered. "You were good enough to listen to me ramble on about myself. Tonight, if you don't mind, I'd like to hear more about your situation and see if there's a way I can help fix some of the damage I've done."

Marian's suspicions quickly rose.

"I agreed to meet with you about your supposedly miraculous recovery from an injury I doubt ever existed. I don't think I want to give you any more information about me. If I've answered the questions you had about our first meeting, it's probably time for us to part ways."

"I don't blame you for being suspicious. But I wanted to tell you, I've looked into your legal situation with some friends of mine – "

Seeing the angry expression shadowing Marian's face, he quickly added, "No names mentioned. Purely hypothetical. But, unfortunately, they came to the same conclusion as your lawyer. This is definitely not as cut-and-dried as I'd assumed. You've got a tough fight ahead."

Marian's face softened and Stan could see the fear in her eyes.

"And what advice did your 'friends' have to offer?" she said sarcastically.

"My friends happen to be an Atlanta District Attorney and a Circuit Court judge."

Marian had envisioned rumpled personal injury lawyers shooting bourbon at a waterfront dive.

"I do have sources in high places," Stan said.

"Anyway, they both agreed the political climate would probably determine the outcome. And we've been riding a conservative wave in national politics over the last several elections."

"So, in their opinions, what's the probable outcome?"

"Not good. Your child may fall outside the current legal definition of human life. It has no genetic material from a male, yet it's not a clone. Sorry I don't have better news."

"Yeah. Me too." Marian was determined not to cry.

"The conservatives are divided on many issues, though. And we may be able to use that," Stan continued.

"We've got a faction of pro-business pragmatists who would happily hand you and your baby over to BiEnCo if they thought it would boost the stock market. On the other hand, we've got the religious right, who would consider it a damnable sin to treat a baby as property, let alone abort it for research. Perhaps we should try to get the religious right on your side."

"That option looks pretty bleak," Marian said distastefully.

"I'm not so sure about that. When it comes to sheer numbers, the religious crowd may have the upper hand."

Marian grew furious upon hearing this.

"I'm a scientist! A genetic engineer! These people would happily dance around me chanting, 'Witch!' while I burn at the stake. And you're saying they're my best shot?"

"If you want to keep your baby, I think you should play the game," Stan said seriously.

Marian stood and began pacing nervously.

"So how do I go about influencing the religious nut-jobs?"

"I can help you," Stan said.

"Oh, no! I've seen the kind of help your articles – "

"Just hear me out, okay? I have plenty of contacts in the mainstream press. I can get this story on the AP wire. This is big enough that every legit paper will run it. Just the legal controversy guarantees interest. The trump card is to let me run the story, with a slightly different spin, in the Enquirer as well."

"And what good would that do?" Marian asked cynically.

"Marian, regardless of your opinion of my employer, do you realize we outsell Newsweek? Do you have any idea how many people think Armstrong's moon walk was Hollywood special effects? How many people think Velcro is alien technology? For better or worse, our magazine has a huge effect on what the average American believes."

"So what's the Enquirer's spin on my story?" Marian asked.

"We go with what we started: 'Is this the second coming of the Messiah?' And, hold on… "

The wheels were turning in Stan's head.

"Oh my God. Marian, when's your due date?"

"November 14th, from what Jenny can tell"

Stan jumped to his feet. "Jesus H. Christ! This is too good. The comet!"

He looked at Marian expectantly, as if she should understand.

"What comet? What are you talking about?"

"Comet Yoshi-Maru. Haven't you seen the news reports? It's a newly discovered rogue comet. It's not in solar orbit. Never passed this way before. From October through December, it will be the brightest object in the sky. It passes closest to the Earth on November 11."

A smile slowly spread across Stan's face.

"My God, Marian, what do you have here?"

"Oh, come on," Marian rolled her eyes. "Not falling for your own story are you?"

Stan spoke slowly, "I've only seen two things in my career I would call miracles. Regenerating a disc in my back was one of them. Wilma Barnhardt's recovery from cancer is the other. You were present for both."

"You're telling me you really believe this baby is the Son of God?" Marian asked incredulously.

"I'm not ready to go shopping for frankincense yet," Stan said, "but something very puzzling is happening here. If we keep the lawyers at bay and get the public on your side, we might buy enough time to find out what it is."

Stan fixed his gaze on Marian. "So what do you say? Can I go with both stories?"

Marian buried her head in her hands. "Fuck. It's totally ridiculous, but I don't have any better ideas."

Looking up at Stan, she decided, "Go with it."

*   *   *

At the house in Washington D.C., where the bearded man kept his secret in the basement, visitors had begun to arrive. Appearing to other residents of the Shaw neighborhood as a stream of visiting family and friends, they had begun filling the underground cinder-block room with hundreds of small, lead-lined cases. The total amount of plutonium was nearing four pounds.

The deadly samples would remain in their cases until the last minute. Sensitive radiation detectors in satellites overhead and on the ground in Washington could register this amount of plutonium collected in one place. When all sixteen pounds were here, the portable smelting furnace would be set up to form the small pieces of plutonium into the two larger interlocking shapes needed for the bomb's deadly core.

Even with the concrete block room lined with lead sheeting, there was a chance small amounts of radiation could penetrate to the outside. The work would have to be done quickly, before the detectors could pinpoint its exact location. The bearded man knew that after his exposure to the plutonium during the smelting process, he would begin a slow death from the radiation. No matter. Before the radiation could take him, the explosion would. And many others with him. Thousands upon thousands.

*   *   *

The following day's Atlanta Constitution ran a story on page two concerning Marian's pending court case. As Stan promised, the article focused on the argument of company-owned property and the legal ambiguities surrounding a fetus conceived by artificial methods without a male genetic donor. He had included statements from BiEnCo's attorney outlining the ways in which Marian had breached company rules by experimenting on herself without receiving proper authorization for human tests.

The company argued, "Given the method of fertilization, and this being the initial attempt, it's almost certain this fetus is not developing as a normal human child. If it were, it's gender would show as female. Our company wishes to have no part in bringing a hopelessly deformed or mutated child into the world. Conscience dictates that we end this pregnancy rather than prolong any false hopes the woman carrying the fetus might cling to."

Stan also had a quote from Marian, "Any mother can understand what I'm going through. When you feel a new life growing inside you, it becomes your top priority. For me, that meant putting aside my role as researcher and scientist and assuming my role as a mother.

"All tests have shown absolutely normal development of the fetus and I expect to give birth to a healthy baby boy. Even though this was a new method of conception, people need to keep in mind that even when a male sperm is involved, an infant has only a 50/50 chance of being male. Perhaps there's an unknown mechanism that maintains the same probability even when a sperm cell isn't involved."

The article went on to add, "Speculation that this child was conceived by normal means was overruled after an amniocentesis was performed. Tests on the nuclear and mitochondrial DNA proved conclusively that all genetic components of the child came from the mother, leaving no doubt that this baby truly has no father."

"Not bad," Marian smiled with approval. "Almost looks like a real news article."

"You're too kind," Stan replied.

"At least people will hear your side of the argument. And the DNA test results lend credibility to the article the Enquirer will be publishing. Oh, speaking of that, I need you to meet with a priest later today."

Marian frowned suspiciously. "A priest? What's this about?"

"He going to be giving an opinion on whether these are actual miracles you've performed."

"Are you serious? He's one of the 'God squad' priests that the Vatican sends out when they investigate possible saints?"

"No," said Stan. "He's a recovering alcoholic priest from a small parish on the South Side. He helps me out from time to time."

"It takes more than this to get the Vatican interested. But we'll have an ordained priest who will give testimony to your baby's miraculous powers."

"And exactly how will he come to this decision?" Marian asked.

"He'll just look over the medical documents from mine and Wilma's cases and give his blessing to them as actual miracles. I also want to get a photo of you and him together. That will be Friday's cover."

*　　　*　　　*

Later that evening Father Bernard Kaplan, a forty-seven year old Franciscan priest, joined Stan and Marian at her apartment. The slightly-built, bearded priest spent a bit of time looking over the MRI's and the interview with Wilma Barnhardt. After hearing Stan's story and Marian's tale of her research experiment, Father Kaplan had an idea.

"Marian, I have to tell you, this is a lot different than most of the stories Stan's involved me with in the past. A scant possibility of truth being the main difference."

Stan laughed as the priest continued.

"What if we add a new twist to this. A little experiment of my own, if you'll humor me. There's a woman from my parish who's been clinging to life for weeks now. She's a terminal cancer patient and is in terrible pain. I've been very close to her family for years. Would you mind visiting her?"

"You expect me to help her in some way?" asked Marian apprehensively. "I don't really believe I'm responsible for any of these things."

"Of course, Marian. I'm not trying to hold your feet to the fire, but if you could humor me...just to see what happens. I'm close friends with the family and if a miracle by chance comes along, she could certainly use it."

Soon the trio arrived at the home of Julie Dunn. Marian paced anxiously as the doorbell chimed the opening phrase of *Amazing Grace*. The door was answered by a rail-thin man in his late twenties.

"Good to see you Father," the young man spoke, "Are these the friends you told me about?"

Father Kaplan answered, "Yes, Roger. This is Stan Wallace and Dr. Foster. Dr. Foster does research on cancer drugs and asked to meet your mother."

They all entered the house and followed the thin man to a small bedroom where an even thinner woman in her late fifties was lying in bed.

"Mom," Roger said, "It's Father Kaplan to see you and he brought a couple of friends along."

"Hello, Julie," Father Kaplan said, "How are you tonight?"

The woman smiled weakly and answered in a strained voice, "Not good, Father. The pain is just too much. I keep praying for God to take me. Why does he leave me to suffer like this?"

"I wish I understood God's ways, but that understanding is beyond all of us. Would you like to pray together?"

"Yes, Father. Please."

Father Kaplan glanced at Marian and Stan. "Could we all join hands?"

Marian looked at Stan uncertainly. Stan gave a slight nod. The priest took Julie's hand and Stan's. Stan took Marian's as she held her other hand out to the woman. Julie meekly took Marian's hand.

As Father Kaplan began his prayer, everyone but Marian closed their eyes. She was watching the woman in the bed.

Father Kaplan was praying loudly, but Marian could hear the woman softly repeating, "Thank you. Thank you." Her voice eventually trailed off and she lay there smiling silently.

The priest finished his prayer and they released one another's hands. Julie Dunn's hand fell limply onto the bed as Marian let go.

Marian asked the woman, "Mrs. Dunn, how long ago were you diagnosed?"

The woman continued to smile peacefully.

Marian leaned closer. "Mrs. Dunn?"

Marian was struck with horror now. She touched the woman's neck. "There's no pulse!"

She leaned her face close to the woman's to see if she was breathing. Marian leaned across the bed and began chest compressions.

"Somebody call 911!" she shouted.

Roger moved close to Marian and placed his hand gently on her shoulder. "Dr. Foster," he said calmly, "please stop."

"Your mother is dying! We have to get her to a hospital!"

"Please stop," Roger repeated. "She has a DNR order and a living will. Please let her go. She's been praying for this for weeks. And to tell you the truth, so have I."

*　　*　　*

The three visitors waited with Roger Dunn until an ambulance arrived. There was no talk wasted on empty attempts at consolation. Roger seemed pleased that his mother had passed with such ease, and with a smile on her face. After Mrs. Dunn's body was taken away with Roger accompanying her, Marian and Stan left to return Father Kaplan to the rectory where he lived.

Marian was extremely upset at the outcome of the visit.

Father Kaplan reassured her, "Marian, don't feel like you've failed. This was God's power at work, not yours."

"Of course I didn't fail. I didn't have anything to do with it," Marian replied angrily.

"I'm trained to help people. That's what doctors do. A person's death is *not* a positive outcome."

"Even if that is what's best for them?" Father Kaplan inquired.

"I don't claim to know what's best for anyone but I *do* know my job as a doctor."

"All negative situations exist so God's work may become manifest as the solution. Many people throughout history have been channels of God's intention. They had no control over the outcome, they were simply the medium through which God worked."

Marian was skeptical. "So you're telling me you think this was another miracle? This woman's death? You actually believe this was God working through *me?*"

"Miracles are, many times, in the eye of the beholder. But do I think God is working through you?" Father Kaplan smiled and looked into her eyes. "I'm becoming more convinced by the minute."

They arrived at the rectory where Father Kaplan lived. As they pulled up to the curb, a younger, sandy-haired priest was walking up to the rectory.

"Thank you both for the ride," Father Kaplan said, exiting the car.

"Stan, there's Father Morris, the new associate pastor I was telling you about. Can you take a moment to say hello?"

"Sure," replied Stan, as he and Marian stepped from the car.

"Father Morris," Kaplan called, "I'd like you to meet some friends. This is Stan Wallace, the writer friend I told you about."

They greeted and shook hands.

"And this is Stan's friend, Dr. Marian Foster."

"Pleased to meet you," Father Morris said, extending his hand.

Marian took his hand and the world evaporated in a flash. As the familiar white fog cleared, she saw Father Morris in a small office with a boy of twelve seated in front of his desk.

Father Morris was speaking, "Danny, I think it's wonderful you think you might want to become a priest. It's a very special calling."

"I really think it would be cool to be like you, helping people get closer to God," said the boy.

"It will take several years of schooling. And you'll have to be willing to give your body, mind and soul to God. Do you think you can do that?"

"I think so."

"It would be a good start to make that commitment right now. Are you ready to do that?"

"Yes, Father."

"Tonight you can show your commitment by giving your body to God totally and completely. You'll need to take your clothes off now."

A look of confusion filled the boy's eyes. "Do I have to, Father?"

Father Morris smiled. "I want you to try on my robes. I want you to see how good it feels. I'll get undressed too, so you won't have to be embarrassed."

Father Morris stood and started unbuckling his trousers.

"Oh my God!" Marian shrieked, pulling her hand away. "You did that!"

Father Morris' face was frozen in terror. He held his hand like a claw in front of him, as if it was a snake poised to strike. He backed slowly away from the three without looking back at them. He continued to grimace painfully at his hand as he backed into the rectory and slammed the door shut.

Marian jumped into the car and shouted, "Get me out of here, Stan! Now!"

Stan exchanged a worried look with Father Kaplan as he got into the car and drove off with Marian. Something told Stan not to ask about what had just happened. He knew he would find out soon enough.

*   *   *

Marian's phone rang early the next morning. It was Stan, sounding very grave.

"I just got a call from Father Kaplan, " he began, "Morris killed himself last night."

To Stan's surprise, Marian remained silent.

"Kaplan found him in the bathtub with his wrists cut. He left a note confessing he had a sexual affair with a young boy in the parish. He wrote, 'God knows what I have done, so I must go to my damnation.'"

Silence again over the phone.

"Marian, is this what you saw last night? His suicide?"

Marian finally spoke, "No. It was worse. I saw him with the boy."

"I have to ask, Marian, did you put any kind of thoughts in his head? Did you feel or think that he deserved to die?"

"No!" Marian shouted, "I didn't possess his body! I didn't steal his soul! Do I care that piece of shit is dead? No!"

She jumped to her feet and began pacing rapidly. "I don't want any of this. I don't want to see anything else or touch anybody else. I just want my life back."

"Father Kaplan says he has to go to the Archbishop. He says it's his duty to report what he's seen."

"So what's next," Marian snapped, "A visit from the local exorcist?"

"No. Nothing like that," Stan reassured her, "He's convinced God is really working through you. But he's scared."

"What's he scared of?" Marian asked, not wanting to hear the answer.

Stan hesitated and then replied, "You. The power frightens him."

Marian began crying. "Please. Please come over. I need somebody. I need - "

"I'm on my way," Stan said. "It'll be O.K. I'll be there soon."

Stan unplugged the coffee pot and pocketed his car keys. He was willing to go try and comfort her. He just wasn't sure he could bring himself to touch her.

CHAPTER 9

Tom Hunt, senior Senator from Indiana, was escorted into the Oval Office for his meeting with President Stanton. Even two years after the election, in which Hunt had won the popular vote but lost by four in the electoral college, his wounds had not healed. Stanton had run as a "man of the people" and had insulted Hunt repeatedly during the debates, calling him an "intellectual elitist, out of touch with American morals."

In the world of modern American politics, a high I.Q. had now become a liability, or so it seemed to Tom Hunt.

"Tom, thanks for coming," Stanton said, offering his hand.

"Mr. President." Hunt shook his hand.

"First, let's just cut through the crap. We don't like one another," Stanton began.

"Agreed, Mr. President."

"We have to put that aside. There's more at stake here than an election. As chair of the Subcommittee for Intelligence and National Security, I know you've seen every report I have. What's your take on China's troop movements?"

"Possibly an attack against India. They have good trade status with Pakistan."

"That's what the Joint Chiefs think too," said Stanton.

"But you can't be sure. China doesn't tolerate a conflict near its borders, unless they're the ones orchestrating it. The chemical attack against Iran has the Islamic nations crying for war. China will almost certainly take some kind of action to reassert their power. It may not be that important who they attack, as long as they show their strength in the hemisphere

"Even though they have decent relations with Pakistan, they know the rest of the world would react more strongly to an attack against India. It all depends on whether they care about the opinion of the rest of the world right now. With their numbers, they could attack both with very little effort."

"Can you find out what's really going on over there?" Stanton demanded.

"Doubtful. The political situation is so hot, even my closest friends in Beijing are keeping their distance."

President Stanton stood and gazed out the window into the Rose Garden.

"Let's talk about that plan you brought up in the House thirty-some years ago. The economic union you thought would eventually replace the United Nations."

"Are you speaking of the plan you tabled discussion on?" Hunt asked dryly.

The President turned and smiled.

"I was the Speaker at the time. It was my job to shut the opposition down. You know that. You've become a master at it."

"Touché." Hunt smiled back.

"So," continued Stanton, "was it just an attention grabbing ploy, or did you really have a plan?"

"Have a seat. Give me a few minutes and then tell me what you think."

The President complied.

"Our current budget dedicates twenty-six billion to foreign aid, including low-interest loans. Our gross domestic product is currently fourteen trillion give or take. So we spend about two-tenths of a percent of our GDP to make friends with the world. Our defense budget is currently 600 billion, or a little over four percent of GDP.

"My plan was to have a group of nations come together with the goals of building global trade and economic stability. A 'club' of sorts. The dues to belong to the club are one percent of each country's gross domestic product."

"So for us that would be one hundred forty billion," Stanton interjected. "Quite a large increase in our friend-making money."

"Yes, but let me continue. Just imagine, on a small scale, the union included us, China, Japan and Russia along with 25 African and Middle Eastern countries. Every country puts up their dues up front. We ask for proposals from countries that need economic help. Their proposals have to utilize that particular nation's natural resources and manpower. The group votes to compose a list of 10 most viable proposals. Each country gets one vote, no matter how much money it puts up. Then, each proposal is taken in turn and the alliance decides how much money is given to each. All money in the kitty must be spent every fiscal year.

"So, at the end of the first year, we would see, for example, a twenty billion dollar automobile industry started in Somalia, a major oil and shipping port in Eritrea, a new silicon chip industry in Iraq, and so on. There would be standing agreements between all members to grant preferred trade status to all other members. The voting process would ensure that competition and supply/demand would have consideration.

"The more countries that become involved and become economically dependent upon each other, the more that global peace is ensured. As more members join, defense budgets globally get smaller. Even with the small group of nations I've just mentioned, I'm sure you'll agree we could cut our defense budget by 300 billion. We've just come out 160 billion ahead, without taking into account the giant boost to our economy."

Stanton rubbed his forehead. "That's just too easy. There's got to be a flaw in a plan so simple."

"Give me a chance to spell it out in detail. I'll bring in a full proposal. Take it to your advisors and challenge them to find the flaw. In the meantime, I'll see what I can find out about China."

*   *   *

Stan had arrived at Marian's to find her near the end of a bottle of wine. She didn't appear to be suffering much effect from the alcohol, although her crying had stopped.

"This is the first time I've seen you drink," Stan said as he sat down.

"I normally don't," Marian replied, "but it was either this or getting my prescription pad out and going for the big guys. To tell you the truth, Father Morris's way out looked pretty good before I started on this bottle."

"I hope you've changed your mind on that."

Marian nodded. "I've got a baby to think about. I shouldn't have had the wine."

Marian eyed the remainder of her glass and poured it back into the bottle. "I just don't know how much more I can take. I'm so confused about everything."

Marian was interrupted by a knock at the door. She rose and answered it.

"Carl! Come in. I'm so glad to see you." Marian held the door while Carl entered carrying two stacked filing boxes.

"Here's the stuff from your desk. Sorry I didn't get it here quicker, but my life has been hell this week," he said, placing the boxes on the floor.

"Join the club, " Marian said, then noticing Stan's questioning look, added, "Carl, I want you to meet a . . . friend of mine. This is Stan Wallace, he's a writer."

"Good to meet you," said Carl, offering his hand.

"Likewise," answered Stan as his cell phone rang. "Excuse me, please"

"So," Marian continued, "what's happening at BiEnCo?"

"God, where do I start? Lots of shuffling in the management teams, several people let go, me included."

"Carl, I'm so sorry. Was this because of me, too?"

"No, not really. The Oncostatin project's been dropped. Everyone involved with Oncostatin is history."

"What happened? Things were going so well."

"Side effects started showing up. Bad ones. Two deaths from strokes, several severe cases of internal bleeding."

Stan hung up his phone and listened as Marian asked, "Do they know the cause?"

"The drug was causing severe thinning and weakening of the blood vessels at a systemic level."

Stan interrupted, "Excuse me. Why wasn't this caught in animal testing?"

Marian answered, "It's one of the things we worry about missing in animal testing. Even though we induce real tumors in the animals to simulate human cases, animals' systems react differently to the stress of constant pain. They seem to develop somewhat of a tolerance to it. Humans don't. The stress of chronic pain often causes hypertension, high blood pressure. And of course, high blood pressure will cause weakened arteries to blow out. The animals may have been showing the same side effects, but weren't caught because their blood pressure never rose high enough to cause a problem."

"Anyway," Carl smiled, "if you hear of anyone hiring submissive lab assistants. . ."

"If I can help in any way, you can count on me. I really was lucky to have worked with you."

Stan interjected, "You need a personal assistant."

"A personal assistant," Marian laughed, "What for?"

"You're going to become a busy person when the publicity really hits, which will be soon. You'll be asked for interviews, TV appearances – "

"What? Are you kidding me?"

"Your story is on the AP wire," Stan replied. "I expect every major paper to run it."

"I hadn't thought that far ahead," Marian said, surprised. "But even so, I haven't got enough money socked away to pay for a staff. I'm unemployed, remember?"

"You're going to need an assistant just to handle your money," Stan said emphatically.

"That was the Enquirer on the phone. Today you received checks totaling $27,000. The article we finished last night hasn't even been published yet."

Marian was stunned. "Did you ask for contributions to a legal defense fund or something?"

"No," said Stan calmly, "All these checks are for the baby."

"The baby?" Marian's head was swimming. "Why the baby?"

Stan smiled, "Our readers are the type of people who contribute quite generously to their churches. Perhaps they feel now is the time to start cutting out the middle man."

*   *   *

Father Kaplan entered the ornate office of the Archbishop of Atlanta, Jerome Newhaus.

The Archbishop greeted him warmly. "It's good to see you, Father. Please, have a seat. I understand you've had contact with the woman they're calling the new Virgin Mother?"

"Yes, Your Grace. The writer of the original article is a friend of mine, and he introduced us."

The Archbishop smiled, "Bernard, we have no audience here, and we've known each other a long time. Let's drop the formalities, shall we? Glass of wine?"

"Thanks, Jerry. I just don't know what to think about this woman. My friend Stan calls me occasionally to come see a bleeding crucifix or a weeping Madonna, but this was different."

Kaplan glanced around the room and leaned close to the Archbishop.

"She shook Father Morris' hand about an hour before he killed himself. He was frightened after she touched him. He appeared to be in physical pain. The woman immediately knew what he had done to the boy. And it appeared he knew what she had seen."

The Archbishop frowned.

"What about these other stories? The miraculous healings?"

"I spoke to the woman who was cured of cancer and saw copies of her MRI's. A four pound tumor disappeared. Needless to say, she's a changed woman. Totally confident that her healing came from God. My friend Stan was healed of a ruptured disc he had suffered with for seven years. Her touch also caused him to relive a memory from his past. This happened at his very first meeting with the woman."

"Does the woman seem to have control over this 'power'? Does it seem like she knows what's about to occur before it happens?"

"No," the priest replied, "She seems scared by it. She doesn't want to claim responsibility for the things that happen."

"Good. It's not unheard of for God's power to work through an unwitting channel. But if she was making conscious decisions about life and death, I would be concerned her power was coming from... another source."

"Is it possible that she could be carrying a child of Divinity? Could the Second Coming of Christ truly be near?"

"It challenges your faith, doesn't it?" asked the Archbishop. "After so many predictions of His coming have passed without event, we've shoved it into the background. It's become an embarrassment of sorts. Since the '60s, we've been 'softening' the Scriptures. Everything is now open to interpretation. The Scriptures are parables, metaphors. We forget that His coming the first time was foretold by the ancient prophets. During His life, He promised to return again. What do you believe, Father?"

"I'll tell you what I know: I'm scared to be around this woman."

"Why is that," the Archbishop inquired, "Do you sense something evil about her?"

"I sense incredible power," Father Kaplan began slowly, "If a burning bush spoke to me, I would be scared. If a spirit hand carved out commandments on a stone tablet, I would be scared. And if a little girl's head spun around spewing green vomit, I would be scared, too. I don't know what the power is, or where it comes from, but I think it's real."

The Archbishop nodded slowly as he took all this in and said, "The world is coming apart at the seams. We've seen political events comparable to prophecies from Revelations several times in recent memory. Today we're closer than we've ever been to a third World War. We've divided ourselves around religious lines and there are about twenty viable candidates for the Antichrist alive right now. Add to this the fact that we will soon have a 'new star in the east' as the comet approaches."

The Archbishop folded his hands and sighed. "We have never needed a savior more than we do right now. I think we need to watch this very closely. I will be advising my contacts in the Vatican of these events."

The Archbishop gazed directly into the priest's eyes. "Father Kaplan, can you overcome your fears enough to stay in contact with this woman? We need someone to keep us abreast of new developments."

The priest knew the Archbishop's return to formality meant that this was more than a request. "I'll do my best, Your Grace."

CHAPTER 10

Marian dreamt of the boy that night. She heard the child's feet padding down the wooden-floored hallway. Just as before, the little boy entered the room where Marian sat in front of a large bay window overlooking a lake surrounded by magnificent golden maples. The boy ran to her and climbed into her lap.

"It's OK, Mommy," he said reassuringly. "Things get better. You'll see."

He leaned to her ear and whispered, "You don't have to be scared. People will protect you. Even when things are scary, someone will always be there to take care of you."

The boy kissed her cheek and slid onto the floor. As he shuffled away, he called over his shoulder, "Don't forget to give all the money away," then ran down the hall, giggling.

The dream replayed again and again in Marian's mind as she made coffee. She tried unsuccessfully to shrug it off. Maybe this was just another part of being pregnant, like the morning sickness. But this seemed to be more than a dream. Instead of anxiety, she felt peace. Things really didn't seem so bad today.

Her thoughts were interrupted by her ringing phone. She glanced at the clock. Seven thirty-five. A bit early, but she took the call anyway.

"Marian," Stan said excitedly, "there are checks here for $119,000. We have to figure out what we're going to do."

"We're going to give it away," Marian blurted out.

"What?"

Marian paused, wondering if it was her voice she had just heard saying 'give it away.'

"Marian, are you there! What's going on?"

"I'm OK, Stan. We have to… give the money away," she said slowly, as if hypnotized by the words.

"Stay right there. I'm coming over."

*   *   *

"Where did this come from - 'Give it all away?' Who is the deserving recipient of one hundred twenty thousand dollars?"

"I don't know," Marian replied. "It's just not right to keep it."

"You're unemployed. And there's a lot of expenses ahead. Travel, hotels, not to mention the best possible care during your pregnancy."

"The best possible care will come from Jenny," Marian affirmed. "Nobody else will touch me."

"What about investments, a trust fund for the baby? That's what the donors want."

"It might not be what he wants!" she shot back.

Her voice softened as she went on, "I had another dream last night - but it was different this time. He was comforting me, trying to reassure me. He told me not to be scared – that things would get better. To know someone would always be there to help me. The last thing he said was, 'don't forget to give all the money away.'"

Stan puzzled over this for a minute, then said brightly, "OK. Who do we give it to?"

"Wow. Quick change. What convinced you?" Marian asked.

Stan smiled, "First of all, I'm going to trust your judgment. Second of all, it's your money. Third, it's great publicity."

"Explain, please."

"When people see that even before his birth, 'the baby' is using their money to do good, this whole thing's going to explode. The donations will flood the office."

Stan now began pacing frantically. "You need to decide who's going to get the money. Think about it carefully. This will be important."

"Me? I need your help with this." Marian begged.

"Sorry," Stan laughed. "This one's all on you. Just play a game of WWJD."

"WWJD?" Marian puzzled.

"What would Jesus do?" Stan replied with a smile.

*　　　*　　　*

Marian didn't know much about Jesus, other than what could be absorbed by being a member of American society. Her parents weren't churchgoers, but her mother believed in God, or so it seemed. No bible stories were ever read in their house, nor was Sunday school ever attended. She had gone to Jenny's church a couple of times, but was totally confused at the goings-on. Religion had not been important for her to think about, until politics became involved. It always seemed to her when politics and religion mixed, personal freedoms were offered up as sacrifice. And from what she knew of Jesus, He promised His way was the path to freedom.

The hypocrisies and contradictions she had seen in the world caused religious beliefs to drop from her consciousness. She easily replaced them with science and logic. Things that no reasonable person could argue about.

Now it became important for her to learn something about the man people were comparing her unborn son to. She went to her storage closet and dug deep into a cardboard box. Her hand reappeared with a worn, leather-bound Bible. This was her one memento of the grandmother she'd never met. Her mother's mother. She went to her bedroom, propped a pillow at the head of her bed and began to read.

It was 6:00 PM when she began Matthew's gospel. She finished John's at 3:30 AM.

She didn't allow herself to become distracted by the inconsistencies or logical arguments her mind kept throwing at her. She was determined to find the essence of the man, Jesus.

One thing for sure, the metaphors of children and parent-child relationships were everywhere. Son of God. Son of Man. The Father. God's children. Suffer the little children to come unto me. You must become like a child to enter my Father's kingdom. Jesus saw children as special, whole. Unblemished by the human condition.

God the Father. And we are all His children. Finally, Marian had her answer.

After a few hours sleep, Marian rose and made a call to Stan at his office.

"I know what to do with the money," she said.

As Stan listened his eyes grew wide. "You're brilliant! I'll set up a press conference for tomorrow afternoon. Carl needs to get working on the details. We have to act quickly."

Marian hung up the phone, feeling quite pleased with herself.

*   *   *

The following afternoon, Marian, Carl and Stan arrived at the Children's Welfare Bureau in downtown Atlanta. They passed through a crowd of twenty-five reporters and four cameramen by Marian's count. Not bad for a novice celebrity, she thought.

As she walked to the podium a reporter shouted out, "Are you a virgin?" Before Marian had a chance to open her mouth, Carl had beaten her to the microphone.

"Dr. Foster is here to make a statement today. She won't be taking questions at this time, but we promise you a chance very soon."

Marian was caught by surprise. She had never seen Carl step up and take charge before.

Passing her, he smiled as if reading her mind. "It's all yours, Doctor," he said.

Marian gave Carl an appreciative nod and began, "Good afternoon. My name is Marian Foster. There's been a lot written about me in the papers lately and a lot of questions on peoples' minds. I'm going to try to answer a few of those, as briefly as possible, because I have a more important reason for speaking to you today.

"First of all, I was a research scientist at a bioengineering firm until recently. I had experimented with a new fertilization procedure that would allow a woman's egg cells to begin growth into a fetus without needing genetic material from a man's sperm. My hopes were that we could learn more about the very beginnings of pregnancy and hopefully prevent some forms of birth defects.

"Unfortunately, I went through a period where I made some questionable decisions. I had the poor judgment to try the procedure on myself. I had noble enough motives, I believed. Not wanting to try a possibly dangerous procedure on another human, it seemed a reasonable thing at the time. But what began as an experiment ended when I went through something all women experience during pregnancy - the moment when I became a mother. I no longer had an experiment inside me. I had *a baby*.

"Something unexpected and still unexplainable happened. Tests showed my baby was a boy. All the theories this procedure was based on say it's impossible. Only a female child can result from this, because there was no donor of a Y chromosome. Yet, DNA tests also reveal there are no genes present except my own. This baby has no father.

"There are several theories floating around in different newspapers about who or what this child might be. On that subject, I have no answer for you. No angels have appeared to me. No burning bushes. There have been some unusual things that have happened to people when I was with them. I won't go into these, except to say the papers have reported them accurately. You'll have to make up your own minds if you think this baby is something special. He's special to me, but simply because he's my baby.

"What I really want to speak to you about today is the donations of money that have been sent by people who have beliefs about who this baby is. Good people have sent their hard earned dollars to help my child. I know that no matter what else my son turns out to be, he'll be a good person. And any good person would put this money toward a good cause.

"When I was growing up, my friends had a lot of fun with my last name. They called me 'the Foster child.' I remembered this last night when I was trying to decide what my son would choose to do with this money. I felt in my heart he would probably approve of it going to real foster children.

"If we accept the view that God is our spiritual Father, then we are all 'foster children' of sorts. He's entrusted us to other human beings to raise and teach and nurture for a while, until we return home.

"Many of our parents do an admirable job of raising God's children. But some have failed, some haven't tried, and some have died and left children alone and scared. For those children who have ever felt unwanted, unloved or without a true place to call home, we want to do something to make their lives a bit better.

"We don't have the means to make sure that every foster child grows up in an ideal environment, but we think we have a way to give them a little extra on the back end: The Foster Child Foundation.

"Beginning today, all money donated to my 'Foster child' will be put into a trust fund that will be used to give no-interest college loans to foster children in this state. The only requirement is that they do their best to pay the money back at some point in their life, so more children can have the same chance. If you choose to continue to support this fund with such generous donations, no foster child or orphan in this state will ever be denied the chance for higher education.

"All those who sent in donations will be given a small token from The Foster Child Foundation."

Marian held up a mockup of a 3" X 12" sticker, white text on dark blue background.

"This bumper sticker that says, 'I'm a Foster Child.' Think of it as a reminder of where we all come from, and who our true Father is. All donors will receive them, as well as anyone who requests one, even if they choose not to make a donation.

"That's all I have to say today. I'll try to make myself available for questions in the future, but for now I don't want anything to overshadow the wonderful work that's made possible by these generous donations. Thank you all."

Stan nodded to himself. A politician couldn't have done a better job. Great presence. Humble and sincere. And as Marian walked from the podium, Stan saw and heard something he had never experienced at a press conference before. A handful of reporters had put their pens and notebooks down and were applauding.

*   *   *

Stan, Marian and Carl met at her apartment that evening to see if the national press would report her statement on the nightly news. They watched the network news for almost the full half hour with no sign of Marian's press conference. The focus was on the Chinese troop buildup, more missile strikes and terrorist attacks in Palestine along with the growing fears that accompanied the fall of the United Nations.

Carl spoke up, "Looks like we didn't make it tonight."

"Just wait," replied Stan, "twenty minutes of bad news. Our story will be the closer."

Sure enough, at 5:52 the commentator announced, "Also in the news tonight, the woman the tabloids have called the new Virgin Mother, Dr. Marian Foster, spoke in public for the first time at a press conference in Atlanta.

"Dr. Foster confirmed reports published by the Associated Press and in the Global Enquirer that she is the first woman in modern times to become pregnant without the assistance of a man. Her pregnancy resulted from research she was performing while an employee at BiEnCo, an Atlanta pharmaceutical manufacturer. She was released by the company two weeks ago and first made headlines in daily newspapers after BiEnCo's lawsuit claiming the embryo as property of the company.

"Readers of the Global Enquirer, the tabloid that originally broke the story, have shown their support of Marian by sending in donations to the unborn child totaling $119,000 as of yesterday. Today Marian Foster announced what would be done with the money..."

Several clips from the press conference were then shown. Marian was saying, "You'll have to make up your own minds if you think this baby is special. He's special to me, simply because he's my baby." The next clip showed her spelling out her proposal for the Foster Child Foundation.

The commentator returned saying, "A divinely conceived child? The jury's still out on that. But in this reporter's opinion, the things we've heard today give proof that a higher love is still alive and well in these troubled times."

He held up an "I'm a Foster Child" bumper sticker and added, "Marian, you're something special. That's the news on this Friday...."

The three stared at one another.

Carl spoke first, "We did it!" he said, giving Marian a high five.

"Fantastic job, Marian!" added Stan.

"My God, I didn't think we could pull this off," Marian added gleefully.

"Now we have to wait and see what BiEnCo does," Stan remarked soberly. "How big will their response be?"

"How can they respond to that?" Carl asked. "There's absolutely nothing in her statement they could touch."

Stan replied, "Nothing in her statement, no. But they could charge embezzlement of funds, hit her again for proceeding with human tests without authorization. And there's the matter of the people dying from the cancer drug she helped develop. They can try to slaughter her character."

The smiles were gone.

"Another buzz kill, Stan," said Marian.

"Don't get me wrong. I think we're in good shape. But we have to remain focused. We have to be ready. You have to address these issues with the press before BiEnCo has a chance to make their case. You can't be seen as hiding things or just reacting to accusations. We have to get your side of the story out first, and then let them try to change the public's mind."

*   *   *

Beneath the minarets of Golestan Palace in downtown Tehran, a meeting was taking place between Islamic leaders and the elected government officials. President Ibn Khamein was fearful of Iran's future given the turn of events in world relations. He desperately tried to convince the new Ayatollah, el-Hamir to end the terrorist attacks.

"Imam, it is vital now for our country to put Jihad on hold. We can't be certain of our support from the other Islamic nations when they are so concerned with their own security. We are very likely to be attacked by the West."

"Concern yourself with the world of politics, Khamein," el-Hamir replied, "and let Allah's work be handled by His devout followers. Jihad will not be put on hold."

"I have stayed out of your affairs," said the President sternly, "even though your ways are endangering our nation. I know your followers are planning to strike the United States and I'm frightened to think what form it may take. I have devoted my presidency to raising my people's standard of living, of bringing this country into modern times. Your ways are destroying every chance of progress."

"Your idea of progress is a model of the society of the infidels," el-Hamir spat. "You would trade our heritage for Western culture. You are no better than those we fight against!"

"This afternoon, I am going to announce to the world that the elected government no longer supports you. If you continue, you will continue alone," said Khamein.

"Bashir," el-Hamir said calmly, "Please summon the presidential guard."

Bashir Pezek stood and opened the door. Eight armed guards entered the room, rifles trained on Khamein.

El-Hamir spoke, "It seems I am not the one who is alone." He produced a pistol and aimed it at the President's head.

"So, you will be the one to make a martyr of me, el-Hamir," he asked.

El-Hamir laughed. "You are no martyr," he said as he fired one shot into Khamein's head. "You are merely dead."

His body fell to the floor.

"Vice-President," said el-Hamir.

"Excellency!" the man seated next to him snapped to attention.

"Inform the Islamic nations of the change that has taken place. Sever all communications with the others. Let them guess about our next move."

"Yes, Excellency."

Bashir Pezek looked on in trepidation. He grew more and more frightened by the actions of el-Hamir. Bashir had known the President well. He was a good man and a servant of Mohammed. It was sinful for el-Hamir to kill him.

Bashir had dreamed many times of the former Ayatollah's dying day. He remembered the words of prophecy the dying man had spoken. Words that had never been given to his people. How he missed the Imam. He had been a true man of God. El-Hamir was simply a power seeker.

Bashir prayed silently to Allah for protection – protection of his family, his beloved country and of the great Teacher that Ayatollah al-Akmed had prophesied. He knew if the old man had seen it, it would come to be true. He will come soon, Bashir thought. He must.

CHAPTER 11

Within a few days, the streets of Atlanta were transformed into a placard for Marian's fight against BiEnCo. At least one out of five cars carried blue and white bumper stickers proclaiming, "I'm a Foster Child". Billboards had sprung up with the same message. Blue and white "FC" banners were seen hanging from office building windows. Similar displays were growing in cities across the nation. The Foster Child Foundation's college fund now topped 1.7 million dollars.

Marian, Stan and Carl made plans for the next day's press conference, where Marian would take questions from reporters for the first time.

"We're going to be fine with everything except the question of the $80,000 in missing funds," Stan said. "We have to have an explanation for that."

Carl interjected, "The truth has worked so far. Why can't we frame this as poor judgment? The people are sympathetic towards Marian."

"We're trying to portray this woman as being worthy of bearing God's child," Stan said emphatically.

"So, she says, 'I stole the money so I could pay an illegal abortionist to kill your savior?' Use your head, Carl."

"And if Dr. Markham's death comes up, I'm sunk," added Marian.

Stan was deep in thought. After a moment, his eyes widened and he said, "O.K. I know this would put a strain on you, but can you pay it back?"

"My God, Stan - I guess I could if I cashed in a retirement account."

"I think you should. Your supporters won't let you go hungry. Do it today and courier a cashier's check to BiEnCo. As a small admission of guilt, you'll claim you were scared your funding would be taken away and so you had it moved to your personal account to ensure that the baby would survive until birth. That's the ticket. You did wrong, but you did it to protect the baby."

Stan smiled proudly.

"I think that could work," agreed Marian. She glanced at Carl, who appeared doubtful.

"What's up?" Marian asked.

"I don't feel good about this. If there's ever an investigation, there's no paper trail to support that story. Then, when the 'mother of God' turns out to be a liar, how do we recover?"

"We're going to put such pressure on BiEnCo, they'll drop the suit, Carl. Then there won't ever be an investigation," Stan said sharply.

"Do what you like, Marian. But I'm not with you on this one. I think it's a mistake."

Marian frowned and decided, "I don't feel great about it either, but I don't see any other way."

*   *   *

Marian dreamt again that night. The soft footsteps coming down the wooden hallway. The door opening into her office. That same beautiful view from her window to the lake nestled in a grove of maple trees. The handsome young boy climbed into her lap once again and began whispering into her ear.

"You don't have to lie, Mommy. If you say what's true, people will help you."

The child's smile faded as he added, "If you lie, I won't be able to be with you. I'll have to leave."

The boy climbed from her lap and ran down the hallway.

*   *   *

The press conference got off to a good start. When questions about the miraculous healings of Stan and Wilma Barnhardt came up, she took no credit for curing them. Marian reported exactly what she experienced at the time and had copies of their MRI's on hand for the journalists to examine. She gracefully said her mea culpas to testing the procedure on herself without authorization. Her explanation that she didn't want to proceed with volunteer testing until she was sure the process was safe seemed to please everyone.

When a question was asked about her religious beliefs, Marian answered, "I believe in God, and I believe in science. God made the universe, and he made the laws that govern the universe. Science is simply the study of those laws. The problem many scientists have is that we want to claim we completely understand them, when we really haven't even scratched the surface. We're not as smart as we like to think we are."

Stan smiled and triumphantly pumped his fist at that reply.

"Is your baby the new Messiah?" one reporter asked as several others began to snicker.

"If he is, I wish he'd cure my morning sickness," replied a smiling Marian. Several reporters laughed.

Marian's not really answering any of their questions, Stan thought to himself, *She'd make a great politician.*

A reporter stood.

"Kevin Sanders, Chicago Tribune. Dr. Foster, BiEnCo is accusing you of embezzling $80,000 in research funds. What's your response to that?"

"First of all, the entire sum has been returned to BiEnCo. I was concerned from the beginning that my funding - Ahhh!"

A searing pain shot through her abdomen. She grabbed her stomach, grimacing. After a moment, it passed. Stan and Carl exchanged nervous glances.

The reporter asked, "All you alright, Dr. Foster?"

Marian recovered, "Yes, excuse me. There's that morning sickness I was talking about. As I was saying, I had concerns – "

The words caught in her throat as another wave of pain seized her. It felt as if something had exploded in her abdomen. Before she could respond, another jolt ripped through her so strongly that her knees buckled and her chin hit the podium. Stan and Carl raced to her side as the crowd of reporters burst to their feet in a frenzy of camera flashes.

A trickle of blood dripped from a cut on her chin as Marian clutched the podium, trying to keep herself from collapsing to the floor. In her mind she heard a small voice calling from far away, "Mommy!"

In a flash she realized these were the pains of miscarriage. She was losing her baby.

Pandemonium was breaking out in the auditorium.

Carl shouted into the mic, "Is there a doctor here?"

The question got no response except to lure the cameramen and reporters closer to the stage, shouting questions and muttering into their cell phones.

Stan shouted at Carl, "We have to get her out of here!"

"No!" shouted Marian into the microphone. She knew what she had to do.

Lifting herself into a semi-upright position, she gasped, "I'm not going anywhere until . . . I answer this question!"

An abrupt silence fell across the auditorium. Marian struggled to regain her footing as the pain subsided to a barely tolerable level. She looked to Stan and Carl.

"I'm alright. You two can sit down."

Marian began speaking to the reporters who had frozen like statues near the foot of the stage.

She wiped tears of pain from her face as she began, "I was going to lie to you. But I can't."

Stan and Carl backed away hesitantly. The reporters held their breath, waiting for Marian to continue.

"When I started my research, I was no different than the people at BiEnCo who are now trying to take my child. I wanted to get the embryo out of me just to see if it was developing normally. Since I had performed the procedure on myself in secret, I couldn't come up with a way to remove the embryo and make sure it remained intact. So I paid $80,000 for an illegal abortion."

The room was instantly abuzz as the reporters took out their cell phones again.

"Obviously, the procedure was never performed. But the money is gone, and I can't get it back."

The room quieted to an ominous silence as Marian's eyes began to tear up.

"Several people have been healed in incredible ways and attributed them to my baby. I can't speak for them, but I know what's happened to me. My baby healed me of the disease that had eaten away at my heart and my soul for the first 29 years of my life. I'm not the same person I was before. What I am is not a scientist. What *I am* is not a doctor. Now I *am* a mother. And I will protect this baby at all costs. I'm willing to die for it."

Several reporters began shouting questions at once, but Marian silenced them.

"Wait a moment. There's one other thing. I dodged the question earlier about whether I thought my baby was something special. I do. I have no other explanation for the things that are happening around me. Is it God's doing, or is at because of the baby's unique genetic makeup? I don't know."

Marian paused and gazed into the faces in front of her.

"But for the first time I know what it feels like to be human."

She abruptly turned and left the stage.

Carl and Stan stared in amazement. Chaos was breaking out among the members of the press.

Carl advanced to the microphone and announced, "I'm sorry, folks. We'll finish this on another day."

Stan raced up to Marian backstage. "Come on, let's get to an emergency room."

Marian kept walking. "No need. I'm fine now."

"But we need to find out what happened. There could be a problem with the baby."

"There's no problem with the baby," Marian asserted. "The problem is with me."

"What do you mean?" Stan asked.

"This is very demanding child," insisted Marian in a quavering voice.

The look in her eyes scared Stan. This was more than just fear. She might be near a psychotic break.

"He was in my dreams again last night. He warned me to tell the truth."

Stan noticed her nervous tics growing in intensity.

"When I began to lie, he was ready to go."

Marian's laughter at her last statement was unnerving.

"He was leaving me, Stan. I felt him pulling away from my body."

"Marian, we need to go and see someone," Stan advised. "I think the stress is too much right now."

"I'm not a good enough person to be his mother!"

Marian's eyes darted from left to right as she gripped and twisted the sleeve of Stan's jacket.

"He won't be born to a mother who's not worthy. Can't you see? If I'm not good enough, he'll leave me."

Her voice was beginning to rise in pitch and volume. She now clutched both of Stan's arms.

"Don't let him leave me! Please help me to be a better person! I have to hold him, I have to- "

Marian's voice trailed into hysterical sobbing as she collapsed into Stan's arms. Stan half-carried her to the car and as he helped her into the rear seat, she sank down and curled up on her side, whimpering softly. Stan reached into Marian's purse and removed her cell phone. He found the entry for Jenny Waters and hit speed dial.

"Dr. Waters? We haven't met, but I'm a friend of Marian's, Stan Wallace. Marian and I need to see you right away. I think there might be a problem with the baby."

* * *

Jenny met them at the door of her office. Stan was supporting much of Marian's weight as they entered the door. Marian looked unsure and uncaring of where she was. She was moving her lips, muttering to herself. Jenny thought she looked like an animal that had been shot with a tranquilizer dart.

"Help her into the chair, please"

Removing a small flashlight from her pocket, she immediately began checking the responsiveness of Marian's pupils.

"She collapsed at the press conference," Stan explained. "It looked like she was in severe pain, then recovered briefly. And as she walked off the stage, she had an emotional breakdown. She thinks the baby is taking some sort of control over her."

Jenny saw that her breathing and pulse were rapid.

"Marian, can you tell me what's wrong?"

"I almost lost him," Marian whispered between panting breaths.

"He's not going to stay with me if I can't become a better person. He told me not to lie, and when I tried to, he started to leave. I don't know if I can do this. I don't know if I can be as good as he wants me to be. It's just too much – "

Jenny knelt on the floor and began undoing Marian's skirt.

"Excuse me, please," she said sternly.

Stan turned his back. Marian checked quickly for signs of blood or fluid and found none.

"Help her back to my office."

Stan helped Marian to lie down on the examining table.

"Wait outside," Jenny ordered.

As Stan exited, Jenny quickly prepared an injection of Valium. Within a few minutes, Marian had calmed considerably.

As Marian's breathing slowed, Jenny asked, "Are you feeling any better?"

"Is the baby alright?" Marian slurred.

"You haven't miscarried. At least there's no sign of it."

"I didn't think so. I think he's alright."

"Can you tell me what happened?"

"I was answering questions at the press conference. We had made up a story about the missing $80,000. When I started to tell it, I felt everything in my gut rip loose."

Marian looked sleepily at Jenny. "I dreamt of him again last night. He warned me not to lie."

"So you think the baby made a decision right then and there to abort himself?"

"I'm not crazy. I heard his voice when the pain started."

"Marian, you know there are many conditions in pregnancies that can manifest psychological symptoms. False labor, pre-eclampsia – there are several logical reasons. Just the hormonal fluctuations can cause thoughts and behavior that seem... well, crazy."

"The moment I made the decision to tell the truth, it all stopped. Instantly!" Marian insisted.

"This baby expects me to behave in a certain way. In these dreams I have, he gives me advice. This is the first time I haven't followed it."

"And you think he was punishing you for disobeying?" Jenny smiled.

"It's not punishment; it's about worthiness. If I'm not up to his standards, he'll have to leave."

Jenny had growing concerns about her friend's mental state. "You've fallen for this Jesus thing hook, line and sinker, haven't you?"

"Damn it, Jenny," Marian shouted, "you don't know what it's like having a voice inside telling you what's right and what's wrong."

"Sure I do. We all do. It's called a conscience. Is this your first experience with it?"

The anger left Marian's face and she began to cry.

"Hey, girl. I'm sorry. You're just not thinking straight right now." Jenny said sympathetically.

"It's OK." Marian said dabbing her eyes, "I keep getting one smack in the face after another. You're right. I never had a conscience. Just make it through the day alive and make sure to come out on top. That was my golden rule. "

"This pregnancy has changed me," she continued. "I just don't know if I've changed enough."

"Becoming a mother changes everyone," Jenny said. "You have no choice but to change. How else could you raise a little alien who's sole purpose in life is to keep you from sleeping and bury you alive in shitty diapers?"

Marian managed a weak smile.

"So this Stan guy's the asshole who broke the story?" Jenny asked.

"Yeah. But he's not really an asshole. He's changed too. Something really weird is going on with everyone who's involved with me right now."

Marian thought for a moment. "Jenny, is it possible? Is this pregnancy a miracle?"

"Whenever I step out of 'doctor' mode, all pregnancies are miraculous," Jenny replied. "But yours is different in a lot of ways. The way the baby was conceived, the weird healings. The priest incident is just *too* creepy.

"Look, I don't know about the spiritual stuff. I'll let the priests and shamans decide. I'm just going to do the best for you that I can."

Jenny placed her hand on Marian's slightly rounded stomach. A slight breeze blew through the room.

Jenny looked around. "Did you feel that?"

"What?"

"Nothing. Air conditioner must be acting up again."

Jenny looked uncomfortable. "It's just the weirdest thing."

"What's up, Jen?" Marian asked.

"Just this thought that popped into my head. I thought your boy might have dark hair, instead of blonde like yours."

"Yeah. That's the way he is in my dreams." Marian yawned deeply. "Are you having visions, now?"

"The face I just saw in my mind was so handsome, so full of love. How weird."

Looking over, Jenny noticed Marian was fast asleep.

*   *   *

Marian awoke in her bed with no idea how she got there. It took a few minutes for the dreamlike events of the previous day to solidify into real memories. *It all really happened.*

She got out of bed, walked into her living room and was surprised to find Stan asleep on the couch. She picked up his jacket, which appeared to have fallen to the floor, and covered him with it.

Marian was both surprised and confused at how her feelings toward Stan had snuck up on her. She had completely forgiven him for the damage his original story had caused to her life. She was beginning to trust, blindly, that he would look out for her interests.

He was becoming her anchor. Marian felt safe when he was around. And she was enjoying his company. She shook off these thoughts. There was too much at stake for her to be distracted by a schoolgirl's crush on a man who would almost certainly let her down eventually, as every other man in her life had done.

She opened the front door of her apartment and retrieved the morning paper. The front page contained the story of her press conference. Her painful episode of struggle with the truth was the focus of the article.

Apparently, her decision to be truthful had paid off. The paper reported she had converted the majority of the readers who were on the fence about whether her baby was divinely conceived. Those that saw her pain and conflict when she had attempted to lie, were overwhelmingly convinced she was a woman whose life and beliefs were undergoing a grand transformation.

A very interesting aside in the article was the assertion that church attendance in all major religions, Christian, Jewish and Islamic, had increased by 35% in the last month.

And several small churches had sprung up across the nation, all under some variation of the name, "Church of the Foster Child," and as a group had applied for tax-exempt status.

Before she could finish the article, her phone rang.

"Hello."

"Marian, it's Carl. Have you heard what happened at BiEnCo? A bomb went off. At least seven people are dead."

"A bomb?" Marian struggled to clear her head. "I just woke up. When did this happen?"

"Less than an hour ago. Turn on the TV right now and call me back as soon as you can. This is awful."

"Do they have any ideas who did it?"

"Yeah, Marian, they do." Carl's voice was quavering. "They say your followers claimed responsibility."

Marian's heart skipped. "My... shit! I'll call you back!"

She slammed the phone down and punched the remote on her TV.

The sound of the TV awakened Stan. He sat up, rubbing his eyes.

"Morning, Marian. I hope you didn't mind me sleeping here. Jenny didn't want you to be left alone. How are you feeling this morning?"

Marian was glued to the television, not hearing a word Stan said.

"Marian. Are you OK.?" Stan said loudly.

"I...HAVE...FOLLOWERS!" Marian shouted, throwing the remote at him.

Stan ducked as it flew past, parting his hair.

"Seven people were killed at BiEnCo by a bomb – set off by *my fucking followers!*"

She turned on Stan, moving closer.

"What have I let you get me into? I let you convince me that we're going to fool the public in order to save my baby, but now people are murdering *in my name!*"

"You have to tell them to stop." Stan said sternly.

"I don't have to tell them SHIT! These people are terrorists. Criminals! I want them in jail. But I DON'T... WANT... FOLLOWERS!"

"Look, Marian," Stan insisted, "the idea was to get the public behind you. It's happened much quicker and on a much bigger scale than we expected. The intention all along was to convince the ones who believed you to put pressure on BiEnCo to drop the lawsuit. We never told them what we wanted them to do."

Marian nervously massaged her temples. "Maybe I see what you mean, but still… Damn, Stan, this is crazy! Am I responsible for every insane notion these bozos come up with?"

"You don't have to take responsibility for individual actions – but, for better or worse, you *are* the leader of a movement. A movement with a defined goal: Save your baby. You *do* have a responsibility to lead this movement and to direct their actions in the way that will achieve your goal."

Marian buried her head in her hands.

"You have to speak to them," Stan affirmed.

*　　*　　*

In the Oval Office, President Stanton met with National Security advisor George DeFontana and economic advisor Sheila McCormick.

"There's been no sign of slowing in the Chinese military buildup along the Southwest border," DeFontana was saying.

"Over two million infantry now, plus at least twenty armored divisions."

"Damn! Where are they going? Don't we have any intelligence over there?" Stanton bellowed.

"No information has been given to any Red Army personnel below the rank of general. Everyone is standing by, awaiting orders. The info we do have says there's a growing belief among the troops that they're preparing for a long-term mission."

"Occupation forces," affirmed Stanton.

"Well, there's a possibility this means something other than the obvious," cautioned DeFontana,

"They know we have satellite and ground intelligence at work. They can be sure we're seeing everything they're doing. This may just be a method of communicating their displeasure over the current diplomatic situation. It may be their way of saying they want a new world forum, something to replace the U.N. They might be giving us a taste of what could happen without a global organization in place."

"In other words, they don't want to be the ones to say that a new organization is needed. They want us to make the overture?" queried Stanton.

"China's line has always been that they don't *need* anyone. Even though that's not exactly true, they're not going to back down from that stance."

Stanton pondered this for a moment.

"Well, that's one reason you're here, Sheila. Has your group examined Hunt's proposal for the economic union?"

"Yes we have, Mr. President."

"Well, what's your conclusion?"

"There are more potential problems than I could even begin to address right now."

"That's what I assumed," the President replied smugly.

"But the consensus was that it *could* work," added McCormick.

"Explain," said Stanton, leaning forward in his seat.

"It all depends on how desperate the nations feel the situation is. Basically, how much are you willing to sacrifice in the short term."

McCormick continued, "For example, it makes sense for countries such as the U.S. and Russia, with fertile farmlands lying dormant, farmers on government subsidies, to put those lands to work to provide food for the world. But in order for that to work, nations such as those in Africa, whose economies are based on primitive, inefficient agricultural techniques, would have to give up all their recent attempts at modernization of agriculture and build a new economic infrastructure based around, say, steel production."

"But then," asked Stanton, "what would happen to our steel industry?"

"We would have to give it up and move those employees to a new type of industry. But to use the example of steel for a moment, we are already protecting that industry with tariffs and price structuring. In a *true* free-trade situation, we couldn't compete with the cheaper steel from Korea and China as it stands."

"Every nation faces situations similar to this," McCormick went on, "The key to success is for every country to abandon the industries to which they have to give extraordinary support to keep them alive, and build new industries based on the unique resources they have on hand. If this is choreographed properly and measures are put in place to ensure compliance, this could be phased in gradually to the point where little economic damage would be done during the transition."

The President was still skeptical. "But after all the dust settles, how would the world economic situation be different than it is now?"

"Actually, Mr. President, it would be infinitely better than it is now. With the worldwide elimination of tariffs and subsidies, everything would be cheaper. We ran this entire scenario on a ten year computer simulation.

Just with the labor force employed during the building of the industrial infrastructure, the per-capita income of third world nations would increase by about 300%. As more people earn higher wages, spending goes up concurrently. And so, production of goods goes up.

If all nations join the organization and we have 100% compliance with the trade agreements upon which the union is based, at the end of ten years we're looking at virtually full employment worldwide."

Stanton was stunned. "OK, damn it, what's the catch?"

"Everyone has to join. If only one nation with substantial natural or economic resources holds out, an eventual collapse is almost certain."

McCormick met Stanton's eyes. "It's an all or nothing deal."

"How detailed is the simulation you've run?" asked the President.

"Very. We've restructured industry worldwide based on tariffs in place, natural resources and available workforce, taken into account local education levels, national and religious customs. We became very thorough with this simulation as we saw the potential developing."

"So you believe in this plan?" Stanton asked.

"I believe in its potential," McCormick said hesitantly. "Putting it together is a different story."

"Get Tom Hunt in here ASAP," the President ordered, "This is his baby. He needs to share in the labor pains."

*   *   *

Marian arrived at CNN studios in Atlanta at 11:30 AM, prepared to denounce those who were involved with the BiEnCo bombing. The network had eagerly accepted her offer to give a live statement during their noon news broadcast. The other major networks were certain to run it as well.

As Marian was in make up for her noon appearance, Stan was giving her some last minute advice for her message.

"Your wording is very important. This is the first time you're giving any direction to these people. There's a danger they'll try to read between the lines. I guarantee people *will* do whatever they *think* you're asking for.

"This group of – sorry, Marian – followers is growing very quickly and they're obviously passionate in their support for you and your child. You have to be very careful. I wouldn't mention the baby. And stay away from the possible religious aspects of the pregnancy. You need to come across as a concerned citizen trying to encourage people to maintain order and calm."

A head popped in the door, "Five minutes, Dr. Foster. They need you on the set."

After some last minute instructions from the floor director, the sound technician came up to clip on her microphone.

"It's a pleasure to meet you, Dr. Foster," the technician said nervously.

"I just want to let you know my whole family believes in you. We're all Foster Children."

He gave her a thumbs-up as he hurried from the set.

The floor director began his countdown and signaled Marian.

"Good morning," Marian began, "There was a terrible occurrence at the offices of BiEnCo Pharmaceuticals this morning. A bomb exploded, killing seven people. People I worked with. People I cared about.

"Someone claiming to be a supporter of mine took responsibility for this terrible act. No one who truly supports me or my child would do such a horrible thing. I ask only for public support in my fight to keep my baby."

Stan grimaced at Marian's words. *I told her not to mention the baby.*

"Violence against innocent people does nothing to help me or my child. The ones responsible for this are murderers, plain and simple. If you have any information about the identities of the people responsible for the bombing, I ask for your help in bringing them to justice. Thank you."

Marian received the "cut" signal and left the set. As she walked toward Stan, she read the concern on his face.

"What's wrong, Stan," she asked, "Did I say something wrong?"

"There was nothing wrong with what you said," Stan replied. "I'm just worried about what people heard."

*   *   *

At 3:30 PM Marian's phone rang. "Hello," she answered.

"Is this Marian Foster?" a voice asked.

"Yes, it is."

"This is Captain Davis, Atlanta Police Department. We'd like you to come down to headquarters to answer a few questions."

"Can I ask what this is about?" Marian said cautiously.

"We'll talk down here. Can we count on you or should I send a car?"

"No, no. I'll be right there," Marian said as fear rose in her chest.

"Thank you, Doctor. We'll be waiting."

*   *   *

Marian and Stan arrived at police headquarters within the hour. As they entered the captain's office they noticed two serious looking men with dark suits sitting alongside the uniformed Captain Davis.

"Have a seat Dr. Foster," the captain said. Looking Stan up and down, he added, "and you are – ?"

"Stan Wallace. I'm her media consultant."

"Wallace of the Global Enquirer," Davis smirked. "I'm not too impressed with your standards for employees, doctor."

Stan bristled, "I'll leave if you need to speak with Marian alone."

"No, please join us. If you're the wordsmith behind this little lady, we may need to hear from you as well."

The captain gestured at the men beside him.

"This is Special Agent Collins, FBI and Agent Rodriguez, Georgia Homeland Security Office. We asked you here today because we have concerns about your organization, Dr. Foster."

"You mean the Foster Child Foundation? The trust funds for college?" Marian asked.

"No, ma'am," replied Agent Collins. "We're talking about the Church of the Foster Child, or whatever name they're using today."

Stan broke in, "These churches have nothing to do with Marian. They sprang up on their own, all over the country."

109

"These churches recognize her unborn baby as a deity," said Agent Rodriguez. "They worship him as God incarnate and look to Dr. Foster as his prophet. They will follow her orders."

"Look," interjected Marian, "I had nothing to do with sanctioning these churches. I didn't ask for them. I didn't organize them."

"You have portrayed yourself as the Mother of God. I can't think of a better way to start a church," scoffed Agent Collins.

Marian was adamant. "I have never spoken of myself in that way! I've done everything possible to avoid that title. I've always been honest about my doubts about who or what the baby might be."

"But your 'media consultant' has done plenty to dispel those doubts," said the captain, opening a folder of front-page clippings from the Enquirer.

"'The New Madonna,' 'The Second Coming,' 'The Miracles of Marian Foster.' Just a few of your articles, am I correct?"

"Yes," Stan shot back, "but each of those titles is framed as a question. My articles only explored possibilities."

"Wait… wait," Marian interrupted, "you think I had something to do with the bombing?"

"That crossed our minds this morning. You certainly have a good motive," said the Captain.

"But this afternoon's events disturbed us even more," Agent Rodriguez continued. "What do you think of this?"

The agent flipped a stack of 8 X 10 photos on the desk in front of Marian.

Marian looked at the first photo. A shot of the front door of the Seventh Precinct police headquarters. In front of the door, three bodies were propped up. Their faces were mangled and bloody. What looked to be cardboard signs were hung around their necks.

The next photos showed close-ups of each of the men. The signs around each of their necks read "Murderer."

Agent Collins handed a sheet of paper to Marian.

"Here's a copy of the letter that was left with the bodies."

Marian read the note: "As the Foster Mother condemned the murderers responsible for the bombing, so do we condemn them. Justice has been done in the Child's name. Love and Devotion, The Church of the Foster Child."

"We can't hold you or charge you with a crime yet, Dr. Foster. But I guarantee we will find a way if anything else happens 'in the Child's name,'" said Agent Rodriguez. "This country has taken a stand that defense against terrorism supersedes an individual's constitutional rights."

"Terrorism?" Marian exclaimed, "These are the acts of a few insane people."

"These are your insane people, doctor," responded Agent Collins.

"This is a violent group of citizens answering to a leader who is not an elected official. They're willing to disobey the law in order to show support to their leader. They've just made a point of murdering people in a way meant to strike fear in anyone who would dream of crossing you – or them. I think that meets the definition of a terrorist group."

"You're a doctor," said the captain, poking a finger at the photos, "so give me your professional opinion of how these people died."

Marian studied the pictures closely. The bodies were lacerated from head to toe. Although there was excessive blood, none of the cuts seemed to be deep. There were just so many of them. From what remained of the faces, it appeared many cranial bones were broken.

Finally, Marian offered, "From what I can tell, it looks like they were severely beaten. Maybe clubbed."

"Think biblical, Dr. Foster," Collins said dryly. "These people were stoned to death."

Rodriguez added, "Get your people under control, doctor. Or else your people will find themselves without a leader."

CHAPTER 12

In its first months The Foster Child Foundation received over $200 million donated by the believers who called themselves "Foster Children." The churches operating in the name of the child were attempting to structure themselves into a unified organization. This was proving difficult, as there was no one person who stepped forward as a leader. Churches of The Foster Child were also arising in Europe, Africa and Russia. In the traditional churches, however, there was much disagreement about the status of Marian Foster's baby.

"Anyone who believes God will return to us by way of technology is being deceived by Satan!" shouted televangelist Reverend Bill Driscoll.

"This is obviously a child conceived by the forces of evil! It will take every cent we have to fight this Antichrist, this abomination to the Lord, so you need to GIVE, my children! I want you to take out your checkbooks right now . . ."

"God sends messages in mysterious ways," mused Rev. Altheus Parker, Southern Baptist minister.

"And this may very well be one of them. Many good people have brought His spirit into the world. Mohandas Gandhi, Rev. Martin Luther King, Mother Theresa. You don't have to be Jesus Christ to do good works. Marian Foster and her child have proven this again."

"The time is right for God to send another messenger," said Brother Raymond DeVille, a Benedictine monk.

"The biblical prophesies are being fulfilled. Some say Armageddon began with the dropping of the bomb on Hiroshima. Since that time we've seen the cold war, Vietnam, religious wars in the Middle East, terrorism, and now, the collapse of the United Nations. We are a people in need of a savior. And God always meets our needs."

*   *   *

Marian placed her hand on her stomach. Her fingers traced the soft roundness where a slim waistline once had been. Not since she was a child had the future seemed so uncertain. The one constant she had relied on for her whole life – her unbending self-confidence – had evaporated. Some people were calling her a saint, the mother of God. But she had never felt more powerless. She had control over nothing, it seemed. Especially her emotions.

She had always believed fear exited her life when her father died. Now, for the first time since, she was scared again. At this point in American history, there wasn't much worse than being branded a terrorist.

The thought popped into her mind: *Jesus was an enemy of the state, too. But he didn't have an army of crazies ready to do his bidding. At least not while he was alive.* She didn't like the sound of that – 'not while he was alive.' What would the government do to her if another incident occurred? Would Stan have a plan?

Stan. Always Stan. Why did her relationship with him have to be so confusing? Her initial hatred had evolved into a necessary alliance. But what else was it? A friendship?

She had confided very little to him about her life and her work. But it didn't seem to matter. He just kept showing up, thankfully. His presence was a comfort. He demanded nothing from her. Stan was instantly there if she needed him and gone if she didn't.

The continuing articles he wrote about her took on a very different slant from stories typically in the Enquirer. They were respectful. Non-intrusive. He was so much unlike any man she had known before. Marian picked up the phone and began to dial. She suddenly felt very alone.

"Wallace," replied the voice on the other end.

"Hey, Stan. It's me."

"Everything alright?" he asked.

He always asks, Marian realized. *Always the first thing he wants to know.*

"Yeah...well, no. Just feeling a little sorry for myself. Uh, you want to go out tonight?"

"Out?" Stan seemed puzzled by the question. "You mean –"

"I mean out. You know. Dinner."

"Well, sure. Is something wrong? Something you need?"

Marian realized she had never called him before unless she needed something.

"Yeah, I need something. I need to tell you who I really am. I want to tell you everything about me."

There was a moment of awkward silence before Stan replied, "I would love to hear all about you. What time should I pick you up?"

"7:00 O.K.?"

"I'll see you then."

"Bye." Marian felt a weight had been lifted from her shoulders.

It was O.K. to call him like that, Marian thought. *He could be a good friend. Friend. Just a friend.*

Things didn't seem as bad now. Where was the fear she was feeling just moments ago?

*　　　*　　　*

Norm Randall remembered the song he had learned for his Confirmation service way back when he was in sixth grade at St. Paul's Catholic School. He tossed an empty beer can in the general vicinity of the trash bin and popped another top.

"We are soldiers in Christ's army," he sang loudly, "Marching to our heavenly goal – "

That was what they sang as they marched up to the altar where the Archbishop awaited. The old wrinkled priest had to slap them on the cheek, a sign of their manhood, symbolically enlisting them in God's army against the devil.

Actually the guy just barely touched them, a great disappointment to Norm after hearing the older kids tell stories about Archbishop Schultz's knockout punches. He and his friends actually practiced slapping each other as hard as they could, just to make sure they wouldn't cry.

The pastor of his Murfreesboro church, Father Vollmer, sure did cry like a little girl last year when Norm broke his nose after the priest refused to give him communion. Vollmer had told Norm he couldn't take the sacrament anymore since he was divorced. Excommunicated, he called it.

You can't throw me out, Norm told him. *I'm a soldier in Christ's army.*

No friggin' pansy in a black dress was going to give him a dishonorable discharge from the heavenly militia. That bastard gave Martha Conrad communion and she screwed everybody South of Nashville. Even Norm.

But the devil's army hadn't arrived in Murfreesboro, Tennessee. So Norm's life had been pretty dull. Until now.

"Jesus is comin' again," Norm slurred. "Gettin' his army together for the BIG ONE."

Norm had finally heard his calling.

"Li'l baby Jesus gonna need some help. Don't you worry, baby Jesus. Big Norm's a comin'."

He rose unsteadily from his oil-stained recliner. He shuffled across the room, kicking aside the old issues of *Car and Driver* and *Guns and Ammo* that carpeted the floor. He opened the drawer under his gun rack and shoved a box of Winchester 30.06 shells in his pocket. After slinging a long, thin case over his shoulder, he staggered to the refrigerator and pulled the door open.

Better take a twelve pack. Atlanta's a long drive.

*   *   *

"Wow," said Stan, "you look great." He was being truthful.

"Thanks," replied Marian, trying not to smile. It had been difficult finding anything other than frumpy business attire that still fit. She had very few flattering clothes left. She couldn't remember ever having more trouble dressing. Not that she was trying to impress anyone. It just feels nice to look good every once in a while.

"Where to?" asked Stan.

"How about Renault's?"

Stan hesitated and finally asked, "Have you really thought about this, Marian?"

"What's to think about? We're friends, right? Friends can have dinner."

Stan smiled. "Well, of course. But I meant... this is the first time you've been out in weeks other than the press conferences and the CNN shoot. Have you thought about what it's going to be like?"

"What do you mean?"

"Marian, your face is everywhere. I don't think you realize what a celebrity you are."

She had never given it a thought. She was so intently focused on her moment-to-moment struggles it never really sunk in that the entire country knew who she was.

"Well, how bad could it be? It's not like I can hide out until the baby's born. We can always leave, right?"

"OK. I'm with you," said Stan, offering his arm.

It was an easy drive downtown, and in fifteen minutes they arrived at Renault's. A parking valet rushed up and took Stan's keys. As Marian got out, the attendant's eyes grew wide.

"You're the Foster Mother! Wow. I'm parking your car?"

Marian was flattered. She approached the young man, smiling and extended her hand.

"Marian Foster. Pleased to meet you."

"DON'T TOUCH ME!" the attendant exclaimed, "It's cool... really. Just don't touch me."

He jumped into the car and drove away.

Marian looked to Stan. He smiled weakly, "You'd better be prepared for all kinds of reactions tonight."

Before they had taken two steps a cab slammed on its brakes and screeched to a stop right next to them.

"Mother Foster!" the cabbie called, "It *is* you! Mother, would you bless my cab?"

Marian stammered, "Well, I don't –"

"Please," the cabbie begged, "Bless the cab, please."

Stan leaned close and whispered, "God bless this cab."

Marian repeated, "God, bless this cab!" as she made a stiff waving gesture with her hand. "And drive safely," she added.

"Thanks, Mother Foster! HA! She blessed my cab!" the cabbie bellowed proudly as he drove off.

"Should I learn how to do that cross thing?" Marian asked, laughing as she made a wild "x" motion in the air with her hand.

Stan chuckled.

Her laughter was cut short by a spray of spittle hitting her in the face.

"Bitch!" shouted a large woman who appeared five inches from her face, obviously the origin of the fluid.

"Devil's whore! I hope you die!"

The two of them hurried past her. Stan offered his handkerchief and Marian wiped herself.

"So much for appetizers," she said dryly.

Looking at the crowd around the door, all gawking in her direction, Marian hesitated.

"Maybe this wasn't such a good idea." Her smile had faded.

Stan said sympathetically, "Let's just get inside. I'll get us a table in the back room."

As the maitre'd hustled them through the restaurant, all heads were turning in their direction. Whispers of, "that's her" and, "Foster" could be clearly heard.

The maitre'd halted in a corner of the room where no diners could overhear.

"We're pleased to have you with us, Dr. Foster, but we would like to avoid any scenes here tonight. Our clientele expects a serene and private dining experience."

Stan replied, "That's what we're here for as well. If you can seat us somewhere in back where we can have some privacy- "

He slipped a bill into the maitre'd's hand.

"We can accommodate you, sir." the man replied, after approving of the denomination.

They were seated at a table in a smaller side room with only one other couple, several tables away. The woman at the table looked up, nudged her acquaintance sharply and both heads stared in Marian and Stan's direction. The man signaled the waiter, said something to him and all three stood and filed out of the room.

"Can't ask for more privacy than this," Stan said smiling.

"What do these people think I am? Do you see the looks I'm getting?"

"They don't know what you are," Stan said gently, "Some are scared. Some think you're a fraud. And some wonder if they're worthy to be in your presence."

Stan saw Marian's self-consciousness growing.

"I'm sorry if I've completely screwed things up for you. I just needed to find a way to help; to make up for starting this mess. I want you to know that everything I've done was because I wanted to protect your baby. I didn't have any idea things would get so. . ."

"I trust you Stan. It took a while, but I know you're trying to do what's right."

She reached across the table and touched his hand. Stan quickly pulled away and picked up his menu.

"What are you going to have?" he asked.

"Oh, I don't know," Marian responded, trying not to sound flustered. "I think I'm in the mood for seafood."

"The stuffed flounder is great," Stan said. "So, you still want to tell me about yourself?"

"What do you want to hear?" Marian smiled.

"What was it like growing up?" Stan asked, "I know you had a lot of trouble when you were young. You seem to have done a great job of overcoming it."

"Not really," said Marian, fidgeting with her fork, "I'm Cleopatra, the queen of denial. Life sucked, basically. I got used to forgetting each day as it passed. There was nothing I really wanted to remember.

"When I was really little, we lived in a big house. I remember that much. My dad had some kind of job with a film production company. Seems like we had money.

"My mom just stayed in her room most of the time. I always thought she was sleeping a lot. When I was five, things changed, there was a lot fighting. Every day things just got worse. I would hear my dad screaming, 'junkie,' at mom. He started hitting her. Soon, he wasn't going to work anymore. That's when things got really bad.

"We moved into a tiny little house in a bad neighborhood on the North side of Atlanta. Mom still stayed in her room most of the time. Dad stayed in the living room.

I remember him pouring drinks out of a brown bottle and sucking powder up his nose through a straw. I'm sure it was cocaine. Every now and then he would become manic, raving about these wonderful ideas he had for movies. He would make phone calls for hours, then become angry and hit the powder again.

When he was really stoned, he would make advances to me. He said I needed to grow up and act like a wife to him, since mom couldn't."

"What a terrible childhood," Stan said, looking shocked.

"Some nights he would attack me in my bed, sometimes when I was in the bath. Luckily he was always drunk enough that I could get away before —"

"Oh my God, Marian. I'm so sorry," Stan sympathized.

"There are a lot of holes in my memory. I've tried many times to remember if he actually raped me," Marian continued.

"Maybe he did, I don't know. Like I said, I learned how to forget a lot of unpleasant things. Anyway, one day, when I was nine, he just left. Mom never even came out of her room that day.

I thought, now things can get better. I'll help mom be happier and we'll have a great life together. I was wrong."

"My new relationship with mom became buying and carrying her drugs for her. I knew all the dealers on the North side. When I was twelve, I finally convinced her to kick. She went cold turkey, stayed off two weeks and went out to celebrate. That night, she OD'ed. Died in her car."

Stan sat in silence for a moment, staring at the table cloth.

"How can anyone live through a childhood like that? I don't see how you kept going."

Marian smiled. " Jenny. I've known her since I was seven, and I always pretended she was my sister. We'd spend time together almost every day. When mom died, I went to live with Jenny and her parents, since I didn't have any other relatives."

"That explains why you two are so close. I'd been wondering," Stan said.

"Wondering if we were lesbians?" Marian asked.

"No, that's not what —"

"It's OK, " Marian smiled. "A lot of people have thought so. No, Jenny is happily married and I have been happily asexual all my life."

The waiter appeared. "Good evening. Are you ready to order?"

Stan and Marian spent the mealtime discussing high school days, college experiences and had worked their way to early career blunders by the time the check came.

"That was a great meal, Stan. I really enjoyed this."

"Me too," Stan said. "This was nice."

The bus boy, a balding man in his forties, was removing the dinnerware from the table. He knocked a spoon off the table which bounced off Marian's lap and hit the floor.

Marian began to reach for it, and at the same time the man said, "I'm so sorry ma'am," and bent to pick it up.

Their hands touched for a moment and Marian heard a small voice saying, "His daughter is dying."

Marian looked around the room. They were still the only patrons in this part of the restaurant.

Marian asked the man, "Excuse me. Do you have a daughter?"

The man looked at Marian, his eyes growing wide with recognition.

"Yes."

"Um, how is she?" Marian asked hesitantly.

The man's eyes grew even wider. "She's... not well. She's very sick."

"I'm very sorry to hear that," Marian sympathized. "I'll, uh, pray for her," she added awkwardly. She had never said those words before.

The man began to turn and walk away but stopped.

"Can you help her?" he asked desperately. "You're the Foster woman, aren't you?"

"Yes, I am, but I'm not sure – "

"You cured that woman of cancer. Can't you help my daughter?"

Marian heard the small voice again. "No," it said softly.

"I have to tell you, I really don't know what cured that woman. I'm not sure I had anything to do with it."

"If God would heal a seventy-eight year old woman," the man said adamantly, "why wouldn't he help a 15 year old child?"

Marian had no answer. Why wouldn't he? Could this be her new purpose in life? Bringing God's healing power to those in need?

"Where is your daughter?" Marian asked.

"Memorial Hospital."

"Stan?" Marian looked to him for approval.

"I'm game if you are."

She asked the busboy, "What time do you get off?"

"Five minutes ago. Can I change?"

"Take your time," Marian said.

Within the hour they were in the girl's room at Memorial hospital. The red-haired teenager was lying in bed, unconscious.

"Last year they told me she had leukemia." the man told them.

"They said with treatment she could probably live five years. But last month she started going downhill fast. She'll probably die this week. See if you can do anything, please."

Marian walked to the bedside and looked at the pale girl.

The nurse said, "She probably won't know you're here. She hasn't been awake for two days."

Marian touched the sleeping girl's hand. She instantly entered the white fog. The girl was screaming. Fighting. A familiar searing pain burned between her legs. The father's grimacing face hovered over her own. The man's voice shocked her back to reality.

"Well, can you help her?" the man asked impatiently.

Marian's mouth was dry. She struggled to speak. "No. I can't," she said weakly.

"Why not?" the man shot back, anger now present in his voice.

"She doesn't want to live," Marian said automatically.

"What are you talking about? Why wouldn't she want to live?" the man shouted.

"Because of what you've done to her," Marian snapped.

The man's eyes grew wide and his face reddened. He shot toward Marian with arms outstretched and clamped his hands around her throat.

"You lying bitch!"

Marian and the man fell to the floor. His hands tightened on Marian's neck as Stan and the nurse fought to get him off. Marian felt her windpipe collapsing and was paralyzed with fear. Not at the thought of dying, but of the terrible power she felt building in her.

"No, please," she croaked, hoping God would hear.

Don't let this come out of me. Her pleading did no good.

Marian felt as if a bolt of lightning was surging through her body. The man's grip turned limp and his face went slack as he fell. She struggled to sit upright and saw the man lying next to her on the floor, eyes open wide.

Stan helped Marian into a chair. "All you alright?"

Marian motioned to her throat and nodded.

"Just can't talk," she said in a scratchy voice.

The nurse was hovering over the man on the floor.

"My God, I think he's dead."

"He is," affirmed Marian.

Stan looked at Marian with a mixture of concern and fear.

"I'm going to have to call security," the nurse said nervously.

Stan, Marian and the nurse related the story to the officers several times until they seemed satisfied Marian had done nothing wrong. The man had apparently attacked Marian and his anger had brought on a heart attack.

The two were told they could leave, with the caveat, "We'll call you if we need anything else."

Marian remained silent on their drive to her apartment. Stan worried if she was near another breakdown like after the press conference. As they entered her apartment Marian began to cry softly.

"Are you going to be alright?" Stan asked.

"Will you stay with me tonight?" Marian blurted out.

"No problem," Stan said softly, "You've got a comfy couch."

"No, Stan. Will you sleep with me?"

Stan's mouth moved but no sound came out.

"What's wrong, Stan. Are you scared I'll kill you too?" she asked sadly.

Stan sat down and considered his response before answering.

"Look, Marian, I'd be lying if I said I wasn't attracted to you, but I've tried to put aside my feelings so they wouldn't interfere with what we're trying to accomplish."

"Well, you have my permission to not put them aside," she said boldly, moving next to him on the sofa. "Consider yourself off duty."

Stan struggled for words. "It would be too easy to fall in love with you. But I can't let myself."

"Why not?"

"Because I believe in you. I think your baby *is* a messenger from God. I'm a…well, I haven't always lived a good life,"

Stan rubbed his face with both hands.

"Marian, to put it bluntly, I'm a sinner! I've drank, smoked, cheated, stolen, committed adultery. Damn, I've broken nine commandments in the span of one week. Since I've met you I've tried hard to change – "

"And from everything I've seen, you have. I think you're a wonderful man " said Marian, moving closer.

"Marian, do you remember what happened when you tried to tell a lie? A simple little lie? You almost lost the baby. What could happen if we made love?"

"I don't know, but don't I deserve to be happy?"

She began crying again.

"Why wouldn't he want me to be happy? I'm his mother!"

Stan said gently, "We can't take this chance. At least I can't. I won't put you or your baby at risk. I promise you I'll stick with you and do everything I can to protect you, but... I'm not good enough for you – or your baby."

"It wasn't a good idea," Marian said, "I'm sorry. You should probably go."

"No, I'm the one who's sorry," Stan said as he opened the door.

Closing it behind him, he heard Marian sobbing softly. He kicked the wall angrily, then turned and walked toward his car.

*   *   *

Big Norm was furious now. Still three hours from Atlanta, raining to beat hell, and he had to make the rest of the trip with a busted headlight.

"Stupid piss ant," he muttered. "Can't understand I gotta take care of li'l baby Jesus. Wants his fuckin' money for gas. Stupid piss ant."

Of course he had to buy gas. Can't get to Atlanta on seven dollars worth of gas. After he filled his tank, he told the man he was going to Atlanta to help baby Jesus. Told him Jesus would pay for the gas. But the man said, no, he had to pay.

Stupid asshole ran in front of his truck to try and stop him from driving away. The guy's head broke out the headlight just before he went under the wheels. Now it was raining, and hard to see.

"Left tread marks on him," Norm chuckled, "Call him the Michelin Man now. Got tread marks on his ass."

Norm thought he would have to stop for beer soon.

CHAPTER 13

Captain Davis of the Atlanta Police Department was having another bad day. He was tired of having bad days and was tired of Marian Foster being the cause of them. Davis had ordered the IT department to have the computers flag her name if it came up on any police reports. And sure enough, here it was already. Connected to a mysterious death.

He called for the officers who filed the report on the man who died after attacking Marian at the hospital.

"So you're sure there were no physical signs of any kind that the Foster woman was trying to defend herself?" the Captain asked the officers.

"Nothing," the younger officer replied.

"We took fingernail scrapings, nothing there. The man had no marks of any kind on his body. The nurse said Foster didn't do anything when he took her down, just said 'no' a couple of times,"

"What about needle marks? Did you check for signs she might have injected him with something?"

"Well, no," said the older officer, "the doctor who was there when we arrived said the guy died of a heart attack. And the coroner agreed."

"Dammit, don't you know who she is?" the Captain shouted.

"Beggin' your pardon, sir," said the young officer, "but I don't believe in any of that shit."

"Neither do I!"

The Captain's face reddened. "She's a doctor, you dumbass, she has access to drugs. People have been cured, or think they have anyway, and people have died in her presence. Don't you think she has the means to cure and to kill people so it doesn't look obvious?"

The two officers looked sheepishly at one another.

"I want an autopsy done. I want every toxicology test done. I want this woman in custody before all hell breaks loose with her and her cult."

Davis leaned nearer the officers to make his point.

"You think Waco was bad? This woman has nutcases all over the country waiting to do her bidding. I want you to find how she killed this guy. Now, get outta here!"

The captain knew in his gut he would have to wait for another time. He was certain the autopsy would find nothing.

*   *   *

Marian was awakened by her ringing phone. She glanced at the clock. 11:00AM.

"Hello."

"Hi, Marian, it's Carl. I wanted to check on you. Stan told me about last night. Are you alright?"

"What did Stan tell you?" she asked apprehensively.

"The trip to the hospital after dinner. The guy who attacked you and –"

"Another one bites the dust," she finished sarcastically.

"Stan was worried about you this morning," Carl said. "He said he wanted to stay with you, but he didn't think it was right."

"Well, Stan knows best, doesn't he. He's got all the answers," Marian snapped.

"Marian, you know he really cares for you."

"So, are you his confidante now?" Marian asked.

"Well, we talk, you know."

"I don't know that I want you two talking about me."

"Don't get upset," said Carl, "Stan asked me last week if there was anything going on between the two of us. I got the feeling he was interested."

"Then he needs to show it a little more," said Marian, beginning to calm down. "He thinks God will strike him down if he lays a finger on the virgin mother."

"Look at what's happened. Can you blame him for worrying?" asked Carl.

"I don't know what I think. I know I've never cared if a man was interested in me before. Now I do, and he's scared to come near me. I would think if he really was interested, all this other crap wouldn't matter."

"To most men it wouldn't," Carl responded, "but he's obviously not like most men. You're an attractive woman. A lot of men would just go for the gold without thinking about what it might mean to you and the baby. I happen to think he's a good guy."

"Yeah, I know," Marian sighed. "I think so too."

"The other reason I called is because BiEnCo has called a press conference for tomorrow morning at 11:00, in front of the Federal courthouse. Stan thinks they're just going to talk about new motions they're filing concerning the lawsuit, but he says there's a chance they might accuse you of being involved in the bombing."

"Great," Marian said grimly.

"He says we should be there so we can respond to the media immediately, if necessary."

"So why didn't he call to tell me this?" Marian asked.

"I think he was afraid you might be upset with him. Can I tell him things are OK?"

Marian sighed, "Yeah, give him the 'all clear'. Tell him to call me."

"Will do."

"Thanks, Carl."

*   *   *

"Colonel, you need to see this."

A uniformed soldier was hunched over a computer monitor.

"What do you have, Adams?" The colonel asked.

"I'm not sure. Satellite picked up something. Sometimes a cosmic ray can trigger a false reading. But last orbit we had a hot spot right in the middle of D.C."

"Right here," he said pointing to the screen. "Showed up as beta and gamma decay. Very small amount, but the computer is flagging the radiation signature as plutonium 239."

"Are you shittin' me, Adams?" the colonel asked, looking at a red circle on the screen centered about 2 miles from the capitol.

"Absolutely not, sir. Nothing was there before. I've checked the last two weeks worth of orbital data and no signals in that location. We'll be getting another shot of the area in about 50 seconds."

"If we get a positive, no matter how small, I want you to report to Homeland Security and get some mobile detectors out on the street."

"Roger that, sir. Wait, we've got new data coming in now."

The men watched as the screen refreshed and revealed a new picture, minus the red circle.

"Guess it was an anomaly, sir. All clear now."

The colonel continued to stare at the screen.

"You keep your eye on that area. Let me know if anything else shows."

"Yes, sir."

*   *   *

The bearded man in Washington, D.C. was cursing his colleagues. Stupid Arabs. Such shoddy work.

Even thought they had delivered one of the largest amounts of plutonium to him, almost two ounces, their lead case had been hastily made. The seams had not been properly sealed and when he dropped the case, the corner cracked open and two small, highly radioactive discs rolled onto the floor.

He picked the discs up with his bare hands and slid them back into the box through the crack, placed some lead sheeting over it, and lit his propane torch. As he was melting the soft lead back into shape, he thought about how foolish people were about radiation.

Even though plutonium has been called the "deadliest substance on earth," he knew the truth. Most of the radiation produced by plutonium could be blocked by a piece of paper. The danger was in inhaling it. He knew he had inhaled some, but his death by fire would come quicker than the radiation could take him.

*   *   *

Norm Randall awoke in a confused state. He squinted around at the strange room he found himself in. After a moment, the world stopped spinning enough for him to clearly see his surroundings. The only familiar sight was a half-drunk pint of Heaven Hill on the chair within arm's reach of the bed. His head was exploding, his skin crawling. Where was he? He knew there was only one way to get answers at a time like this.

"Come here, ol' buddy," he said, reaching for the pint. He downed half the remainder and waited for relief to come. He laid his head, throbbing and pumping, back down onto the drool-stained pillow and began to feel the warmth coarse through him. His headache started to subside and the first answer came to him. Atlanta. Next question was, why?

Norm sat up and finished the rest of the pint. On the table beside him were two more full pints.

Thank you, lord. Also, there was a wallet. Not his. He opened the wallet. One hundred forty bucks. And a Florida driver's license with the name Joseph Cameron on it. He stared at the picture until it came into focus. As the next wave of Heaven Hill spread through him, he remembered the face. A tourist he met outside of the liquor store last night. A man who hadn't wanted to be generous when he asked for a donation to help save baby Jesus. Took a little persuading in the alley to make him see the light.

Baby Jesus! That's why he was here. Baby Jesus needed Norm's help. He broke the seal on the second bottle and took a good whack. Now he was starting to feel better.

He looked over and saw his H&K rifle in the corner, still in its case. He reached into his jacket which was draped over the chair and drew out the box of ammo. Unopened. At least he hadn't used ol' Hatfield yet. He felt the whiskey bringing back his strength.

"I'm a soldier in Christ's army," he sang, "marching to my heavenly goal."

But he still wasn't sure exactly what his goal was. He had seen the Foster Mother on TV asking for help and Big Norm was ready to respond. Now that he was close by, he could act at a moment's notice once he got his instructions. He took another slug from the bottle and flipped on the TV.

Headline News was showing highlights from the previous day's baseball games. Norm wasn't much of a baseball guy. Since coming back from Iraq in '91, nothing seemed like much of a sport if there wasn't a chance of bones being crushed or blood being spilled. Even regular army were a bunch of pansies to Big Norm. He was a Marine. *Is* a Marine. *Semper fuckin' Fi, assholes.*

He got his discharge after his best bud had been killed in an ambush outside of Tirkut. He had killed the assailant and then mounted the guy's head on his jeep like a hood ornament. When he drove back into camp that night, his commanding officer put in for an immediate discharge for Norm. It was revised to 'dishonorable' after he made a half-successful attempt to gut the C.O. with his bayonet.

It was the top of the hour now, and the headline stories were on. The anchorman was saying the C.E.O. of BiEnCo Research would be holding a press conference on the steps of the Federal courthouse at 11:00 AM in Atlanta. They had filed something or other in court that said the Foster baby belonged to them and they were going to take it. Take it right out of the mother.

"Uh-uh," shouted Norm at the TV, "not gonna take baby Jesus! You workin' for the devil! You in the devil's army! I fight for Jesus!"

It was time for Norm to get dressed.

*   *   *

Stan and Carl arrived at Marian's apartment at 9:35. They knocked repeatedly until the door finally opened and Marian appeared, squinting at the bright morning sun.

"What time is it?" she asked groggily. Marian was still feeling the effects of the Ambien she had taken to sleep last night.

"It's time to go." Stan said. "What the hell are you doing?"

"Uh, sleeping, I guess."

"Hurry and get dressed. We really need to be at this announcement."

Stan tried to hide his annoyance. "Do you mind if we come in?" he asked sarcastically.

"Oh, sorry. Come on in. I'll hurry." The men entered and Marian rushed to her bedroom.

"Traffic is horrible out there. What's been going on?" Stan shouted to her.

Her voice echoed from the rear of the apartment, "Couldn't sleep. I had terrible dreams all night. Moved to the couch about 3:30 for a change of scenery. I guess I couldn't hear the alarm."

She didn't want to admit to the sleeping pills.

Carl and Stan looked at each other. "Bad dreams?" Carl said softly.

"I really didn't need to hear that this morning," Stan grumbled.

He thought for a moment, then asked, "Carl, does Marian seem alright to you? You've known her a while. Is she just that good at keeping things inside, or is it possible she's suffered another breakdown?"

"Even though I've worked with her for a few years," Carl replied, "I can't say I really know her. She's always been tough as nails. Could out-curse a drill sergeant. She seems a bit more human now."

Carl deliberated before continuing. "I think she's O.K. I try to remember what she's lived through. Her life would either make you strong or kill you."

"You're right about that," Stan said.

"But she definitely has changed. She's not the person I worked for at BiEnCo," said Carl.

"Change is in the air," Stan replied. "The world's changing. And I think I can say: You ain't seen nothin' yet."

"OK, I'm ready," Marian said as she rushed into the living room.

"Foster, you better have a miracle up your sleeve this morning or we'll never make it on time." Stan said, trying to appear annoyed.

"I had a miracle ready last night, but you weren't interested." Marian smiled coyly through bleary eyes.

Carl and Stan shot each other a look and after an uncomfortable silence, Carl exclaimed, "All righty, then!"

*   *   *

Someone was working miracles that morning, because they made it to downtown Atlanta in record time for a workday morning. They arrived seven minutes before the scheduled start of the press conference. There were twenty reporters impatiently milling around near the steps of the courthouse.

Behind them, a loosely formed crowd of a hundred or so had gathered to hear the announcement. Several of them were loudly voicing their support for Marian.

Stan, Carl and Marian - wearing a large floppy hat and sunglasses - found a spot near the back of the crowd as the microphones were being placed at the podium at the top of the steps.

Within a few moments, Alvin Hedstrom, the man that had taken Dr. Prevost's place at BiEnCo, stepped up to the mike.

"I'm glad you all could be here this morning," Hedstrom began.

"Hey asshole! You suck!" Shouted a college-aged man with a goatee. His friends on either side flipped a middle finger at Hedstrom.

"This morning, our company has filed a motion with the court to have Dr. Foster deposed to give testimony concerning all of the details of the procedure she supposedly used to become pregnant. We have also filed a motion to have Dr. Foster undergo a battery of physical and genetic tests to see if she indeed became pregnant through egg-cell fusion.

"We have been unable to duplicate her results and suspect fraudulent research reports were made. If that is the case, we will pursue additional criminal and civil charges against her. If she did indeed succeed in impregnating herself by a method owned by our company, we will continue in our pursuit of the fetus as the property of BiEnCo."

"Our company is also cooperating with the FBI and the office of Homeland Security in their investigation of the bombing at our office. If Marian Foster is found to have any connection to this act of terrorism carried out in her name, they promise she will be dealt with swiftly and harshly."

Hedstrom droned on, but Marian wasn't listening to what he was saying. She was hypnotized by his face. *Last night. He was in the dream. Something bad happened. What was it?*

An overwhelming sense of dread was coming over her now. Something she had seen. Marian gripped Stan's arm forcefully.

"Something's going to happen, Stan. Something bad!" She looked very worried.

Stan looked around the crowd. "What are you talking about?"

"Someone's here who shouldn't be!" she said in a voice verging on panic. She began looking all around. For who or what, she wasn't sure.

"Have you seen something again?" Stan asked. He was beginning to worry too.

"This is all too familiar," she said, still looking around. "I think I dreamed this last night."

Stan thought to himself, *get ready. This could be what we've been dreading.*

Her eyes darted over each face in the crowd. No. No. The truck. Truck? Her eyes fell on a rusty white Ford pickup with a broken headlight. Now the panic truly flooded through her.

She broke from Stan and Carl and shoved her way violently through the crowd.

As she pushed aside the reporters and the onlookers she began shouting, "Alvin! Get off the steps! Get away from the podium! Alvin!"

She pushed her way up to the security detail where two officers stood shoulder to shoulder blocking her, less than 15 feet from where Hedstrom stood.

"Alvin! You have to get away! Get out of here!" Marian waved her hands frantically.

"Dr. Foster?" Hedstrom muttered in surprise, but quickly regained his composure. "I'd expect at least a bit of professional courtesy from you."

"You have to get out of here! They're going to kill you!" Marian screamed.

"Are you —" Hedstrom had meant to finish his sentence with, *threatening me?* but he never got that far before his shoulder exploded.

The impact of the 30.06 payload spun him halfway around. Hedstrom looked into the crowd desperately as if they might be able to tell him what was happening. He staggered, pondering why his right arm was hanging limply, unable to move. He looked down at his shoulder and saw the broken ends of three bones protruding from his powder blue shirt, quickly staining with blood.

Marian began to scream. But before Hedstrom's scream could come forth, the left side of his face burst into a pink cloud as the second bullet struck. As he dropped to the concrete, the security officers rushed to him, leaving Marian screaming hysterically. Stan shoved his way through the pandemonium to Marian. He leaned over, grabbed her around the waist and slung her over his shoulder.

He broke into a dead run, with Marian draped over him. He raced toward the curb where Carl screeched to a halt in Stan's car. Carl reached across the seat and threw open the door. Stan unceremoniously dumped Marian, still screaming, into the passenger seat. Stan jumped into the back and the car sped off.

Captain Davis of the Atlanta Police Department was also at the courthouse for the press conference. He saw it all. And he knew he had Marian Foster now.

He raised his radio. "The Foster woman is in the crowd somewhere. She was right in front when it happened. I want her apprehended. Don't let her get away."

Marian had curled up on the front seat, sobbing softly now. Carl was at the wheel, breathing hard.

He looked back at Stan, "This is it, huh? We follow the plan?"

Stan opened his cell phone and began to dial. "Yeah. Follow the plan. Head towards Buckhead and take 41 North. We need to pick up the other car."

"You got it," said Carl. "You really called this one. I'm glad you were thinking ahead."

"I'm just scared at what I might've missed. Hello," Stan said into the phone. "It's happened. Call them together. Yeah, we're on our way. We need to see a man about a car, first."

* * *

Marian had fallen into a deep sleep and was happy to be back in the familiar dream. She turned in her chair, the one that overlooked the beautiful lake, to see her son trotting toward her.

The young boy climbed into her lap and said, "Don't be scared, Mommy. There are lots of people who want to help you."

He frowned for a moment, then continued, "Some of the people don't understand. They think they're helping you, but they're doing bad things. You need to make them understand, so they'll stop."

His eyes sparkled as he spoke. "But there are even more people that are doing good things for you. You'll meet them soon. Also, there's a man who lives in a white house. You'll have to talk to him. Don't forget."

He climbed out of her lap and scurried away. He shouted back to her, "I like Stan. He should be my Daddy."

And then he was gone.

CHAPTER 14

Marian woke in the front seat, startled to realize the car was no longer moving. She sat up in the seat and looked out into a suburban neighborhood. Carl and Stan were on the front lawn of a house talking to a man in a policeman's uniform.

Stan walked back and opened the driver's door of the car and Marian heard the policeman saying, "Pull it into the garage."

Stan started the car and pulled into a driveway leading to a three-car garage. "Everything's going to be OK, Marian. Don't worry."

"What's up with the police, Stan?" Marian asked, trying to control her growing fear.

"Just hang on. I'll explain."

They parked in the garage and Stan led Marian by the hand to face the officer.

"Steve, this is Marian Foster. Marian, Steve Lucas. *Officer* Lucas I should say."

The policeman offered his hand. "Ms. Foster, it's a pleasure — and an honor to meet you. I'm glad Stan called me to help. My family are all believers."

"Thank you," said Marian, taking his hand gingerly. *Nothing this time. Why does it only happen sometimes?*

The officer turned back to Stan. "Here are three sets of I.D.'s for you and Ms. Foster."

"That's 'Doctor' Foster," Stan corrected.

"Sorry," said Lucas, smiling at Marian, "Didn't mean to be disrespectful."

"No problem," Marian returned the smile uncomfortably.

"Anyway, like I was saying - these I.D.'s will pass any background check."

He handed the I.D.'s to Stan.

"Here's your car. A beige Camry. Most common car on the road." He handed keys to Stan. "And registration papers. Make sure you use this set of I.D.'s while you're on the road. The DMV records for the vehicle only match these."

He pointed to licenses in the names of Tony and Judith Bergeron, from Slidell, Louisiana.

"The others are in case of emergency, and...oh yeah, these credit cards." He handed a MasterCard and Visa to Stan.

"Now, Ms. – I mean Dr. Foster, is there anything you need from your apartment? I can have it picked up and sent to your next location."

"I... I don't understand. Where are we going?" Marian asked, looking from Carl to Stan.

"You haven't told her?" Steve asked. Stan and Carl shook their heads.

"Ma'am, there's a warrant out for your arrest. You're wanted for murder. You can't go back into Atlanta."

Marian eyes began to tear up. She looked at the officer and said, "Why are you helping me? All these things - "

"Ma'am, there are a lot of people on the force who want to see you and your baby safe. A whole lot," said Steve, smiling. "Even more where you're going. You'll see."

Stan interrupted, "Time to go. Carl, just keep the Foundation running. Put two million in the account I told you about and stick to the story."

"Roger that," Carl replied.

"You know how to reach us. Use the VoIP account only if it's an emergency. Talk to you soon."

Carl flashed a thumbs up.

"Thanks, Steve," Stan said to the officer.

"No problem. Good luck to you." The officer turned to Marian, "And to you. Keep that baby safe. We need him."

"I will," Marian replied. "Thank you so much."

Steve Lucas and Carl waved as Marian and Stan drove away.

Carl turned to the policeman and asked, "If you don't mind - what happened when she touched you?"

"I knew she was for real," Steve replied as he watched the car round the corner.

*   *   *

Big Norm was on the road too. He was a happy man, tooling down the highway on a beautiful day. His first assignment as a soldier in Christ's army was behind him now, and it felt good.

"Mission accomplished!" Norm shouted, taking another belt of Heaven Hill.

No more beer for Norm on this trip. He knew once you got on a jag like this you had to keep moving up the ladder of alcohol content. Can't go back to beer.

He was proud that he'd remembered what he'd learned from his Marine buddies before he was discharged. Nobody had even turned a head in his direction when he fired the shots at that skinny little baby killer. Home-made silencer did the trick. Made from a lawn mower muffler.

"Private Randall reporting for duty, Jesus. What's my next assignment?"

Norm drove in silence while the voices in his head spoke to him.

"No shit?" Norm responded to the voices. "Kansas, huh? Ain't never been to Kansas." He began singing again, "I'm a soldier in Christ's army. . . "

*   *   *

"You want to tell me what's up, Stan?" said Marian. "You and Carl obviously had some sort of plan worked out? It's time to let me in on it."

"Yeah, we had a plan," Stan replied, keeping his eyes on the road ahead. "I knew something was going to happen sooner or later. Eventually you would have to drop out of sight for a while. You didn't think you were going to make it through the entire pregnancy living life as usual, did you? Not while people think you're carrying God's child. If you're not already, you soon will be the most famous face on the planet."

"I've never thought that far ahead," Marian replied. "I'm too busy just making it through each day."

"I know. That's why I haven't told you about a lot of the things that are going on with your church. You'd had enough to worry about."

"Well, I don't know where we're going, but it feels like it's going to be a long drive. Maybe this is a good time to fill me in," Marian said, crossing her arms and peering at Stan.

"OK," Stan said, "First of all, the people who believe in you have gathered into two separate factions. One faction, who call themselves the True Believers, are some of the ones we're going to see now. They are the typical members of the Church of the Foster Child. A well-organized group who want to prepare the world for the child's birth."

"The second faction, who we call the Zealots, are a little harder to pigeonhole. They range from those who are committing acts of civil disobedience to bring attention to the fight for your baby, to those who feel a need to start Armageddon, so the scriptures are satisfied. The shooter today was almost certainly a Zealot. The Zealots are not well-organized. A bunch of small groups and individuals with virtually no communication network. Mostly just shooting from the hip - no pun intended. We're getting very worried about them."

"You say 'we'. Who's 'we'?" asked Marian.

"The True Believers," said Stan. "I am one, you know."

"I haven't heard anything about the True Believers or the Zealots," Marian said, puzzled.

"These names are just used by the people in the Circle," Stan said.

"The 'circle'?" asked Marian.

"Those of us that feel called to provide leadership to the other followers."

"Called? You mean like to the priesthood, or something?"

"Not exactly. Some of us just seem to be getting...messages, I guess you could call it."

"Who are these 'messages' coming from?" asked Marian.

Stan turned and looked deeply into Marian's eyes. "You're not the only one who's having dreams, Marian."

Marian's mouth dropped open. "You –"

"There are seven of us so far. We keep in close contact. We felt something big was coming and so we made plans to keep you and the baby hidden for a while. One member of the Circle says there will eventually be twelve of us who receive messages through dreams. 11 of them will be true believers, one will be a zealot. It kind of makes sense it would be that way."

"Why does that make sense?" Marian asked.

"Because that's the way it was before. Twelve disciples. Eleven from various walks of life that became enthralled by the living story of Jesus, and one zealot. That was Judas."

"What are your dreams like?"

Stan smiled again. "I'm going to wait till we get to Asheville, so you can hear the whole story."

"Asheville? North Carolina? Who are we going to see there?"

"Someone you know. Woman named Wilma Barnhardt. She used to have cancer." Stan winked at her.

"Her dreams have been incredible. And always right on the money. If this church survives, she'll probably be the first 'pope'."

"What do you mean, 'if this church survives'?" Marian asked.

Stan didn't reply. As he turned his attention back to the road, his expression turned grim.

*   *   *

Tom Hunt and President Stanton were still struggling to make sense of the puzzling situation in China. Hunt had just returned from a clandestine trip to visit 'friends' in Beijing.

"I've never seen the atmosphere so tense. These people are scared."

"Damn it, Tom, so am I," the President responded.

"Do you know how long it's been since the President of the United States couldn't pick up a phone and immediately be speaking to the Chairman of the Communist Party in China? Over thirty-five years!"

"There appear to be some very big problems brewing internally. From what my sources tell me, the troops don't appear to be immediately preparing to move out of China. For right now, they seem to be more concerned with sealing the borders."

"There are probably no more secure borders anywhere in the world," said Stanton. "Are the Chinese actually expecting an invasion?"

"I don't think so. It seems they're determined to prevent any of their people from leaving the country."

"That's nothing new."

"Well, a lot of people are trying to get out now. Perhaps millions. There's some sort of religious upheaval going on. I don't have a lot of information, but it has to do with some kind of prophecy that came from the Tibetan Buddhists. Several of their lamas claim the Buddha himself is about to reincarnate."

The President chuckled, "Sounds familiar. But doesn't this stuff happen all the time over there? Every few years some child is claimed to be the reincarnation of Buddha."

"Well, that's not quite right," Hunt interjected. "Their spiritual leaders are selected at a very young age by elders that proclaim the children to be reincarnated lamas, highly revered holy men from generations ago. They even will identify the particular lama they believe has returned. But never before has there been a prophecy that Prince Siddhartha himself, the actual Buddha, was going to reincarnate. The people want to go to where he will be born."

"So what if millions of Chinese are trying to cross the border into Tibet? They've occupied Tibet for years." Stanton asked.

"No," said Hunt methodically, "they're trying to get to the United States. That's where they say the Buddha will be born."

Stanton's eyes widened. "No wonder they're not communicating. Do they think we're behind this, encouraging it somehow?"

"I don't get that feeling. There's enough animosity between them and the native people of Tibet. They don't have to look any farther than that to find a scapegoat. However, I wouldn't be surprised if they activate more troops. Tighten things up even more."

The President changed the subject. "How was your proposal for the Global Economic Union received?"

"My contact accepted the proposal, but I have no idea who will see it, or when. I think they have their hands full," Hunt replied.

"We have got to make headway with this idea of yours," said Stanton. "Russia is very receptive, but they want to hold out to see what China does."

"So, you've presented to Russia," said Hunt with a smile. "You sound like you're behind this idea now."

"I have to admit I am, Tom. I had my doubts, big ones. I really don't want to start liking you either, but you're damn smart. Not a one of my advisors could shoot holes in this plan."

The President added quietly, "This may be our last and best hope."

"By the way, what's your feeling on the religious movement going on here in the U.S.?"

"The Foster Child business? I'm concerned," Stanton confided. "Homeland Security has been on my back to shut 'em down. They wanted me to label them a terrorist group after the bombing in Atlanta. It's getting even worse now, since the assassination of the BiEnCo chairman."

"So, why haven't you shut them down? Their leader has a warrant out for her arrest."

"It's that freedom thing, Tom," Stanton smiled. "We didn't shut down the Baptists when a few abortion clinics were bombed. Hell, we haven't shut down the Catholics when dozens of priests are buggering schoolchildren and their leaders conspire to obstruct justice. I've always felt that Americans have to take a bit of the bad along with the good. The 'price of freedom,' you know. And the Foster people *are* doing a lot of good. Besides the college fund, they're holding anti-racism seminars, food drives, free childcare services for the poor."

"But don't they feel a lot like 'moonies' to you?" Hunt asked.

"Tom, do you know the demographic breakdown of the Foster Church? 72% white. 12% black. 12% Hispanic. 4% Asian. 51% women, 49% men. It's an exact duplicate of the demographics of the whole country. There's never been a religion that's attracted such a diverse group of followers. And their churches aren't about worship, they're about action. What good works can *you* do today? Their 'services' are more like strategic planning sessions."

Hunt laughed. "So are you ready to convert?"

"I'm very interested in what they're doing," said the President. "A politician can only dream about motivating people like this church can."

"And that's where the worry comes in?"

"Yeah," affirmed the President. "I allowed the NSA to put some moles in the church so we can keep tabs on what they're up to."

"What happens when you find out where the woman is?" asked Hunt.

"We bring her in for questioning. But I really don't believe we'll find out anything that would allow us to legitimately hold her."

"You don't think she ordered the shooting?"

Stanton shook his head. "I don't *want* to think that. I would love for this church to turn out to be a good thing. I just don't know."

CHAPTER 15

Stan and Marian crossed the North Carolina state line at sunset. Just before 8:00 PM they turned off the main highway and took a winding gravel road through the foothills of the Smokey Mountains. After fifteen minutes the road ended at a gate in a split-rail fence. Beyond the gate was a two-story farmhouse, white, trimmed in light blue. Looked to be circa 1930.

"Is this Wilma's house?" Marian asked.

"It's the house she grew up in," Stan answered. "She bought it after you cured her. She said this was a message in one of her first dreams: Return to the place where you were a child."

"So these dreams started immediately after I met her?"

"About a week after she left the hospital the dreams started. And the person in her dreams is the same one who spoke to her when you touched her. The one who told her she was cured."

Stan pulled the car into a graveled area surrounded by beds of wildflowers and parked. He opened Marian's door and they walked to the front porch of the house. Marian admired a hand made cane-back rocker as Stan rang the bell.

The door opened and revealed a vibrant, youthful-looking Wilma Barnhardt.

"Stan! It's so good to see you again," the woman said, hugging him enthusiastically.

"And, you," she said, turning to Marian, "the troublemaker."

Stan and Wilma laughed, making Marian even more uncomfortable.

"Come in, darlin'," Wilma said, smiling grandly. "What do you think of all this ruckus you've caused?"

She leaned in close to Marian and whispered, "Ain't this the livin' *shit!*"

They walked through a large living room, decorated with items that a woman of 78 could be expected to gather throughout her life. Mismatched lamps, chairs in three different styles, a modern sectional sofa accented with patchwork quilt pillows. Knickknacks overflowed the shelves and bookcases in the room. Styles of every era from early American to art deco were on display in Wilma's living room. Marian found it charming. She had expected for them all to be seated in the living room, but Wilma kept walking, so she and Stan followed.

The entered a larger room, which Marian deduced to have been the dining room and master bedroom before the wall separating them was knocked down. This space had been turned into an artist's studio. Where the exterior wall once stood there were now ceiling-to-floor windows. On an easel, Marian saw a large painting at least five feet by three, a work in progress. Marian halted in her tracks. *It was her boy!* The familiar face from her dreams smiled down at her. Behind him a miraculous sunset over breaking waves on the ocean's shore. She then noticed other paintings on the walls. All of them in different styles, but all most definitely portraits of her child.

Marian gasped, "It's – "

"Him," finished Wilma, "I know. Not bad for my first painting, huh? There's something not quite right about the eyes, though. Something I haven't captured."

"It's beautiful!" Marian exclaimed. "He's exactly the way I see him in my dreams."

"It's the way we all see him. Those paintings on the wall, they're not mine. Those were done by other members of the Circle."

Wilma began walking again. Stan followed, but Marian slowly lagged behind to take in these other portraits. They definitely weren't going down in history as great works of art. It was obvious most of the artists had never held a brush before. But there was no mistaking the subject of these paintings. The essence of the boy's face had been captured in each work.

She saw her boy seated in a forest, surrounded by small animals. Her son on a mountaintop, overlooking a large city at dusk. And the one that touched her most deeply – her boy as a shepherd, in a white robe, surrounded by fluffy white lambs.

She walked through the door where Wilma and Stan had exited and was shocked to find herself in some sort of hi-tech communications center. Four oak desks were in the foreground of a maze of smaller cubicles. On each desk was a flat-screen computer monitor. Wilma had taken a seat at the largest desk, Stan sitting in front. He motioned to the empty chair next to him and Marian walked over and sat.

"What is all this?" Marian asked in amazement.

"I guess you could say it's the unofficial headquarters of the Church of the Foster Child," replied Wilma. "No one knows about it, though, except for the Circle and a few trusted believers."

"How many people do you have here?" Marian inquired.

"It varies. Today it's only me and Carver. He's the techno-geek that keeps everything running. He's a sweet boy; don't let his appearance fool you."

Wilma leaned forward and spoke softly as if breaking a confidence, "He was one of those hackers, you know. He wrote computer viruses. Nearly brought down the whole Defense Department last year. But that was before his miracle."

A young man in his late teens entered the room. His orange, spiked hair was accented by shining silver rings in his ears, brow and nose. He walked behind Wilma's desk and bent over her computer keyboard.

"I gotta change all the accounts again. Someone's trying to hack our e-mail server." He glanced up briefly at Stan and Marian. "Hey, whassup," he mumbled as a greeting. His eyes grew wide as he stared at Marian open-mouthed.

"It's her! She's here!" Carver looked at Wilma. "Why didn't you tell me she was coming?"

Then he said to Marian. "Wow, it's great to meet you, man. This is *so cool!* Are you going to be staying here now?"

"Just a short while, Carver," answered Wilma. "And this is TOP SECRET, understand? That's why I didn't tell you. No one can know she's here. There's a warrant out for her arrest."

Carver looked at her with admiration after this last revelation.

"Very cool," he chuckled. "I hope you can stay a while. I gotta get back to work, but I'll talk with you later, okay?"

As the boy strutted away, Stan called out, "By the way, I'm Stan Wallace."

He lifted his arm in a half-wave and without turning around mumbled, "Yo, dude."

"Please excuse his manners," Wilma said. "Kids, you know. It takes a lot to impress them."

Stan turned to Marian and stuck out his lip in a mock pout. Marian laughed and blushed slightly.

Marian turned to Wilma. "You mentioned his 'miracle.' What did you mean by that?"

"That's how this Church came to be," Wilma responded. "Everyone who made a donation to the Foster Child Foundation has experienced some kind of miracle in their life."

Talk of miracles raised Marian's suspicions again.

"If 'miracles' have been happening, why haven't they been publicized?" she asked skeptically. "I haven't seen one mention of it in any paper or newscast. Not even Stan's articles."

Wilma smiled. "When we first became aware of these occurrences, we needed to determine if they were real, first of all. After we became convinced that something unusual was truly happening, we didn't want any outside attention until we found the mechanism through which they were occurring.

"It soon became clear the miracles were directly tied to the donations. Initially, we made phone calls to each donor asking that, if anything out of the ordinary happened after their donation, they tell only one other person about it, ask them to donate and pass the same rules on. We told them that any person who broke the rules would also break the chain of miracles."

Wilma chuckled, "I doubt that's true, but by this time we had decided we didn't need any extra attention drawn to the church."

"A chain letter from God?" Marian asked incredulously. "And people followed the rules?"

"Oh, yes. Because they worked."

"So, who made up these rules?" Marian asked.

"They weren't made up. They came in a dream," Wilma explained.

Marian turned to Stan. "Why haven't I heard about any of this?"

Stan began to answer but was interrupted by Wilma saying, "You weren't supposed to hear about it."

"Let me guess. Another dream?" Marian said skeptically.

"My dear, you have to try to get a higher understanding of what's going on here," Wilma said, suddenly sounding like a seasoned corporate executive rather than the eccentric old woman Marian had been sitting with.

"There are many changes happening all over the world." Wilma continued. "Changes that *must* happen. In order to make these changes come about, all of us have a role to play right now. Your role is being played out through this pregnancy, through the Foster Child Foundation and, most of all, through this journey you now find yourself on."

"Tell me about my 'journey'." Marian demanded. "On the way here, once I had a chance to think, I wondered why I was running from the authorities. If I just turn myself in, answer a few questions, make them see I had nothing to do with the shooting –"

"And you would never be seen again," finished Wilma. "The time will come to confront the authorities, but this is not it. There's too much fear in them. The one thing people in power fear is other people with power. And, baby, you've got the power!"

The old Wilma was back, laughing loudly.

Marian struggled to muster a smile. "Please, I'm trying not to sound belligerent, but I know less about this church than anyone here. I don't like being kept in the dark."

"Tomorrow we'll start filling you in." Wilma reached over the desk and brushed Marian's hair from her face. "Don't worry darlin'," she said sweetly. "You won't be left in the dark."

Stan finally spoke. "Where will we be staying, Wilma?"

"Good question. This old body is about ready for bed. Your bedroom is upstairs, end of the hall on the left."

Stan stammered, "But – we don't – I mean…"

"Are you kiddin' me?" Wilma laughed loudly. "You two haven't figured it out yet?"

She shook her head in mock disbelief. "It's hard to believe two young people are so stupid they can't just do what comes naturally."

She pointed her finger at Stan's nose.

"You have one room for the two of you. Understand? If I catch you sleeping on my sofa, I'll set your socks on fire. I'm going to bed now."

Stan face had turned five shades of red while Wilma scolded him.

Marian asked, "Wilma, what about Carver? Does he just work nights?"

"No, he stays here too."

She leaned closer to Marian and Stan, whispering, "So you all better make sure you know which room is yours. Come into the wrong room and you might get an eyeful."

The woman laughed heartily, "If my room's a-rockin', don't come a-knockin'."

She headed for the stairs, still laughing loudly.

Marian's mouth fell open as she watched the woman climb the stairs.

"She's not serious, is she?" Marian asked Stan.

Stan, looking more than a bit shaken, replied, "Nothing about her would surprise me."

*   *   *

Marian awoke before dawn and made her way downstairs as quietly as possible. She had been aware through the night of Stan's pitiful efforts to get comfortable on the floor, where he had insisted on sleeping. Marian stepped cautiously over his sprawled body and closed the door slowly behind her as she entered the hallway. She was met by Carver, in t-shirt and shorts, carrying his toothbrush toward the bathroom. She was somewhat relieved to see he had come from a room other than Wilma's.

Marian descended the stairs into the kitchen, where she found Wilma preparing coffee.

"And I thought I was an early riser. You look like you've been up awhile, Wilma."

"Good mornin', dear," Wilma said. "Been up about an hour. I've had to adjust my sleep habits so I can be sure to remember all my dreams. If you don't wake up at a certain point in your sleep cycle, amnesia sets in and you can't remember shit. Coffee?"

"Please," replied Marian. As Wilma poured her cup, Marian continued, "You said last night, you'd fill me in on what's up with the church. Would this be a good time?"

"Good time to start," chuckled Wilma. "There's a lot, though. We're going to take it slow. I'm going to give you the back-story, so to speak, and then I'll try to answer your questions. OK?"

"Sounds good," said Marian, sipping her coffee.

"There's a great cleansing taking place in the world right now," Wilma began, speaking again in the strong voice that resonated with timeless wisdom.

"The age of peace stands before us. But first, the fears we have created and nurtured for two thousand years must be overcome – swept away. Armageddon is almost over. It's been going on for a millennium. One continuous war, moving from place to place, year after year. The warriors have different faces, but it's the same old war. A war not of good and evil, but a war between our true nature and our fears.

"The time has come to express our true nature and banish fear, once and for all. That's why the Master is returning. This is the final ultimatum. Either we abolish fear and begin to evolve, or this grand experiment will be brought to an end. Back to the drawing board."

Marian's skepticism surfaced again as she smiled at the woman. "Are you telling me if we don't get our act together immediately, it'll be the end of the world?"

"Not the end of the world. Just the end of us."

"Look, I don't know much about religion," Marian continued, "but I thought the new idea of God was one of pure love and forgiveness. No more of the hellfire and damnation."

"You're on the right track, dear." Wilma replied. "This is all about love. When you love a pet dearly, with all your heart, and it becomes ill and begin to suffer for a long period of time, what do you do? You end its suffering."

"Surely you can't believe that," Marian exclaimed. But the woman just smiled back at her.

"What do you believe, dear? Do you believe your dreams? Do you believe miracles have occurred? Do you believe you have healed people and seen inside their lives?"

Marian hesitated, realizing she hadn't evaluated her beliefs for quite a while. What did she believe? Somewhere along the line – she didn't know quite when – her disbelief had transformed into acceptance. She also knew, without a doubt, something was special about her son. But a *messiah*?

"Is my baby the Christ child?" Marian blurted out. "Is this a divinely conceived child?"

Wilma's face was a blank stare. For several moments, she appeared to be looking at something in the far distance. Finally, she spoke.

"Belief in that is the key to everything. You must believe. The world must believe. There is nothing else that can motivate people to fulfill the enormous change that has to take place."

"There's a lot we don't know," Wilma went on, "much we can't know yet. But you have to come to terms with the fact that you are the point from which salvation will spring. Your courage will be tested, as will your faith. You will be pushed to the brink of the bottomless pit – and you will have to jump. You will have to be willing to sacrifice everything you have and everything you are. You will have to be willing to walk alone in the darkness."

Marian felt the fear rising again. "That last sentence scares me more than anything else you've said."

Wilma looked at her with sadness in her eyes. "Your dark night of the soul is coming, dear. There's no way around it."

She placed her hand on Marian's.

"I don't envy you."

CHAPTER 16

In the days following Marian's flight from Atlanta, Carl was kept busy dealing with the many government agencies that were frantically searching for her. The 'official' line he held to was that Marian had foreseen the murder only moments before it happened and had tried to warn Hedstrom. This part was true, and there were witnesses, real ones as well as those planted by the church, that gave testimony to hearing Marian's shouts of warning.

The second part of the story was that the trauma of witnessing the shooting had caused Marian to go into early labor and she and Stan had disappeared to parts unknown to seek medical treatment and sanctuary from the stress of the public eye.

Investigators from the Atlanta police department, FBI and Homeland Security scoured Marian's apartment and Carl's offices for evidence of her whereabouts. Nothing helpful was found, though, due in large part to friends of Officer Steve Lucas who were pouring through Marian's apartment even as she and Stan were picking up the car and their fake I.D.'s.

The heat was off Marian temporarily, as least as an accomplice to the murder, although the warrant for her arrest was still in force. Attention was now turning to a rusty, white Ford pickup that was seen leaving the scene immediately after the shooting. Several bystanders had reported hearing muffled popping noises followed by a smell of gunpowder.

Big Norm, however was oblivious to the new attention directed at him. He had a new ride, courtesy of a gentleman who had stopped to offer help to a good old boy who had run out of gas on a dark road in Western Tennessee. His body would not be discovered for nearly a year.

Big Norm had put the good Samaritan's lifeless body inside the dead Ford pickup and rolled it into Lake Obion. Norm's head was swimming in pain now, from lack of alcohol for almost eighteen hours. But still, he drove on, pushed ahead by – *what?* He knew he was losing his focus, could feel the fear mounting that he done a lot of BAD THINGS he would have to answer for, but Wichita was his destination, and he *had* to get there. Then he would know what to do.

But first, a stop at a liquor store. That was next on the agenda. The wallet he had lifted from Burton Embry's corpse contained a few hundred dollars and half-a-dozen credit cards. Soon he would be clear again. Soon he would be ready for action.

Norm heard the familiar verse of, "I'm a Soldier in Christ's Army," beginning to play in his head. He slammed the steering wheel with his fist.

"NOT NOW, DAMMIT!" he screamed as tears began to flow down his cheek.

Christ, I need a drink. Please, Jesus, find me a liquor store. And, as God answers all prayers, he soon saw the flashing neon signs ahead that pointed to *Cy's Beer Barn, open 24/7.* Norm sobbed once and began to relax. Things would be good again soon.

*   *   *

Bashir Pezek looked out the window of his modest apartment into the streets of downtown Tehran. Hundreds of men in suits and turbans wound their ways through the maze of merchants and beggars that stretched as far as he could see. He said a prayer of thanks for his good fortune.

He was among the privileged, thanks to his association with el-Hamir. A few years earlier, he had more in common with the filthy men begging for food and money on the street corners. Those men in suits were part of the "New" Islam. They embraced the ways of the West. Traded in currency and stocks. Many were government officials.

His brethren were those that had nothing. El-Hamir's followers were the unwashed majority. Devout followers of fundamental Islam, anxious to become martyrs if only to bring an end to their pitiful existence. Bashir thought, *if this truly is Allah's path, why is he continually punishing us with poverty, disease and death?*

Many such thoughts filled his head in recent days. Since el-Hamir's assassination of the Prime Minister, nothing had changed for his people. Except for the fact that el-Hamir now occupied the Palace, it was business as usual. There were no new decrees to end Westernization, no rules about adherence to the traditional men's attire of Islam. Not even a harder line against crime. In fact, many of Iran's worst criminals had been set free and absorbed into el-Hamir's inner circle.

Bashir's reverie was broken by a ringing phone. He picked it up and heard el-Hamir's voice on the line.

"Excellency!" answered Bashir.

"Blessings upon you, Pezek. Today I call you to serve once again. Your days of glory await."

"How may I serve?"

"You must go see our friend in Washington. The day of reckoning approaches and I need you to ensure everything happens as planned."

"Is there a problem with Hamoud?"

"I have concerns about his dedication to our struggle. He has many family members who live in America. We cannot allow him to be overcome with cowardice at the last moment," el-Hamir replied.

"Excellency, will I be...remaining in America?"

"A jet will take you to Al Jubayal where you will get a Saudi passport and identification. From there you will fly into Washington. I will be in contact with you soon after."

"Please excuse me, excellency, but when will I return home?" Beads of sweat were forming on Bashir's brow.

"Your service to Islam will not be forgotten, Pezek. Your rewards in heaven will be great. You must prepare to leave now. A car will pick you up at 9:00 tonight."

Bashir was silent.

El-Hamir's voice changed to an accusatory tone. "I'm not hearing your joy at being given this honor. Is there a problem?"

"No, excellency," Bashir answered, "I was saying a prayer of thanksgiving."

"That is only proper. For such a great honor you should be thankful."

El-Hamir was pacified now.

"Prepare your things. And be strong. Allah be praised!"

"God is great!" responded Bashir. The phone clicked dead.

He was about to become a martyr for El-Hamir's plan. But the promise of virgins in paradise did nothing to displace the very strong desire to hold his son right now.

*　　　*　　　*

The past few days of solitude had done wonders for Marian. Wilma had refused to answer any more of her questions. She told Marian it was time to clear her mind of the stress of the past two months. Any time Marian had shown her face around the offices while Wilma, Stan and Carver were together, she had been told, basically, to get lost. She spent many hours walking the neatly manicured paths through the gorgeous forest of sugar maple and pine. The streams that flowed through the limestone hills were abundant with fossilized shellfish and ferns.

She had forgotten how much she loved fossil hunting as a girl. The ability to hold in her hands something that lived before dinosaurs were a thought in God's mind was miraculous to her. Each treasure taken home was a connecting link to an ancient time when life was new. Already today she had discovered a fern imprinted in shale and a cast of a small ammonite. As the sun began its descent toward the horizon, Marian headed back to Wilma's house, anxious to show the others the treasures she had found.

Marian entered the back door into the kitchen where Wilma was preparing dinner. Before she could open her hand to display her discoveries Wilma began, "Good. You're getting it."

"Look at this, Wilma. Did you know your land is covered with fossils? I found these in the creek bed."

"Yes," Wilma replied, examining them. "They are beautiful. You've discovered something wonderful today."

"Well, I don't know about wonderful. These are pretty common in this region."

Wilma laughed, "I'm not talking about rocks, dear. You've discovered something from your past. You need to keep going."

"I don't understand what you mean, Wilma."

"Jesus said, 'You must become like little children to enter into the kingdom'. That's what you need to do right now. Reclaim what you had as a child. The awe and wonder. Magic and miracles. Intuition and wisdom. And most of all, the belief that anything is possible."

"You worry me when you start talking like Yoda," Marian said with raised eyebrows.

"You're a damn dingbat!" spat Wilma, throwing a skillet noisily into the sink.

"These are tools you will need to carry you through your journey. Your doctor's diploma won't help you where you're going. Nothing you have learned from any man or woman will help you. The only tools that will serve you now are the ones you were born with."

Marian had never seen her angry before.

"Sorry! This is just moving a bit fast for me. We haven't even talked for days and you act like I should know what to do next."

"Things aren't moving fast enough," said Wilma. "You don't have the luxury of forty days and nights in the desert like Christ had to discover his path. You've got to figure it out quickly. You're almost out of time"

"What do you mean, 'I've got to figure it out'?"

"My God, girl! Don't you understand? No one can guide you from here on. You have to find your own path. Whatever comes next has to be your decision. The fact that I know what you have to do is meaningless. You have to see it for yourself."

Wilma turned back to preparing dinner and added, "Just go and get cleaned up now. We're having company tonight."

"Who's coming?"

"The Circle is coming together again. We have a new member to welcome - two actually, including you."

Cars began arriving as the night fell, and when Marian answered the call for dinner there were several new faces at the large table that had been set up in the studio.

She was a little unnerved by the paintings of her son covering the walls of the room where they gathered. Wilma joined the group and began the introductions around the table.

"It's so good to see you all again," Wilma began. "The circle is growing larger, as it was foretold. Now it's time for us all to be reacquainted."

She motioned to a barrel-chested man with a turquoise bolo tie seated at her immediate right. "Ames Campbell. The first person to send a donation to the Foster Child Foundation."

The middle-aged gent stood and made a half-bow in Marian's direction and addressed her in a Texas drawl, "Howdy, Ms. Foster. It's a real honor to be in your presence."

Wilma smiled at his response. "Would you tell Marian what happened to you, Ames?"

"Well, an hour after I put my donation in an envelope and mailed it," he began, as a single tear ran down his cheek, "I, uh, I found my mother."

Ames squinted his eyes closed as several more tears followed. He quickly drew a handkerchief from his pocket, wiped his eyes and continued.

"I had been looking for her for seven years. I was a foster child. A real one, I mean. I grew up in five different homes. The state took me when I was two. My mom had left me in a hotel room in Dallas. She was turnin' tricks at the flop houses out by Love Field. Seems one guy took a likin' to her, had some money, and offered to take her to Oklahoma City. Didn't want anything to do with a kid, though, so I got left behind. I never knew that story until about a month ago. The Dallas cops didn't either. To them, I was just another abandoned kid. I belonged to the system until I turned eighteen."

"I got work in the oil fields when I got older, saved my money, finally bought a drill rig of my own. Got married, had a couple of sons. One of 'em died seven years ago. I had never felt such pain in my life. I don't think anything could hurt worse than that. I got to thinkin', how bad life would have to be for you to give up a child on purpose. After all the years of hating my mom, I started feeling sorry for her. Things must have been really bad for her to leave me behind."

"I found out how to use the Internet to look for people. There's lots of help there for people like me who didn't know what they were doin'. Anyway, seven years pass, and the afternoon I sent my donation, I get a call."

His handkerchief came out again.

"She was living in public housing outside of Vegas. Slept in a sleeping bag on the floor."

Ames was briefly overcome by his tears. He blew his nose and began again.

"She lives with me now. And she's a fine woman. Life just wrecked her when she was young and she was so busy surviving, she never had time to heal."

"I'm so glad you found her," said Marian.

"Nothin' but blessings, ma'am," responded Ames.

Wilma gestured now to the man seated to the right of Ames. The thirty-something man in a gray suit and close-cropped dark hair stood and extended his hand.

"I'm Clay Parker. It's a pleasure to meet you, Dr. Foster."

"Good to meet you, Clay." responded Marian.

"I work for the National Security Agency. I'm a mole. My assignment is to report back to Homeland Security about the inner workings of the Church of the Foster Child. In particular, to report any intelligence on *your* whereabouts."

Marian looked frantically to Stan and Wilma for support, but they avoided her gaze. She started to become dizzy from the fear that was surging through her

"O.K. That'll be enough of that," Wilma said after a few tense moments.

The group broke into laughter.

"I'm sorry about that, dear. I just couldn't resist." Wilma chuckled as she slapped Marian's knee. "Clay's actually telling the truth. He just left out the part where he became a double agent. He feeds the government innocuous information about our church, while keeping us up to date on what's really going on in Washington."

"I do apologize, Dr. Foster," Clay said. "It was her idea, really."

"No problem," Marian responded, her voice cracking.

"I joined the church with every intention of doing my job, as assigned. But at the first meeting I attended my world got turned around. I made a generous contribution to the Foundation, hoping to get closer to the inner circle. But, instead, like everyone else, I had an experience that changed my life. I listened to a lecture on how the current human condition was dictated by fear; about how we had to overcome fear in order to express our true nature."

"When I left the meeting, in a warehouse in downtown St. Louis, it was late. I was thinking about what I'd heard in the lecture. It really made an impression on me. On my way to my car, a guy came up behind me, stuck a gun in my back and shoved me into an alley.

"Remember, now, I'm NSA. I have a license to kill, and I'm armed to the teeth. I began planning how I was going to first humiliate this punk, and then kill him, but my hand started to burn. The heat coming from it was intense, like I had stuck my hand into an oven. A weird feeling came over me. Like I was an observer outside of my body, watching everything that was happening. It didn't feel like I was in control of myself.

"Anyway, I held out my hand that was burning and said, 'Take it.' The guy put the barrel of the gun right between my eyes and said, 'What did you say?' I told him, 'Take my hand.' I could see the guy getting really scared then. His hands started shaking and I could see him tightening the grip on the trigger. I just stood there, with my hand out. He began to lower the gun, slowly, and believe it or not, he actually took my hand."

"I felt the heat leave my hand, and the guy just bursts into tears and drops the gun. He sank down to his knees, crying like a baby. And I heard myself say, 'Come with me.'

"I took the guy back to my apartment, fed him, gave him a bed and the next day we both went to another church meeting. That guy is now leading a new church group in St. Louis. Needless to say, I was hooked."

"Do all of you have stories this incredible?" Marian asked, looking around the table.

Unanimously nodding heads responded to her question.

Wilma gestured to the table, "You'll notice there are a couple of empty chairs here. That's just my little flair for the dramatic. Those people are here, but I think they need to make a grand entrance, just for your benefit."

She turned toward the kitchen and shouted, "Gordon! We're ready."

Wilma turned back to Marian and said, "I'd like to introduce you to the fourth member of the Circle."

Around the corner from the kitchen walked Dr. Gordon Prevost, former CEO of BiEnCo Pharmaceuticals.

"Marian, you just can't stay out of trouble, can you?"

"Dr. Prevost!" Marian shouted as she stood and gave him a hearty hug. "I can't believe it! The one person from the company I've truly missed."

"You didn't make many friends there, did you?" Prevost laughed. "I've missed you too, Marian. I always knew you had big things in your future, but this tops all!"

"Alright," Marian said, "what's your story?"

"Very simple. I'm alive," Prevost said.

"When I was let go from the company, I was already in my last days there. I was diagnosed with MS about six months ago. Marburg's variant."

"My God, I had no idea," Marian said, shocked. "Marburg's variant is usually terminal within a few years."

"Yes," said Prevost, "and mine was progressing extremely rapidly. I had stopped driving two weeks before I was fired. Every day was a huge step downhill. It was a particularly bad day when I saw you on TV. You had just announced the money that had been sent to you was being used to begin the Foster Child Foundation. I was so impressed with you. I saw the person I always knew you were on the inside. I got out my checkbook, ruined two checks because I couldn't control my hands, but finally wrote out a donation and put it in the mail."

"The next morning I had an appointment with my specialist. His office was only six blocks from my place, so I usually walked, even if it was a struggle. That morning I felt wonderful on my walk. I made such good time, I even stopped and shot a few baskets with some kids at the park.

"I told my doctor how good I felt that day, but he just attributed it to a mild remission. Something inside told me to make him run the diagnostic tests again, and, reluctantly he did. He called me a few days later to tell me there was absolutely no sign of myelin damage. I did *not* have MS. I already knew that, though. I had just gone and bought a new Harley," Prevost chuckled.

The three others at the table introduced themselves and offered their stories. Janet Conwell was a young mother whose autistic son began to speak after she made her donation.

Arnie McCullogh was a farmer whose land had been repossessed when the bank foreclosed. He won the Michigan lottery.

And Rosie Velasquez. She had been waiting for a kidney transplant. After her donation, she went to her dialysis appointment and was told both of her kidneys were functioning at higher than normal levels.

"And finally," said Wilma, "let's fill this last chair. This is the newest member of the Circle, and the first time he's met with us all. Father, would you come in, please?"

Father Bernard Kaplan, the priest Stan had introduced to Marian, entered the room and sat. He smiled at Marian, but remained silent.

"This is the biggest surprise of all, Father," exclaimed Marian. "How did you come to be in the Circle?"

The priest silently placed his hands on the table and began to remove a pair of soft leather gloves. He held his hands up in front of his face and peered at Marian through holes in each of his hands that gently oozed blood. He then unbuttoned his shirt and revealed a jagged wound on his left side. He lifted his graying bangs from his forehead to display a band of small cuts reaching from one side of his head to the other.

Marian was thoroughly shocked. "What happened to you?" she exclaimed.

"The stigmata," Wilma replied, in a tone of awe, "the wounds of Christ. Hands, feet, heart and head. Isn't it wonderful?"

"Wonderful? I hope you're getting medical treatment." Marian said, appalled at the wounds.

Father Kaplan smiled broadly at this statement.

Wilma continued, "For a Catholic priest, there's no greater honor. This is something he has prayed for all his life. He's in constant communion with God now. He hasn't spoken since the day the wounds appeared. Father Kaplan has been the source of our greatest insights since the Circle was formed."

"How's that possible, if he hasn't spoken?" Marian asked.

Kaplan bent over the table, then held up a napkin for all to see. On it was written, "I can still write, stupid."

Everyone at the table laughed, including Marian.

"But everyone else's miracles are so wonderful. Yours seems like such a burden."

Kaplan hunched over the table with his pen once again. He sat up and gave Marian another napkin.

It read, "You have no idea what it feels like on the inside. Pure peace and love."

Wilma added, "He's performed many miracles of healing since the stigmata came. He's a very holy man. I personally have seen him levitate when he prays."

Kaplan shrugged and waved his hand at Wilma.

"He hates when I tell people that. He doesn't like to perform."

"Stan," Marian asked, "what about you? I've never heard how you joined the Circle."

Wilma interrupted, "It's time we ate. We have business to discuss."

The group ate, mostly in silence, punctuated by occasional small talk. After the meal, the dishes were cleared away by Wilma and Carver. Marian rose to assist them. As she placed a stack of plates near the sink, she turned to Wilma.

"Why didn't I get to hear Stan's story tonight, Wilma?"

"Well, dear, Stan's a bit embarrassed to bring up his miracle, especially around you."

Marian asked, "Why is he embarrassed?"

"For one, he doesn't feel his miracle was as grand as the others, although I personally think it's more so. Second, he thinks he's not worthy of what he aspires to."

"Can you tell me?" Marian whispered.

Wilma hesitated thoughtfully for a moment then said, "Alright, my dear. If you knew about Stan's life, you'd grasp how huge this miracle actually is. After he interviewed me for the first time he could tell there was something special about me, even though I didn't tell him about my dreams. He called me several times over the next few weeks and finally I told him about the miracles that were happening to those who donated to the Foundation. He gave it a shot – an experiment, he called it. Sure enough, something miraculous happened."

"Well?" Marian asked anxiously.

"He fell in love," Wilma said as she turned and walked back to the studio.

CHAPTER 17

After dinner, the mood of the group shifted as if a switch has been turned. They moved in silence to a sitting area in the far corner of the studio. Wilma joined the group and began.

"What do we know?" she asked.

"Kansas is next. Wichita, I think," Ames said.

"I've got Wichita too," said Rosie.

"Any idea who?" Wilma asked.

"The President is crying," said Gordon ominously.

The members all turned to Prevost.

"When did this come?" asked Janet.

"Last night."

"Consensus?" Wilma asked, looking around at the group.

Marian watched in confusion as everyone closed their eyes for a moment.

"I think it's good," Arnie replied.

"Feels right," said Stan.

"I'll go with it," added Clay.

They all turned to Father Kaplan who was nodding, eyes still closed.

"Any idea if it's a personal matter or a political one?" Wilma asked Gordon.

"No," responded Prevost.

"I get a bit of both," said Rosie.

Father Kaplan was nodding again.

"What about our boy in the white truck?" asked Wilma.

"He's heading for Wichita, but not in the white truck anymore," said Ames.

"Does anyone know what he's driving or where he's heading?" Wilma asked.

Everyone in the group shook their heads negatively, except for Father Kaplan, who was writing on a pad. As the group noticed, they waited patiently with all eyes upon him.

He held up the pad, which said, "He's killed another man. If we don't act soon, we'll lose him completely."

All eyes then turned to Marian, who shifted uncomfortably.

Wilma continued, "I got something this morning. More mischief. Not our boy, but a zealot group. I think it's going to be bad."

Stan asked, "Where?"

"I keep getting Wichita. I don't know if I'm getting crosstalk from the dream about 'big boy' or if something else is going to happen there, too."

Rosie spoke up, "I think I have something new. A new player in the game. Arriving from the Middle East. He's coming to supervise something. It doesn't feel good."

Wilma looked very concerned. "Can he be stopped?"

"I think so. I don't get that this is a 'have to happen' thing."

Wilma continued, "Perhaps we should get a group together. Any idea on his entry point?"

Rosie began to answer, but was interrupted by Father Kaplan tapping his pen loudly on the pad. The group turned to him and he raised the pad.

He had written, "Leave the man alone! It is important that he continue for now!"

"When is she going to be ready?" Janet asked impatiently, gesturing to Marian.

"Don't –" Wilma responded, raising a finger to Janet.

"You know what's at stake here, and how it has to happen. She carries a larger burden than any of the rest of us. Remember what we learned at the very beginning: World transformation through personal transformation. This is all about transformation, one by one."

Wilma smiled again, "Let's hear how all the groups are doing."

Talk then turned to growth of the individual church groups, their successes in affecting the communities they resided in. After about an hour the group stopped to retire for the night.

As they disbanded, Arnie said to Marian, "We didn't hear about your dreams, tonight. I was really anxious."

Marian was embarrassed, "After hearing you all, I don't feel I have much to offer. The dreams I've had have all been very personal, nothing as important as yours. And – I haven't had any dreams for over a week."

Arnie smiled, "You have a whole lot to offer, girl. You just don't know it yet. And by the way, the dreams about personal things are the most important of all. Remember – world transformation through personal transformation."

Father Kaplan held up his pad as he walked past the two. It read, "She'll dream tonight. She'll know tomorrow."

*   *   *

That night Marian did dream. A dream unlike any she had experienced before. It began like the others, with her in the spacious home office that overlooked the lake surrounded by golden maple trees. The little boy joined her, as usual, but this time looked very serious. Instead of climbing into her lap, he took her hand. As he guided her gently, she rose out of her seat. The boy led Marian to the window and she turned, expecting to see the beautiful lake. The lake was not there.

Outside the window, a war was going on. The scene was of an urban business district. Police in riot gear were preparing to battle typical American citizens. Men, women and children, young and old, were standing their ground with firearms, clubs, bricks and stones as the police marched forward.

A single shot was fired. By whom, Marian couldn't tell. Then, instantly, the carnage began. Automatic weapons fire, tear gas, and small explosions from grenades and home-made explosives produced massive injuries and death on both sides of the battle. The citizens seemed to be getting the worst of it, but more and more of them came, in seemingly endless numbers. The police were soon joined by uniformed military forces whose firepower decimated the civilians. Still, the people advanced. The gutters were filling with blood.

The scene changed and Marian now was looking at the Capitol building in Washington, D.C. Like watching a child blow away a house of cards, Marian saw the Capitol crumbling to pieces and being swept away in a brilliant flash of light. The Washington monument toppled and shattered.

When the blinding light subsided, every one of the buildings symbolizing the ideals that define the nation were gone. Piles of alabaster rubble were all that remained. The scene was framed in a sinister silence. There was no movement, no cries of the wounded, for there were no wounded. Of those elected to lead the country, there were none left.

The vision of destruction dissipated and Marian now saw a dark green Range Rover weaving along an Interstate highway at a high rate of speed. Her view changed to a nearer angle, with a clear view of the driver. A very large, muscular man in his late thirties was taking a big slug from a bottle of Heaven Hill. He sang a song, something about being a soldier for Christ. He appeared to be quite intoxicated.

"This man thinks he is helping you."

Marian was startled to hear the boy speak. He spoke in a powerful voice resonating with ageless wisdom.

"He is strongly connected to Spirit, but the messages are being scrambled by hallucinations from the alcohol. He's trapped in his own violent past and continues to turn to violence because it's all he's ever known."

The boy turned back to watch the man as he continued singing.

"Not all the things I've shown you tonight have to happen. Some of them will, but they don't *have* to. This man is one of the hinges on which the future turns. He is dedicated to you and your safe pregnancy. He is focused and determined. He is also psychotic and an alcoholic. There is only one human voice he will respond to, and that voice is yours."

The boy looked deeply into Marian's eyes. "This man is important in ways you can't understand now. His personal transformation is being blocked by his addiction to alcohol and his transformation is key to your success. Your help is necessary for him to break through his barriers. He has killed several people and is near the point where transformation will no longer be possible for him."

Marian spoke, "So I'm supposed to go and stop him from killing?"

The boy smiled, "You're not *supposed* to do anything. Everything that happens in your life, happens by your choice. If you wish to be successful in bringing about the transformation of the world, then the next step is to help this man begin his transformation. He will be in Wichita, Kansas tomorrow. And he won't be there for long "

Marian sensed that her time with the boy was almost over. She wasn't ready to leave him yet. "But how do I find this man? What's his name?"

"You'll have to watch for signs along the way," the boy smiled again, "That's the next part of *your* transformation. The development of intuition, and faith in it. Just remember, wherever there's conflict, there's a troubled soul."

The dream ended abruptly and Marian shot up in bed. No white fog, no gentle footsteps, no warm hugs from her son. This was more like an intelligence briefing from a four-year old general. Quite disturbing. And much too real.

It was nearly four-thirty. Marian knew that further sleep was impossible at this point. She got up, stepped over Stan, and made her way downstairs.

Seeing the light in the kitchen, she knew Wilma must be awake as well. As she entered, Marian saw that Wilma had already prepared a cup of coffee for her. She joined Wilma at the kitchen table.

"You know now," Wilma solemnly began.

"Yeah," replied Marian, sitting down at the table.

"So?"

"I guess I have to go. The things I saw were terrible."

"Everything is by choice, dear," Wilma said softly.

"God, that was all real, wasn't it?" Marian said, desperately hoping she was still dreaming.

"American citizens – *civilians* – were being massacred by the police and the army. Washington was destroyed. No one was left."

Wilma sat up abruptly. "What did you say?"

"It looked like a nuclear bomb had hit Washington."

Wilma jumped out of her seat and began pacing. "*That's* where it is. We were so far off," she muttered to herself.

"What is it?" asked Marian.

"We knew there was a nuclear device being built somewhere. We were guessing Los Angeles at first. Then Wichita started coming up from all directions. But, Christ, Washington!"

Wilma's adrenaline was pumping now. She continued in a rapid-fire pace. "You see how this works now? Everyone gets a piece of the puzzle, but we're all ignorant fools until we work together. This is an example, on a small scale, of how the world should work."

"So this dream is an example of the way things are for the rest of the Circle?" asked Marian.

"Yes. Although everyone's experience in the dreams are unique. Some are very symbolic, some very verbal, some very visual."

"Mine was like a lecture. Everything was spelled out quite plainly," said Marian.

"I guess that means God thinks you're either very special – or very stupid," Wilma spat, still pacing in tight circles.

Marian smiled weakly.

"I have to tell the others. You need to take this time to decide who's going with you."

"You mean I don't have to do this alone?" asked Marian.

"You will be quite alone, even though you'll have a companion," Wilma said ominously.

"One of the rules we follow is that none of us goes on a mission alone. The one who feels called for the mission chooses another member of the Circle to accompany them. You can choose anyone except Stan."

Marian's heart sunk. "Why not Stan?"

"These missions rely on intuition and clarity. You must be present and focused. The feelings you and Stan have for each other would get in the way."

Marian sighed, "OK. If you say so."

Wilma's mood lightened and she gave a small laugh.

"You took that much better than I expected, dear. Stan, on the other hand, is going to be royally *pissed!*"

*   *   *

"That's ridiculous!" Stan exploded when told he would not be accompanying Marian. "She and I have been together through everything since the beginning. She knows I'll do anything for her."

"Stan," Wilma explained gently, "you know very well that any member of the Circle would lay down their life for Marian. I understand how much you care for her, but you haven't been on any assignments of this nature before."

"Neither has Marian, and that's the point!" fumed Stan.

"Exactly why someone should go with her who can help her through this. Someone who can keep her focused and in tune with her intuition. We can't take the risk of decisions being made based upon human emotions. We have to be above that."

Ames spoke up, "I'd like to go with you, Marian. From what I can tell about this guy, he's a country boy. Might have a few things in common with him. Also, I'm the only one of us close to his size, in case things get physical."

Marian took notice of Ames' size. He was an imposing figure, although his gentle demeanor made him seem incapable of violence.

"You should consider this, Marian," Wilma offered. "Ames has proven very capable in these situations. And his intuition is quite good. He could teach you a lot."

Marian considered this for a moment and then said, "Alright. It's you and me, Ames."

Ames smiled proudly.

"So when do we leave? We don't have much time, obviously. Do we fly to Wichita?" Marian asked.

"It's not that easy," said Stan, still disappointed. "The ID's we might not pass the TSA agents at the airports. A random check of recent death records and you'd be caught. You'll have to drive. And no Interstate highways. You'll have to avoid attention."

"That could take two days!" exclaimed Marian.

"Count on three, unless we really get lucky," said Ames.

Father Kaplan entered the group hastily and placed a writing pad in Wilma's hands.

"It's already started in Wichita," she said grimly. "Dozens of people are dead."

"What's happened?" asked Marian.

Wilma looked at Father Kaplan, who shook his head. She continued, "We're not sure yet. Maybe a transportation accident, a plane or bus. Maybe another bombing. But whatever it is, it's being connected to us, and we have to do whatever we can to prevent more lives being lost."

"Ames, I guess we should start packing," said Marian.

"I'm already packed," Ames replied.

Marian and Stan looked at Ames suspiciously as he slowly broke into a sheepish grin.

"I dreamt about this last night."

*   *   *

President Stanton had just been told about the abortion clinic in Wichita. A group of Foster supporters had claimed responsibility for the bombing, which happened just as the clinic was opening for business.

"Get me an update on casualties," Stanton ordered his aide.

"Yes, sir," answered the young man as he rushed from the Oval Office

National security advisor George DeFontana asked, "Has your wife landed yet?"

"No. She'll be on the ground in about fifteen minutes. I spoke to her a few minutes ago and she was determined to go ahead with this idiotic speech, although she *is* going to postpone it until after the victims' families are notified."

"I can have her security force beefed up. I got a good group of Special Ops at Marshall. I can have them in Wichita in two hours."

"No, George, she'd have my balls. She's all about being the 'people's First Lady.' I can barely get her to stay with the Secret Service detail. She's got to be accessible, you know."

"Sir, with all respect, this is madness," said DeFontana. "The Foster people have just murdered again and she's going to show her support for them?"

"Dammit, George, I know!" shouted the President.

Calming himself, he continued, "I know. You realize she only agreed to my candidacy because I promised to let her have a forum for women's issues. Otherwise, I would have been going through a divorce while I was running. The RNC shit gold bricks when I told them I wasn't going to have a Right to Life plank in my platform."

"But the few democratic states you pulled because of that was your winning margin," said DeFontana.

"I know, but now I have to deal with this bullshit while she goes to play patty-cake with the feminists."

The fear in Stanton's eyes was obvious. "I'm scared for her, George."

"You *are* the commander-in-chief, sir. Would you like me to have her brought back?"

The President eyed DeFontana and snorted, "I'd rather attack China!"

*   *   *

Marian and Ames crossed the Kentucky state line at dusk. The two lane highway led into the town of Bowling Green, where they planned to stop for a quick meal. Marian had hoped for at least some lively conversation to ease her nerves during the trip, but that hadn't come to pass, as Ames had slept most of the way.

"You must be feeling pretty rested, Ames," Marian said. "You've been asleep for quite a while."

"Not asleep. I'm trying to keep a connection going," Ames said adamantly.

"Everything's so much easier when more of us are together. It's a real struggle for me to get much besides the dreams when I'm on my own."

Marian was a little concerned. "Wilma was praising your intuition before we left. You must be selling yourself short."

"Well, no, there's a big difference between getting hard facts and getting feelings. I do have a knack for making the right choices, but I can't say why I make them," Ames said, shrugging his shoulders.

"They just feel right. But I'm trying to get some real information right now. Like exactly where this guy is and what he's up to. Wichita's no one-horse town. We could spend days trying to find him, and we don't have days."

Marian asked, "Have you got anything yet?"

"I think maybe I do," Ames replied. "The guy's using a stolen I.D. with the name Burton on it."

"Like Richard Burton?" Marian asked.

Ames squinted his eyes shut in concentration. "Nope. I think that's the first name. I also have a feeling if we don't stop him, the powers that be are going to come down on us hard."

"I had a dream like that the night before we left," Marian interjected.

"The police and the Army were killing civilians. People kept coming by the thousands, but were being massacred by the soldiers. You don't think they were church members, do you?"

"I think so," Ames said grimly. "After this last bombing, I wouldn't be surprised if they were already getting ready for another Waco. These things the zealots are doing could bring it on."

He added forcefully, "And you know if it comes down to it, we *will* fight. There's not a one among us who doesn't believe that we have to survive in order for the world to survive."

Marian wondered if the church had been preparing for war. Had the Circle known violent confrontation was in their future? Were there stockpiles of weapons? Secret bunkers?

Suddenly, Ames perked up. "Hey, there's a Waffle House!"

Marian's look left no doubt that Waffle House was not the dinner she had in mind.

"Oh, come on, Marian," Ames pleaded. "It's fast, and there ain't no better food on the highway."

Marian gave in, "It would be fast, and we've got a lot of miles to cover."

"Yeah!" Ames exclaimed, and then quickly tried to hide his excitement. "I, uh – really like Waffle House."

Marian had to laugh at his blushing face as she turned into the parking lot.

*   *   *

Norman Randall was living the high life. He had taken $1500 in cash advances on Burton Embry's credit cards and decided to live it up in a Motel 6. No more Heaven Hill for him, either. Nothing but Jack Daniels Black Label from here on out.

He lay in the king-size bed, oblivious to why he was here in Wichita, Kansas. This was the longest drunk he had been on in quite a while, and it was taking its toll on his brain. He knew he was waiting for something. But what?

He could no longer remember the words to, "I'm a Soldier in Christ's Army." That golden oldie had been replaced by visions of people from his past. His mother. His buddy from the Army, disemboweled on the desert sand. His ex-wife. And the most disturbing one, the one that kept coming no matter how much he drank, this little kid he had never seen before.

The kid would appear, telling him how much he loved him. Begging him to stop sippin' the Jack. Telling him the world depended on him.

No fuckin' rugrat was gonna tell Big Norm what to do. Every time he appeared, Norm would get even drunker out of spite and now, he was dangerously close to alcohol poisoning. Thankfully, the kid hadn't come around for a couple of hours.

Norm sensed he was close to the edge. The booze was affecting him differently than ever before. He was getting a little scared, but if he could just get to the commode and puke once, he was sure he would be O.K.

He tried to get out of the bed and stand, but his legs gave out and he tumbled over the nightstand, hitting his head on the window ledge. He grabbed the window blinds as he fell and ripped them from the wall. As the pain from his bleeding head registered in his brain, his system finally reached overload and a stream of vomit mixed with blood sprayed out across the floor. Norm thought, *not much except blood there. Whole lotta blood.* And then Norm was unconscious.

∗   ∗   ∗

Marian and Ames ate heartily. Marian had donned the brunette wig and reading glasses Stan had hoped would conceal her identity during the trip.

"I told you," said Ames. "You can't beat a Waffle House."

"This is pretty good, I have to admit," said Marian over her second helping of peach cobbler.

"S'cuse me, ma'am," Ames motioned to the waitress, "would you mind turnin' the TV up? News is on."

The waitress smiled and clicked the remote. " – death toll in the Wichita bombing has reached thirty-one this evening as another nurse succumbed to injuries."

The anchorman spoke over aerial photos of the clinic.

"A group associated with the Church of the Foster Child has claimed responsibility for the bombing at the Mt. Carmel Family Planning Clinic, saying they will not rest until the BiEnCo lawsuit is withdrawn and Marian Foster is given immunity from prosecution. A Justice Department official is quoted as saying, 'The Church is under investigation at this time, but we're assuming for now that these terrorist acts are those of a renegade faction, not representative of the Church as a whole.'

"This highly popular church, with followers numbering in the millions, has no apparent leadership on a national level. Our sources report it actually consists of a loosely-knit, diverse group of many smaller community organizations that have sprung up in light of Marian Foster's unusual pregnancy.

"Across the country, local church group leaders have distanced themselves from these illegal actions, saying their churches exist only to promote love and understanding, and to banish fear so all of humanity can raise its spiritual consciousness. The one figure at the center of this controversy, Marian Foster herself, is still in seclusion. Her whereabouts are unknown."

Marian unconsciously adjusted her wig as the newsman continued.

"First Lady Susan Stanton is scheduled to speak at the National Organization of Women's conference tomorrow in Wichita. It was originally thought her speech would be cancelled in light of the bombing, but the First Lady has confirmed that she will speak at the conference. She will also make an additional appearance at the site of the bombing. The time of that appearance has not yet been confirmed."

The waitress appeared at their table and asked, "Can I get you anything else?"

"No, thank you, "Marian replied, handing a twenty to the waitress, "Everything was great."

The waitress took the money from Marian's hand and their fingers briefly touched. Marian was aware of a sensation like static electricity passing between them. Marian glanced up to see the waitress staring intently into her eyes. The waitress began to walk to the register, holding eye contact just a bit too long for Marian's comfort.

"Ames," Marian asked, "Do you think I could be recognized in this wig?" She kept an eye on the waitress who was putting the money in the register, but still glancing in Marian's direction every few seconds.

"Stop worrying. The brown hair should fool anybody."

"I don't think it fooled her," Marian said, nodding toward the waitress.

Ames turned to look and saw the waitress quickly turn her eyes away and walk back into the kitchen where she began talking animatedly to a cook.

"Let's go," whispered Ames. "Keep the change!" he shouted toward the kitchen as they left the restaurant.

"Get in the car, quick," he ordered Marian.

Ames bent to grab a plastic shopping bag from the ground and quickly tucked it over the license plate as he walked to the driver's door.

Ames started the car and gunned out of the parking lot back onto the highway, the way they came into town.

"Damn," he exclaimed softly. "This is going to cost us time. We'll have to bypass Bowling Green. Head back down into Tennessee."

"Did you hear what the newscaster said? The President's wife is going to be in Wichita tomorrow."

"I heard. Does that mean something to you?" Ames asked.

"I have a bad feeling, Ames. We have to get there fast." Marian replied.

"I'm going to go with your feelings. Want to risk taking the Interstate?"

Marian thought for a moment. "Yeah. I think we have to."

CHAPTER 18

Wilma sat silently at the antique roll-top desk in her bedroom. She ran her fingers over the letters "W.B." that had been scratched into the mahogany top. Her initials. From Christmas 1943 if memory served. Wilma had sat on her grandmother's knee at this desk

Grandma Barnhardt had been a special person in Wilma's life. She read the Bible to her when she visited. Taught her to pray. And she had the Gift. Grandma was the one you came to when your best earrings had been misplaced. Always knew if the baby was going to be a boy or a girl. Always lit a candle just before the neighbors arrived to announce a death in the community.

She had told Wilma many things about her future. Told her that she would witness a miracle first-hand. Told her that God had a special plan for her when she was older. At seventy-six, having watched every member of her family, including two of her own children, die before her, Wilma was alone.

She remembered thinking a few months back, *If God's special plan for me is a glass of beer every day at sunset while I pray for my own death, then Grandma's still batting a thousand.*

Then the diagnosis of cancer came. Wilma had thanked God and asked to be taken quickly. But that's when the party started. Marian Foster's touch.

Wilma's first dreams hadn't been of the child, but of her grandmother. If her instructions had come from anyone else, even Jesus Christ in person, she would have ignored them. It was too late for this kind of "special plan." She was old, tired and ready to move on.

But Grandma could be a persistent old coot. Wilma finally agreed to accept her role, and the instructions began to come, step by step. And Wilma followed dutifully.

As the Circle began to form and the path became more clear, she became passionate about her mission. There was a very real possibility of a new world unfolding, and she would be one of God's instruments to bring it about.

But then the instructions came about Marian's arrival. The deception. She began questioning the source of her dreams. Surely God wouldn't work his will through lies. This poor young woman had such a burden to bear. Surely she should know the truth.

Then, for the first time, Wilma was shown the entire plan. She thought she knew how Jesus had felt in Gethsemane when He prayed for the cup to be taken from him. But this was her cup.

Wilma opened the bottom drawer of the desk and took out a box of stationery. She pulled a sheet from the box and ran her finger gently over the embossed rose at the top of the page. Her grandmother's special stationery. Taking a pen in hand, Wilma began to write the most difficult letter she'd ever written. A letter that wouldn't be read until after her death.

"Dear Marian. . ."

CHAPTER 19

Norm Randall awoke in the Wichita motel. He groggily rolled over and tried to push himself off the floor, but his hand found a pile of bloody vomit.

"Shit," he mumbled as he shook the mess from his hand and sat up. He looked around at the strange surroundings. *Where am I?* was the familiar question that first came to mind, followed by the also familiar, *What day is this?*

He was used to the blackouts, sometimes spanning several days, but this time was different. Norm was terrified. The first wave of pain struck him then, and he clutched his head with both hands. *Please, Jesus, make this go away. Just make it stop.*

He knew what would ease the pain. It was right across the room on the table. Black Jack. The overwhelming feeling he had done *very bad things* over the past few days caused him to hesitate. He knew every time he got in trouble, it was because of the booze. And he knew he could be in *very bad trouble* this time. But, God, the pain. Just one sip, so the pain would go away. That's all he needed. No more, then.

Norm wobbled and almost fell as he stood up. He was shaking badly. Just one sip, that's all. He staggered to the table and unscrewed the cap from the bottle of whiskey. The aroma alone made him feel a bit better. He put the bottle to his lips and tilted it back. He felt the burn in his throat and the warmth spreading through his body, and he knew he would be OK. His journey was almost over. He could feel it. Norm tipped the bottle a second time and the world became even clearer.

He turned toward the window and squinted at the bright sunlight that streamed in from where he had torn the window shade from its brackets. Something was happening down below. Norm saw people gathering across the street from the hotel around the burned out shell of what looked like an office building. They were carrying placards and banners. A partially burned sign in the parking lot read, "Mt. Carmel Family Planning Clinic".

*   *   *

George DeFontana rushed into the Oval office carrying a heavy stack of papers.

The President asked, "What's the problem George? You sounded panicked on the phone."

"When did you present Hunt's proposal to the European Union?" DeFontana asked angrily. "I'm supposed to know about these things, Mitch!"

"It's 'Mitch', now?"

"I beg your pardon, *Mr. President*," DeFontana said sarcastically, "But as National Security advisor, I need to know when issues like this are being discussed."

"I have only presented this proposal to the Russians. Hunt gave it to his Chinese contact. No one else has seen it."

"Not according to these!" exclaimed DeFontana, tossing the stack of papers onto the President's desk, many of them fluttering to the floor.

"The European Union is unanimously endorsing this proposal. As are 17 African nations and a handful of Pacific rim islands. There are copies of this proposal everywhere!"

"Hunt must have leaked it," said the President angrily. "And I thought I could trust him!"

DeFontana calmed a bit and replied, "No, that doesn't make sense. He understands that unless all nations agree to join, the whole thing falls apart. He would work the most powerful nations first." DeFontana paced around the office.

"It had to be the Russians," he finally said. "They would stand to gain a lot if this were seen as their proposal. And their overinflated egos might make them think the rest of Central Asia would automatically line up behind them."

"Does this hurt our position any?" the President asked.

"Maybe not," replied DeFontana, "the key to this is still China. And they continue to refuse to talk to anyone. Nothing can happen without them."

*   *   *

Marian and Ames were thirty miles outside of Wichita a few minutes after noon. Marian had been driving again for the past four hours as Ames remained silent, much of the time with his eyes closed. He suddenly rose up straight in his seat.

"Get off at this exit," he exclaimed, pointing to a sign that read "State Road 451."

"What's up? " asked Marian nervously, while moving into the right lane.

"He's at number six," Ames said emphatically.

"Number six, what?"

"I don't know, yet. But he came in town on a smaller road. A two-lane. 451 comes in from the Southwest, and that's where he would have come from."

Ames was glancing all around as they turned onto highway 451.

"What are you looking for?" asked Marian.

"I don't know. There's this big number '6' that just keeps flashing in my head. Do you see anything that looks like a six?"

Marian looked around, "Nothing here like that, Ames."

"Just keep looking. We're close."

Marian noticed Ames had broken into a sweat.

*   *   *

Big Norm had almost polished off the last of the Jack Daniels. He slouched in a chair, oblivious to the television newscast telling about the First Lady's speech. His stupor was shattered by a loud voice.

"You're a disgrace, soldier!"

Norm quickly looked up in the direction of the voice. He knew that voice. It was the voice of his commanding officer from Desert

Storm. A figure slowly came into focus, approaching him from the door to his room.

"You drunken faggot, come to attention when I'm talking to you!"

Norm stood up, still trying to focus on the man in officer's combat fatigues that was moving nearer to him.

"You couldn't make it in the United States Marines, and now you want to be in *my* Army? Don't make me laugh!"

The uniformed man came even closer and Norm saw that it wasn't his old C.O., but a man with shoulder-length brown hair, blue eyes and a beard. On top of the man's head hovered a glowing golden ring. A halo, like the angels in the old cartoon shows.

Norm's eyes grew wide. "Jesus?"

He dropped to his knees and bowed dramatically. "Jesus! My Lord and my God."

"Randall, you make me puke," the specter said. "Get on your feet before I kick your cowardly ass."

Norm unsteadily got to his feet. The figure blurred in and out of focus.

"Look out that window, scumbag," the figure said. "Do you know what that is?"

Norm gazed at the building across the street, then turned back, shaking his head.

"That's an *abortion* clinic, dumbass! That's where they murder babies. They wanted to take Mother Foster there and rip me right out of her guts."

Norm stared at the vision, blinking.

"Thank God I've got some *real* soldiers in my Army. They bombed the fuck out of that place!" the man exclaimed, smiling.

"But the job's not finished, Randall. And since you're the only one here, I thought I'd see if you had enough guts to do it."

"I . . . I'm ready," slurred Norm.

"Yeah," the figure laughed, "I'll bet you are."

He turned his back to Norm and gazed out the window.

"There's a woman coming in an hour to give a speech right over there. She's going to tell all those people it's O.K. to kill babies." He spun around at Norm. "She's going to say it's O.K. to kill *me!*"

"That - that's a sin," Norm stuttered.

"Fuckin' A-right it's a sin. Burn in hell for that shit, you will. But you're going to shut her up, Norm. You're not going to let her talk about killing babies."

"I'll shut her up!" Norm exclaimed loudly.

"That's the spirit I'm looking for, Norm. You take care of it."

"You can count on me, Lord," Norm said, saluting.

The figure laughed. "Oh, yeah, one other thing, Norm. This is your final assignment. We can't have any evidence left layin' around, know what I mean? It's time for you to come home and collect your reward."

Norm's eyes got wider, "You mean – ?"

"It's time, Norm. Aren't you tired of all this horseshit? The booze. The pain. The voices in your head. You come back home and everything will be fine. No more pain. You'll never want for nothing."

Norm tried to imagine what that would be like.

"I've got a seat saved for you, Norm. At my right hand."

Norm nodded slowly. "O.K., Lord. I reckon I'm ready."

The figure flashed Norm a thumbs-up. "Good man." He turned toward the door and began to fade away, muttering under his breath, "Dumbass. . ."

*   *   *

Ames was growing more excited, frantically looking in every direction for the "6" he had seen in his vision. Marian had to slow the vehicle because of traffic congestion on the small road.

"Must be a wreck," she said, "People are stopping up ahead."

Ames squinted, trying to see what was up ahead. "Son of a bitch!" he exclaimed. "Pardon me, ma'am, but that's the clinic that was bombed."

Marian strained to see into the distance but could make out a partially burned sign that said, "Mt. Carmel Family Planning Clinic."

"And there's the 'six'," Ames shouted, pointing to the opposite side of the road. Marian saw the huge Motel 6 sign on top of the red brick building.

"Turn into the gas station," Ames said, "I think it connects with the motel parking lot."

Marian did as requested and as they entered, they immediately saw a dark green Range Rover at the corner of the building.

"That's it," Marian said. "That's his car."

"Don't park by it," Ames said, looking around the lot. "Over by the dumpster."

Marian backed the car into a spot by a large trash bin. Ames looked around nervously.

"What's the plan? What's the plan?" he muttered to himself.

"Are you alright?" asked Marian.

"Things are always in order," Ames said, continuing to survey the area as he muttered to himself. "You'll always have everything you need. You just have to find it."

Next to the dumpster, Ames spotted a large trash container on wheels.

"O.K.," he said. "Call the front desk and get the guy's room number."

Marian hesitated, "But we don't know his last name, only 'Burton'."

"Just make the call," replied Ames. "Trust yourself to say the right things."

Marian dialed information on her cell phone and was soon connected to the front desk of the motel.

"Front desk, may I help you?"

"Yes," Marian said, "Can you give me Mr. Burton's room number?"

"One moment," said the man. "We don't have anyone by that name, here. Oh, wait, did you mean Mr. Embry? We do have a Burton Embry staying with us."

"Yes, of course. That's him."

"Would you like me to connect you?"

"Uh - no," said Marian, "I just need his room number."

"I'm not allowed to give out room information, miss."

Marian thought quickly, then said, "Mr. Embry was my eighth grade English teacher. I haven't seen him in fifteen years. I heard he was in town and I'd really like to surprise him."

There was silence on the other end, so Marian continued, "No one else believed in me. If it hadn't been for him, I might not be alive now."

Silence again for a few moments, then, "You didn't hear it from me, but it's room 217."

"Thank you so much," said Marian, hanging up.

"217!" she shouted to Ames who had gotten out of the car. He had removed his plaid shirt and was now wearing only a t-shirt and his gray pants. He opened the trunk, took out a battered John Deere baseball cap and put it on. He grabbed the trash receptacle and began pushing it toward the motel.

"If anyone comes, or you sense any danger, just get out of here," Ames ordered. "Don't wait for me, understand?"

Marian nodded and watched him heading toward the service entrance.

Ames looked to see that no one was watching and then entered the door. In front of him was an elevator. He got on and pushed the button for the second floor. When the elevator stopped, Ames got off and walked down the corridor looking for 217.

A man emerged from room 203 and asked, "I've been calling all morning for towels. Can you get me some?"

"Yes, sir," Ames replied. "Got one room to do and then I'll take care of it."

Ames waited for the man to round the corner and then proceeded down the corridor. He stopped in front of room 217 and looked around. From inside the room he heard the sound of breaking glass.

Ames knocked loudly on the door. "Housekeeping!" he shouted.

He backed away from the door, preparing to charge and put his shoulder through it, when a man and woman emerged from the room next door. Ames quickly turned to attend to his trash container.

The man and woman paused outside their room, chatting about the morning weather. *Hurry up!* Ames was thinking to himself, when a sharp popping sound came from the room, followed moments later by another.

The woman turned to Ames, "What's going on in there?"

"Uh - repairs. Gotta take out a wall in the bathroom to get to a broken pipe." Ames replied.

The woman looked at her husband. "A broken water pipe of all things! Go make sure no water's getting into our room."

The man sighed as he opened the door and his wife followed him back into the room.

As soon as their door had closed, Ames put his entire weight into the door of room 217, which sprung open, wood splintering from the frame.

Inside, Norm was seated on a chair with the muzzle of his rifle under his chin. He was straining to reach the trigger with his left hand. Ames raced into the room, and in one motion pulled the gun from Norm's hands, swung it around and planted the butt in Norm's temple. The huge man instantly toppled to the floor.

Ames glanced out the broken window at the spreading pandemonium across the street.

"Shit!"

He raced to the doorway and pulled the trash container into the room. "Lord, give me strength," Ames said as he bent to lift Norm's limp body.

He nearly buckled under the strain. Norm outweighed him by at least thirty pounds. Ames thought he was lucky he didn't have to fight him. He tossed Norm into the container, grabbed the top sheet from the bed and stuffed it on top of him. Ames wheeled around and quickly pushed toward the service elevator.

"Come on…" Ames mumbled as he waited for the elevator to open. He pushed the container on and as the doors started to close he heard a voice.

"Hey, you!"

Norm turned and saw two men in dark suits and sunglasses racing toward the elevator.

The doors continued to close as Ames pretended to push buttons and shouted, "I can't stop it now. I'll be right back up!"

The younger suit said to the other, "Want me to go get him?"

"He's the garbage man." The older man said, "He's not going anywhere. Start checking the rooms."

Ames exited the elevator and pushed across the parking lot. Sweat was pouring from him. He glanced around at the men in black who swarmed over the motel like ants. *Keep steady*, he thought. *Don't push too fast. Take it slow. No attention.*

He reached the car where Marian waited, opened the back door and tipped the trash container over. Marian gasped as Norm rolled out.

"Little help, please," Ames said breathlessly.

Ames took Norm's legs as Marian pulled his upper body into the back seat. As soon as they were able to get the doors closed, Marian started the car.

"What now?" she asked. "They've got men all over the parking lot."

Ames paused for a moment and they both became aware of a roaring sound that was getting louder. Ames stuck his head out of the window and looked skyward.

"It's a MedEvac chopper. As soon as it's overhead, put it in reverse and go!" Ames ordered.

"There's a fence behind us!" Marian said, beginning to panic.

"That wooden fence will turn into splinters. The chopper will cover the noise."

The helicopter was just passing overhead, it's engine a deafening roar.

"Floor it!" Ames yelled.

Marian put the car in reverse and hit the gas. There was a small impact when they hit the fence, but just as Ames had said, it collapsed easily.

"Get back on 451. They'll roadblock the interstate first."

"What happened back there?" Marian asked, dreading the answer.

Ames rubbed his neck nervously. "I think he shot the President's wife."

*　　　*　　　*

"How can we get the Chinese moving, George?" the President asked. "With the responses we're seeing from the European nations, I'm starting to think Hunt's idea might actually work. The last thing we need is for everyone else to jump on board and let China hold us hostage."

"Maybe a face-to-face with the Chairman. Would you be willing?" asked DeFontana. "Security would be a major concern. Traveling could be dangerous right now."

The door to the Oval Office burst open and Press Secretary Helen Dollison entered and closed the door behind her.

"You're early Helen. Our meeting is at – "

"Mr. President," she said, looking very ill. "It's your wife, sir. She's been shot."

"What . . .where is she?" Stanton demanded, rising from his chair.

"She's on a helicopter en route to Munson Hospital at Fort Leavenworth."

"Helen," the President whispered, "is she...?"

"She's critical," Dollison said, as tears began. "She hasn't regained consciousness."

She moved toward the President and placed her arms around his neck. "I'm so sorry, Mitch," she sobbed.

Stanton embraced her and said softly, "George, get me in the air. Now."

"Right away, sir," DeFontana said, then quickly left the room.

"Helen, do you know what happened?" the President asked.

"She was arriving at the clinic to give her speech. She had just gotten out of the limo when she was hit. They found the sniper's nest at a motel across the street. The weapon was still there, but the shooter was gone. The whole Midwest is on the hunt for this guy. Rest assured, he'll be caught."

The President sat back down and cradled his head in his hands. "Where was it, Helen?"

"Sir?"

"Where was she shot?"

Dollison swallowed hard.

"She was hit in the head, Mitch," she said softly.

Mitchell Stanton sat in silence, head in hands. Helen Dollis on watched as the President's silent tears fell onto the mahogany desk that Roosevelt, Truman and Kennedy had once occupied.

The leader of the free world is weeping, she thought.

Helen Dollison had never been so scared.

CHAPTER 20

Marian was heading southeast on Highway 451 at 80 miles an hour. The passenger in the back seat was still unconscious. Ames was on his cell phone with Carver back in Asheville.

"We've got him. A little too late, I'm afraid. We're on 451 heading away from town. Is there a safe house nearby?"

"Hold on," said Carver, "let me see who's close." Ames could hear rapid typing on a keyboard. "Head for Tulsa. I'll call you back."

Ames put the phone down and told Marian, "When you see the 169 exit, head South for Tulsa."

"What the hell are we going to do with this guy?" Marian asked anxiously. "Every cop in the country is looking for him. Sooner or later, we're going to get caught."

"Focus on one thing," Ames replied sternly. "He has information we need. That's more important than anything else, right now. Whatever happens later, happens."

Marian exploded, "What do you mean, 'whatever happens, happens'? This guy shot the President's wife. If we're stopped, I don't expect to be kept alive long enough to make it to prison!"

Ames sighed and replied calmly, "You still don't get all this, do you? We take one step at a time. Don't worry about what *might* happen next. The Circle needs to get the information this guy has, so we're gonna make sure that happens."

"What information could he have that will stop the lawsuit?" Marian shot back.

"Forget about the lawsuit, Marian. Right now, we're trying to prevent a global war. Your baby won't be born if the world's not at peace."

"What the hell are you talking about. I haven't heard anything about this."

"You haven't dreamt about it?" Ames asked.

Marian thought back to her dream of Washington destroyed by nuclear attack.

"I guess maybe I have," Marian said reluctantly.

"I'm sorry, Ames. I can't get used to taking these dreams as reality."

"Better get used to it," Ames said. "For a while they're all you're going to be able to count on."

The cell phone rang. "Yeah," said Ames. "Hold on."

He took out a pad and began writing. "Got it. What? OK, I'll tell her." Ames hung up the phone.

"We're going to be staying at a farm outside of Tulsa for a few days," said Ames. "Carver and Stan are going to come and meet us there."

Marian's spirits rose slightly at the thought of seeing Stan.

"Oh, and Wilma has a message for you."

Marian was anxious for any words of encouragement. "What did she say?"

"She said you're going to have to talk to the President."

"What!" Marian exclaimed.

"Talk to the President? What am I supposed to say? 'Mr. President, I have your wife's murderer here with me, but he's going to help us save the world, so everything's A.O.K. You have a nice day'."

Ames' patience with Marian grew thin.

"I don't know what the hell you're supposed to say to him. Everything will be clear when the time's right. You've got to get that through your thick head, just so you won't go crazy. Just look back over what's happened to you the past few months. Every time you would expect things to hit a dead end, something happens that takes you a bit further. That's the way things are now, at least for the True Believers."

He drew a deep breath and continued in a calmer voice, "Just keep moving forward. Take one step. Look and listen. Take another. We're on God's timetable now. As long as you remember that, you'll be fine. If you try to rush things – well, just don't, O.K.?"

Marian couldn't mistake the hint of warning in Ames' tone. She decided to take it seriously.

*   *   *

At 4:30 P.M. the President left his wife's bedside for the first time since his arrival at Munson Hospital. She'd been struck once in the left rear of the head by a large caliber bullet. The portion of her brain that controlled breathing had been destroyed and she was being kept alive by a respirator. The doctors held no hope of emergence from her comatose state.

The Chairman of the Joint Chiefs of Staff, Gen. Harold McCullogh, had accompanied Stanton on his trip and was in the waiting area as the President emerged from his wife's hospital room. The look in Stanton's eyes answered his questions even before he spoke.

"Is there any change, Mr. President?"

"No, Harold. None is expected."

"Is there anything I can do for you, sir?"

The President stared at the floor for a moment, and then said, "Yeah. Yeah, there is."

He turned to face the general.

"Get these sons-of-bitches," the President snarled.

"I've played footsie with this goddamned Foster church for too long. This is my fault for not shutting them down sooner. These people are terrorists, and I want them treated like terrorists. Whoever shot my wife is from one of these groups. I don't care what you have to do, I want them – as a predecessor once said – dead or alive."

"Mr. President, I'm not sure we can do that," the general cautioned. "They're a legitimate church, and the public supports them. I can promise you, I'll have NSA agents so far up their ass, they won't be able to sneeze without us knowing about it. As soon as we have some evidence, we'll go in with full force."

"Screw evidence!" the President shouted. "We took out the Branch Davidians in Waco, and they hadn't assassinated anyone.

You tell DeFontana that I want an NSA finding that labels them a terrorist organization. Everyone in that church can then be considered co-conspirators."

"Sir, that kind of action is probably unconstitutional. These *are* American citizens," the general said.

The President squared off to McCullogh and stared into his eyes.

"The last time I checked, I was commander-in-chief of the armed forces. When several million Americans are found to be members of a terrorist organization, I'd say that constitutes a national emergency. What I'm ordering you to do falls squarely within my powers during a national emergency. So, do you have a problem with that?"

"No, sir," the general answered softly.

He made a mental note to speak with the Vice-President about his willingness to assume command if Stanton was found to be mentally unfit to serve. He also made a mental note to phone his wife and tell her to skip the church meeting tonight.

*   *   *

"What if he wakes up, Ames?" Marian asked with a nervous glance into the back seat.

"The way this guy reeks, he been on a bender for a while. Between the booze and the love tap I gave him, he's going to sleep a long time."

Ames turned to check on Norm.

"He's pissed himself, too," he said with disgust. "I'll take that as a sign he's still alive."

"What happens when we get to the farm?" Marian asked.

"First thing will be to dry him out. From the looks of him, I'd say we're lookin' at a few days of D.T.'s before he's in any shape to talk."

"Will we be able to handle this ourselves? This guy is obviously dangerous."

"You're a doctor," said Ames, "so I'll be counting on you to watch his vital signs. I'll help him get through the D.T.'s. I've been through this before, many times."

"How's that?" asked Marian.

"I've been through it on both sides," Ames replied.

"I've been in AA for nineteen years. I've sponsored folks in just as bad shape as him."

Marian turned to Ames in surprise. He *was* the perfect guy for this mission.

"See how everything works?" he asked. "We have exactly what we need, between the two of us, to handle the situation. That's the way it always is."

"What about that weird message from Wilma?" Marian asked anxiously. "I'm transporting the guy that shot the First Lady, and I'm supposed to talk to the President! I don't know if I have what I need to deal with that."

Ames smiled. "Open your eyes, girl. You have *exactly* what you need to deal with this situation. Wilma can vouch for that," he added with a wink.

"You're not talking about trying to heal her?" Marian exclaimed. "I can't get anywhere near her without being shot! And besides, I don't even know if I can help her!"

"You think about this hard, Marian. What's the one thing that could set everything right?"

Marian thought for a moment. "I understand what you're saying, but how do I even get his permission to see his wife if he suspects I'm involved in her shooting?"

"Maybe the right question to ask is: How do you get to see her without his permission?" Ames said mischievously.

"Shit! Like I need more adventure in my life right now!"

Ames grinned. "What else is life but an adventure?"

"If my life has to be a movie script, I'd rather it was *Sleepless in Seattle* instead of *Mission: Impossible!*"

"It's neither one of those," Ames laughed. "It's *The Greatest Story Ever Told. – The Sequel.*"

*　　　*　　　*

Bashir Pezek looked out the airplane window at the clouds beneath him. He was hypnotized by the tranquility of the billowing shapes. One could hardly suspect that below their undulating beauty lie a world in such turmoil. He tipped back the last sip of ginger ale and reclined in his seat to enjoy the clouds while he could.

Soon he would be landing in Washington, D.C. His name was now Muhammed Hamari, a Saudi national whose wealthy family had large investments in American energy and pharmaceuticals.

He wondered if the real Hamari was still alive. Perhaps he had become another unsuspecting martyr, simply because of a trick of fate that caused him to bear an uncanny resemblance to Bashir. El-Hamir had created a great number of unwitting martyrs. Bashir knew that he, too, would soon be added to the list of names so highly revered by the Jihadists.

He thought about the rumors he had heard in Al Jubayal. Rumors of a newfound hope and joy in America. Rumors of a new spiritual teacher and master who would soon be born. He had heard things were changing in the land of decadence and deviltry.

Millions of people had joined a new church that asked people not to donate their money to it, but to donate their money to educate children. Communities were feeding their poor. The poor were cleaning up their communities. People of all races and religions were coming together not to argue their differences, but to celebrate what they shared. The citizens of the land of selfishness and greed were offering themselves in service to others. All because of a pregnant doctor.

Bashir had heard stories of miraculous healings the Foster woman had performed. Now she was wanted by the police. Members of her church had claimed responsibility for two bombings and he had just heard on the plane they were suspected of the attempted assassination of the First Lady.

What kind of woman was this? Certainly, a much different sort than he had ever known in his country. A woman who inspired courage in the common citizens and fear in the leaders. This was a woman he wished to meet. He had a job to do in Washington, D.C., a job from which he would never return home. He would complete his mission, he decided, but first, he was going to meet this Dr. Marian Foster.

CHAPTER 21

"Oh, God! Make it stop! They're eating my legs! Sweet Jeeesuuus!"

The screaming had completed unnerved Marian. Her background in research had shielded her from the harsh realities of practical medicine. She sat with her back against the bedroom door, trembling at the thought of being face-to-face with this…this animal who was tied to the bed, purple-faced from hours of screaming.

"Jesus called me home! You have to let me die! PLEEEEEASE, LET ME DIE!"

Ames appeared in the hallways and looked down at Marian.

"Hey, girl," he said gently, "you're going to have to go in there soon, you know. He can die from this. D.T.'s need to be closely monitored."

"Just because I went to medical school, don't assume I know what to do, Ames. I don't. And I'm scared to death of him. I can't go in there."

"He needs a saline IV to re-hydrate his brain," Ames said impatiently. "And he's going to need sedation so he doesn't break any bones from struggling. We've got Valium. He's also going to need B-12 and thiamine within the next day, or this will go on even longer. We have all the supplies we need. But you have to do the work. I can't put in an IV line."

"You said Mrs. Collins was a nurse," Marian said, "let her put in the IV."

"She was good enough to sneak these supplies from her office, and to let us use her home, but we can't – " Ames hesitated. "You have to do this, Marian. You're the one."

Ames knelt down beside Marian.

"You gotta remember, in his mind, he did all this for you," he said sternly. "You'll be able to calm him down at least a little. Your presence can take his mind off the horrible things he's going through right now. I hate to say this, Marian, but you owe it to him."

Marian looked aghast. "I owe him? How can you say that?"

"I'm not saying you're responsible for what he's done," Ames said, "but to him, everything he did was to save your child. He deserves to see you."

Marian's head sunk onto her knees. "Will you come in with me?"

"Won't leave your side," Ames replied.

Marian took a deep breath. "Alright. Let's do it."

The two of them stood and Marian opened the door. The man's back was arched high off the bed, frozen in a position Marian had only seen in patients who had to be electrically shocked to restart their hearts. His body seemed to be trying to levitate, held down only by the sheets that bound his hands and feet. Every tendon in his arms and legs seemed ready to burst from his skin. Marian cautiously approached the bed, clinging desperately to Ames' arm.

"Hey, big guy," Ames said, "everything's gonna be O.K. We're friends and we're here to help you."

Norm turned his head slowly towards Ames. His body shook violently as he struggled to form the words, "Make – them – stop!"

"Alright, fella. We're going to help you," comforted Ames. "Tell me what you see."

"D-d-devils," Norm said, his eyes growing wider, "Satan's army. THEY'RE EATING ME ALIVE! OOOHHH GAWD!"

The screaming began again.

Marian jumped back, but Ames grabbed her arm, steadying her.

"It's alright, guy. It's O.K.," Ames said over the screams.

"Listen to me. SHUT UP AND LISTEN!" Ames grabbed Norm's chin and the screams stopped.

"You don't have to worry about devils anymore," Ames continued. "Do you know who this is?"

Ames nudged Marian forward towards the bed. Norms eyes rolled wildly in their sockets, unable to focus.

"This is Marian Foster. Look at her. Marian Foster. It's her." Ames said, watching as the man's eyes settled for a moment on her face.

"God's power works through this woman. Devils are powerless over her. Devils fear her. She can cast them away."

Norm looked helplessly at Marian, "P-p-please?" he begged.

Ames whispered to Marian, "Do something dramatic."

"What?" she whispered back.

"Anything. Just make it good."

Marian stepped forward and said weakly, "Devils –" Ames gestured to her to take it up a notch.

"DEVILS BE GONE!" she said forcefully. "BY THE POWER OF GOD I CAST YOU OUT! YOU SHALL NOT TORMENT THIS SERVANT OF CHRIST! IN GOD'S NAME, BE GONE!"

Marian swept her hands down both of Norm's legs, as if scraping away the demons that tortured him. Norm's body immediately relaxed onto the bed and he began to cry. Marian watched in amazement as the intimidating giant transformed into a three-hundred pound child.

"What's your name, friend? I'm Ames."

Between sobs, he managed to say, "Norm…Randall."

"We're gonna take care of you, Norm Randall. Don't you be scared," said Ames.

Norm turned to Marian, still crying loudly, and sputtered, "I saved your baby."

Marian touched his hand as a tear rolled down her cheek.

*   *   *

Bashir Pezek left the U.S. Customs area and walked through the terminal of Dulles International airport. He walked past a group of workers removing a sign that said, "Give to the Foster Child Foundation" from a deserted kiosk.

Bashir made his way to the taxi stand and hailed the first available cab. A turbaned driver helped get his bags into the trunk.

"Iran?" asked the driver, smiling.

"Al-Jubayal," answered Bashir. "My parents were Iranian."

"Welcome to America. God is great."

"Allahu akbar," replied Bashir, entering the cab.

"Where can I take you, my friend," asked the driver.

"Hotel Monticello in Georgetown."

"Very nice," said the driver. "Will you be staying long?"

"I'm not sure how long my business will take," said Bashir.

They spoke of their families in the Middle East during the 45 minute drive into Georgetown, Bashir faithfully recalling all the family members of his new identity, Muhammed Hamari.

As they approached the hotel, Bashir asked the driver, "Do you know anything of the Foster Church?"

"The Church of the Foster Child has been banned by the government. Any who profess ties to the church are subject to arrest," the driver answered.

"When did this happen?" asked Bashir.

"Just yesterday. The government says they are terrorists. Why are you interested in the church?"

"I had heard of miracles the woman supposedly performed. And an Imam in my land predicted the birth of a child that sounds much like the Foster Child. I had hoped to meet the woman while I was here."

"I doubt if that's possible. No one knows where she is."

The driver eyed Bashir suspiciously in the rear view mirror and then added, "There are some church meetings still taking place."

As they pulled up in front of the hotel, Bashir asked, "Do you know how I can find one of these meetings?"

The driver paused and rubbed his beard, then turned to Bashir. "I will be attending a meeting tonight."

Bashir was surprised, "I had assumed you were a Muslim, my friend."

"I am. My life is devoted to Islam," the driver responded. "The Child's Church stresses that there is one God for us all. The Child comes to bring peace and wisdom to all mankind. He will unite us and make us see we truly have no differences. He will bring an end to fear."

Bashir thought for a moment, and then asked, "May I join you tonight?"

The cabbie turned and stared intently into Bashir's eyes. He seemed to be searching for something. Finally, he replied, "I'll pick you up at 7:30. Allahu akbar."

*   *   *

Bashir unpacked his bags and made a call to the phone number he was given when he left Saudi Arabia.

"I have arrived safely," he spoke in English, "And will be contacting the board of directors tomorrow."

Bashir hung up the phone, having let his superiors know his arrival and entry was successful. He turned on the TV and sank into his chair.

America. It was always difficult for him to feel he was in an enemy land. He had been here several times before, transporting large amounts of cash in and out of the country, some of which had funded the deaths of American civilians here and abroad. But it never felt like traveling in hostile territory. It was much more fearful to visit a city in Iran where a different Muslim sect was in control. Your name, your accent, your style of clothing would point you out as an enemy. And you were treated as such.

He had heard Americans speak of racism and religious prejudice in their country, and it was hard for him not to laugh. They had no idea of the hatred fellow countrymen could feel for one another.

His attention was caught by the television newscast. It was showing scenes of rioting in an American city. Behind the newscaster, policemen and soldiers could be seen firing on the crowd. Bashir turned up the volume.

"…unprecedented use of force against American citizens. About three hours ago, Atlanta police and Army Special Operations conducted a raid against what was claimed to be the group responsible for the BiEnCo bombing. Thirteen members of The Church of the Foster Child were killed during the raid in North Atlanta. Government sources report that 800 pounds of plastic explosives were found on site as well as several RPG launchers and numerous assault weapons.

"When word of the raid was broadcast by local media, supporters of the Church took to the streets in great numbers, prompting the confrontation you see unfolding behind me. We have no word on casualties at this time, but from what we've seen, they will number in the dozens at least.

"The Church has no official spokesman, and apparently no leadership at a national level. However, several members were willing to talk to us earlier today, after the initial raid took place."

A man in his mid-fifties appeared on camera, "I'd just like to know what happened to the constitution. How can a country founded on religious freedom declare a church to be illegal? There are some crazies out there, no doubt. So go after them. Leave those of us alone that want to do God's work. We won't be stopped, I can promise you that. If the government doesn't back off, this could turn into civil war."

*   *   *

Marian and Ames were leaving the room where Norm Randall slept.

"My God, that was a lot of Valium I just gave that man," Marian said.

"You'll have to watch him closely," Ames replied. "But he had to get some sleep. When a guy's in D.T.'s, every brain cell just starts firing like crazy. Heart rate goes sky high. Metabolism is out of whack. When a guy dies, it's because his brain and internal organs literally burn out. You have to calm him down for his own good."

"When are Stan and Carver going to get here?" Marian asked.

Ames chuckled, "Will you stop, already. They'll be here today sometime. You'd think you hadn't seen your man in a year."

"He's not 'my man'," Marian blushed, "Oh forget it. You don't understand."

"I understand you've asked me once an hour since we got here. He'll make it just fine."

"Ames, he's a friend. He's the only man I've ever been able to get really close to. He's helped me through this whole thing. I just feel better when he's around."

Ames laughed again, "All I know is, the way sparks fly between you two, you best keep away from dry wood."

Marian decided to change the subject. "Do you have any idea yet what information Norm Randall might have for us?"

"Maybe the location of the bomb in Washington, maybe information about a zealot group planning something. Who knows. He might just be here to lead us to someone else."

"Like a scavenger hunt?" asked Marian. "One clue just leads you to the location of the next one?"

"Yeah, that's about the size of it. We just know he has a big role in everything that's happening. He's a key player."

"He's also a murderer," said Marian. "Have you heard any more about the government's crackdown?"

"Several more dead in Atlanta," Ames answered.

"Dallas and New Orleans have had some raids too. At least a couple dead in each case. One thing I'll say – so far, they seem to have only hit zealot groups. Every one of these raids were on locations where they had some serious firepower stockpiled. If they move on any True Believer groups... well, I just don't want to think about it."

A voice from the living room shouted, "The cavalry is here!"

Carver's head popped from around the corner. "S'up, big man! Did you miss me?"

Ames gave him a hearty hug, "Hell no, weasel. I've been enjoyin' the quiet. All that shit you got pierced through your body, you sound like a sack of tin cans when you lope around."

"How ya doin', Dr. Foster? This redneck hasn't driven you nuts yet?"

Marian gave Carver a hug, "I'm learning how to handle him."

"Food's the key, right?" Carver said grinning. "Am I right? He made you eat at a freakin' Waffle House, didn't he?"

Marian laughed with them. She had forgotten how good it felt.

"I can't believe Maw-maw let you out of her sight," Ames continued. "Does she even know how to turn her computer on?"

"Hey, she learned from the best, dawg. That granny can hack a medium-security site on her own now."

"Marian – "

It was his voice. Marian turned and immediately buried herself in Stan's embrace. They kissed and she found herself alone with him in a faraway place. For a brief moment, nothing existed except for the two of them.

Ames said to Carver in a mocking voice, "Good friends. She says they're *good friends*. Is that the way you act with your friends?"

"No way, dawg. Few beers. Maybe some Playstation. In my world, friends don't suck other friend's faces."

Stan gave them the finger behind Marian's back.

Carver continued, "You know, Wilma says they're so hot for each other, when they finally do it, they're gonna spontaneously combust."

Marian finally broke the embrace, "I heard that!"

"I'm gonna bring the bags in," Carver said. "You two, get a room!"

"Are you holding up okay?" Stan asked. "I've been so worried."

"It's been quite a trip, but I'm alright. I missed you."

"There's someone else here to see you, and she can't stay long, so…"

Stan led Marian into the living room where Jenny Waters was waiting.

"Oh – my – God." Marian ran to embrace Jenny.

"Girl, it's so good to see you!" Jenny exclaimed.

"What is this? What are you doing here?" Marian asked.

Stan spoke up, "I knew Jenny was the only one you wanted to take care of you during your pregnancy. You're several appointments behind schedule, so she agreed to come and examine you. Make sure everything is going the way it should."

Stan turned to Jenny, "I'm going to leave you two alone. The owner of the house is a nurse. She said everything you need will be in the master bedroom inside the wardrobe. Just yell if you need anything else."

Jenny gave Stan a peck on the cheek. "Thanks. You're the best."

Marian and Jenny began to walk toward the back of the house. "I can't even imagine what you've been through, Marian. I can tell just by looking at you that you've changed."

"There's no way you could go through what I have and come out unchanged," said Marian. "It's just been *so much*. One part of me feels things I've never felt before, and another part has become numb – almost fearless. Here I am, hiding the man who shot the First Lady and it's like… no big deal. Five minutes ago, I was laughing with my friends."

Marian sat on the edge of the bed and fidgeted with her hair. "I think I need you to convince me I haven't gone crazy."

Jenny answered, "You know from your research how incredibly well a subject can adapt to stressful conditions. I'd say you've done the only things you could to *keep* from going crazy."

"But you don't think I'm responsible for this mess the whole country's in? You don't think I'm… evil, do you?"

"I believe in you, Marian. And in your child. If you're following your heart, you're doing what needs to be done."

"So, you've actually bought into all this? The coming of the age of peace?"

"Yeah," Jenny smiled. "I have."

"Wow," Marian replied, mildly shocked.

"What's up? It sounds like you're the one who hasn't bought in."

"I guess I have, sort of, but I never think about it, Jenny. I'm always reacting to some bizarre situation, doing whatever I have to do. When I actually do stop and think about it, it's...unreal."

"The situation the world is in right now is what's unreal. It has to be changed. Thank God some things are starting to happen."

"You know, I have no idea what the Church is even doing. I've never been to a meeting, never really heard what was being accomplished. I've just been running."

Jenny smiled. "The way my group leader put it, was, 'How well do you clean your house when you know your mom's coming to visit?' The mother, father, whatever, of the whole human race is coming to visit. We've got a lot of housecleaning to do."

"What hooked you?" Marian asked. "What made you believe?"

"Same as everyone else. The miracle."

Jenny opened the wardrobe and began taking out the equipment needed for the examination.

"Stan called me when you left Atlanta. After Hedstrom was shot. I thought he was still just preaching this messiah stuff to get the public on your side, like at the beginning. He convinced me to donate to the Foster Child fund, which wasn't that difficult. It's a good cause on its own. Anyway, he asked that if anything out of the ordinary happened, I tell one other person about it and ask them to donate. I thought it sounded silly, like some chain letter scam, but I agreed. A week later I was pregnant."

"That doesn't seem like such a miracle, unless you and Steve stopped having sex."

"Marian, I don't have any ovaries. I developed cysts on both while I was in med school. They were removed."

Marian was stunned. She felt ashamed for not knowing such information about her friend.

"Jenny, I had no idea. I just assumed you and Steve decided against children. Why didn't you ever tell me?"

"When you were in med school you barely gave me the time of day. We didn't speak for months on end," replied Jenny. "If you can remember the old you, you'll remember a person who was extremely self-centered. You were a friend only when you needed a friend."

"I'm sorry. It's hard to believe that was me just a few months ago. It seems like a different lifetime. I was really a shit, huh?"

"Yeah, you were. *Were* being the key word. World transformation through personal transformation."

"Everyone keeps saying that. Where does that come from?"

"From the church. That's what it's all about in a nutshell. The True Believers know it's pointless to try to change the world. Just change yourself and everything else will happen automatically."

"How is it that everyone can accept these miracles so nonchalantly?" Marian asked. "What has happened to you is every bit as miraculous as my situation. Yet, to you it's just, 'Ho-hum, here I am, pregnant with no ovaries'."

Jenny smiled, "Get undressed from the waist down. It's not like that at all. The first reaction is disbelief, followed by more disbelief. Then finally, when it sinks in, joy at the realization that *this stuff really happens!* It validates the religious ideas we hoped were true when we were young, but just pay lip service to as we get older. Eventually, you have to accept that the world is different than you thought. Everything becomes exciting and filled with possibilities. Time to take a look inside, now."

Marian spread her legs as Jenny continued her examination. "Why aren't these miracles being reported in the news? It would make the church's job a lot easier. Who wouldn't become a believer?"

"We're asked to only tell one other person about our miracle," Jenny replied.

"Of course, people tell their families and spouses. And those of us in the church spend a lot of time talking about our experiences. This church is different, Marian. It has to be. The other churches haven't worked that well. This is a church of action, not words. It's about direct experience, not gilded philosophy. Talking about God can't compare to being touched by God."

Jenny stood and snapped off her gloves. "You look fine. From what I can tell, right on schedule. I'm going to stick with November 14. Too bad I can't see a sonogram, but from the look and feel of your belly, I think the baby's right where it should be. I do want to take some blood so Mrs. Collins can have it run at the hospital."

*   *   *

"Let me out of here! You have to let me go! I'm going to DIE!" Norm shouted, tendons bulging in his arms again.

"We're all going to die, Norm, but nobody's going to die today," Ames responded calmly. "The booze almost killed you. We're going to make you better."

"IT HURTS! God, my head is going to explode!"

"You're doing real fine, buddy, if that's your only complaint," said Ames. "No more devils on your legs?"

"What're you talking about? Who are you?" Norm asked, a look of paranoia spreading across his face again.

"We're just trying to keep you alive. We work with Marian Foster, remember?"

"The Foster Mother?" Norm asked with eyes wide.

"Yeah. You've met her already. You just don't remember. Don't worry. She'll be in to see you soon."

"I saved her baby, y'know. I – " Norm's sentence was interrupted by a stream of vomit that barely missed Ames.

"I know. I know. Have some water and wash that taste out."

Norm took a small sip and spit it on the floor, "Damn, that's nasty! Can't I get a real drink? That would really fix me up."

"No can do, big guy. It'll get better every day, I promise."

"Where's the little kid?" Norm asked, looking around the room.

"What little kid?" asked Ames, wary of any more signs of hallucinations.

"The little kid who comes in when you all leave. The one who says he knows me."

Ames quickly sat at the bedside. "What does he tell you?"

"He tells me that he forgives me. And he loves me. I don't know who he is. He keeps saying there's something I have to tell the Foster Mother."

"What is it?" Ames insisted. "What do you have to tell her?"

Norm opened his mouth, but only vomited again. This time a weak dribble that ran down his chin onto his shirt.

"Never mind, fella," Ames said, toweling him off. "Just get some rest. We're real close."

CHAPTER 22

Bashir entered the modest apartment in Arlington, accompanied by his cab driver, whose name he had learned was Adel Khazaneh. Looking through the living area into the kitchen, he could see several men gathered around the table, several more standing along the wall.

A thin black man rose from the table and approached them. "Whassup, bro," the man said embracing Adel.

"Another one?" he asked. "Man, I'm gonna have to start takin' up a collection for a bigger apartment if you keep bringin' in more members." Adel and the man laughed.

"This is my friend, Muhammed. Muhammed, meet Terell Pittman."

"Please call me Bashir," he said as he extended his hand. Shocked at himself for breaking his cover, he quickly added, "That's what my family calls me."

"Peace, Bashir," answered Terell. "Glad you could join us. Come on in."

As they entered the kitchen, Terell announced, "Got a new guy tonight. Bashir."

Bashir walked through the kitchen nervously. There was an elderly white man in a brown sport coat, a young man, early twenties, with numerous piercings in his face, two police officers, one white, one black. There was another fierce-looking black man, arms like small trees, covered in prison tattoos. And a catholic priest. All greeted him warmly and enthusiastically.

"Are all of your groups for men only?" Bashir asked.

"I wish!" said one of the officers, generating laughs from the group.

"No, man," replied Terell, "but with the government against us, we think it's safer to leave the women home for now. They're still involved in the work."

"Come on, we got stuff to do," said the pierced young man. "Shake down the new guy and let's get going."

Bashir understood that to mean he would be searched. He held his hands in the air. "I assure you, I am not armed."

This generated even more laughter. The large tattooed man fell from his chair and rolled on the floor. Finally, Terell put his hand on Bashir's shoulder.

"No, bro. That's not what he means. It's a custom to ask all new members to donate money to the Foster Child Foundation. Have you heard of it?"

"It's to generate money for education of children without parents, I believe," replied Bashir.

"Right. Here's the scoop. Your donation is a symbol that you're ready to offer yourself in service to others. In exchange for that, something good will happen in your life."

"I don't understand," said Bashir hesitantly.

"Didn't Adel tell you his story?" asked Terell.

"I didn't have the chance," spoke Adel. "He began asking about meetings before he even knew I was a member."

Terell looked into Bashir's eyes. "No shit? That's a good sign."

He smiled at Bashir. "I have a feeling you're a very important man, my friend. You're here for a reason. We'll find out together what that reason is."

Terell turned away and paced the floor, speaking as if to himself. "Very important. This is good. This is good."

As if struck by a revelation, he turned back to Bashir. "Well, before I ask for a donation I have to follow the rules. I got a story to tell you. Have a seat."

One of the policemen stood and offered his seat to Bashir who bowed slightly and sat. Terell stood over the tattooed man and cleared his throat loudly. When the man didn't respond, Terell grabbed his chair and began shaking it. The man abruptly stood up, chuckling in a deep voice. Terell flipped the chair around and sat in it backwards, arms propped on the back.

"Bashir, do you believe in miracles?"

*   *   *

"I think tomorrow's the day," said Ames. "He's seen the child and has a message for Marian. He's almost coherent enough to talk to, but he's got a ways to go. I think between Mrs. Collins and myself, we can take care of him till he dries out."

"So it's a road trip again for Marian and me," said Stan.

"I'm guessin' that's the case. I can only hope he's going to tell us where she needs to go next."

"What about Carver?" asked Stan. "Do you need him to stay with you?"

"Let's see what Norm has to say tomorrow. I think there's a good chance you might need him."

"Have you thought any more about what to do with Wilma?"

"About moving her, you mean. She's not gonna go anywhere, Stan. You already know that."

"The government is going to find her house, soon. There's too much communication flowing from there."

"Carver warned her all the time," Ames said in disgust. "There was only so much he could do to cover their tracks."

"Clay is their mole," said Stan. "Can't we use him to misdirect them?"

"We can't let him blow his cover. He feeds us too much information."

Ames' eyes brightened and he added, "But maybe there's something more important he could give them. Something that would take their attention off our headquarters."

"Like what?" asked Stan.

"Like the location of Marian Foster."

Stan slapped his shoulder. "You're so good, you're bad."

"Ain't it the damn truth," chuckled Ames.

*   *   *

Bashir arrived back at his hotel room after the meeting. He was more confused than ever. After hearing Terell's story, he gave a one hundred dollar donation to the Foster Child Foundation. Something had touched him deeply while in the company of the group. He did feel important. As if he had a purpose here he was not yet aware of. A purpose other than ensuring the destruction of the American capital.

There were so many good things being done by the group. Two rival gangs were fighting for drug turf on the West side. Five gang members had been shot in the last week. Next Thursday they were going to bring the two gangs together in an attempt to make peace.

Bashir had been told the Foster Child Foundation had generated more money than it could spend on educating only children without parents. The Foundation was now preparing to offer scholarships to troubled youth of all kinds, and these gang members would be recipients of the first such grants.

The people he had encountered on this trip to America were not evil. He wondered how he could ever have thought such a thing. Certainly, their living conditions were far better than those of his people, but they had the same concerns. They worried for their families; worried about their future. There was discontent with the state of their nation, and of the world, but they were taking actions that didn't create growing lists of martyrs. He felt drawn to help them. If only...

The ringing phone interrupted Bashir's reverie. "Hello."

"Papa?" answered a small voice on the line.

"Farid? My boy, is that you?" Bashir replied incredulously.

"I'm coming to see you, Papa."

"Are you alright, my son? Where is your mother?"

"She's here, Papa. We're fine."

Tears had begun to roll down Bashir's face. What could be the terrible circumstances behind this call. They must have been taken prisoners, being held to ensure he would complete his mission.

"Can I talk to your mother?" Bashir asked.

"Yes. Papa, I love you."

"I love you too, my son."

"Bashir?" a woman's voice spoke.

"Salma, what is happening? Have they hurt you?"

"We are alright. We are leaving the country tomorrow."

"Where are you? Who are you with?" he asked anxiously.

"With friends of yours. People who were loyal to the Imam al-Akmed. They told us where we could find you. Many here are displeased with the things el-Hamir has done since he assumed command. He is not Islam. He is a devil. There is a group of us leaving tomorrow for Al Jubayal. Several are coming to America. The remainder to Turkey and Greece."

"Praise Allah," Bashir muttered. "I've wanted nothing more than to see you and Farid."

"We had been told you were martyred. I never expected to see you again."

The pieces of the puzzle came together in Bashir's mind.

"It's a miracle, Salma. I'll tell you about it when you get here. For now, I'll just say – God is with us. Finally and surely, God is now with us. I have found the true path."

"I love you, Bashir. Be safe."

"I'll see you soon, my love. Travel with God."

Bashir placed the phone in its cradle and slowly sunk to his knees. He bowed forward in prayer and began weeping loudly. He gave thanks until he was exhausted and then sank into a peaceful sleep. He now knew his purpose, and for the first time in his life, was certain God walked with him.

*   *   *

"It's time," Ames said.

Marian followed him into the bedroom where Norm was now sitting in a chair, unrestrained for the first time in three days.

"Good morning," Ames said to him. "You have a visitor."

Norm looked at Marian and tried to stand, but his unsteady legs wouldn't support him. He plopped back into his seat.

"It really is you," said Norm, reaching for her hand. She offered it and Norm took it gently and placed it against his cheek.

"You're the mother of God."

Marian glanced at Ames nervously.

"Mr. Randall told me he's pledged his life to you," Ames said, giving Marian a look that told her this was for Norm's benefit. "He wants to serve your cause in any way he can."

Marian responded, "That's very kind of you, Mr. Randall. I'm glad you're here with us, and that you're feeling better."

"My name's Norm and I'm not better," said Norm shaking his head. "Not better at all. I did bad things, but I can't remember. I'm really, really sorry."

"From what I understand, God forgives all of us when we're sorry. You don't have to worry," Marian reassured him.

"But what about you?" Norm asked. "Do you forgive me? Even though I don't remember?"

"I forgive you, Norman. No matter what you did, I forgive you."

"Just, please, please, make your baby be born. So things can be better. So people don't have to hurt anymore. I'm tired of hurting."

"My baby will be born. And you won't have to hurt anymore."

"Excuse me, but…I have to go to the can," Norm said, blushing.

"Let me help you get there," said Ames, helping him up.

Ames closed the bathroom door and returned to Marian.

"I don't know how much he's going to be able to give us. The booze really tore up his brain. Now that he's sober, there doesn't seem to be much left of him."

"That's not from the booze," Marian said. "That's Norm. He's borderline retarded. Pretty much like a big ten-year old."

Ames rubbed his head. "Now, how did you figure that one out?"

"When he took my hand, I knew everything about him. His father was a devout Catholic, slightly schizophrenic and an alcoholic. Norm dropped out of school at sixteen while he was making his third attempt at the eighth grade. He enlisted in the service when he turned seventeen; thought he was going to get to play Army for a while.

"Unfortunately, Desert Storm happened the following year. He was scared, almost unable to fight, but had a friend in his platoon who looked after him. One day while they were on patrol, they walked into an ambush and Norm went back wearing his friend's guts on his shirt. He snapped, got a dishonorable discharge and came home. Today is the first day since then he's been sober."

"Christ!" said Ames. "All that from a touch?"

"When it happens, that's the way it comes."

"So what does that mean to you?"

"Well, the first thing that comes, is that his mental state might keep him from being executed when the authorities finally catch up with him."

"I mean, did you get anything about the message?"

"No," responded Marian, "only that he's seen my son."

From the bathroom, Norm's voice called, "Mr. Ames! Can you help me?"

Ames helped Norm back into his chair.

"Can you tell me about the little boy you've seen?" Marian asked.

"I like him. I used to not, when I was drunk, but I do now. He makes me laugh sometimes."

"Do you see him when you're dreaming?"

Norm thought for a moment. "No. He's real. He's not a dream. He knows all about me."

"Do you know who that boy is, Norman?" asked Marian.

Norm shook his head.

"That's my son. My baby."

Norm looked puzzled as he glanced at Marian's protruding tummy and then back at her face.

"He's a big-un, huh?"

Marian smiled. "Did he tell you anything I should know?"

Norm stared into space and then his eyes brightened.

"Yeah! Yeah, he did!" Norm licked his lips, obviously using all his concentration. "He said... to heal the President's wife, and...and find the Basher."

"Did you say, 'the Basher', Norm? What is that?"

"It's not a what. It's a who. It's a guy and that's his name."

Marian wasn't sure she wanted to find anyone called 'the Basher.'

"He sounds a little scary. Do you know anything about him?" asked Marian.

"He's not scary. He's a good guy. He can help you save everything."

"Save everything? What do you mean?"

"He knows about the bomb. He knows where it is."

Marian and Ames looked at one another nervously.

Ames asked, "Did he tell you where she could find the Basher?"

"No. But it won't be hard. He's trying to find her, too."

*   *   *

Bashir quickly dialed the number Adel had given him. He heard the phone begin to ring. "Hello."

"Adel, this is Bashir. I need to talk to you."

"How can I help you, my friend?"

"I need to speak with you in person. I have to tell you who I really am, and why I came here."

"Bashir, when we leave our homelands, we all carry secrets with us. It is a hard life over there. There's no need to feel - "

"I have to talk to you now! Many lives could be lost. Thousands. I need help from the Church."

There was silence for a moment before Adel responded. "I'll be right over."

*   *   *

"So 'the Basher' knows where the bomb is hidden?" asked Stan, skeptically. "And we're going to look for him?"

"I'm just telling you what the man said," replied Marian. "You know all of these messages are filtered through the consciousness of the person receiving them. He's slightly retarded. The message might be distorted, but I know he's telling the truth as best he can."

"Did he give you any clues on where to look?"

"No. Norm just said it shouldn't be hard because he was looking for me, too."

"Washington would be a good place to start," interjected Ames. "We know the bomb is somewhere in the capital."

"Wait a minute!" exclaimed Marian. "Ames, you told me we have to take one step and then wait for a sign to know what to do next, right. You told me that on our way to Wichita."

"Yeah, but – "

"Looking for 'the Basher' wasn't the first thing he told me to do. The first thing he said was, 'heal the President's wife'. Maybe that's what we should be concentrating on."

"You're catchin' on quick, girl. I missed that one. Could have been a big mistake."

"And I've been thinking about a way I might be able to get in," Marian continued. "It's pretty 'cloak and dagger', but I guess it's no worse than what we've done so far. Anyway, here it is: Tell me if this is possible…"

CHAPTER 23

Adel had turned pale, and was feeling faint at hearing the news that a nuclear device had been constructed within the city of Washington, D.C.

"This cannot be true! Why are you telling me such things?"

"Because now I must stop it!" Bashir exclaimed.

"I was having doubts before the phone call, but now, I have no choice. My family has a chance to live in freedom. I cannot let them come here so I can watch them die"

"Where is the bomb?" Adel asked.

"I don't want to tell you. You would be in great danger if you knew. I can't take the chance that you or the others would try to act without my help. It would only make things worse."

"My friend, how can things be any worse?"

"The bomb is scheduled to be detonated next week, when congress reconvenes. My mission is to see that it happens on schedule, but there are other safeguards in place, as well."

"Such as?" inquired Adel.

"From the time the bomb was armed, the man guarding it has been wearing a remote switch that allows him to detonate it instantly if he deems necessary. In addition, there is a keypad in which he must enter a number every six hours. If he misses the scheduled time, the bomb explodes."

"So if he's killed, the bomb detonates automatically," added Adel. "Do you know the number that must be entered?"

"It changes each time. He has received thousands of copies of the Koran. In each one there is an encoded verse that tells him the next number. All he has to do is go through the cases of books in the correct order."

"Can you break the code? Would you be able to enter the numbers?"

"Yes," replied Bashir, looking ashamed. "My job was to kill him if he showed signs of weakness and detonate the bomb myself."

"Then there is hope," affirmed Adel.

"I will not tell the members of our group about this. It is too big for us alone."

Adel pondered for a moment, then continued. "Very few people know this, but there is a group of people who are the real leaders of our church. They are called the Circle. They have a very strong connection with God. They will know what to do next."

"I don't want to put anyone else in danger," Bashir pleaded.

"The Circle has protected us from the very beginning. Let go of your fear before it destroys you. You have received a miracle. Do not let your faith waver. All will be as it was meant to be."

Adel paused and then added, "You may very well get your wish to meet Marian Foster."

*　　*　　*

Another night passed at Munson Hospital, with the First Lady's condition still unchanged. A respirator was breathing for her and there were no signs of higher-brain activity. Dr. Brad Tarnow, chief neurologist, conferred with Gen. McCullogh about her status.

"How long before we can move her to Washington, doctor?" McCullogh asked. "We need to get the President back there and he refuses to leave her side."

"Nothing has changed in days and nothing will. I could authorize her transfer tomorrow. We'll just have to get the equipment ready to travel. I can't guarantee how she'll handle the trip, but the only way her condition could get worse would be death. That's going to be the eventual outcome even if I keep her here."

"Let's start the preparations, then," said McCullogh. "I'll try to get the President comfortable with the idea."

A young Secret Service agent sprinted down the hallway, narrowly missing a nurse pushing a crash cart. He had a cell phone raised over his head like a runner carrying the Olympic torch

"General, it's her! You've got to take this!" He slid to a halt in front of the general.

"Who is 'her', Agent Bradford?"

"It's Marian Foster, General! She says she's on her way here!"

"Son of a bitch!" the general sputtered, almost dropping the phone the agent was handing him. "Get a trace on this call!"

"Already on it, General. Just keep her talking."

The general put the phone to his ear and un-muted the phone.

"This is General McCullogh."

"General, this is Marian Foster. I'm on my way to the base. I'd like to see the First Lady. I believe I might be able to help her."

"Well, we'd really like to see you, too, Dr. Foster. What kind of help do you think you could offer her?"

"Don't worry about tracing the call, General. I'm almost there now. I'll be at the front gate in five minutes. Please don't try to stop me. I'm determined to see her. One way or another, I will."

"Dr. Foster, I'll have to see what I can arrange." The general heard only silence over the line. "Dr. Foster? Dr. Foster! Damn it!"

He threw the phone to the floor.

"Did anyone get the location?" he bellowed.

Bradford raced to his side once again. "She's on K-net. And she's on the local cell. That means she's within a twenty mile radius. We're trying to triangulate her exact position."

"Keep one agent with Mrs. Stanton. Get everyone else to the front gate. I want Special Ops in position surrounding the front gate too, but out of sight. I don't know how much firepower she's got, but we need to take her alive. Alive! Understand?"

"Yes, sir."

*   *   *

Marian Foster attached the badge to the front of her nurse's uniform that gave her clearance to the First Lady's floor and left the nurse's lounge. As she walked past the surgical unit, she marveled at the fact she had made it this far.

Thank God for the popularity of her church. Carver and his computer skills could find True Believers anywhere she needed them.

And it so happened that one of the nurses with clearance to the First Lady's ward was a member of a Wichita group. With her badge and uniform Marian walked in as a registered nurse with security clearance.

This time she wore a pair of thick glasses along with her brunette wig. The soldiers at the gate accepted the badge, no questions asked and allowed her to enter the base. Marian stayed on the first floor, out of sight, to avoid having to answer any questions until she made the call which she hoped would clear most of the guards from the First Lady's floor.

She had to play this perfectly. *Let's see, what would a nurse be delivering to a comatose patient? Simplest would be a glucose I.V. and urine collection bag. That wouldn't raise any suspicion.*

She saw the medical supply room up ahead and made her way inside.

Marian located the refrigerator with the glucose containers and retrieved one. The urine bags proved harder to find. As she was digging behind boxes on shelves, another nurse entered.

"Exactly what are you doing here?" the nurse asked.

"I need a urine bag for floor seven. I already found the glucose."

"And you can put it right the hell back. That's MY inventory and it stays on this floor. If you need something for seven, get it on seven."

Marian turned on her heels and held the badge on her chest up for the nurse to see.

"We're out on seven. And whom should I tell the President is preventing his wife from getting the supplies she needs?"

The nurse put both hands on her hips, sizing up Marian. Marian met her gaze and kept her hand on the badge. The nurse finally relented and reached into a box on the top shelf and shoved a urine bag into her chest.

"Take the damn bag. And stay off my floor."

"The President thanks you for your help," Marian said trotting out the door.

"Hope the damn thing leaks," the nurse muttered under her breath.

Marian strode to the elevator, entered and pushed "7".

She was carefully controlling her breathing now. Couldn't let nerves get to her. She was in her element, now. In a medical setting, she had always been top dog. Just being in this environment should give her confidence.

But she knew things could get dangerous. If she was recognized, would she be shot on sight? Hell, would they shoot her just for being a face that hadn't been seen on that floor before. *Gotta trust,* she thought. *Gotta have faith.*

The door opened on the seventh floor and Marian felt a wave of adrenaline rush through her. She took a breath and walked at an authoritative pace down the corridor toward a door at which a single man in a black suit, earpiece in place, sat reading the sports page.

Marian strode up to him. "Good evening," the man said, not looking up.

"Good evening," Marian replied, glancing at the medical chart in the holder outside the door. In the usual place, the bottom left corner, she saw the name of the floor's chief RN, Nancy Statler.

"Nancy said she'd be due for a bag soon, so I'm going to leave one after I get her I.V. started."

"Fine," the agent said, still mesmerized by the American League standings. Marian began to open the door.

"Whoa!" said the agent, putting his newspaper down.

Marian broke a sweat. She tensed her muscles so her trembling wouldn't be obvious.

"You know the drill," said the agent, grasping her badge and scanning it with a laser pen attached to something that looked like a pocket calculator.

"What time you got?"

"Uh...three-seventeen," said Marian, checking her watch.

The agent entered the time into the keypad and sat back down and retrieved his paper.

Marian entered the room and closed the door behind her. When she turned, she was shocked at what she saw.

The First Lady was almost unrecognizable. The elegant, statuesque woman she had seen so many times at the President's side had been replaced by an open-eyed mannequin, a graying shock-wig of hair splayed across her pillow, hands already beginning the transformation into claws common to comatose patients.

Marian bent over the bed and looked into the blank eyes. *Is there still anyone in there?* she wondered. Would a soul remain tied to a body in such deteriorated condition? *God,* she thought, *please be here now. I'm really trying. I'm trying so hard. Please, no tricks. No surprises.*

Marian took her hand. She began to pray. She had never wished so hard, not even on those nights when her father was hurting her.

Heal her, God. Heal her, God.

Suddenly she felt a familiar wave of energy building up inside of her. It felt as if her hair was standing on end. A flash of unbearable heat began at the crown of her head, shooting down her neck and shoulder and out through her arm. The first lady began convulsing. Marian released her hand, becoming more frightened when the convulsions didn't stop. An I.V. line ripped from the woman's arm and then, as suddenly as the seizure began, it was over.

Marian's relief was shattered by the sound of a loud, high-pitched beeping. A crash alarm. The woman's heart had stopped. She looked at the monitor above the First Lady's bed. The EKG was a flat line. Blood pressure, zero over zero. Pulse, zero. Marian leaned over the bed and began giving CPR chest compressions as she heard a stampede of feet coming up the hall toward the room.

The door burst open and first in was the chief RN. "What the hell are you doing?" she shrieked.

Next was Dr. Tarnow, who glanced at Marian, turned and grabbed the Secret Service agent by the collar and shouted, "Who is this woman?"

General McCullogh was next in the door. He pulled the badge off her chest and scanned it with Agent Bradford's laser.

"Joan Casey," McCullogh began, "you've lost about 70 pounds since yesterday, Nurse Casey. And your blonde hair . . ." he pulled off her wig. "Oh, *there* it is."

"You're good, Dr. Foster," McCullogh said as he shoved her into a chair in the corner of the room.

"You got in. I don't know why you needed to kill her, though. It was going to happen on its own. Or was this an act of kindness on your behalf, ending her suffering?"

"I came here to try and heal her," said Marian softly. "The Church didn't want this to happen."

Dr. Tarnow shouted, "Get the defibrillator in here, stat."

The doctor turned to Marian. "Just tell me what you did to her. I might be able to save her."

"I just held her hand and prayed," said Marian.

"An I.V. line is out, but none of the other equipment has been touched, " added the Chief RN.

"I was praying and she began having a seizure. Then she coded and I tried to revive her. I want to help her."

"Clear!" shouted Tarnow as he applied voltage to the defibrillator paddles. He saw no change on the monitors.

"Charge to 300. Stand by with lidocaine. Clear!"

The First Lady's body arched off the bed again. Still no sign of life on the monitor.

"Clear the room, General. I'm going to have to open her chest."

"NO!" said President Stanton, entering the door. "My wife will die with a shred of dignity."

His eyes moved to Marian. When Marian saw the mad rage in them, like a starving animal moving in for the kill, she was terrified. He held his gaze, veins in his temples throbbing, for what seemed an eternity.

Without turning his eyes from Marian he ordered, "General, take this terrorist into custody."

"Yes, Mr, President. I'll have her taken to FBI headquarters in Wichita."

"No, General. That would afford her all the freedoms of an American citizen accused of a crime. This woman is a terrorist. She will be handed over to NSA officers in Washington. She will be treated as a prisoner of war."

General McCullogh fought the vision of Marian Foster, figurehead of America's most popular church, living in a tent village on Guantanamo Bay. He knew what those "POW's" were subjected to.

"Mr. President – " McCullogh began.

"If you choose to argue this order with me, General, it will be the last order you ever argue," Stanton bellowed.

"She is your responsibility. Don't let her out of your sight until you get to Washington."

"Yes, sir," the General saluted. He turned to Marian. "Come along, miss."

Marian rose and allowed the General to lead her out by the arm. She was too numb to be afraid. *This can't happen. I did everything. I had faith. I had no fear.*

The general flipped out his radio.

"This is McCullogh. I need a secure HumVee, driver and two Special Ops for a prisoner transfer. Washington, D.C. Right. You have ten minutes."

The general entered the elevator with Marian in his grasp.

"Miss, you have no idea how much trouble you're in. Our Commander-in-Chief says you're a prisoner of war. You no longer have any freedoms or constitutional rights. There will be no phone call, no lawyer, and we don't even have to acknowledge that you're in our custody. You will be tried by a military tribunal that can order your immediate execution. And the worst part of all this is my wife thinks the future of the world lies in you. She believes in you."

"Not in me," said Marian despondently. "In my child."

"Yeah, right. Your child." McCullogh thought of what life in the terrorist camp would be like for a pregnant woman. Not pretty.

They exited the elevator, greeted by three saluting soldiers.

"As you were," the General said. "Soft cuffs for the woman, please."

He released Marian into the hands of a sergeant who cuffed her with plastic straps. The other two soldiers guided her into the back of the HumVee and took their places on either side.

"You're in front," the General said pointing to the one on the driver's side. "I need to ride with the prisoner."

* * *

Dr. Tarnow slowly staggered into the waiting area where the President sat, head in hands. The doctor was quite pale and trembling.

"Excuse me. Mr. President?"

"Not now, Doctor. Just let me have some peace for a while."

"Mr. President. Your wife – "

"Talk to my press secretary," the president growled. "She can handle the arrangements. She can handle it all. I want to be left alone!"

"Your wife…" Tarnow stammered, "is asking to see you."

CHAPTER 24

"Can you loosen these a little?" Marian asked, holding up her bound hands.

The general looked at her hands, which had turned beet-red and reached over to adjust her handcuffs. Marian instinctively grasped his hand in hers and felt the familiar surge of energy pass between them. The general paused for a moment, a look of surprise on his face and then loosened the plastic straps a bit.

"Better?" he asked.

"Yes, thanks." Marian replied. "Your wife was right, you know. It was a miracle."

"I think it's best if you keep quiet," said McCullogh sharply.

"One of the hardest things for anyone to accomplish is to change. Anytime it happens, it's something of a miracle. Your wife knows that."

"I'm telling you now to shut up!" McCullogh shouted as his cell phone began to ring.

"McCullogh," he answered. "You're positive of that? What about Foster? Yes, sir, I understand, but if it's true shouldn't we – No, sir. We'll proceed as planned."

The general rubbed his face as he stared intently at Marian.

"You knew, didn't you?"

"That she woke up? Yes, I knew."

McCullogh pounded his fist on his thigh, obviously waging a battle within himself.

"I also know the President told you that I was to be held anyway; that I was dangerous. That holding me might be the only thing that prevents my followers from striking again."

McCullogh rode in silence for several minutes, then announced, "We're going to stop in Emporia for lunch."

The soldiers glanced at each other and replied in unison, "Yes, sir."

Thirty-five minutes later they exited the Interstate and motored into the town of Emporia. The general directed the driver to pull off at a drive-in burger joint.

"O.K., here's the deal," the general announced. "You boys are going to take an hour lunch break. I'm going to take the prisoner for a little one-on-one interrogation. President's orders. If anyone asks, this never happened. We never stopped for lunch. We never pulled off the road. Is that clear?"

"Yes, sir," the men replied.

"I'll need your radios and your sidearms. Chop-chop."

The soldiers handed over their gear as the general asked.

"I'll be back. Don't leave this location and don't contact anyone, understand?"

"Yes, sir," the men parroted again.

The general slid into the driver's seat and headed toward the edge of town. He drove without speaking until they reached a large, nearly deserted truck stop at the city limits. The general parked at the farthest possible location from the restaurant. He unlatched a holster on his belt and opened a large single-blade knife. He turned and reached into the back seat. Marian screamed and slid to the far side of the vehicle.

"Hold out your hands," said the general calmly.

Marian complied and McCullogh swiftly sliced through the bands.

"Now, let's talk," he said.

"I took the hook," McCullogh continued. "Let's see if you can reel me in."

"It was the evening after your wife attended her first church meeting. What made you decide to contact your son on that particular night, after all these years?"

McCullogh's face went slack. His eyes suddenly looked old and tired.

"I couldn't bear not having my son in my life any longer. We had a great relationship when he was young. When I was off duty, we were inseparable. We hunted, fished together. He was everything I ever hoped my son would be. Honor roll in high school, captain of the football team. He was offered a scholarship to West Point. I thought he was going to follow in my footsteps. Then he told me he was gay."

"I thought in the 'new' Army that didn't have to stop you," Marian interjected.

McCullogh chuckled. "He knew as well as I, that 'don't ask, don't tell' was a joke. I just couldn't bear it. Every time an enlisted man looked at me, I knew what he was thinking: 'Must run in the family.'

"I loudly and publicly denounced him every chance I got. I erased him from my life and forced my wife to do the same. I made her give up her son for my career. That night, I just had to call him. I wanted my son back."

"That was the miracle," said Marian. "Something in you changed that night."

The general gazed into Marian's eyes as if trying to uncover a grand secret.

"What is it you people are all about, anyway? You obviously have some kind of mission to change the world, so your child can be born, right?"

"Not to change the world," Marian replied. "To change people. One by one. As people change, the world takes care of itself."

"World transformation through personal transformation. I heard my wife say that several times."

The two sat in silence for a moment. Marian asked, "So what now?"

The general sighed heavily. "How long would it take your people to pick you up here?"

"Probably about an hour," Marian answered.

"I'll give you two. Hop out."

Marian was astonished. "What are you going to do?"

"I gave my men orders to wait there for me. If I left them there for two months, when I return they'll just get in the car without saying a word."

McCullogh gazed into the hills. "What am I going to do? I think I'll take a walk in these woods for a while. This is beautiful country."

"What will the President say when I don't show up in Washington?"

"The President and I have been at odds for days now, ever since he started this 'war' against our own people. If he doesn't come to his senses soon, I'll be fired whether I get you to Washington or not. It'll all work out."

He looked at his watch.

"You have an hour and fifty-eight minutes now. Better hit the road."

Marian got out of the HumVee. "Thank you, General."

"Whatever it is you're doing – keep doing it."

Marian waved and headed off toward the restaurant. The general looked off into the hills once again. What a beautiful day for a walk.

*   *   *

Wilma Barnhardt doused the pilot light on the water heater in the utility room just behind her kitchen. She took the crescent wrench and began loosening the fitting that connected the gas line to the regulator.

This is the day, she thought. *I have to make sure, though.*

She placed the wrench on the floor and closed her eyes tightly. *Are you sure, God? I'm really not too keen on this plan. What was it your boy said - If it be your will, let this cup pass from me?*

Wilma let out a sigh and continued her job.

When the fitting was loose she pulled the flexible copper line from the regulator. The room began getting heavy with the stench of natural gas. She got a telephone from the kitchen and stretched the phone line into the utility room and placed the phone on the floor next to the water heater. Wilma checked that the doors to all the rooms on the ground floor were open, then went into her modestly furnished living room and closed the door tightly behind her. She looked out the window and saw three black sedans raising clouds of dust as they sped up the dirt road to her house.

She sat down on the couch and pictured Marian in her mind.

Take care, girl. Stay on the path.

An image of Stan then came.

Mister, hurry up and marry that woman. Get off your ass before it's too late.

The cars were parked in her graveled driveway now, and several men in dark suits were coming toward the door.

Ames, you are the rock on which this church is built.

Two men were now walking up the steps to her porch.

Carver, you made me wish I was fifty years younger.

A knock at the door.

Wilma answered it. "I've been expecting you."

"Wilma Barnhardt?" said the man.

"That's me," smiled Wilma.

"FBI. We have a warrant to search this house."

"I know," said Wilma as she pushed the speed dial button on her cell phone.

No one heard the phone ring.

CHAPTER 25

Stan and Carver arrived at the truck stop in Emporia shortly after 2:00 PM. As planned, Marian was waiting for them near the trash bins at the far corner of the parking lot. They pulled to a stop as Marian ran to the car and hastily entered the back seat.

"We better get out of this town, fast," Marian said, peering out the rear window, "I think the man at the cash register recognized me."

Marian turned to the two men, neither of which looked at her. Stan put the car in drive and turned onto the highway. Carver wiped his reddened eyes. He looked like he'd been crying.

"What is it? What happened?" Marian asked anxiously.

Stan looked at her in the rear-view.

"Wilma's dead."

Carver began quietly sobbing as Stan continued, "The FBI showed up at the farm and she had it rigged to blow up. Gas explosion."

Marian clamped her hand to her mouth in disbelief.

"Oh my God. I thought Clay was going to misdirect them - to have them looking for me somewhere else."

"We moved too slowly," Stan replied softly. "Planning to get you into the First Lady's hospital room became the priority. We never were able to contact Clay."

"How is Ames taking this?" Marian asked.

"Not well. He blames himself for not acting when he first had the idea. He thinks he betrayed us by not following his intuition. He sees that as his role. He represents the intuition of the Circle."

Marian's mind raced. "Can't you remind him that some things have to happen? Maybe Wilma was aware all along that her role would end in this way."

"He won't hear of it. He's starting to believe we all might be doomed to failure."

Marian felt the fear growing inside. "Why does he think that?"

"The Circle can't be complete, now. We all dreamed our final number would be twelve. There are only ten of us now, with no leader."

"So Ames thinks we're doomed," questioned Marian. "What do you think?"

Stan stared ahead at the road that meandered into the foothills.

"I think I'm scared, Marian. Maybe we should try to leave the country. Just let the baby be born in safety and see what happens."

A wave of raw anger washed over Marian. She slammed her hand into the back of Stan's seat.

"God damn it, Stan! If we don't finish, my baby WON'T be born! You're not going to screw me over after taking me on this roller-coaster ride. If all of you are going to turn into a bunch of whimpering pansies, I'll do this myself. I was just set free by the goddamn Chairman of the Joint Chiefs of Staff of the United States of fucking America. I don't think that happened so I can piss away my time on a beach in Acapulco!"

Stan stared at the angry eyes in the rear-view mirror. "So what do you think we should do?"

"Call the Circle together. Now."

Stan glanced to his right, "Carver?"

"I've got everything I need in my laptop. I can contact them."

"Have them at the Collins place tomorrow night," ordered Marian.

"I'll have them there," replied Carver, drying his eyes.

*   *   *

"We've got a positive ID from the prints on the rifle, Mr. President," said Special Agent Hiller.

"A Norman Randall, from Murfreeboro, Tennessee. 37, ex-Marine, served in Desert Storm, dishonorable discharge for aggravated assault on an officer. Severe learning disability, possibly borderline retarded. Worked as a temp day laborer, married two years ago, divorced three months later. Disappeared from Murfreesboro about a month ago, but a truck similar to his was reportedly seen at the site of the BiEnCo shooting in Atlanta. Trail goes cold after that."

"So what are his ties to the Foster church?" asked Stanton.

"None that we can see, sir."

"Ridiculous. He's obviously working for that church."

"We've searched his house. He doesn't own a computer. Doesn't even have a phone. There's no sign of contact with the church at all."

"No matter. We've got Foster in custody now. We'll find out what this Randall's connection is."

"I don't think so Mr. President," said McCullogh, entering the room.

"What are you doing here? Where's Foster?" bellowed the President.

"I've let her go. She and her church had nothing to do with this."

"You!" the President's face reddened. "You have disobeyed a direct order. You're relieved of your command, immediately. Hiller, arrest this man for treason!"

"Mr. President, we're not at war," Hiller stalled.

"Has everyone forgotten who's in charge here? I said arrest this man!"

McCullogh offered his hands to the agent. "It's alright, Hiller. It'll all work out."

A woman's voice rose over the commotion, "Has everyone here lost their minds?"

It was Susan Stanton, standing in a hospital gown in the doorway.

"Mitch, you always told me Harold was the one military man you could trust. He was the first person you put on your list of appointees. Don't you think you owe him the chance to talk?"

"Sue, what are you doing out of bed? The doctors haven't finished the tests yet."

"I don't need tests to know that I'm fine," said the First Lady. "I'm very worried about you, though. Haven't you seen what's happening to your country?"

"Yes! I've seen that we have a very large and powerful terrorist organization posing as a church. They've caused chaos across the country, killed dozens of people – you being one of their targets."

"And your response to them was to kill *hundreds* of American citizens, in the name of what? National security? This church, this movement has sprung up in a matter of just a few months. There is no leader. This church is just an idea, a passion that entered the mass consciousness. This is nothing but energy. Energy that had one focus – to change things."

"How do you claim to know so much about this?" asked the President angrily. "You've been in a coma while all this was happening."

"I saw everything, Mitch. I was everywhere, seeing everything."

"You've been hallucinating, Sue. Your brain was severely damaged."

"Brain tissue does not grow back, Mitch. That's a medical fact. Mine did."

"Look, I'll admit your recovery defies explanation, but to claim that a miracle – "

"My God, Mitch! Miracles are happening everywhere. Open your damn eyes before it's too late. All this is for real!"

The President sat and crossed his arms defiantly.

"O.K. I'm listening. Convince me."

"Then let this sink in: For the last several days I have been with Marian Foster's son."

*   *   *

The Circle assembled in the modestly furnished living room of the Collins farm. Everyone except Clay Parker, the NSA agent had arrived on schedule.

"We need to get started," announced Stan. "Has anyone heard from Clay?"

"He said he would be here as soon as possible," said Arnie McCullogh. "He said something big was happening in Washington he had to finish up."

"Clay knows how important this meeting is. It must be very big for him to be late." added Rosie Velasquez.

"Alright. Let's dive in," said Stan.

"First, the prophesies about the size of the Circle: We were at ten until yesterday. We were told that before our work was complete, we would have twelve members. What does Wilma's death say about our chances for success?"

"I need to get clear on something," said Marian. "Who determined when a new member would be allowed to join the Circle?"

Janet Conwell answered, "There was no person who selected or approved members. The sole factor was dreaming about the child. If the child appeared in your dreams, you were in the Circle."

"But how was contact initially made?" Marian continued. "I mean, how did you come to discover people had been dreaming about the child?"

Gordon Prevost spoke up, "We found that when the dreams would begin, the person would eventually tell his group's leader about the messages. They in turn would tell the person who brought them into the church, and so on. Quite soon the path would lead to one of us. That's how all important information comes to us."

"That seems like a pretty inefficient way to communicate," Marian said, skeptically. "Especially if the information is time-sensitive."

"Not at all," Stan replied. "Think of it like this: The average size of a group is ten. There are ten of us. Each one of us was responsible for the formation of at least one group. Every church member, on average, brings in ten new members."

"I see," said Marian. "A geometric progression. Each original member was the initial cause of hundreds of thousands of members joining the church."

"Right. With our phone tree, we can reach 100,000 members with just five generations of calls. That also means it will take no more than seven phone calls for any member in the country to eventually reach a member of the Circle."

Father Kaplan, with gloved hands to cover his wounds of stigmata, had been writing rapidly on his pad. Finished, he held it up. It read: "The circle grows larger."

"What does that mean, Father?" asked Marian.

The priest began writing again, and all at the table anxiously awaited the response. Finally he showed: "Susan Stanton".

"The First Lady?" asked Marian, "She's been dreaming of my son?"

The priest nodded, then wrote more: "She has been with the boy for days. She is working with us."

"So we have a friend in high places?" asked Marian, smiling.

"We have many friends in high places," added Arnie McCullogh. "More and more will be showing their presence, soon."

"What do you mean?" asked Janet Conwell.

"My brother is General Harold McCullogh. The man who set Marian free. There are many more in the government who are unhappy with the President's actions. They'll be speaking out soon."

Father Kaplan was tapping his pad loudly. He held it up: "The Circle grows larger."

"Yes, Father," said Stan, "and we're all very thankful."

But Kaplan shook his head imperatively and added another word, large and underlined, so the message now read: "The Circle grows larger, NOW!"

At that instant the door opened and Norm Randall's head appeared.

"Mr. Ames, where is the T.P.? I can't find none in the bathroom?" Norm peered around the room. "Why is everybody lookin' at me?"

All heads turned back to Father Kaplan who was pointing insistently at Norm.

Ames rubbed his chin and said, "Norm, why don't you come join us?"

"Did I do somthin' wrong, Mr. Ames? I didn't mean to bother you all."

"No, Norm, there's no problem. We just think you should be talking with us too. We're all here to help Marian's baby, just like you are."

Norm quickly pulled out a chair and sat. "I'll do anything for him. Just tell me."

Stan asked, "Have you still been having dreams about the boy?"

Norm smiled, "Oh, yeah. Almost every night."

"What have your dreams been like, Norm?"

"Mostly just playin' games. He like to play school with me. He says I'm really pretty smart. Other people don't think so, but he does. He says he can teach me things."

"What have you been learning?" asked Gordon.

"About the world. Other countries and stuff." Norm's face brightened. "Did you know that in China they have over a billion people?"

"That's a lot of people," replied Gordon, smiling back at Norm.

"Yeah. And they don't quite know what to do. They're getting ready to fight a war, if they have to."

"Who are they going to fight with?" asked Stan.

"Don't know. They haven't figured out who the enemy is yet, but when they do...PKOW!"

He spread his hands wide to demonstrate a huge explosion.

"That's new," said Gordon, eyeing the rest of the group.

"And disturbing," added Stan. "Norm, anything new about the 'basher?' "

"Oh yeah. Ms. Foster will meet him soon."

"Norm," said Stan, "this is important. Is the 'basher' dangerous?"

Norm frowned, deep in thought. Finally he answered, "He's OK. But what he knows – oh, what he knows – now that's dangerous. Ms. Foster will have to go with him. And that'll be scary. I don't want her to go with him, but the little boy says she has to."

There was a knock at the door. It opened a few inches and Carver's hand thrust through the opening holding a cell phone.

"Somebody might want to grab the phone. It's your dude from the Agency."

Ames hurried over to take the call. "Clay? I hope you're on your way. We really need you here."

"Sorry to say I'm not. I've got a bit of a dilemma." replied Clay.

"How so?"

"I'm sitting here having coffee with the man who knows where the big prize is in Washington."

"You mean – "

"Don't say it!" warned Clay

"I understand, but – you have the guy right there with you?"

"Yeah. He's from a faraway land. The big prize was supposed to be his project."

"But he's going to help us stop it, right?" asked Ames.

"Well, that's what he claims he wants to do – and I believe him. But he won't tell me where the thing is."

"Clay, I'd say that in this circumstance, you would be right to do whatever it takes to get that information."

"I've thought about that. But I decided against doing anything extreme, until I talked to you all. This gentleman wants to speak to the woman."

"You mean Mar – ?"

"Ames, dammit, you have to be more careful. Yes, that's who he wants to speak to. He says he will only tell her the location of the device. I need to know what to do."

Ames looked around at the group, who were all gazing anxiously at him. "Call me back in five minutes on the backup number."

He put the phone down on the table. "Clay says he's with a man right now who knows where the bomb is. The guy claims he wants to stop it, but will only tell Marian where it is."

Stan chuckled, "Clay's NSA. He could get any information he wants from the guy."

"I know," said Ames, "but you know he doesn't like to use those kinds of tactics anymore."

"I'll talk to him," announced Marian. "If Clay thinks he's on the level, I have no problem. Let him come."

"No. He can't come here," said Stan.

"We can't attract any more attention to this house. Besides, somebody might be watching Clay. Those paranoid Agency bastards are always spying on each other."

"Then I'll go to Washington," Marian said in exasperation. "I should have known I'd end up there sooner or later. Marching right into the lion's den."

"So that's what I'm telling Clay?" Ames asked, looking around at the others. "No one here thinks this is dangerous?"

"Which part?" asked Arnie. "That there's a nuclear bomb in Washington, or that Marian's going to meet the guy responsible for it?"

"He's right, Ames," said Marian. "To talk about 'danger' at this point is absurd. Just look at what we've been through so far. And we always knew it was going to get worse the closer we got to the end."

"I'm going with you this time," said Stan, defiantly. "Don't even try to talk me out of it."

"Don't worry, Stan," she replied, touching his face. "I won't. I need you on this trip. I want to be with you, no matter how it comes down."

Ames' cell phone began to ring. "That's going to be Clay."

He looked at Marian. "You're sure you want to do this?"

Marian nodded solemnly.

He inhaled deeply as he removed the phone from his pocket.

"Yeah. She's coming. Stan too."

Ames frowned as he listened, then responded, "That doesn't sound too promising. You're sure we can trust this guy? Alright, then. Wait! What did you say his name was?"

Ames jaw dropped as he looked around at the other members of the circle. "O.K. She'll be there," Ames muttered distractedly.

As he folded his cell phone, Ames announced, "All the pieces are coming together pretty quickly."

He turned to Marian, "You'll be meeting with an Iranian national, Mr. Pezek. *Bashir* Pezek."

"The 'basher'," Marian whispered. She placed her hand on her round belly.

What am I getting myself into? What am I getting him into? Norm says he's on our side, but then, Norm's retarded. Father Kaplan says Norm's to be a member of the Circle, but then, he bleeds from every orifice.

Marian's mind raced and the terror grew within her until she was distracted by a soft, familiar voice saying, "Trust." It was so real that Marian had to look to make sure no children were around. The voice served to calm her and she felt herself coming back into the moment.

"That's not who I am anymore," she whispered.

"Are you alright, Marian?" Stan asked.

Marian didn't reply. She was concentrating on a feeling that emanated from her midsection. A small, subtle warmth spread throughout her body. She focused intently on the origin of that feeling. And suddenly she knew everything would be just as it should be. There was no other possible outcome.

That simple knowledge, which she would have labeled mindless acquiescence just a few months prior, gave her confidence. More than that, it gave her a sense of detachment, a feeling that she was nothing but an observer watching actors on a stage. Now, that portion of her, the actor, knew what was on the next page of the script.

"I'm fine," Marian announced. "We're wasting time. Get what you need together now, Stan. We're leaving in fifteen minutes."

She turned to the others and asked, "Rosie, can I speak to you for a moment? Janet, can you come too?"

"What is it?" asked Rosie.

"I've spent less time with the two of you, than any others in the Circle. I don't know you both as well as I'd like. Maybe that's why I'm more comfortable telling you this."

Janet and Rosie exchanged looks and waited for Marian to continue.

"I'm not sure if you know Carl Fontenot. He's the man who's been taking care of the Foster Child Foundation since I've been in hiding."

Marian was taken aback by the knowing smiles the women gave to each other, but quickly composed herself and continued.

"Carl is a brilliant man – although I never told him that – and I know he's made wise investments with the money in the Foundation's accounts. There are probably millions just in interest, by now. If things don't turn out, you know, like we expected, I want the members of the Circle to share the interest that's been earned. All of you deserve it. And if something happened to me, there's nothing else I could leave for Stan. Everything I've ever owned is gone. Will you see that this happens?"

Rosie and Janet shared a quick look and unsuccessfully tried to stifle their snickering. After Janet broke down into outright laughter, Rosie doubled over, slapping her thighs with both hands. After a few moments of resistance, Marian had to join in the laughter as she saw them clutching at each other to keep from falling down.

"O.K., I give! What did I say?" Marian struggled to be heard through the laughter.

"You still haven't got it?" asked Janet.

"The dreams!" Rosie added emphatically.

"No, I haven't 'got' it yet. Will someone please tell me what I haven't 'got'?

"Look, Marian," Janet began. "Have any of the dreams ever been wrong?"

Marian thought briefly, then replied, "No. I guess not. At least not any I've heard of."

"And none we've heard of, either," added Rosie. "And who is always in your dreams?"

"My boy, of course," Marian answered.

"Which tells you – what?" Janet asked playfully, as if giving Marian a test.

"Look, I'm dense," Marian exclaimed. "Just spell it out, O.K.?"

"Sorry, Marian," said Rosie. "We're having too much fun at your expense. You need to understand that the dreams we have are very different from yours. They may be just symbols that we see, or just feeling a certain way, or rarely, a direct message of what we need to do. We're led just one step at a time. We're never shown an outcome to the things we're asked to do. There is always a doubt about whether we'll be successful at what we're asked to do.

"When you arrived, Janet and I understood what many of the others haven't. That's why our faith is so strong. You have seen your outcome. You will hold your child in your arms. That means success for us all. None of us knows what will happen to us individually, but we know the child will come. That's what keeps us going."

Marian drew the two of them close and hugged them tightly. "I love you all. I can't believe how much you have done for me."

Janet replied, "Wilma used to tell me, 'Doing what's best for others always turns out to be the most selfish choice you can make.' I'm just starting to understand what she meant."

CHAPTER 26

Marian knocked on the door of the bedroom where Stan was packing his bag.

"Can I come in?"

"Sure," Stan said, with a hint of a grin. "You're sure we've got time to socialize right now?"

"Knock it off. I didn't mean to sound so bossy back there. I just got this feeling all of a sudden."

"I know exactly what you mean," Stan empathized. "It's happened to all of us. We don't pay each other much mind when it happens. It's like a huge charge of confidence, of knowing exactly what to do, right?"

"Yeah, that's it. I just wanted to come in because I haven't had a chance to tell you how much I've missed you. I haven't had a chance to do much of anything except, well... you know everything that's happened."

"Just playing Wonder Woman all day long," Stan said moving closer to her. "I can't believe all the things you've done. When I look at you, I'm just so – "

"Stan, I'm no Wonder Woman," Marian said, taking his hand. "But when everyone believes in me so strongly, things seem so much easier. Knowing that you believe in me makes me think I *can* perform miracles."

"I've seen them, Marian. You *should* believe it."

241

"You know, all the while I've been on these adventures, you were always on my mind."

Marian, slightly embarrassed, picked an imaginary speck of dirt from her sweater.

"I know we're going to be so busy the next few weeks, there's not going to be much private time for us. I just want you to know, when this is all over, I want there to be an 'us'. I really think I'm in love with you, Stan."

Stan put his arms around Marian and hugged her gently.

"I can only imagine how you've been confused by the way I've acted toward you. I'm just afraid to say, 'I'm in love with you'. I know Wilma, and probably several of the others, have told you that I am. In my heart, it's true, but I can't bring myself to say it. I can't afford to be the one who screws this whole deal up. I feel so lucky to be a part of this, to be able to make up for the terrible person I was for most of my life. I can't be selfish now. You need to be able to focus on the big picture, and not worry about me or my feelings."

Marian took her arms from around him.

"Gee, thanks," she said sarcastically, "That's so thoughtful of you. Since you've decided to do your penance, I have your permission to turn my feelings off. WHAT THE FUCK, STAN!"

She pounded her fists into her thighs.

"I'm supposed to just wait around until you think you've suffered enough for being an asshole? I don't need to pay for your sins! You say you can't be selfish? You're willing to pass up something we both want so you can punish yourself and feel noble about it. Why not just get a robe and a pair of sandals and you can walk around beating yourself with a leather strap for the rest of your life?

"Just - fuck - off! There! How's that for focusing on the big picture?" Marian turned and walked toward her room.

She stormed past Ames, who had heard the end of the conversation. Ames hesitated in the hall, then walked to Stan's room. He entered and took a seat on the bed while watching Stan throw clothes into a suitcase on the floor.

"You're screwin' up, son," Ames said gently.

Stan froze, but didn't reply. The shaving kit he held in his hand went flying into the wall at full force. The sound of glass breaking inside the kit was followed by a strong scent of after-shave that filled the room.

"Mmm. Nice," said Ames. "I always figured you for an 'Old Spice' kinda guy."

Stan turned, "I'm really not in the mood for a fatherly talk right now."

"Well, Stanley, I wouldn't know how to talk fatherly to you, since I never raised a kid as stupid as you are."

"You should get out now," said Stan, his face reddening.

"If we're going to have it out, I guess now's the time – but I'm going to say what I have to say."

"Make it fast," said Stan continuing to throw clothes into his bag.

"What do you expect from her?" asked Ames.

"What are you talking about? I expect her to focus on her role in this... this mission, or whatever it is. Ever since I've been in the Circle, I've been told that each one of us has a particular job to do. I don't want to screw up either one of us by bringing a relationship into the picture."

"Everyone's doin' their jobs just fine right now, Stan. Except you."

"And what's that supposed to mean?"

"Come on," Ames sighed, "we all know what your miracle was. You finally learned how to love someone. Same thing happened to Marian. I know the both of you are in unfamiliar territory here, but at least she's willing to accept her gift. You just spat on yours."

"That's not true! I do love her. It would be the easiest thing in the world for me to just ride off into the sunset with her on my arm. I've spent my whole life doing the easiest thing. Doing whatever felt good at the time. Booze. Drugs. Affairs. I ruined dozens of people's lives just to get stories published. I started out doing that to Marian. I'm through with all that. I'm going to prove I don't have to think about myself all the time."

"So who is it you're doing this for?"

"Marian, of course," replied Stan.

Ames just stared back at him in silence.

"Who else would I be doing this for? Haven't I always been there for her?"

Ames rubbed his chin. "When she needed someone to save her life, yeah, you were there. But when she needed someone to love her – no, Stan, you weren't."

He rose from the bed, put his hands in his pockets and turned toward the door.

"Don't be a fool, man."

*　　　*　　　*

Stan and Marian crossed the Illinois border in silence. The autumn colors had just begun to touch the forests that outlined fields of soybean and winter wheat. Marian stared out the passenger window at the blur of greens and browns as the Public Radio announcer droned on about a county fair in Saginaw.

Stan cleared his throat. "It's going to be a long trip if there's no conversation."

"I'm focusing," Marian said sharply, without turning from the window.

"I'm sorry about last night," Stan began. "I'm just really confused."

"I hope you can work it out," Marian said sarcastically. "I've got my own problems."

"Don't you know how I feel about you? Haven't I shown you over and over?"

"I've come to the conclusion I really don't know a damned thing," Marian spat. "Except that you're using me."

"Using you?" exclaimed Stan, "How do you get that?"

"I get to be the recipient of all the new, wonderful deeds the new, wonderful Stan Wallace sees fit to bestow upon me. Because he's a 'changed man'. And he's going to use me to prove it at every opportunity. Screw that."

"That's what you think?" asked Stan.

"I repeat: I don't know a damned thing."

"Well, I spent a lot of time last night thinking about the future. About how it would be when the baby came. I know it won't be easy for you and I'd really like to be around to help you."

"As what? A nanny?" Marian's temper began to boil.

"No," Stan offered meekly. "As a husband, you know. At least if you'd have me."

Marian exploded.

"You want to be my husband because you think I can't take care of a baby! I'm supposed to what – fall into your arms now? Good old Stan wants to marry the poor woman out of pity. By God, why don't we stop at a motel and celebrate this happy occasion with a sympathy fuck. Whatta ya say? Are you up for that, Stan?"

"That's not – "

"Stop the car. Now!" she shouted.

"Marian, you can't – "

She grabbed for the door handle and opened it slightly. "Stop the car or I'm jumping out!"

Stan grabbed for her arm as he slammed on the brakes, the car skidding as it came to a halt on the shoulder.

"Let go of me!" Marian cried as she tried to pry Stan's hands from her wrist.

"Please, just calm down," Stan begged, as Marian began punching at his chest with her free hand.

"I said let go!" Marian slapped his face hard.

"I'm not letting go! I love you!" Stan bellowed.

Marian's body went limp and she began to cry. "How?"

"What do you mean, 'how'?" asked Stan. "I said, 'I love you'."

"How can you love me?" Marian sobbed. "No one could love me. I'm a crazy *bitch*. I'm wanted by the feds. I'm carrying something in my body and no one knows what hell it is. Everyone who comes near me is in danger. I DON'T KNOW WHAT THE FUCK I'M DOING ANYMORE!"

Stan drew her close as she cried inconsolably in his arms. "Don't hurt me," she whimpered.

"I would never hurt you," Stan replied.

"There's no one else in the world who can hurt me. Just, please...don't."

The sun had begun to set over the Illinois plains.

*　　　*　　　*

Susan Stanton sat with her husband in the lounge of Munson Hospital's psychiatric ward. Two days of extensive testing have found no psychological damage from her gunshot wound or her days in a comatose state. Prior to that, an MRI showed a complete regeneration of tissue in her cerebellum, which had been almost completely destroyed by the bullet.

"You can have them run tests as long as you like, Mitch. What I'm telling you is the truth. What's happening in this country, is happening around the world. There's a new consciousness growing, and it's not just a 'religious thing'. It's Muslims, Hindus, Christians,

Jews, even atheists. They can sense something is about to happen and they want to be ready for it."

"All I know is the whole goddamn world is going mad," responded the President. "This country is depending on me to rise above this insanity. Somebody has to be minding the store."

"Mitch," she said, touching his hand, "you're wrong. And if you don't wake up, you're going to find out too late just how wrong you are."

"What? I'm going to miss the rapture?"

"No. You're going to be removed from office," his wife said bluntly.

"What the hell are you talking about, Susan? I was beginning to be convinced you really were alright."

"McCullogh and DeFontana have been speaking today to the party leaders in both houses. Bradley's being prepared to step in."

"You're insane. Bradley's too chickenshit to cross me. He'll piss down his leg if I say 'boo'. And how do you propose to know so much? Did you become psychic when your brain grew back "

"I'm warning you, Mitch, you've completely lost touch with the people. Do you know more people believe in Marian Foster's child than voted for you in the election? Do you know that congressmen all over the country are fielding phone calls demanding your impeachment. You've declared war on half the population of the United States. Your agents have killed civilians."

"These people are armed, damn it! They're dangerous!"

"People are allowed to be armed, Mitch. It's in the constitution. Don't you remember why that right was originally put there? To ease the people's minds that had become frightened of the idea of a powerful central government. They were allowed to keep and bear arms not so they could defend themselves against terrorists. It was so they could defend themselves against the *government* if they had to. That same fear of government has been growing again for years. You've just proven how right they were."

George DeFontana entered the lounge, escorted by two M.P.'s.

"Mr. President, Ms. Stanton," he stiffly greeted the two of them.

"So George, have you plotting a coup today? Is that a dagger in your pocket, or are you just happy to see me?"

DeFontana stopped in his tracks, stunned. "Who have you been speaking to, sir? I'm supposed to be the one – "

"Jesus fucking Christ! So this is actually true?" Stanton asked, looking from Susan to George, with a growing smile. "You actually think you can pull this off!"

"I'm sorry, sir," DeFontana said, handing the President an envelope. "But it's a done deal."

"What the hell is this?" Stanton snapped, grabbing the envelope from his hand and ripping it open.

"It's a letter of intent from a joint session of congress. 69% of the members will vote to have you removed from office unless you call off the raids on the Foster Church and relinquish your executive powers under the Homeland Security Act."

"You're full of shit, George! What kind of bluff is this?"

"It's no bluff, sir. A lot of us don't like what this country has become. There's been too much power put in one man's hands and recent events have proven that out."

An Army officer rushed into the room with a cell phone, handed it to DeFontana, saluted and exited.

"Yes." DeFontana said gruffly. "You're sure? How many did you say? All this is confirmed? Yes, yes, just keep me posted. I want updates every ten minutes!"

He snapped the phone closed. "The Chinese are on the move."

"Where?" the President demanded.

"They're moving through India, almost to Islamabad. My God, Mitch, they've got over a million troops moving. Tanks, mobile rocket launchers, and *trucks*! Thousands of regular 18 wheelers!"

"No air support?"

"No planes have taken off yet. And the strangest thing is, they haven't been engaged in any combat yet. The Indian army hasn't even responded."

"India warms up the nukes if somebody spits across their border. What the hell is going on here?"

"The Chinese army hasn't stopped moving for a moment. They haven't tried to hold any positions, take any goods or prisoners. It's like they're just...passing through."

"Passing through?" Stanton snarled. "Passing through to where?"

CHAPTER 27

Marian and Stan reached the Indiana/Ohio border just before midnight. The warm night air swirled in through the open windows, bringing with it the smell of freshly mown hay. The sky was clear, and Marian was reacquainting herself with the constellations she had known so well as a child.

"Stan, look at that blurry patch, right next to the handle of the Dipper. That can't be Andromeda, can it?"

Stan bent his head low to see out her window.

"I don't think so. That could be the comet. Yoshi-Maru. It's near the time they predicted it would become visible."

"That's the comet you told me about when we met, isn't it? The one that would be brightest when the baby's due."

"Yeah. It's going to pass much closer than they originally thought. Earth will pass right through the tail."

Marian gazed at the patch of light.

"Could this really have anything to do with the baby? This part has to be pure coincidence, right?"

"I really have no idea. It's a rogue comet. If it's ever passed by us before, it's been thousands of years. Astronomers have already calculated the paths of all the known comets that are in solar orbit, but occasionally one will pass by that's on its way...somewhere else."

"How bright do they say it will be by November?" she asked.

"As bright as the full moon. It's tail should cover a third of the sky."

"Coincidence or not, it's a wonderful gift." Marian stared at the fuzzy patch of light, imagining where on the Earth it would be directly overhead.

*   *   *

"The Chinese troops have passed Islamabad with no signs of conflict," DeFontana reported. "They're using the main roads. From satellite photos, it appears the highways have all been closed to traffic."

"India must be working with them. They obviously know the plan," offered Stanton. "They have to be heading for Pakistan. India must have finally made a deal with the Chinese to get rid of their nearest enemy."

"Sounds good in theory, sir, but they're not turning south. It appears Kabul is the next major city in front of them."

"But why Afghanistan?" pondered the President. "Neither India or China has had any problems with them to speak of. Unless – "

"What, sir?" asked DeFontana.

"The oilfields. Between the two of them, they have the manpower to take the whole Middle East. Afghanistan's government is still a shambles, they'll have no problem there. If they mass their forces after Kabul falls, they could form a line along the northern border of Iran and just start moving south and west. They wouldn't meet any real resistance until they reached Saudi Arabia. George, we need to move on this now. Get Air Force One ready to fly."

"I'm sorry, sir, but we have unfinished business."

"You're not going to start on this Foster shit again! Not now, of all times."

"I'm afraid so," DeFontana replied. "If you attempt to use any of your executive powers without the approval of congress, the Surgeon General is ready to state under oath that you are mentally unfit to lead. Then we will begin the process of removing you from office, unless you choose to step down."

"This is *criminal*, what you're attempting to do, George!" Stanton shouted. "This is blackmail *and* treason, and I won't stand for it!"

"Mitch. You don't own this nation. We're going to put this country back on track. You can either go down in history as the

President that gave the country back to the people, or as the President who was impeached because he tried to steal it. What's it going to be?"

Stanton pounded his fist on the arm of his chair, his face tensing into a grimace.

"What is it you and your goddamn cronies want? To rule the country from the shadows with me as your figurehead?"

"No, Mitch. We want you to come and speak to a joint session of congress. We want freedoms restored that were taken away by the Homeland Security Act. And we want you to give credit to the Foster Church for the good they've done in the country."

"Absolutely not! I will not praise the people who almost killed my wife!"

"You have no proof of that," said Susan Stanton, entering the room. "I don't know who it was that shot me, but I know who saved me."

"Damn it, Susan. I'm in a meeting. Don't just come walking in here —"

"I trying to keep you from making the biggest mistake of your life."

"You don't know what they're trying to do," the President said in exasperation.

"They're going to have you removed from office," Susan responded calmly.

The President turned on DeFontana, "*You're* the one who told my wife about this!"

"Don't be ridiculous. You know my security clearance."

"Then how does she know?" Stanton bellowed.

"Calm down, Mitch," the First Lady continued, "I told you I know what's going on now. And stop worrying about the Chinese. They're not going to touch your precious oil supply."

She sat down next to the President and took his hand.

"Mitch, I know I don't tell you that I love you very often, but I still do. I don't want you to go down in flames. There are some wonderful things about to happen in the world and I'd like you to be one of the people who helped bring them about."

She placed her hand on his shoulder.

"You can be. Go to Washington and speak to congress. Do what George is asking. Your place in history is already assured. It's up to you what the caption under your picture says."

The President stiffened, "I don't have any choice, it seems. But I guarantee that after I speak to congress, I will have a whole new staff in place. You can start getting your resumé in order, George. I won't work with a traitor."

"Don't worry, George," the First Lady assured him, "he'll calm down after things start happening. And make sure you have a slot on the agenda for me. I'll be wanting to speak to congress as well."

"You!" Stanton snorted. "Why should you be allowed to speak to a joint session of congress?"

"For the same reason I always need to speak, Mitch," Susan smiled. "Because I have something important to say."

*　　　*　　　*

It was just before noon that Marian and Stan arrived at Bashir's room at the Hotel Monticello in Georgetown.

"Marian, Stan, it's good to see you," welcomed Clay. "This is my friend, Bashir Pezek."

Bashir offered his hand with bowed head. "It is an honor to meet you, Dr. Foster."

"And this," continued Clay, rolling his eyes emphatically at Marian and Stan, "is his *wife and child*."

Marian and Stan glanced at each other. Bashir's family was not supposed to be here. They surely knew nothing of what was happening.

"My wife, Salma, and this is my son, Farid. They have come over… unexpectedly, to join me."

"It's a pleasure to meet you both," said Stan.

Marian smiled weakly and waved.

"Will you excuse us while we conduct our business?" Clay said to the woman.

Salma smiled and nodded as the others moved to the balcony.

"Thank you for coming, Dr. Foster," Bashir began.

"The situation is terrible, but I think we have an opportunity to prevent a disaster. It's more important to me than ever since my family arrived here."

"I have to know something," Marian asked, "Why did you insist on only telling me about the location of the bomb?"

"My spiritual leader foretold your son's birth just before he died. He ordered his followers to stop the plans for the bombing. The new leader, though, is evil. He would not let the Holy One's words reach the ears of the people. As he lay dying, the Imam said the birth of the child would bring a new age of peace among all men. When I heard about you, I remembered his prophecy.

"I was led to a meeting of your church, where I saw a group of men, many races and religions, all working together. Working to improve their community. I saw this was the way things could be in the world. I feared for my life and that of my family, but I knew that if you were here with us, we would be safe. It is selfish, I know, but to be in the presence of a holy one guarantees success in holy endeavors."

"I am honored to be here with you," Marian replied. "Millions of lives will be saved because of you."

"This will not be easy, but with you here, we can accomplish this."

Bashir told them of the plan for detonation of the device, of the precautions that had been taken to ensure it would not be stopped. He told them of the coded Korans which held the numbers that had to be entered into the bomb's keypad every six hours to delay detonation.

"I can enter the codes myself, once we have overtaken Hamoud. Then we can call in the authorities to defuse the bomb."

"Why can't we just call in the authorities first? Let them take the guy out, then defuse the bomb?" asked Stan.

"The guy's got a remote that he wears constantly. If he suspects anything is amiss, he's to set it off before the target date," answered Clay.

"When is the target date?" Marian asked.

"Next Tuesday, when congress reconvenes from Labor Day. The President will give an address on that day, full attendance by both houses. They'd take out everyone in the chain of succession to the presidency."

"So when do we move?" asked Stan.

"I'm supposed to meet with him on Saturday night," said Bashir. "I can overpower him, and after I've input the code for the next six hours, you can get the authorities."

The air was suddenly filled with the sounds of sirens and a brigade of motorcycle policemen zoomed down Georgetown Avenue. A trio of black helicopters flew low over the hotel, headed toward the Capitol.

Clay watched nervously as they passed, "I don't like this. Bashir, turn on the television. Let's see what's going on."

They walked inside and Bashir clicked the TV on.

"…with all the secrecy behind First Lady Susan Stanton's miraculous recovery. We should know more about that in two hours when President Stanton addresses a joint session of congress. The main session will be closed to the public, but we have been told there will be a speech to the American people from the Congressional chambers immediately following."

"No. This can't be," Bashir mumbled, wiping his brow.

"What's wrong?" Marian asked.

"This will change everything. When Hamoud hears of this, he will detonate the bomb during the President's address. A joint session of congress, televised, no less. He will do it!"

"So we have to move now," Clay said.

"It's our only chance, but very dangerous. I am not supposed to see him until Saturday. When I show up early he will suspect something is wrong."

"Why will showing up early be dangerous?" asked Marian.

"We only make contact on a pre-arranged schedule."

Clay ordered, "Marian, you and Stan get on the road, now. Get as far away as you can, as fast as you can."

"No!" Bashir demanded. "She comes or I do not. We have little chance of success on our own. If she is with us, we will succeed."

"Look, fella, you'd better get over this idea or you and I are going to have problems," said Clay, pushing his jacket back and placing his hand on a pistol. "I'm not screwing around."

"She must come!" pled Bashir. "The boy has told me so."

Clay unsnapped the strap on his holster. "I don't care what –"

"What did you say?" Marian exclaimed, running between them. "What boy told you so?"

Bashir sat down and sighed. "I am not insane. Everything he has told me has proven to be true. He has told me exactly what to do. It is because I listened to him that my family is now here with me."

"Tell me what boy!" Marian said through her teeth.

"The boy who comes in my dreams," said Bashir as a tear trickled down his face. "He comes every night now. My beloved Ayatollah is with him. My master tells me the child is blessed by God. He says I must do as he asks."

Marian looked at Stan.

"The twelfth member of the Circle," Stan said.

Marian touched Clay's hand.

"It's alright. I'll go with him. I have to."

CHAPTER 28

"Where are they now, George?"

The President ducked the prop wash from the chopper and hurried across the White House lawn, his wife on his arm.

"Almost to Herat," DeFontana replied.

"They've bypassed Kabul and have gone completely across Afghanistan without as much as a skirmish? This is insane!"

Secretary of State Hugh Turner turned to DeFontana. "You mean to tell me we have absolutely no intelligence on this situation? We have operatives all over that region!"

"Our operatives," growled DeFontana, "are all filing their reports as scheduled."

"And what are they reporting?" demanded Turner.

"The same thing," he spoke with growing exasperation.

"The Chinese troops are moving forward toward an unknown destination. They seem to have no interest in taking or holding territory. The people in their path seem to be aware of their approach. They're staying indoors, speaking to no one about what's happening. To our agents, it appears the people are preparing or clearing the way for the Chinese."

"So what do we tell Congress?" bellowed Turner.

"Only what we know and nothing else," DeFontana replied sternly. "No speculations."

"And let them know our intelligence system has failed? We're supposed to know what's going on."

"And we do. We're getting minute by minute accounts of exactly what's going on. As far as divining the future or reading the minds of the Chinese, our crystal ball is on the fritz," DeFontana added sarcastically.

"You sound like a bunch of schoolkids," laughed Susan Stanton. "Worried about how tough you look to everyone else on the playground."

"The kids in our schoolyard carry a lot more than brass knuckles and penknives," said Stanton.

"You'd better wise up fast," said Susan, "or you'll get your ass kicked."

"What do you mean by that?"

"People aren't going to respond to the politics of fear anymore. You have to inspire them to act through faith and confidence."

"And how do we accomplish that?" Stanton smirked.

"You have to change the way you make decisions. You can't inspire people with decisions made to change poll numbers or to gain political clout. You have to make decisions based on what's right."

"It's that simple, huh?" the President deadpanned.

"It's not simple at all. It's the most difficult decision you can make, but the only one whose outcome is assured. Just decide what's right, and tell them that's what you're going to do."

*   *   *

Bashir and Marian turned off "U" street and headed into an older neighborhood of D.C., a mix of nightclubs, office buildings and ghettos.

"You must wait in the car. When I have eliminated Hamoud, I will come to get you."

"Eliminated!" exclaimed Marian, "This is the first I've heard of murdering anyone."

"Many thousands of people are about to die. I don't want that to happen. I have to proceed in the only way I know how – the way I was trained."

Bashir parked the car and pointed to a one-story wooden house about half-a-block away, surrounded by a low chainlink fence.

"That is where the bomb is kept. Until Hamoud is out of the way, I won't know how much time we have before the next code must be entered. It could be hours; it could be minutes. I will need your help searching through the Korans for the encoded passages. With the key I have we'll be able to determine the correct number sequence to delay the bomb for another six hours."

"Please be careful," Marian asked.

"God walks with me," said Bashir, leaving the car. "Keep your head down. I'll return soon."

He headed for the house.

Upon Bashir's knock, the door opened far enough for a single eye to peer out.

"What are you doing here?" a suspicious voice growled.

"My cell phone was stolen. I wanted to make sure you heard the news," answered Bashir.

The eye inspected Bashir from head to toe, then demanded, "Get inside, quickly."

Bashir entered into a living room containing a couch, a small table and a television set tuned to CNN. The floor was covered with copies of Iranian newspaper clippings.

"I have heard," Hamoud said, "and I have adjusted accordingly. I am surprised to see you have the courage to be here at the moment of Satan's defeat."

Hamoud kept one hand inside the pocket of his sweatshirt as he talked. Bashir knew that in that pocket, Hamoud held the detonator. Bashir couldn't risk shooting him while he held the device in his hand. Muscle spasms at the moment of death could trigger the bomb. He would have to be patient.

"Our leaders have doubted your commitment. I did not expect you to show up," said Hamoud.

"And I was told the same about you. That's why I was sent – to see that you completed your mission."

Hamoud laughed. "You are a fool. You were sent to ensure your death. This mission was constructed in such a way it could not be stopped. Our Imam has seen you faltering in your loyalty. It is well known you have never stopped mourning for al-Akmed. He became weak before he died. His cowardice has tainted you."

"If I have been sent to my death, at least I came willingly. That should tell you where my loyalties lie."

Bashir glanced quickly toward Hamoud's hand. He showed no sign of releasing the detonator.

"That means nothing. You know very well that if el-Hamir wishes you to die, you will die. Where you are makes no difference."

"If you believe that, then kill me now," Bashir reached into his jacket and tossed a pistol toward Hamoud. Hamoud withdrew his hand from his sweatshirt and caught the pistol.

"I will be happy to. A coward like you has no right to be martyred in our moment of triumph. You will be executed like the traitor you are."

Hamoud leveled the pistol at Bashir.

"One thing, Hamoud," said Bashir. "That pistol is not loaded." The hammer of the pistol made a dull click as Hamoud pulled the trigger.

"This one is," said Bashir, pulling another 9mm from a shoulder holster and firing a bullet through Hamoud's left eye.

Bashir swiftly crouched over the fallen body and retrieved a device from the pocket that resembled a cell phone with a large red button on the side. The numeric display read 17:23, and the numbers were getting smaller.

Bashir dashed out to the car and jerked the door open.

"We must hurry. There are seventeen minutes left and I fear this will be even more difficult than I had thought."

Marian joined him in running back to the house. "You have the code to reset the detonator, right? We just need to find the boxes of Korans."

"It seems I have been lied to. I will be very surprised if the code given to me works."

"If it doesn't work, then what?" Marian asked with alarm.

"We improvise."

"I've been doing way too much of that lately," Marian replied.

They dashed in the front door but Marian hesitated at the sight of the dead body.

"Come," said Bashir. "The basement."

Marian followed Bashir into the kitchen where he opened a door and began descending the stairs.

"Fifteen minutes," he said. "There will be several boxes of Korans here. We must find the opened one and hopefully it will be easy to see where the last book was taken from."

As they reached the bottom of the stairs, Marian slowed to gaze at the gleaming steel cylinder.

"Is that it?" she asked.

"The Korans! Just worry about them."

Marian glanced at a stack of large boxes in the far corner.

"Over here!" Marian shouted as she began checking the seals.

She quickly found a box that had been opened and ripped the lid back. There were three stacks of books reaching to the top of the box. Four books were left in the remaining stack.

"It looks like he left off here."

Bashir grabbed the top book in the short stack and flipped through the pages. He ran his finger down the page as he searched for the correct passage. He took a small card from his wallet and glancing from it to the book, entered a series of numbers in the remote. As he entered the final number, the display began flashing, but then returned to the screen of descending numbers, which now read 12:52.

"Get the next book!" Bashir exclaimed, breaking a sweat. Marian handed the book to him and he repeated the procedure. The numbers once again flashed several times then displayed 9:15.

"I'm going to have to try and disassemble the bomb. Even if I can't stop the detonation, if I can get the plutonium core out it will only be a charge of plastic explosives when it goes off. Get out of the house and wait for me in the car. It should be far enough away to be safe."

Marian ran to the top of the stairs and wrenched at the door knob. It wouldn't turn. "The door's locked!"

"Use your shoulder and try to break it," Bashir shouted back as he frantically looked for tools.

Marian put her shoulder into the door, but the result was only a sharp pain in her collarbone.

"I can't do it!" she cried.

"I'm coming," replied Bashir.

"No! Just get the bomb dismantled and we'll leave together."

"I need tools!" Bashir shouted. "A pipe wrench, crescent wrench, anything!"

Marian raced down the stairs and began pulling open drawers.

Her fingers eventually ran across an eighteen inch pipe wrench which she held out.

"Will this work?"

"Perfect. There are six bolts on top of the device. When they're off, I can get to the core." The display read 6:49.

Bashir quickly overturned a crate and climbed upon it to begin unscrewing the bolts. The first two came easily, but the third wouldn't budge. "Can you find a piece of pipe? Anything hollow I can use for more leverage?"

Marian scrambled through the dusty basement looking frantically under tables and in cabinets. She finally found a two-foot length of steel pipe which she raced to Bashir.

Bashir placed the pipe over the handle of the wrench and put all his weight into it. The bolt made a small groan and broke free. The display now showed 3:22.

"Time is running out. Get under that desk and get as far back against the wall as you can."

Marian crawled under the desk and was able to draw her legs up against her chest enough to fit in the space where a person's legs would normally be.

Bashir removed the second-to-last bolt as his thoughts raced. *God walks with me. God walks with me.*

The last bolt was frozen as well. He jumped from the crate to put the pipe back on the wrench's handle. A mighty push and - nothing. He braced his back against the wall and pushed again. The bolt remained stubbornly in place. The display read 1:12. He wedged both feet against the wall so that his body was suspended in the air and pushed with all he had. He felt something slowly began to give. He tightened his legs even more as the wrench began to turn. There was a small 'pop' as the head of the bolt broke off and skittered across the floor. 45 seconds showed on the display.

Bashir wiped sweat from his brow and began pummeling the top of the cannister with the wrench.

"Move! Just an inch! Allah help me!"

He saw a slight crack begin to appear between the lid and the side of the cylinder. He threw the wrench to the ground and grabbed the back of the lid with both hands and placed his feet on the side to try and open it further. He saw that the display read :07.

Bashir glanced at Marian, who was trying desperately to sink further under the desk. He leapt from the crate and threw himself in front of the opening of the desk.

He shouted *"God walks with me!"* as the world dissolved in a flash of white.

CHAPTER 29

". . .the President of the United States of America!"

There was sparse applause as President Stanton and his wife entered the Senate chambers, waving. Very few waved back. They were followed closely by George DeFontana and Hugh Turner. As the President turned toward the podium, he was stopped by his wife's hand on his shoulder.

"I'll let you know when it's your turn, Mitch. Besides, you'll be getting a phone call."

Susan headed toward the podium and left Stanton standing dumbfounded. He quickly regained his composure and tossed a wave and smile to the crowd as he took his seat

The House Speaker, confused, returned to the microphone and cleared his throat. "Um, the, uh, First Lady of the United States, Ms. Susan Stanton."

There was an explosion of applause as the entire chamber rose to its feet. Susan smiled and waved until the crowd began to seat itself again.

She then began, "Rumors of my death have been greatly exaggerated." The chamber erupted in another standing ovation.

The President grabbed DeFontana's shoulder. "What the hell does she think she's doing?"

"Let it go, Mitch. Tonight's going to be tough. You could use a good warm-up act."

Susan Stanton continued, "There are things of great importance to be said tonight, so I won't take up much time. But I know many of you have wondered about my recovery, so I'd like to fill you in.

"A large portion of my brain was destroyed when I was shot. Almost a fourth of it. The doctors believed it would take a miracle for me to ever be more than a vegetable. But you and I know about miracles, don't we?"

She looked around the chamber.

"We can all stop pretending. It's happening to everyone."

She raised her hand. "How many here have experienced a miracle?"

The audience was silent.

"Senator Crenshaw, you know I lunch with your wife. She told me about your last checkup."

An elderly man in the front row shifted uncomfortably.

"What about Congresswoman Hutchins? Shirley, how's your mother doing?"

A portly red-headed woman smiled and mouthed, 'Just fine.'

She looked toward the wife of a Senator in the balcony.

"Kathy, you're the one who told me about the Foster Foundation. You have an amazing story too."

She turned back to the full chamber.

"I'll ask again. Who here has experienced a miracle?"

Slowly, hands began to raise throughout the hall. Within a minute well over half the hands were raised and the chamber was starting to buzz.

"I'll be damned," said the President. He looked at the sea of hands in awe.

An aide brought a cell phone to DeFontana, who took the call and quickly raced offstage.

Within a minute he returned and leaned to whisper in Stanton's ear.

"There's been an explosion in Shaw. It was a nuclear device."

"What!" the President shouted.

"The nuclear core failed to detonate, but the C-4 used to trigger it damaged several houses on the block. The core stayed intact. Agency crews are there now cleaning it up. There were three people in the house. Marian Foster was one of them."

"Was she – ?"

"From my reports, she's injured, but alive. The other two are dead. One had been shot. The seal on the core container had been broken open. Enough of the blast escaped to keep the plutonium from igniting. Foster and one of the men were in the room with the bomb when it went off. It looked as if someone had been trying to dismantle it right up to the time it exploded."

Susan Stanton was wrapping up her speech.

"…snuck into the hospital in disguise, risking arrest, in order to heal me. And now I'm going to ask my husband to come up and tell you some news we've just received - Marian Foster has once again put herself at great risk to save lives. Mitch, come tell them what you know about the explosion in Shaw."

The great hall erupted with a cacophony of muttering voices.

Susan passed her husband on his way to the podium.

"How did you know about that?" he whispered, with a frown.

"They're warmed up, Mitch. Don't screw this up."

Stanton stepped to the podium.

"We have just received word that a bomb has exploded in the Shaw district. There was a nuclear device as its core, which failed to detonate. Several houses were damaged, but the plutonium has been retrieved and there is no further danger to the neighborhood. There were two casualties that we know of, both were inside the house. A third person, Marian Foster was also in the house. All we know at this time is she's alive. We – "

The audience erupted at the mention of Marian's name. The President saw DeFontana waving frantically at him from the entrance wing. Stanton waved him forward.

DeFontana rushed to the podium and whispered in Stanton's ear, "The Chinese have begun their attack. It's centered on a government building in downtown Tehran. They have also destroyed several sites we suspected were being used to train terrorists. The offensive is completely contained in those few areas, at least for now. No reports of any civilian casualties. That's all I have."

"Thanks, George." President Stanton turned back to the crowd.

"I was just getting an update on the movement of the Chinese Army. After passing through India, Pakistan and Afghanistan without taking any aggressive actions, there are now reports that the Chinese have engaged in an offensive against select targets inside Iran. There are no reports on casualties at this time. I'll be giving you further information as it comes in. Now, returning to the explosion in Shaw this afternoon – "

Hugh Turner rushed to the podium and placed a sheet of paper in front of Stanton, then retreated to the wing. The hastily scrawled handwriting read: "The new <u>President</u> of China wishes to speak to you!!"

Stanton gave Turner a puzzled look. Turner responded with a shoulder shrug and mouthed, "I don't know!"

The President's confusion was interrupted by a hand touching his shoulder.

"Go take your call dear," Susan Stanton said, smiling. "I'll fill them in on the explosion."

Stanton looked back at Turner who was frantically beckoning him offstage.

"Don't say anything stupid," he whispered to his wife.

"Wouldn't think of it."

She turned to the audience and continued, "There's obviously a lot happening right now, and the President has several critical developments to oversee. But it was important to him to be here with you all today. I hope you will excuse him for a moment, while he attends to a matter of great urgency.

"To give you a little more information about the bombing attempt in Shaw: a device had been built by operatives working for the Islamic Liberation Front, headquartered in Iran. It was constructed over a period of many months with stolen plutonium from sources in the old Soviet bloc. Our intelligence agents had no knowledge of this operation. The credit for preventing this terrorist attack lies solely with Marian Foster and members of her church.

"An Iranian national entered this country with the intention of assisting with the plot, but after attending meetings of the Foster church, sent a message to Marian Foster informing her of his desire to stop the bombing. There were such extreme safeguards in place for the attack, it seemed impossible to involve government agencies without endangering our citizens. The Iranian national and Marian Foster together subdued the guardian of the bomb and prevented the nuclear device from exploding…"

*　　　*　　　*

Stanton entered a private office where a young Marine officer opened a briefcase containing a red phone. The President picked up the receiver.

"This is President Stanton."

"Good day, Mr. President. This is Zhi Sheng, acting President of the Democratic Republic of China. You may remember me as the previous Minister of Finance."

"*President* Zhi? The *Democratic* Republic of China? Obviously you have much news for us."

"Yes, yes," he laughed. "More than you can imagine. But I first want to inform you of our intentions in Iran."

"I would appreciate that very much," replied Stanton.

"There has been a disruptive element operating in Iran, as you know. My country desires to join you in your endeavor to construct a World Economic Coalition, as was proposed to us by Senator Hunt. However, many things had to change before that could happen."

"Like the government of your country?"

"Yes, of course, that was a big one," Zheng said jubilantly.

"But, we also knew the Iranian extremists would be a stumbling block that could not be overcome. We saw that they must be eliminated before any positive steps could be taken toward a global agreement."

"It seems you have taken care of that matter in short order," Stanton said suspiciously. "Typically, if a country's intentions are honorable, it would inform others of its plans and try to build a coalition of support."

"With all respect, Mr. President," Zhi explained, "that hasn't proven an effective solution in the past. Our philosophy is still one of pragmatism. If we are to join the world as a modern democratic society, we open ourselves up to the same problems they face. Terrorism is a problem we choose not to have."

"I see," replied Stanton. "I admire your resolve, but what are your plans in Iran?"

"The religious extremists are no longer in power. Our forces are already withdrawing, but we will leave troops behind to ensure the safety of the remaining elected government officials. We have also brought a large amount of food, clothing and medical supplies for the citizens. They have been badly mistreated by their leaders."

"That's what all the trucks are? There must be enough supplies for the entire country."

"Chinese tradition is to bring a gift when you visit a friend. We wish to have many friends."

The President smiled. "You've just made another one."

"I hope so. Our country will be drafting a new constitution next year, with elections following shortly after. I would like the input of a man who knows the ways of freedom."

Stanton's smile faded. "Thank you for the kind words, but I believe I have a bit of brushing up to do on the ways of freedom. You have my support, President Zhi, and I promise my assistance in any way possible."

"Thank you, President Stanton. I'll be in touch."

* * *

Marian squinted to shield her eyes from the bright light. She had awakened to a roaring sound in her ears and a blinding radiance that seemed to come from everywhere.

"Am I dead?" she asked.

Her own voice sounded like it originated from miles away. Her eyes quickly adjusted to the light and she saw a soldier in HazMat gear crouching over her.

"Everything's going to be alright, ma'am," the man replied, but Marian heard only a muffled murmuring

"I can't hear you!" she shouted.

The man examined the side of Marian's head where a bit of blood trickled from her ear. He took a pad and pen from his pocket and quickly wrote: "You may have a ruptured eardrum. We're going to get you to a hospital."

"There was another man here," said Marian.

The soldier kicked at a shape on the ground, turning him over and shoved his rifle barrel into the dead man's chest. It was Bashir. His clothing was charred and there were several large pieces of metal embedded in his torso.

Marian jumped up and began swinging, hitting the soldier once in the face. "Don't you dare kick at him, you bastard!" she shouted.

The soldier shielded himself from Marian's blows and shouted, "That man is a terrorist!"

Marian was able to make out his words and shouted back through tears, "That man is a hero! He saved your life! He saved all of us!"

The soldier shrugged and waved to a pair of paramedics who helped Marian onto a stretcher and carried her up the stairs.

*   *   *

"...I hope congress will quickly ratify our charter membership in this economic organization. We will be working with the European nations, Russia, China and Japan to iron out the details of the pact. We have every reason to expect unanimous acceptance from the other nations of the world. When you're given the details, I think you'll see that this economic union could spell the end of wars forever."

The President's explanation of the proposal for the Global Economic Union was greeted with a standing ovation that continued for over a minute.

"I'll be giving an address to the nation shortly, in which I will spell out the general scope of this proposed organization. In addition, I'll announce that I am asking the Homeland Security Agency to review the laws currently in place and consider loosening the restrictions we have placed on our citizens while attempting to defend ourselves from terrorist attacks. In many ways, we have helped the terrorists further their goals by placing restrictions on the freedoms Americans have enjoyed for over two hundred years. It's time to act like Americans again."

Another standing ovation interrupted the address.

"And finally, it's time to correct a grievous mistake in judgment on my part. A mistake I made because I was blinded by fear and anger. I want to thank Marian Foster and her organization for the awakening of the American people.

"Spurred on by her church, the citizens of this country have cried out for change. When we refused to give it to them, they made it happen for themselves. For problems the government refused to solve, they found solutions. The great number of people who have given themselves in service to others far surpasses even what we saw during the days of President Kennedy."

Another ovation.

"And leading the way was Marian Foster. Even while she was fleeing from those of us who sought her capture, she continued to sacrifice herself on behalf of others. Her courage has saved our country from the ultimate disaster, and has given me the greatest gift possible – the chance to spend the rest of my days with the woman I love. Please join me in praying for Marian Foster's rapid and complete recovery."

CHAPTER 30

"Marian? Can you hear me?"

Her eyes slowly opened. She felt like she was leaving one dream and entering another. Stan's voice sounded far away even though he was inches from her face. She could barely make out his words.

"Yes. Kind of. You sound funny," she replied groggily.

"The doctors had to repair one of your eardrums. The blast ruptured it."

Marian's hand brushed against the left side of her head and felt a large gauze pad held in place by a bandage wrapped around her head.

"The hearing in your other ear will get better. Maybe not as good as it used to be, but you'll be able to hear. And Jenny's given you a thorough exam. The baby's fine."

"Bashir –" Marian began.

"I know. I had to tell his family. It was hard."

"He saved my life, Stan. If he hadn't dove in front of the desk I was hiding under –"

"His family is proud of him. They know he'll be remembered as a true martyr for saving you and the baby."

"Is this almost over, Stan?" Marian asked, as her eyes began to tear. "Please tell me it's over."

"I think it is. Stanton gave an address this afternoon and called you a hero. He had high praise for the church and its charitable works. He also said that an economic union of nations was forming that would replace the U.N. It'll take a small miracle to pull it off, but the idea really sounds good.

"And I heard from Carl that BiEnCo has dropped the lawsuit. There's no one left in the company that cared to pursue it. No judge wanted to hear the case, anyway."

"So I can finally just think about having my baby?" she asked, hopefully.

"Well, I was hoping I could get you to think about one other thing,"

Stan's eyes shifted nervously.

"How would you feel about planning a wedding?"

Marian smiled. "Whose wedding would I be planning?"

"Will you marry me?" Stan asked, taking her hand.

Marian fought to contain her joy. She knew there was an important question to be asked.

"Why?"

Stan was caught off guard by her response. "Well, because I want to be with you while you have the baby – and for a long time after, and – because I love you so much."

"Good answer, Stan. Yes, I would be willing to take on the immense task of planning a wedding."

Marian threw her arms around Stan and pulled him into the bed with her.

"And I love you too," she said as their lips met.

CHAPTER 31

Stan and Marian were married in Athens, Georgia on October 27th by Father Kaplan, who ended his vow of silence with one word, "Yes," when asked to perform the ceremony.

Marian asked if he regretted losing his ongoing communion with God, and he replied, "I do miss that, but you can have the Stigmata. I ruined more pairs of socks!"

Ames served as Stan's best man, Jenny as Marian's maid of honor. The rest of the members of the Circle stood in the wedding as bridesmaids and groomsmen. Norman Randall, a free man after a presidential pardon, had the honor of bearing the rings.

With less than three weeks until the baby was due, Marian and Stan did their best to stay out of the spotlight and, remarkably, people seemed willing to grant them a bit of privacy. There was a consensus they deserved it. The birth of the child, however was a different matter.

Because of the worldwide anticipation surrounding the birth, Stan and Marian agreed there should be a way that everyone who wished to could share in the event. The Chinese alone had requested 7.2 million temporary visas for citizens wishing to come to America for the birth. There was obviously no way to accommodate all those who wanted to be present.

The government asked the church for advice on how to handle the requests, but the Circle wisely made a decision to give an answer that would be repeated many times in the future:

"Constitutional separation of Church and State dictates that we refrain from interference in government policy."

Marian, however, had a suggestion: Televise it.

"Nothing embarrassing or intrusive. One wide-angle camera shooting from a position overhead and behind me. No sound. No close ups of my face, or my – well, just leave it at *no close ups*."

Jenny was given the authority to choose the hospital at which Marian would give birth.

"North Fulton County Medical Center in Atlanta. Even if this is the savior of mankind, he would want his mom to be taken care of by these folks. Southern hospitality beats Mayo Clinic technology any day. They know how to make a mother feel special."

North Fulton had agreed to reserve a labor suite for her for the entire month of November.

On November 14th, at 6:24PM, Marian Foster's water broke. After four hours in a private room, Marian was wheeled into the maternity suite at 1:37AM, in full labor. A single remote-operated camera transmitted the proceedings to the world.

Even with over two hundred channels of digital television available, nothing could be found on TV that night other than a wide angle view of Marian's delivery. In cities all over the world, the scene was being watched on giant outdoor screens and projected onto the sides of buildings.

The most spectacular scene of all was in New York City, where Times Square was filled with a crowd rivaling New Year's Eve of the millennium. Hundreds of thousands packed the streets of Manhattan to watch the birth on screens around the Square. And in the clear sky overhead, brighter than the moon, blazed Comet Yoshi-Maru, her tail swooping majestically toward Earth.

The crowds were ready to celebrate in grand style. A Chinese family grilled burgers on hibachis to share with those around them. Two young men, one white, one black, rapped free-style as a group of girls cheered their performances. A Mormon prayer group temporarily abandoned their vigil to admire the Harleys owned by the Hell's Angels across the street.

At 2:12 AM loudspeakers blared to life around the Square and news anchor Walt Phillips announced, "We're told the birth is very close. The family has requested that no sound be broadcast from the labor room, but ABC's medical reporter, Dr. Jane Favrot, will be giving a running commentary on what we're seeing. Dr. Favrot?"

"Thanks, Walt. From all appearances, things are progressing very quickly now. There appears to be a lot of activity around the business end of the table. From Dr. Water's position, I'd say she's expecting to see a crown very soon."

*   *   *

"Damn you! And your husband! And your kid! On behalf of every woman you ever convinced to have a natural childbirth, I CURSE YOU!" Marian panted.

"Yeah, yeah. That's what they all say. We've got a head here. Shut up and push."

"Damn it, I can't push anymore! Please just make the pain stop," she cried.

"It's not going to stop hurting until it's over," said Stan. "Just one more big push. You can do it."

Marian gripped his hands. Her fingernails glistened with blood oozing from Stan's palms.

"AHHHH!"

"That's it!" said Jenny. "Don't let up! Yes!"

Marian wept with relief as the pain subsided. Suddenly she felt empty.

Jenny cut the cord with lightning speed and wrapped the newborn in a towel. Her face was strained.

"Let me hold him," Marian asked.

"It'll be just a minute," replied Jenny, curtly.

She beckoned the attending nurse with a tilt of her head and walked rapidly toward the door of the labor suite. On her way past the camera, Jenny quickly put her leg through a loop of cable and kicked hard. The cable broke free at the camera and dangled from the mount.

*   *   *

"We seem to have lost the picture from inside the hospital. We'll get that back up as soon as possible," said Walt Phillips. "But from what we just saw, it appears Marian Foster has just given birth!"

The crowd erupted with cheers. Fireworks were launched from New York Harbor and the Marine Band struck up, "God Bless America." Champagne corks flew and beers were poured over celebrating faces. The marquee around Times Square flashed, "FOSTER CHILD BORN! GOD BLESS US ALL!"

As the throng waited for the television picture to be restored from the hospital, the newscaster began a retrospective on Marian Foster's pregnancy. Scenes from the BiEnCo bombing, surveillance camera photos of Marian in a Waffle House while running from the law. The shooting of Susan Stanton. Interviews with her college professors, grade school classmates and co-workers at BiEnCo.

After an hour and ten minutes, the celebration was showing signs of strain. As the news crew struggled for filler material, the obvious tension in the ABC studios was infecting the crowd. People had become quiet, beginning to pace and bite their nails. The comet filled half the sky as the Earth began its journey through the path of its tail. At 3:35 AM, a very ashen Walt Phillips returned to the screen.

He stared into the TelePrompTer hypnotically. His mouth formed a few words, but no sound came. Finally, two words found their way from his throat.

"Oh, my - " he quickly covered his eyes with his left hand, his breath rattling as he inhaled deeply.

"At 2:45 this morning...the Foster child was pronounced dead at North Fulton County Medical Center."

He let out a loud sob and continued as tears streamed down his face.

"It was reported that the baby never took a breath after its birth."

The newscaster was now crying shamelessly.

"Please pray! We have to pray. God help Marian Foster," he wept. "God help us all!"

The streets below were eerily silent. Tears fell from one hundred thousand faces, with hardly a sound being made. Strangers embraced one another in sorrow. Families wept shoulder to shoulder. Men looked skyward in agony, arms outstretched, begging their God for an answer. The nation, the world, together mourned a loss more devastating than they had ever felt. They mourned a loss of hope. A loss of what might have been.

And as the Earth moved into the tail of Comet Yoshi-Maru, a stream of thousands upon thousands of shooting stars rained down through the night sky, leaving glowing trails of peach and lavender.

A five-year-old boy looked skyward from the arms of his weeping mother at the heavenly display. "Look mommy, God's crying too."

SEVENTEEN MONTHS LATER

"Can you believe this day?" Stan asked, inhaling deeply. "Beautiful. A lot warmer than usual for April."

"Mm-hmm. It's very nice," Marian responded, as she watched the greening trees and blossoming wildflowers blur past.

The trip through upstate New York was taking longer than she had expected. Too much time to think. She yearned for the chaos of downtown Atlanta, a blaring stereo, a raucous Hawks basketball game, anything to drown out her own thoughts.

Conversation with Stan wasn't an option. He'd been trying hard for the past year, but there was just too much that couldn't be shared; too much that couldn't be understood. His patience and understanding would have put a saint to shame, but the relationship was strained, nonetheless. You can only walk on eggshells for so long before you begin giving in to the temptation to just *stomp on the damn things and be done with it.* The only reason Marian hadn't bolted from the marriage was out of respect to just how hard he kept trying, even after all she had put him through.

Stan had attended the funeral by himself. An event attended by thousands, covered by worldwide news on the scale of the passing of a head of state, he faced alone. She was in a psychiatric ward, recovering from the effects of barbiturate overdose, the result of her failed suicide attempt the day after the stillbirth.

The public had been respectful, to a point. They accepted Stan as the family spokesman and gave Marian the distance a grieving mother deserved. But, as time passed, there was a growing need to hear from her, to validate or refute the opinions that were flying. She had adamantly refused to discuss the subject.

There were those who felt deceived, that they had been taken for a cruel ride. Sure, the world *was* a better place, but were we tricked into creating it? Others proffered the view that the child *was* the Messiah, but had no need to come into the world in physical form, since His work had already been done. His presence in spirit was enough to change the world. Still others claimed his death was a necessary part of the drama, just as the death of Jesus was necessary, to make a lasting emotional impact on the world, to ensure that he and his ideals would be remembered.

Marian had no room for any of these opinions in her life. Yes, she now believed in God, but He was her sworn enemy. Her faith, her courage, her selflessness had been rewarded with pain, anguish and psychosis. All she had gained – her ability to feel, her ability to love – had been lost in that moment when her child refused to take his first breath.

And all of this had transpired on the world stage, for all to see. There was no privacy in her mourning. At least one great secret had been kept between Stan, the doctors and herself. The news media reported her baby was missing a vital portion of its brain, the part that controlled breathing. The secret was that the child was missing the exact portion of its brain that had been miraculously restored in Susan Stanton's. If Marian had to hear that tidbit repeated every time the First Lady's face flashed on TV, nothing would have prevented her from taking her own life.

The Foster Child Foundation was still a strong entity. It could survive indefinitely just on the interest from the wise investments Carl had made. The board of directors of the Foundation, which Carl had formed from some of the largest contributors, had voted to give Marian a lifelong stipend of $100,000 a year. At first she had adamantly refused, but finally agreed to accept a smaller sum after much persuasion from Stan.

Neither of them chose to profit from their experience through books or speaking engagements. Stan had become so concerned with Marian's mental state that he didn't want to be away from her for the hours a normal job would require. He finally convinced her it was the least they deserved, after all they had been through.

The remaining original members of the Circle continued in the work they had begun through the church, although, bowing to Stan's wishes, had renamed all the charitable services in ways that recalled no connection to the Church of the Foster Child.

A different story, though, for one of the Circle. The one Marian felt the strongest empathy toward. Two months after the birth, evidence was uncovered that connected Norm Randall to the deaths of 3 men in towns between Atlanta and Wichita. His rifle was also proven to be the one used in the murder of Alvin Hedstrom, CEO of BiEnCo.

Norm had almost immediately received a presidential pardon for the shooting of Susan Stanton, but not even the President could risk a pardon for a serial killer. Norm's claims of amnesia were supported by polygraph tests, but his deeds, even with impaired mental capacity combined with alcohol induced psychosis, warranted nothing less than long-term incarceration in the eyes of a jury. He was shown great leniency when the judge instead sent him to a mental institution from which he had little chance of emerging. To Marian, just another example of how God turns His back on those who do His work.

Marian felt a flash of heat rising from her stomach. "Pull over, Stan," she said, licking dry lips.

"We're only a few miles from town. Can you hold it till we get to a gas station?" Stan asked.

"Pull over!" Marian insisted, now feeling a cold clamminess spreading through her.

Stan braked and pulled onto the shoulder. Before the car had come to a stop, Marian had opened the door and was vomiting into the gravel. She retched twice more, spat, wiped her mouth and leaned back into the seat, slamming the door.

"I'm good," she replied matter-of-factly.

Stan gazed at her, doubtfully, but put the car in gear and eased back onto the highway. He was learning when to keep his mouth shut.

Damn it! Marian thought. *Why didn't I take care of this when I had the chance? Soon it will be too late, again.*

She cursed herself for giving in that night. That night when the combination of anti-depressants and alcohol mixed in the just the right combination to cause her to open her legs to Stan. One of the very few occasions they had made love. And of course, she was pregnant again. *Thanks a lot, God. This must be the most fun you've had since you taught kids to burn ants with a magnifying glass.*

But He wasn't going to get the last laugh this time. She still had time to get rid of it and she damn sure would, even if it was done by a one-eyed hunchback with a rusty coat hanger. And Stan would *not* be told. The last thing she needed to hear from Saint Stan was a speech on how this pregnancy could be a "new beginning for them." A way to "pick up the pieces and move on." She felt like puking again.

Stan had tried to persuade her to go to the reading of Wilma's will. Something about closure. She had refused. He returned with an envelope Wilma had left for her, with instructions to open it "when she was ready." She had wanted to toss it in the fireplace, but couldn't deny that the old woman held a special place in her heart. So the envelope had lived in her purse for the past sixteen months, unopened.

As the World Economic Council began putting its ten-year plan in place to restructure manufacturing and agriculture on a global scale, the world had already changed dramatically. The sheer scope of planning and organizing, let alone the task of rebuilding and reconfiguring industries around the world had brought virtually full employment to all nations.

Yep, things sure were peachy, here on good old Planet Earth. Marian's anger grew with every smiling, optimistic news report. How dare they be happy, while she struggled daily to keep from slitting her wrists. Didn't they remember her part in all this? Why didn't they share her sadness?

She was at least able to show a few feelings for Stan when his mother died two months ago. Didn't she cry with him, when they heard the news? Well, OK, maybe part of it was because sadness was the only thing they've had in common since the baby died. But, still, she was there for him, right? She hadn't attended the funeral, but she had shared in his loss.

Right. That was too much of a stretch for her to even pretend to believe. The fact that Stan was mourning again had just given her a reason to quit hiding her feelings for a while. For a short time she didn't have to rely on medication and acting skills to get through her days.

She had been able to feign a bit of excitement when Stan had told her they were going to visit his Mom's summer home he had inherited. He had been grasping desperately for something, anything, to lift Marian from her depression. He was hoping she would fall in love with the place and agree to move there. Cue the "new beginning" speech.

She hated the North. Particularly the Northeast. Despicable weather. Despicable food. Despicable accents. These people actually believed there was a city named "Nah-fuck."

She was wondering now why she had even agreed to come. No sense of indebtedness to Stan was worth having to spend this much time alone with her own thoughts. If she couldn't escape from this car soon, she would just have to scream.

They turned into a graveled driveway that wound its way a few hundred yards up a gradual incline. Stan parked the Volvo in front of a large ranch-style home. The unmowed yard was at least four acres in size, bordered by gentle hills dotted with several decade-old northern pines. Even in its present state of neglect, Marian had to admit it was beautiful. As they climbed a short rise of steps to the front door, Marian's eye was taken by a distant cluster of trees whose tops jutted above the horizon.

"You alright?" Stan asked.

"It's very pretty."

Stan smiled. "You ain't seen nothin' yet. The inside'll really hook you. Do you have the envelope I gave you with the keys?"

Marian fished in her purse and offered a manila envelope to Stan. Stan dumped the keys into his hand and probed inside the envelope with his finger.

"There was a paper in here with Mom's code for the alarm system." He help up the envelope and peered inside. "Could it have fallen out in your purse?"

"I don't think so, but I'll check." Marian sat on the front step and began removing the contents of the purse. When it was empty, she turned the purse over and shook it.

"Sorry," she said.

"Damn. Mom's security system was tight as a drum. Every door and window are alarmed, every room has a motion sensor."

Stan looked around, hoping for an idea. "I might be able to kill the power at the main. At least we could get in to look around before it gets dark. I'm going around back to the breaker panel."

"OK," Marian said, "Be careful."

She began gathering the contents of her purse and putting them back inside when a gust of wind took an envelope and carried it down a few stairs. She walked down to retrieve it and picking it up, saw it was the letter from Wilma. She climbed back to the top step and sat back down, staring intently at the letter in her hand.

"Damn it, Wilma," she said softly, "how am I supposed to know if I'm 'ready'? Ready for what? Dinner? Armageddon? Ready to blow my brains out? I just know I miss you. And I need you now. I hope that's enough."

She put her thumbnail under the flap, slit the envelope and withdrew its contents.

"One page? That's it?"

Marian had nightmares that the letter contained some enormous and dangerous secret, like the location of the Holy Grail, the last prophecies from Fatima, or the precise kung-fu maneuvers to defeat the four horsemen of the Apocalypse.

She unfolded the page and began to read.

Dear Marian,

If you're reading this, you're obviously feeling pretty low right now. Unfortunately, this might not be the pick-me-up you'd hoped for. I'm sure you've struggled with feeling used and deceived by the way this whole thing turned out. The truth is, you were deceived, and I did it.

I know there's no way I could ever feel what you've been feeling the past year, but I want you to understand I had a burden to bear as well. I knew exactly how this would end, and I couldn't tell anyone. I really loved you, Marian, and that made it a very hard secret to keep. I do have to make the point that even though I deceived you, I never lied to you.

Remember when you asked me if the baby was really the Messiah? I almost cracked right then, but I answered, "It's important everyone believe that." That sentence was the absolute truth.

I'm not trying to absolve myself from guilt, but all of you in the Circle could easily have seen what was coming. I relied on my belief that you would all get so caught up in the drama, you wouldn't analyze the situation too much, and that proved to be the case.

It was never told in any of our dreams that the boy who spoke to us was the one you were carrying. How could it have been? This is the boy who will grow up to teach men how to live like gods. To take us up to the next level of our existence. Just as with Jesus, how is he supposed to teach us if he has no idea what its like to be <u>one of us</u>?

It took the man from Galilee thirty years to discover his path. During that time he experienced all the pain, grief and suffering of men of that time. Had he born to a royal house, anointed Messiah at a young age, with all the world knowing his purpose, what would we have learned? How to be followers of the powerful? He needed to show the very least of mankind that what he did, they could do also. That if this poor son of a carpenter could lay his faith, his love, his life on the line for others, so could they.

The same is true for the child who will come. He can't be born in the spotlight. Raised with the world anticipating his first miracle, rather than his first step, or his first word. He'll have to have the chance to be raised as a man, not a god. He'll have to have the time to find his own path, whether it takes thirty years, or sixty. And his parents will have to be the keepers of the greatest secret in two thousand years.

There were no lies told to you, Marian. You must believe that. As I told you before, everything in the dreams of the boy have come true. Eventually all of them will. I want you to think hard about what I'm saying here. If it's not clear now, it will be soon.

Just remember I love you, kiddo. And I'm always with you. Kiss that hunk of a husband for me.

Love,
Wilma

Marian had never felt so empty, so totally wrung out. She couldn't even muster up an emotion. There was nothing left inside.

She had hoped to be lifted up, somehow, by Wilma's letter. Perhaps some encouragement, some guidance. No, nothing but an admittance that she had been brutally used. Wilma knew all along she was fighting a losing battle for a stillborn child. She couldn't even feel anger at such blatant manipulation. There was simply nothing there.

That's it, she decided, *I'm through. Fuck it all. If I see pills, I'm taking them. If I see a gun, the barrel's going in my mouth. If Stan's got a razor, I'm whittling my wrists tonight. I'll see you soon, Wilma. And when I do, I'm gonna kick your sorry, wrinkled ass.*

Stan emerged from around the corner as Marian crumpled the letter into a ball and tossed it aside.

"I think I finally got it disarmed. Let's go in before the sun starts going down."

"Whatever you say," Marian replied mechanically.

Stan turned the key in the lock and opened the door gingerly. No alarm.

"Yes! Who's the man?"

"You the man," she replied with a forced smile.

They entered a large split-level great room, the lower level with a tiled floor and plush area rug framing a huge fireplace. The upper level was a luxuriously carpeted sitting area with a wet bar. Marian gazed up at the exposed beams in the cathedral ceiling.

"What do you think?" asked Stan.

"It's gorgeous," she said, her mood softened by the beauty of the house. "Quite a spread for a father you called, 'Mr. Blue Collar.'"

"Dad never saw this place. But he believed in life insurance. He had quite a policy he'd been holding since the '50's. After he died, Mom finally had a life. Shame they couldn't have had one together."

Marian's guilt rose even further at this last statement.

A man like Stan deserves a life with someone, and I can't give it to him.

They toured the elaborate kitchen, the dining rooms and bedrooms. Stan finally announced, "Now, I've saved the best for last. Follow me."

They backtracked through the great room, past the fireplace, and turned down a hallway they had bypassed before. Marian noticed the sound her feet made on the wood floor. That sound was hypnotic. She had a slight sense of vertigo, a feeling that the sound was carrying her off to a distant place. Marian felt like she was entering a dream. She continued behind Stan as he opened the door at the end of the hallway.

"This was Mom's room. I thought it would make a perfect office for you."

Marian entered the room and faced a large bay window. Outside the window she saw a shimmering lake nestled in a grove of maples, sporting fresh spring foliage. She felt the blood beginning to rush from her head.

This is the room from my dreams!

Her knees became weak and she clutched at the chair behind the computer desk facing the window.

She fought the strong urge to faint as thoughts swirled through her head.

She said all the dreams would come true. It's THIS child. This child. And I will hold him. IN THIS ROOM I WILL HOLD MY SON!

Marian burst into tears. She emotions she thought had fled her, were now bursting forth. She could see it all now. Finally, she could see.

Stan watched as her emotions finally peaked and began to subside.

He asked cautiously, "Are you O.K., babe?"

Marian wiped her eyes and fixed her gaze on the maple trees across the lake. Those gorgeous trees.

She inhaled deeply and turned to Stan with a smile. The first real smile he had seen in over seventeen months. She held out both hands to him.

"Come and sit with me, Stan. I have something to tell you…"

EPILOGUE

I'll ask again: Have I ever lied to you?

I told you I was the only one who could fill in all the blanks in this tale. You now know the whole story of how we got here. This be-yoo-ti-ful world we're all sharing now.

No more war. Everyone's working. Everyone's prosperous. Isn't it great?

It's boring. That's what it is.

And I'm not quite sure what to do about it.

So for now, I'll keep up the pretenses. Being a child is simple. And at least a bit of fun.

Mom and Dad think it's so cute when the animals follow me home. We've got five cats and three dogs. I found them all dead on the roadside but I became aware of my talents when I was five. I'm eight now.

The thing people don't realize about reanimating the dead is that they don't get their own souls back. That trick isn't allowed. They get a bit of me instead. It's a good trick, though. The Lazarus thing got me a lot of attention, but he really wasn't much fun to be around after he came out of the tomb. His wife wouldn't sleep with him anymore. She could tell. The wife can always tell.

So what do I do?

I came here with a plan. I heard the prayers and felt the emotions of billions calling for me. So I show up ready to kick ass and come to find that everybody's happy. So content. Never been better.

Is there even a need for me to be here? I haven't figured that out yet, but I can tell you I don't hear any prayers these days. No one's asking anything of me.

I do hear something else, though. A voice from a different place. One I haven't heard in two thousand years. Last time, I ignored it. But I'm listening this time. It's interesting. And very tempting. If I agree, it would certainly end the boredom.

I don't know.

What do you think I should do?

ABOUT THE AUTHOR

Lawrence Peter is a writer, film maker and clearing practitioner in the philosophy of Dynamism. He has a beautiful wife and two handsome and talented sons. You can call him Larry.